SECRET BUDDIES

SECRET BUDDIES

A NOVEL BY

MIKE NEWMAN

GLB Publishers   San Francisco

Published in the United States by
GLB Publishers
P.O. Box 78212, San Francisco, CA 94107 USA

Cover by Curium Design, San Francisco

ISBN 1-879194-09-0

First printing, July, 1992
10 9 8 7 6 5 4 3 2 1

This little wet dream of a story is dedicated
to the memory of my dear lover, Randy.

He was the first to read it and afterward
gave me his highest compliment:
"Boy, are you queer."

Yeah, my buddy. Queer for you forever.

And thanks to Bill Warner
of GLB Publishers, my coach.

1

In my mind I could still see every detail of Duane's dick. I could picture it as clearly as if I had a color photograph of it right in front of my nose. Staring absently through the tinted bus window, I got lost in my daydream again, the same old one about that afternoon in Duane's car. Two years had passed since that day, and he'd never let me touch his cock again, but the memory of it was still more vivid to me than the scenery of Idaho flashing in front of my eyes outside the bus.

It was inches from my face, poking straight up between his legs, aimed at my mouth. It wasn't very big, because Duane wasn't a big guy. It wasn't very long. Five and three-quarters inches long, fully erect, to be precise. It wasn't really special in any way, except that it was Duane's dick, and Duane was my best friend, and when we were alone together we could do secret things with each other, forbidden things.

I knew his cock as well as I knew my own. I knew exactly how thick it was at the base; I could still hold my thumb and fingertips apart as if I had it between them again. I could draw a map of the veins on it. I knew how short it was soft, and just how much it expanded when I held it. I knew how, when Duane got really excited, it would extend out exactly one inch longer than his longest pubic hairs, if I pulled them out straight along the top of it.

I knew all about his pubic hairs, too. I'd watched every one of them sprout down there, back when we were thirteen. His hairs were coarse, mine were fine. His were black, mine were brown. His were curly, mine were wavy. I'd measured their growth at least once a week for months, just as I'd measured the growth of his dick, and he'd measured mine.

We had started fooling around with each other in the seventh grade, back when we both still had our boy peckers, short skinny things the size of our little fingers. By the time we got into high school both our dicks were man-sized, and jacking off together had become a weekly habit.

Somewhere along the line Duane had started bringing a

Playboy along, plopping the damn magazine down right between us with the Playmate folded open. I didn't mind the magazine so much, but it made an awfully long reach to get my hand on his dick.

That's what I remember liking the most, the feel of Duane's warm, hard cock in my hand, and his hand holding mine. We never went all the way like that, though. Right when I was really getting into it, really getting turned on, he'd push my hand away. He'd always insist on finishing the job himself. We always shot off separately, with Duane pounding his pud and staring intently at the Playmate centerfold, and me beating my meat and staring just as intently at Duane's dick.

But the one afternoon that I keep remembering was when we were parked on our favorite back road in the woods, whacking away in the front seat of his mom's car, and everything changed. We were both tensing up, breathing hard, jacking each other off faster and faster, only this time when he stopped beating my meat he didn't let go and push my fist off his dick.

He held onto it and looked over at me, and when our eyes met he gave my cock a special squeeze and said what I'd thought about for years but always been afraid to suggest.

"One thing I've always wanted to know," he said, "is what a blowjob feels like."

I probably answered too quickly, now that I think back on it. "I'll do you if you'll do me," I said, right away.

He was grinning. I was shaking with nervousness.

"It's a deal," he said. I should have known better.

I could see it happening again like a movie. Duane had his pants down to his knees. He was holding his shirt up out of the way for me. His dick was rigid, throbbing, as I leaned across the open Playboy magazine on the car seat between us.

I got my face right up to his hard-on. I put one hand on his leg, on my best friend's thigh, right next to his thick bush of curly black pubic hair. Touching his leg got me so turned on I almost creamed all over myself, just looking at his dick. He pushed my hand off his leg, and I should have stopped right then.

But he said, "Suck it, Billy, suck my cock," and he was my best friend, so I did.

I'll never forget the feel of his dick in my mouth that afternoon, prodding against my tongue, so hard, so urgently stiff, and yet with such soft skin surrounding it, thin, silky soft skin that slid up and down so easily between my lips as I sucked on it gently, pulling it into my mouth, licking at it tentatively, waiting for him to give me some sign that it was as exciting for him as it was for me.

Damn him. I was being good to him. Why did he do what he did? Bastard. We'd had a deal.

The bus jolted and swayed. I shifted in my seat. Oh, fuck, here I go again. Dick, dick, dick. It's all I ever *think* about.

I stared through the window, bored out of my gourd, as the bus rumbled into the afternoon sun. Boise would be coming up pretty soon, after dark. No, not Boise. Lewiston. We did Boise already. In Lewiston I'd have to change buses for the last time.

Maybe then I'd get to see the big trees. I squinted at the horizon. We were crossing a vast valley of farmland, and on either side, miles away, I could see a jagged blue line of mountains, ridges with white lines of snow topping them, but they were so far away I couldn't make out much about them. I was disappointed. I'd expected mountains everywhere, like in Colorado.

Maybe after Lewiston things would change. Maybe then I'd see the big trees, the tall, straight, pointy kind I'd seen in magazines, the kind that only grow out West.

Slouching toward the window, I braced my elbow against the wall to try to make the vibration go down my arm, so my palm would do a buzz job on my hard-on.

I can't ride for hours and hours without getting horny. *Real* horny. I mean raging-hard-on-bent-in-half-inside-my-Jockey-shorts horny. I mean, I could see the headline in one of those supermarket newspapers:

GIANT PURPLE BONER FROM OUTER SPACE
HITS TEEN ON BUS, WON'T LEAVE CROTCH—
CAN MODERN SURGERY SAVE THIS LAD?

It's because of all the vibration, riding along like this for hours. When I was a kid I used to hate having to mow the yard, until I got one of those spurts of growth that made me tall enough so the handle of the lawn mower no longer pushed against my stomach. About age thirteen I hit six feet tall, and the handle started to hit a little lower on my anatomy, down below the belt. The vibration gave me an instant hard-on. I cut the grass a lot after that.

My father said I was in love with the lawn mower, but that wasn't quite right. I was just dating it. I was just taking it out for cheap thrills. One sweaty hot Saturday afternoon I closed my eyes for a few extra minutes, leaning forward, letting that handle vibrate like mad against my private part, and it felt so good my knees went wobbly and my eyes crossed inside my head.

What I got that day was a spurt of growth nobody had warned me about, another kind of spurt entirely. I was standing there like a geek, with my eyes closed and my mouth wide open, and I didn't even know what was happening until I felt something dripping out from under my shorts and running down the inside of one leg.

Talk about dumb. My first ejaculation, and I thought I'd peed on myself, right there in front of Duane's mom, who was planting tulips or something just on the other side of the fence. If I hadn't been worried she would see it, I'd probably have stood there until dark, trying to make it happen again.

I moaned to myself. I'm probably the only guy in the whole world who came of age with a gasoline motor instead of a girl. I'm probably perverted for life.

I slumped even lower in my seat. There I go again, thinking about sex.

If I just had a car everything would be okay. Not perfect, I know that, but a hell of a lot better. Mainly, I wouldn't have to be sitting on a goddam Greyhound bus for three days and nights with every other scuzzy misfit who wants to get from Bumfuck, North Carolina, to Bumfuck, Idaho, and can't either drive it themselves or come up with a plane ticket.

It is not normal for a person who has passed the age of eighteen, which I did many months ago, to have to take a bus. And, if I just had my own car, I could pull over for about ten minutes and *GET RID OF THIS GOD DAMNED ETERNAL HARD-ON.*

My name should be Billy Beat-off.

I took a deep breath and tried to focus on the outside world. We were driving across some rolling hills for the first time all afternoon. The blacktop pavement was patchy, and it followed the hills exactly, without any cuts and fills. I could see half a dozen humps in the road ahead, like a roller coaster ride. It was the main highway through the state, but it was built like a farm road.

Maybe it really was just a farm road. In all directions there were endless parallel rows of turned-over soil plowed in waving lines that followed the contours of the hills. It was still as boring as the Midwest, only with bumps.

For most of the afternoon we had gone for hours through a canyon above a muddy river, on an even shabbier highway that was notched into the canyon side. The road was barely wide enough for the bus, and it seemed to be falling into the river in places. I would notice little red triangles on wire stakes beside the pavement, and minutes later the bus would hiss to a stop. Construction crews would be carving into the hillside to move the road over, and when they waved us around, I'd look down at a gaping hole in the road where the land had slipped right into the river.

Everything in Idaho seemed new, and raw, and temporary. The canyon would widen, and the road would drop down to a little village of trailer homes up on blocks. What few buildings there were seemed unfinished, bars and trading posts that no one had bothered to paint outside, as though everyone expected to move on when the river flooded, or when the trees were all logged, or when the gold was all panned out.

All the guys drove muddy pickups with gun racks in the back window, and they all wore plaid shirts, and ball caps, and big, black boots with mud cleats an inch thick. Everybody's hair was shaggy. Back home, guys drive pickup trucks, but they wash them every Saturday. Guys wear ball caps, but their hair doesn't stick out from under the edge. Nobody goes more than a week without hitting the barbershop. Nobody wears suspenders either, except fat old whitehaired men who smoke cigars. Here in Idaho, even sexy young guys all seemed to have on red suspenders holding up baggy black workpants with rips in them. And below the muddy cuffs, boots, boots, boots. And they sure as hell didn't look like any of them wasted any time daydreaming about their best friend's cock.

Got to watch that shit, Billy, I told myself, straightening up in my seat. Forget the Billy Beat-off shit. You're Out West now. Be a man. Hell, I should stop calling myself Billy, too.

From now on I'd introduce myself as Bill. "Hello," I'd say, sticking my hand out. "Name's Bill. Bill Bartholomews." Make a change. Make a new start.

And back home, everybody always leaves the "s" off. That really gripes me. Not that I'm real picky, but it makes me feel like I'm invisible or something. I'd have to put an end to that, too, right from the get-go. These things are important. "It's Bartholomews," I'd say, right from the first. "With an 's,' please."

No, no. That sounds fruity. Forget the "s" bit.

This is Idaho. Be a man. It's 1979. The sexual revolution started ten years ago. At least it did for everybody else except me. But in Idaho, there are probably tons of women out there just waiting to have sex with me. This year, I'm gonna do it. This summer, right here in Idaho, I'm gonna become a man.

The guy across the aisle from me twisted in his seat. He was in an army uniform, got on in Boise. He'd taken his coat off and loosened his tie, and was leaning back against his window, propped up to nap. He had both his hands cupped in his lap, too, like me, even in his sleep. It's the vibration. He had left his reading light on, and I watched him snore in his seat as the darkness grew around us.

His forearms were thick, muscular, covered with black hairs. In his face he was just a slack-jawed kid, with his hair cut that real short way they do in boot camp. But his arms were powerful like a man's. Hairy like a man's.

I wanted arms like that. Hell, I was out of high school already, six foot two, and still only weighed 168 pounds. That's scrawny, really scrawny. In fact, I actually only weighed 163, but I always told people it was 168. I'd have rather said 170 if I'd thought I could get away with it.

Well, that was one of the reasons I was on my way to the back side of Idaho, to work for the summer in the Forest Service, goof around in the mountains and maybe put a little weight on the old bod. I was on my way to get some muscles, like his. And a car. Well, my folks expected me to put all the money I made toward tuition at school in the fall, but there'd be enough for a car first. And once I had a car, the girls would be next.

The bus lurched. Soldier boy moved his chin, swallowed, and stretched in his seat with his arms straight down to his lap. He squeezed himself. I could see it plain as day. I could see his hard-on sticking out from under his hand, underneath his green trousers.

I felt my own erection jump a notch under my palm. His army uniform was thick, but his cock was growing, visibly, snaking out under the cloth, twitching every few seconds until it extended a half inch beyond his fingers, then pushed out a full inch, maybe more. It must have been humongous. I wondered if he was dreaming about fucking. My dick ached in my hands.

Another lurch. The soldier boy stretched again, locked his fingers together backwards and lifted them out straight. I got a good look at the whole bulging thing standing up rigid in his pants, before he turned his back to me and heaved a sigh.

That was it. That was more than it. Billy Beat-off can only take so much. I pulled myself up and into the aisle, and headed for the crapper in back, to take care of business.

Some guy was going in ahead of me. The lock clicked, and I flopped into the last seat to wait.

Dick, dick, dick! It's all I ever think about! Nobody could see me in the back, in the dark. I worked my boner out of my Jockey shorts and pointed it down inside my pants leg, like the soldier's had looked. My cock was pretty long. At least I thought it was.

I remembered when Duane and I first tried measuring ourselves, back in the seventh grade. He'd brought a ruler along in his back pocket one day when we went out in the woods together after school to jack off. It's actually a pretty confusing business.

Do you put the ruler on top? If you do, it makes a serious difference which way you point your dick. Straight up, full-out hard, it only comes to like maybe four inches on top. Push it down toward your knees and you go off the scale they have in anthropology books. And if you put the ruler underneath, forget it. You get readings that nobody would believe anyway.

Duane and I settled for the top measurement, pointed out perpendicular. We were changing fast, so we had to check it at least once a week. If you must know, my best was six and a half inches. Well, Duane said six and a quarter, but I round it off.

It's funny. My parents kept track of how tall I was growing with marks on the kitchen doorway. They couldn't understand when I didn't want them to do that any more. Fact is, I didn't really want to get any taller. I was too skinny as it was. The only measurements that counted were the ones Duane took on my cock, but I couldn't have told them that in a million years.

How long could that guy take to piss? I was shifting in my seat when I saw the army kid stand up and start toward the rear. The lock clicked, the toilet door opened, and the guy inside went back to his seat. I was next, but I didn't move.

The soldier headed for the toilet. When he reached the door the light inside flooded over him, and he wasn't even trying to hide how stiff he was. It flipped by my face, big as a baseball bat, strong enough to lift his pants leg out in front.

I tried not to stare at it too long as he passed. I got a good look and then pretended to stare into space as he pushed into the toilet and closed the door.

Guys get the wrong idea if you check them out too much. I would never let what happened with Duane happen again.

I closed my eyes and went over it again, remembering how surprisingly far Duane's hard cock had protruded into my mouth, how excited I had gotten when his sweet fluid had seeped onto my tongue, that first clear, slippery stuff you get when it's starting to feel real good, and then—he hadn't even said a word, or grunted, or anything like that—just, pow, he'd shot off right into my mouth. The slippery stuff had suddenly changed into thick, ropey spurts, a mouthful of cum exploding against the back of my throat.

I don't know why I was surprised, but I was. It had just poured out of him, filling my mouth up in seconds. I'd gagged at first, trying to hold it all in, and then, what's a guy supposed to do? I'd swallowed it. Before I could think about it, I'd swallowed it. Hell, it was my first time. I hadn't planned any further than sucking on his cock.

If I just had thought to spit it out the window, everything would have been different.

I raised my head up, and Duane said, "Well, aren't you gonna spit it out?"

Too late for that.

"I don't fucking believe it," he said, staring at me with his eyes wide. "You swallowed my cum? God damn, Bartholomews," he muttered, jerking his pants up and buttoning them. "I always thought it, now I know it." He looked at me again and sneered. "You're queer, aren't you? You're a fucking queer!"

It was agony. Worst moment of my life, definitely. I swear he told me to go first, and then he'd do me. I'm positive he said that. Hell, I'm not some queer. We were best friends, and we had a deal.

Bastard. Talk about a slam right to the old balls. I never had the nerve to bring it up again, and I'm still waiting for my turn to find out what a blowjob feels like. See, you just can't let on to anybody about this stuff, not even your best friend.

Damn, that soldier was driving me crazy. I knew exactly what he was doing in there. He was swinging that baseball bat of his.

I wanted my turn, fast. I'd get inside there and, sha-ZAM! I'd become Captain Hardcock, zooming through space on the rocket between my legs, riding on the blast of my trusty beat-off boner, my best buddy, my hard dick. I lifted my hips in the air and squeezed my pants leg until it looked like it stuck half-way down to my knee.

We hit a bump. *CLICK*! The toilet door swung open. *FLASH*! The spotlight was on me, Captain Hardcock, arching up in my seat like a fool with both hands gripping my blaster through my pants. How fucking embarrassing. I looked up slowly.

The soldier wasn't coming out. He was still pissing. The guy wasn't even looking my way, and no wonder. He had plenty to look at of his own. He was still hard, and it was sticking out so stiff he had to push down on it with one thumb to hit the toilet.

I lowered myself slowly, gawking at the soldier pissing through his hard-on. He made a few last squirts, then stretched the loose skin all the way down, and back up, and down again. That was when he turned his head and looked straight at me. His eyes followed my arms down to my midsection. When he saw what I had in my hands, he started to smile. The corners of his mouth curled up.

The bus swayed around a curve, and the toilet door swung between us. The soldier moved over, kicked it wide open, and propped his foot against it. Staring at me, he slowly unbuckled his belt and lowered his pants. He had on white shorts, and when he dropped those to his knees his dick popped up. He raised his shirt with one hand, and rubbed his belly, staring down at himself.

Damnation. The guy liked being watched. He was showing it off.

And, oh, lordie, what a sight it was. His thighs bulged above his shorts, and like his arms they were thick with tight muscles, covered with dark hair, a real man's legs. His belly was a solid mass of black curls. Out of the tangle below his navel protruded his stubby slab of a cock. It wasn't very long, but it stuck straight out, rigid. It didn't even bounce with the swaying of the bus.

The soldier turned his head toward me again. His eyes stared into mine for a long minute. I couldn't look away. I froze with both hands on my crotch. He glanced down, then back up. He raised his eyebrows and tossed his head toward the front of the bus.

I knew what he meant, but I was too petrified to move. If I answered his motion, I'd be into something with him. He frowned and tossed his head again.

I leaned out and looked up the aisle. Most of the lights were off. My heart pounded. I could feel a wet spot spreading where my boner poked against my leg. Nobody was coming.

I looked back into the toilet and slowly shook my head. It was just me and the soldier.

He reached under his shirt and plucked at both his nipples. His hard-on twitched up, then dropped back down. He shoved his shirt all the way up and tugged his nipples out, like two inches out, and his dick raised up again and held there at an angle. He stared down at it, smiling proudly. It bulged. It turned red. A silver spot appeared at the tip. He pulled his nipples out so far I thought they'd rip off, and more juice oozed out from his cockhead. The goop moved slowly down the underside of his dick and stopped where the skin had a little fold. A clear drop formed there, halfway down the stub of his prick, and hung suspended, swinging from side to side, glistening.

Then his eyes burned at me again. He narrowed them and raised his chin. I couldn't swallow. My dick was about to explode in my pants. He motioned again, sort of squinched his face at me, like, "Come on." My hand trembled as I unzipped my pants, right there in the back of the bus, with other passengers nodding and swaying in their seats just a few feet in front of me.

He watched as I flipped myself out. I felt skin down there at last, instead of cloth. Soft, warm skin over a rod that was already steel inside. I held it up in the light and squeezed out a drop of my own slickness. My ears roared. I spread my palm over myself, working the slippery head of my dick around in my hand.

I stared back at him, openly gaping at him. He turned his hips so I could see it better, positioning himself just so, showing it off for me, and checking to make sure I was watching.

Then he faced his own image in the mirror. Still pinching both his nipples, he leaned forward a bit. He moved his jaws, working up a wad of spit, and let it dribble out, aiming it down below. I stared as he let it hang down toward his cock, then cut it loose and let it drop right smack on top of his hard dick. He looked over at me and grinned. I almost shot off right then, but I held it in. If he could last, so could I.

He reached down and got a grip on himself. Still pinching his tit with his left hand, he worked his cock with his right hand, and it swelled even more in his grip. The head bulged. It was an animal thing, a beast in his hand. I leaned forward until I could see him and his reflection, two massive cocks pointed tip toward tip, two fists riding up and down, slowly. He twisted his fist around it and narrowed his eyes, and from the way his arm muscles tightened up I knew he was letting loose inside. I tried to hold myself back, but I felt my own load start moving up.

He made three hard pumps, grunted, and then his head rocked back against the metal partition, *THUNK!* A long white stream of cum jetted out from the slit in the tip of his big cockhead and hit the mirror. *THUNK!* he rapped his head back again as another shot exploded out of him. *THUNK!* Squirt. *THUNK!* Squirt. He kept it up, shooting off and banging his head back again and again until he had blobs of cum hung all over the mirror, thick, gooey wads that first stuck to the glass and then slowly dribbled down in white streaks.

I arched my back. It was all so forbidden, all so dangerous. If anyone looked back, they'd see me, see me jacking off in the back seat. I didn't care. I stared at the soldier as he squeezed the last drops out of his hard-on, and a thrill of excitement shot through me as I imagined I was in front of his dick, imagined I was down on my knees, with my mouth open, sucking on his dripping cock. I could taste Duane's cum again, feel it thick and hot in my mouth, feel it slide down my throat. I groaned and raised my hips again and felt my own cum spurt hard against my palm.

I hardly moved my hand, just held it like a cage around the

head of my cock as all that good stuff poured out of my nuts and flooded up through my dick and out between my fingers. I locked both hands around the glob of thick juice that was finally free from inside me, shuddering with sexual pleasure.

Slowly, I sank back onto the bus seat in relief.

Soldier boy slumped against the wall and sucked in air like he'd just come up out of water. After a minute he took a paper towel and wiped himself off. He raised his trousers, tucked in his shirt, buttoned up, and adjusted his tie in the mirror. He looked down at me for a moment, then his lips curled in another strange smile.

Reaching for the towel dispenser again, he grabbed a handful, stepped out into the aisle, and dropped the towels on the seat beside me. He clicked his heels together and gave me a little salute, just touched his forehead and popped his wrist, and then slowly made his way back toward his seat.

The air brakes went *PSHHHW*. Gears in the transmission ground together behind my back as the driver tried to make a shift and missed it. My breathing slowed to normal. I cleaned myself up with the towels and zipped my pants.

Damn, what was that all about? Nobody had ever looked at me like that before. At least the guy wasn't queer or anything. I mean, he hadn't tried to sit down beside me and grab at me.

Lucky thing nobody saw us. We'd be off the bus right now. We'd be in jail right now.

Well, my grandmother warned me not to leave North Carolina. She told me I'd see too much of the other world, and then I'd come back a stranger. She used to say, "The Devil always has a smile on his face."

Was that the Devil? He sure was smiling. She didn't tell me he'd drop his drawers right in front of me, though. She didn't say anything about him showing up in a toilet, with a hard-on.

Damn, why did I get so turned on watching him shoot off like that? Why did I keep thinking about Duane's dick?

Fuck, all that cum he let loose!

At least I didn't go in there with him. I mean, I was gonna jack off anyway. I think that was all right, just to watch.

2

"Yeah, yeah, yeah," Steve called out over his shoulder. "You can all just kiss my rusty ass, you hear?" Standing just inside our cabin door, he cupped his hand to his ear and listened to something from outside. The after-dinner volleyball game had just broken up, and all his macho buddies had to yell insults at each other before they went to the showers.

Still looking outside, he motioned down at his gym shorts. "Eat it, Preston," he sneered. "Tonight, okay? Right after lights out, you come over here and bite the weenie, okay?"

Steve was the most muscular guy I'd ever seen up close. His shoulders were so broad he had to turn sideways to fit through our cabin door. From where I was scrunched down on my bunkbed I could peek over my book and watch him stand there with no shirt on, just his green gym shorts, his white sneakers, and his huge, half-naked, monster body.

He wasn't very tall, but his big bones and his solid-meat arms made him seem to take up twice as much space as regular people do. Blond fur covered his barrel chest and made a fuzzy fringe on his thick forearms and wrists. With the late afternoon sunlight streaming in over his shoulders, he glowed around the edges like a model in a TV commercial.

Fondling my paperback, I watched his gym shorts tighten over the humps of his butt while he twisted around. Below the curves of his ass his thighs swelled out into powerful, beefy legs, big muscles stretching the cloth so snug that his shorts followed every stocky contour of his legs. Golden leg hairs curled up over the bottom edge of the green fabric. I could see the outline of his jockstrap under the tight shorts.

Damn, I thought, some guys have all the luck. Talk about built like a truck. Mmmh.

He turned inside. "Hyah!" he said, twirling his volleyball on his fingertips, grinning at us. He was always grinning, always. I guess if you look that good you have a lot to grin about. He strutted inside. "Hey hey hey, we won," he shouted at us.

"Us" meant me and my other roommate, a creepy little guy named Stanley. He had the bunk across the room from me, the bottom bunk, underneath Steve's. He was listening to music on a headset, but his eyes followed "Muscles."

Bam, bam, bam, Steve bounced the ball over to his locker in the far corner and tossed it inside, *CRASH.*

"Hey, fuckers, did you hear me?" His thick arms flexed as he held onto the metal bedframe and pulled off his sneakers, shaking the bunkbeds and rocking Stanley's head around. "We won. Fifteen-fuckin'-three, man. Whupped their asses. Hyah!"

I hate all that sports crap. "Grasshopper legs," somebody called me once in school. One of the real drags about being tall and skinny is how everybody keeps asking you if you play basketball. I don't.

Steve looked like he probably played everything. The white waistband of his jockstrap showed above his shorts in back as he bent over. He kicked his shoes into the corner, next to his mirror and set of weights, and turned around, beaming like an idiot.

"Nobody cares but you," Stanley said, and turned up the volume on his tape player. Steve slammed his locker shut. Stanley squinched up his eyes and groaned through his clenched teeth.

Steve propped his elbow on his top mattress and ducked his head under the rail. "Whatcha listening to, man?"

Stanley ignored him, keeping his eyes closed. Steve grabbed the metal frame of the bunkbeds and shook it, repeating his question until Stanley sat up, red in the face, and yelled, "Mozart, goddammit, Mozart! Now shut up."

"Hey, I was just asking," Steve said, raising his hands and making an innocent, wide-eyed face. "You classical guys are so fucking touchy. This place is like a morgue, you two lying around reading and listening to 'Moot-zart.' Just checking to see if you're dead or alive, okay, huh?" He rattled the bed again. "Obviously dead, both of you."

Stanley gave him the finger. "Don't you ever get tired?" he asked. "We've all been working all day. I'm tired. I'm sore. I'm not a muscle-bound freak like you, so leave me alone, please?"

"You guys aren't in shape, that's all." Steve turned to his weights, picking up two dumbbells. "You think you can sit on your butts all winter in school, and then come out here and work in the woods just like that, but you're not ready for it. You're all brains and no-o-o-o brawn. All that reading won't get you jack shit in the Forest Service."

FWOOSH, he sucked in air as he pumped the black iron over his head.

Stanley adjusted his headphones.

Steve was right. I was in lousy shape, and I wasn't at all sure what they'd have us doing once the whole crew was in camp.

The only thing I really knew about the job was that a friend of mine back home had a brother who worked here one summer and said it was great. The job description I'd gotten in the mail had said we'd maintain hiking trails and help survey logging roads. We were also supposed to be training to fight forest fires later in the summer. That's when you make the big money, my friend's brother said. On a fire, he said, you get paid around the clock, overtime and all.

Everybody in camp talked about the big fires they fought last summer, but it was still early June and so far they just had us cleaning toilets, mopping floors, opening the place up after it had been buried in snow all winter. It was pretty boring, but it wasn't school, and best of all there were those granite-tipped mountains around us, the Bitterroot Range that forms the backbone of Idaho.

On the last ride of my trip they had put me and some other guys on an old converted school bus, and I'd finally gotten sight of those big pointy trees I'd waited so long to see. We went for hours on dirt roads leading high into the mountains, and at last I was really out West, a Southern boy in the Rocky Mountains, and there was real ice still melting under real ponderosa pines, right on the hill behind our cabin.

I was just dying to see it all, but working up in the mountains left me too pooped out every night to do much of anything. Every night after dinner I just collapsed into my bunk to read and drowse until time for lights out.

Steve, however, never collapsed. After work, he played volleyball. Then he lifted weights. And all the time, whatever he was doing, he made noise.

His giant shoulders bunched and relaxed. Soon his body glistened with sweat, and his gym shorts turned dark wet at the base of his back. I made myself look at the pages of my book. Five days in camp, and I was still reading the same novel. Well, it was one of Henry Miller's books, and I did tend to read the dirty parts more than once, but mainly it was because Steve bothered me. Even now, not talking, just working out, he radiated energy. It was sexual energy. It made me restless.

Stanley was lost in his classical music again. I wondered how he had ever gotten this job. He was even shorter than Steve, and skinny. His thick mop of curly black hair only emphasized how pale his skin was, and how thin his neck looked. I was squinting at him so no one would know I was watching him, when he put his arm behind his head, and then I could see he was squinting, too, looking at Steve over his feet. I wasn't the only one fascinated by that sexy, slightly dangerous body.

"Muscles" dropped his weights and stood up to flex in front of the full-length mirror he had propped against the wall in his corner.

"Gee," Stanley's voice squeaked. "I wish I had a mirror like that." He looked at me. "Funny, when I checked in they gave me a bunk and a blanket and a pillow, but no mirror. How about you, Bill? Did you get a mirror?"

I grinned back at him. "Nope. Maybe we should complain to the management."

Steve was ignoring us. Stanley kept needling him. "Maybe they didn't think we were good-looking enough to need one. We just aren't pretty-boys, are we? I hear Steve is from L.A. Maybe the Forest Service thinks everybody from Hollywood has to have a mirror—"

"I'm not from fucking Hollywood," Steve interrupted without looking around at us. "I'm from Santa Monica. And I brought this mirror here myself. I got it in town."

Stanley sneered. "Hah, I can just see it. Fifty miles of dirt logging road to get out here, and he's going along at five miles an hour, over all those holes. He's got one hand on the wheel and one hand on the mirror, sweating out every bump, going, 'Oh God, please don't let it break. I won't be able to see my beautiful body.'"

Steve dived across the room and grabbed his leg. Stanley scowled and kicked him away. "Lay off, asshole. Go chase a rabbit or something."

Steve turned to me and crouched. My heart skipped a beat.

"Bill, baby, let's have a go at it, huh?" He held his hands out from his sides like a gunfighter, bobbing back and forth. His shoulders sloped down from a neck as thick as his head. His arms were pumped up, huge. That massive chest loomed over me. "C'mon," he motioned. "Let's wrestle."

My mouth was dry. I didn't want him to start calling me a wimp, but I really hate that macho stuff. I picked up my book and tried to sound casual. "Nah, man. Some other time."

He stepped toward me, still grinning. For such a big hulk, he had delicate blue eyes, fringed with lashes and eyebrows so blond they looked white. He loomed over me, ready to pounce. I could smell his sweat.

"Steve, you're a fucking gorilla," I began, and then he was on top of me. I tried to push him back, but he grabbed my wrists and easily forced them behind my back, hugging me. I strained, but couldn't move. Suddenly I felt weak, and it wasn't just his strength that overwhelmed me. He was physically hot, hairy as a bear, and I was suffocating. I couldn't even struggle.

"You fight like a pussy," he said, dragging me off my bed by one arm. "You're not even trying."

At least I was taller. When I got to my feet he had to look up at me, and his grip loosened on my wrist. I told him, "Look at your arms, man. You've got arms bigger than my legs. I can't fight you."

He looked down and proudly displayed himself for me, puffing up and holding his elbows out. I put both of my hands around his thick biceps muscle. It was bigger around than my hands could encircle. When Steve held his breath and clenched his fists his muscle flexed up hard as a rock in my hands. I squeezed and poked my fingers into the cleft between his arm and his chest, touching the tuft of hairs sprouting from his armpit. The curls were wet. My own sweat trickled from under my arms. I felt a stirring inside my underwear.

I watched his face to see if I was giving away how much his body excited me. Men have a way of admiring other men's builds without actually saying they're sexy, but I've never been good at making that distinction. Holding his arm and getting a hard-on didn't seem like one of the best ways to do it.

Steve liked the attention, though. He wasn't even looking at me anyway. He was staring down at himself, flexing and posing. I wanted to touch him all over, to cup my palm around one of his enormous chest muscles, to slide my hand down and feel his furry belly. Then he twisted away and danced over to the other bunks.

"Stanley, baby," he said, jabbing at the boy. "How about it? How about a little arm-wrestling, huh?" He pulled the headphones from Stanley's head.

"Oh sure," Stanley said. "Right." He plopped his pillow over his face.

Steve dropped the headset and went to his corner, shaking his head. "Ah, you guys. You never worked here before. You don't have any idea how goddam hard they're gonna push our butts. Wait'll we really get out in the woods and have to carry a pack all day, cross country, sometimes straight up and down. You'll wish then you'd worked out some like me. It's gonna be work out or wash out, you'll see."

He yanked off his socks and then shoved down his shorts and jockstrap with one motion, showing the white triangle where his butt wasn't tanned. Suddenly naked, he admired himself in the mirror again as he used the wadded-up cloth to wipe out his armpits, then tossed it into the locker. He wrapped a towel around his waist and strutted outside to the showers.

Stanley sat up on his bunk, gathering his headset. For a moment the room was silent, then he asked, "What does he mean, 'wash out'?" He looked up to me. His face was long and thin and pale. Even his eyes were a colorless gray. And they bulged out too much, as though he couldn't believe what he saw around him. His lips were too thick, so they barely closed over his buck teeth. Everything about Stanley looked vaguely defective.

"Is there going to be some kind of physical to pass here or something?" His black eyebrows almost touched together in a worried frown.

"Not that I know of," I said. "I hear we'll get lots of shit-work to do this week, digging ditches and chopping wood and stuff like that. It's supposed to get us used to working at this altitude so guys won't have heart attacks later on."

His eyes widened. "Heart attacks?" Stanley wrapped the wires around his tape player.

"Oh, don't take him seriously. Look around. We're all just regular guys, except for Muscles. He's the only one here who's really big."

Stanley stared down at the floor. Absently he raised the back of his hand to his face. His littlest finger was overwhelmed by one of those fake gold rings with a big, cheapo stone. He touched the ring to his lip for a few seconds, then got up to undress.

Looking at his hairless, skinny legs as he climbed into bed early in his underwear, I had to admit he looked like a loser. Maybe no one else in camp was as big as Steve, but no one else was as small as Stanley, either.

At ten o'clock Steve was reading a Mad Magazine at the table, sitting in his blue bikini underwear and nothing else. He never seemed to get cold. His lips moved, but he flipped pages without changing expression.

"Lights out," Stanley piped from his bunk.

Steve made a disgusted face at me and mimicked, "Lights out," in a high voice, dropping the magazine. "Bedtime, girls." He bounced up onto the top bunk and flopped back without pulling up his sheet.

I undressed and reached for the light switch. The last things I saw before the bare overhead bulb went out were Steve's blond hair on his pillow and his furry chest, and his hand cupped around the lump in his tight little blue shorts.

His image hung in my mind as I settled into my bunkbed. I saw him in the door again, so cocky, glowing in the sunlight. Damn, those huge arms. Even his jaw was big and square and masculine. Trying to get comfortable, I turned onto my stomach and squirmed against the unfamiliar, lumpy mattress. Why did he have to start that wrestling crap? Doesn't he know what a body like his does to another guy's hormones?

No use trying to get to sleep. There was a lump under me that wasn't in the mattress. I felt pressure growing in my own shorts, and thinking about Steve's body wasn't going to make it go away. Slowly, I rolled over and slipped my hand down and over my briefs. My erection lifted up under the cloth, demanding attention. I cradled my prick in my palm and petted the poor, neglected thing. It was time for Billy Beat-off to take care of business.

Back home, I'd just drop my shorts, whack off and be done with it. But this wasn't at home, it was in camp, and now I had roommates. I yawned, playing with myself. Were they asleep yet? Steve began to snore. I squeezed my dick, and it reared back at my hand. What the hell, I lifted my hips and slipped my underwear down over my thighs. My hard-on sproinged up at the covers. Ah, much better.

My belly felt so smooth and hairless. Not like Steve's at all. Sexy fucker, all that body hair. All those muscles. Maybe I'd get big like him, working out here in the mountains. I rubbed my pubic hair. At least I had as much of that as he did, maybe more. I pushed my fingers through the bush until I touched the shaft of my dick. It throbbed again as I slowly wrapped my fingers around the tube of sensitive, tingling skin. I pulled up, and pleasure surged though my belly. Slowly, I moved my hand around the head of my cock.

The image of Steve motioning for me to wrestle passed through my mind, and as I saw him moving on top of me and forcing my hands behind my back, I felt the first seepage wet my palm. I lifted my hips, lowered my fist, and dropped into that rhythm I love so much, pumping my hard cock, feeling my guts melt with the warm glow of sexuality. I turned my cheek to my pillow, remembering his arms around my body, and felt his chest hair, his sweaty chest hard against mine, and somehow that all mixed with the vision of the soldier jacking off in the toilet on the bus. Steve was on top of me, jacking off onto me, rearing back like the soldier, shooting cum like the soldier, shooting off his load all over my belly as I twisted and arched my back beneath his weight. Oh, fuck, it felt so good, jacking off together, jacking off underneath him. . .

Steve snorted.

AGH!

Springs squeaked in the darkness as he rolled over in bed.

Shit! The big fucker was awake. I realized my hand job was making the bedframe bump the wall. With the upper bunk empty, I could hardly move without making the whole contraption sway. I waited, listening to every sound from across the room, but how do you listen for someone else listening?

I heard a snore. Safe again. I raised my hand up slowly and licked my palm. When I slipped my wet fist around my dick, Steve's image came back.

He was pulling his tanktop over his head. I was standing next to him. We were both sweaty from lifting weights together, both pulling our clothes off. With his arms up, I could see the hairs in his armpit, blond hairs, almost orange against his pale skin. He dropped his shirt, and looked me in the eye. I dropped my shirt, and looked back. His blue eyes twinkled. One eyebrow went up, and I smiled. He pushed down his shorts. I pushed down my shorts. His dick was hard. My dick was hard. He reached out for me, and I felt his hand down there, pulling my prick. I reached for him, and took his dick in my hand, and then my cum began burning inside me, rising up, as his hand worked my cock, and my hand worked his. I put my other hand on Steve's arm, squeezed that thick biceps muscle again, oh shit, his arms are so big, his chest is so hairy, and then his beautiful blue eyes narrowed, and he smiled proudly as his cum splashed hot against my dick. . .

I arched my back, held my breath, and shot off. I bit my lip, forcing myself not to make a sound as I got what I needed at last, trembling in my bunk, feeling spurt after spurt spring out of my dick and drop across my belly.

I relaxed slowly. Shit, Steve would kill me if he knew I jacked off thinking about him. Sometimes I embarrass myself. Damn, why do I keep dreaming up stuff like that?

This will not do, I thought. I cannot go three months like this. I'd have to hunt around camp and find some place to jerk off. I needed to find some secret place where I could be alone, have a little privacy. A guy with a sex drive like mine can't just dink around like this. I have to have my fun. I need time to really get into it, flop around some, make some noise. These other guys, they don't understand. I can't really get off unless I'm completely alone.

Tuesday morning I woke up hard as a rock, my cock throbbing inside my briefs, ready to repopulate the whole planet, as usual.

Steve jumped down first and gave a big stretch. He tugged at his crotch a few times and snapped the elastic of his bikini shorts before he stepped into his work pants. I'd seen him in the showers, and for all his muscles he wasn't very big between the legs.

Stanley rolled out of bed next. He got into his pants with his back turned. Eyes to the floor, he hung a towel around his neck and followed Steve down to shave, although I don't think Stanley really had anything there to shave.

I got up last, hulking over to my locker with a boner that didn't go away entirely until after breakfast.

We got our work assignments every morning at the office, which was at the far end of camp. It was a new building with dormitory rooms in back for the permanent staff, and, although nobody actually came out and said it, we all knew it was off limits for the summer crews except when we were supposed to meet there at eight AM.

As the crowd walked across the parking lot, I lagged behind. The older guys all wore thick work shirts, down vests, bluejeans, and heavy logger's boots that left cleat marks in the mud. I felt silly in my old corduroy school pants. Even my boots weren't right. Back in North Carolina, I'd bought a pair of the brown construction kind, with flat soles, and they slipped in the puddles.

Stanley was the only one jerkier-looking than me. He had loafers on for work, the dummy; black ones, and black pants and a black windbreaker. He looked fruity. I avoided him.

Somebody I couldn't see read out, "Parking lot crew," and then a bunch of names, including "Bartholomew." They always leave the 's' off. We all trooped over to a barn in the middle of camp.

The barn was being used as a garage. Instead of hay and horses there were rows of lime green government pickup trucks, and a room at one end full of tools and backpacks and saw blades. We lined up at the counter and I was handed a shovel.

Out in the parking lot they started us digging a ditch to drain a small lake of mud left by the melting snow. A dozen of us scrabbled in the rocky ground. Everybody on the crew was new. I pried at a chunk of stone, already out of breath in the thin air. Idaho must be solid rock under about three inches of dirt.

A pickup bumped past us, and Steve called out from the back, "Rake those rocks, you turkeys!"

Stanley and I looked at each other. I pried harder.

Stanley kept up, I have to admit. While he was trying to pull a rock loose somebody stepped on his hand, and his face showed how much it hurt, but he didn't even whimper. Then the crew boss yelled at him, "Take off that goddam ring while you're working. You want to get it caught on something and rip your whole fucking finger off, man?"

Stanley turned red and put the ring in his pocket, but I have to admit, the little fruit kept up.

We raked rocks all afternoon. At the five o'clock bell, tired and sore, I dragged myself to the cabin. Undressing in my corner by the door, I wrapped up in a towel and walked outside.

We were at the end of the row of cabins, and next were the showers in a separate building by the parking lot. After work every guy in camp went by our door on the way to clean up, wearing only a towel. It didn't take long for all of us to realize there were no women around for about fifty miles, so each night a few of the ballsier ones would stroll down bare-assed, carrying their towels and letting it all hang out in the wind.

It was my favorite time of day.

Inside, in the steamy tiled room behind the toilets, I waded through the naked butts to find an empty shower head. At first I kept my eyes down on the wooden slats that let the water drain, but I couldn't help checking out the nude guys.

In school I'd always managed to talk my way out of physical education classes, and I'd never seen as many bare cocks at once as I saw every night in the showers. This was my chance to make up for lost time. Every evening I gaped at all the different shapes and sizes, big fat ones that swayed in the suds, long skinny ones that whipped against their legs when they dried off, and short ones like Steve's that stood out more once the hairs around them got wet.

The rest of them jabbered on about curves on girls and jiggling titties. The curves I was fascinated with were on the other guys' behinds, and the jiggles that caught my eye were between their legs. I sneaked looks, until I noticed other eyes darting toward the door.

It was Stanley. He'd never come into the shower room while I was in there before, and for the whole week we'd been bunking together, I'd never seen him undress all the way in the cabin. As his white body moved toward me, I saw why everyone was staring at him. The kid with the body of a boy had the biggest schlonger I'd ever seen. It was so long it had a double wiggle as he walked, the fat middle going one way with each step, the tip swinging the other way. It was uncircumcised, too. Every eye was on it.

In the silence, a bar of soap dropped onto the slats. Somebody said, "Don't bend over to pick that up with Steve behind you." Everyone laughed suddenly. Grinning, Steve scooped up the soap and chased the guy into a corner. "You'd like that, wouldn't you?" he growled, with one sudsy arm around the boy and his other hand on his butt, pretending to push the bar up between his legs. They were wrestling up against Stanley, and when Steve started smacking the boy's bare ass, Stanley began to get hard.

We all watched in awe as it swelled. It moved, growing, reaching almost to his knee before Steve saw it. When he shut up, the only sound was running water. Stanley turned red.

Steve whistled. "Hey, Stanley, I knew you were a donkey dick, but, god damn—"

"Don't call me donkey dick," Stanley snapped. "I hate that." He rinsed off and left.

The guy next to me said, "If I was hung like that, I wouldn't care what you called me."

"It's wasted on the fag," another voice called out, and I'm sure Stanley was still drying off outside, where he could hear every word.

A sound in the night woke me up. I listened for it again, but heard nothing. I turned my head against my pillow. The cabin roof cracked. I opened my eyes. Was something up there? A pop came from over in the corner. Maybe a cat on the roof? Maybe a wildcat!

I listened in the dark. Nothing. Steady breathing from across the room. I sighed and closed my eyes.

"The fag." I saw Stanley in the showers again, nude and wet and skinny. The guys all laughed at him, pointing at his prick. "It's wasted on the fag." Glad it was him and not me.

I turned my head and snuggled against my pillow, remembering how Stanley's huge schlong had swung back and forth between his legs as he washed himself. The others all vanished, and I was alone with him. I could hear the water running. I could see him take his dick in his hand and start to pull on it. I could see how the loose skin moved over it, how it flopped back and forth as he soaped it up. He skinned it back and showed me the pink tip, glistening wet.

My dick throbbed in my Jockey shorts. I sighed. Just a quickie wouldn't hurt. I wiggled my shorts down and raised my knees to give myself some whack-off room under the blanket. I imagined soaping myself up, lathering my crotch and making my pubic hairs froth up, and then sliding my soapy fist down over my dick, with warm water cascading down my back and between the cheeks of my ass and running down my legs.

And Stanley, the fag, standing next to me.

His long, thick, uncircumcised cock was swelling up in his hand. It was a big fat sausage, it was a donkey dick, it was a horse cock. I spread my knees under the covers and beat my meat furiously. Stanley the faggot turned toward me. The faggot, I thought, grabbing my nuts. Stanley the faggot. He pointed his enormous hard-on between my legs. He peeled it back. The head was red, swollen, as I watched it slide under my balls.

I gripped myself tighter and arched my back. I felt his horse dick force its way into the soapy slot between my legs. Sliding my index finger under my nuts, I clamped my legs together and pressed three fingers up against my crotch, pressed up hard against the base of my cock, pumping madly, feeling Stanley the faggot fuck me between my legs, gonna cum, gonna cum, gonna cum, you faggot. . .

"Hey!" Steve barked from his bunk. I froze, dick in hand. The pit of my stomach turned to ice. I thought sure they were both asleep, this time. It was the middle of the fucking night!

"None of that shit in this cabin," Steve said gruffly through the darkness.

I didn't answer. At moments of absolute humiliation, to speak is to die. I couldn't budge.

Moments passed. I didn't move. Then Muscles threw his blanket back and dropped down onto the floor. I panicked, thinking he was coming after me, but instead he went outside, stomping his bare feet on the boards going toward the bathroom.

I was beginning to contemplate suicide when I heard Stanley sit up. Not making a sound, he crossed the room and stood beside my bed.

I could make out his pale form over me. I took a breath, still holding my dick, as the little guy knelt beside me, and then I felt my blanket slipping slowly down to my knees. My fingers were still hooked under my balls. Stanley unplugged my left hand from my crotch, and tugged my right hand off my dick. I closed my eyes. Steve would be back any minute. Stanley carefully lowered my briefs down to my knees.

My heart raced. His fingers were cold, and my nuts shrivelled up inside me when he touched them. But when his fingertips went around the base of my dick, it wasn't shrivelled at all. It was so stiff he had to pry it up from my belly.

It was all very formal, sort of mechanical, as though we'd rehearsed it. Damnation, eighteen years I'd waited for this moment, and I was almost too nervous to feel anything. My back was as stiff as a board. I kept listening for Steve's footsteps on the walkway.

I felt a puff of warm breath, just a brush of air around my pubic hairs, and then Stanley pressed his mouth against the side of my dick. He kissed it, down by the base. He kissed it again, and again, moving his lips up higher each time. He pointed my cock straight up, leaned forward, and kissed the tip of it.

I felt one spindly arm snaking around behind my back. He lifted me up a bit and slipped his other arm under me, still holding the tip of my cock with his lips. It was like being hugged by a grasshopper. I heard a shaky "Mmmmh" from him, and then my eyes opened wide as I felt a wave of pure pleasure, warm, slippery wet, tight-sucking pleasure, the hot sensation of his mouth wrapping around my dick and sliding down all the way to the hilt, enveloping my hard cock right down to the hairs on my belly. "Shit!" I whispered. "Oh, shit!"

Ah-h-h, at last, the sweet ecstasy of a real blowjob. My hands tightened on the bed. It was true, everything I'd heard was true. Please, God, keep Muscles away just one more minute. Stanley's mouth moved faster, pulled tighter, as I felt the hot sap rising up inside me. Oh, Lord, just give me thirty seconds. My dick was swollen, enormous, and my cum was gathering, flowing out those secret tubes and channels inside me, headed for that glorious last surge up and out through my cock. Twenty seconds more, and I won't care what Steve does to us. *JUST LET ME GET OFF IN SOMEBODY'S MOUTH, FOR ONCE, GODDAMMIT!*

The door of the toilet building slammed outside as my bed began to spin and then, oh, glory, my dick started doing what it's designed to do, at long fucking last!

"I'm gonna shoot!" I tried to warn him, before I let loose right in his mouth, but it was too late. I heard Stanley go "Mmmm-hmmm!" as I finally found out what it's like to get your rocks off without having to use your own hands—to shoot your load in another guy's mouth, to cream inside a pair of willing, sucking lips.

He didn't seem to mind it a bit, getting my cum in his mouth. He just sucked harder. I grabbed his neck and held his head down as I heaved my hips up, driving my dick into his face as I shot off. When I drew back I felt his jaw work a few times around my cock. He gulped, and sucked some more. I held his scrawny neck and fucked his mouth, and every time I pulled back he swallowed and went "Mmm-HMMM!"

Steve's footsteps thudded toward the cabin, but I couldn't help letting out a long groan of satisfaction as Stanley pulled burst after burst of cum out of my dick. The doorknob turned before I finished pumping it all into him, but I was too turned-on to care.

Stanley cared. He popped loose and jumped up in a flash.

I was still twitching and dripping cum onto my belly as he tossed the blanket over me. He turned around just as the door creaked open.

Wiping his mouth, he pushed his way out past Steve without a word.

I lay there grinning in the dark, still leaking jism under the blanket and trying not to breath too hard. Muscles hesitated, then climbed into his bunk and pulled up his covers. He snorted a couple of times and then rolled over.

In a few minutes Stanley came back in and slipped quietly into his bunk.

The cabin was quiet after that. I tugged my Jockey shorts back up and patted my half-hard dick.

Maybe this would work out after all.

3

Stanley didn't even look me in the eye the next morning. He avoided me when we lined up to shave in the head, and at breakfast he sat at a table off by himself. I decided that was okay by me. I didn't really want to be associated with the camp creep. We stayed apart at work in the parking lot mudhole.

By noon we were all a muddy mess again, so we used a hose behind the barn to get some of the mud off our faces and arms, and then we sprawled under a tree to eat the sack lunches we had packed at breakfast. I really wanted to go crawl into my bunk and sleep, but my pants were plastered to my legs below the knees. After lunch I stretched out on the grass and tried to nap.

"Oooo-wee!" Steve's volleyball buddy Preston was crew leader that day, and he was mouthing off about sex. He was a big guy with dark eyebrows that made a sharp "V" on his forehead, so he always had this heavy look like he was planning to pull out a dead rat or something and throw it at you and then laugh.

"Her pussy was so tight, man. . ."

I stared up at the tree above me. We were supposed to be learning to identify them. Pine tree, definitely. Growing up in the South, you get to know pine trees. Silvertip? Sugartip? Something like that.

"I'm not kidding, I had eight orgasms that night, and shit, she must'a had about a thousand."

He didn't have to say that. Eight orgasms? In one night? Rolling onto my side, I propped myself on one elbow and drank my little can of apple juice. I stared at his crotch. He looked like he had a lot crammed into his underwear. All I could think was, didn't it start to leak out? Where does all the cum go after you shoot off eight times inside a girl? But you don't go asking questions like that, or everybody can tell you're inexperienced.

Maybe he had been using a rubber. Can you use a rubber eight times? Probably not. Probably he wasn't using one anyway. This was all back in the days when nobody worried about safe sex, or getting pregnant. The only thing I worried about was not getting any, period.

I checked my watch. We had twenty minutes before lunch was over. I got up to look around for a little privacy.

The cabins were no good. Across the lawn from them stood the mess hall, but the cook lived in a back room, so that was out. I went the other way. The building with the toilets and showers would be too busy. It had a laundry room, but that was too small. Only the barn was left. I walked up to the big door and felt a cool draft from inside.

I could go and sit in a truck to do it, but what if someone came in the barn?

I kept going, around behind the building. At the hose I had noticed a shed tacked onto the back of the barn, and when no one was looking I ducked inside. It was a woodshed. The door creaked and wouldn't quite close behind me, but I thought maybe I had found the secret place I needed.

Sunlight streamed in through gaps between the planks of the walls. I could see out through the cracks, but I knew that no one could see me inside as long as I stayed out of the bright shafts of light. I moved to the darkest corner and sat on the stack of wood, leaning back onto the rough chunks. With my shirt off, the bark scratched my bare skin. I liked the feel of being muddy and half-naked. I moved my hand to my crotch and squeezed myself.

I felt my whole body relax. Something clicks in my brain whenever I get my hand on my dick. Something about grabbing myself by the root sends me into another world, where everything is peaceful and safe. I rubbed my stomach and my eyelids drooped. My prick throbbed through my pants. I felt my arm muscle. Firming up okay. Not anywhere close to Steve's, but not bad for a new kid. I unzipped my pants and poked my finger inside, tracing the lump in my shorts. This is my refuge, I thought, this is my safe place, this is where I can get away from all the assholes of the world.

Something stuck under a chunk of wood caught my eye. I pulled out a folded-up magazine. The cover had a picture of a naked woman with her legs spread apart. Her fingers stretched her cunt wide open, showing pink, wet folds of skin. Somebody else in camp had a problem in his pants. Most of the pictures inside were black and white. I turned to the color centerfold.

The pages were stuck together. My dick strained in my pants as I peeled them apart, tearing the paper. Damn, those were cum spots. Some other guy had come in here to hide and beat off over the magazine. I touched the dried spots and wondered how old they were. Could have been last night.

The picture showed a naked man kneeling between the woman's legs, ready to insert a huge penis into her. I stared at it. He was just a kid, with a goofy grin on his face, but he had a dick the size of Stanley's. The big head was just pushing the lips of her pussy apart.

I flipped through the pages. On the back cover there was one more color shot, a close-up that showed the guy's dick all the way inside her. The girl's twat was swollen up, crammed so full of his meat that the lips bulged around it. I wondered what that must feel like, to be wrapped around a man's hard cock like that.

Dried cum was splattered on that page, too. I imagined another boy whipping off, groaning and sprinkling his load over the magazine. I touched the wrinkled spots, wondering whose cum it was, which dick it had come out of. I slipped my fingers inside my Jockeys and touched my hard-on. I was just flipping it out when I realized the dinging sound in the distance was the cook's triangle, the signal to go back to work.

This is how guys get blue balls, I thought, putting the jack-off book back where I'd found it, and then stuffing my dick back into my pants.

Well, at least I knew I had a good hideout when I needed to get into some serious jerking off. I could come back after work, when I had some time.

Okay, so I overdo it, I admit that. I could stand to cut back, maybe hold it down to a few times a week. But quit cold turkey? All summer long?

No way.

After work I was so tired I could hardly drag myself to the showers. I was almost late for dinner. Everyone was crowded outside the mess hall, and the door opened as I walked up. We all rushed to sit on benches around four long tables covered with tacked-down oilcloth. Every night was a feast, served family style.

The mess hall used thick white porcelain dishes and coffee mugs. Each piece of crockery had a green stripe around the edge, and in the center a shield with "US Forest Service" and a big tree on it. I liked that.

They always served two or three kinds of meat, and heaping bowls of good, simple vegetables, mashed potatoes, sweet potatoes, peas, corn on the cob, beans, everything, and then thick, gooey desserts. We could eat fried chicken, ham, and roast beef, all in the same meal, or we could eat three steaks in a row. They never told us to quiet down, and they never, ever, ran out of food.

"Long as you men can eat it," the cook always said, "my job is to keep it coming at you." He had a big belly under his apron, and he looked like he knew all about putting food away. "You ain't never going hungry out here," he'd say. "You want more later? Door's unlocked until ten o'clock. Eat all you want, wash your own dishes, and don't throw nothing away."

It was paradise. I could feel myself growing bigger as I ate.

After dinner I shuffled across the lawn, stuffed and sleepy. At the cabin I had to detour around a car parked at an angle, blocking our door, right under the "Do Not Park Here" sign. It was an old blue convertible with the top down, a boxy Oldsmobile with a Montana plate dangling from the bumper. A spray of mud streaked the door.

Inside the cabin I found an army surplus duffel bag on the bed above mine. My heart dropped a bit, because I'd hoped that bunk would stay empty, but I was too tired to care. Whoever had put it there wasn't in the room, so I kicked off my shoes and fell onto my bed to read myself to sleep.

My eyelids were drooping when the new guy walked in and tossed something onto the upper bunk. He leaned down and took a toothpick out of his mouth. "Guess we're gonna be neighbors," he said pleasantly. "My name's Donnie." He stuck out his hand.

With the bare lightbulb glaring in my eyes from behind him, I couldn't make out much of his face, but I could see that he had a bushy brown mustache and long sideburns, much shaggier than anything my mom ever let me get away with. He seemed a lot older than me, at least twenty, maybe twenty-one.

"Bill," I said, taking his hand. "Bill Bartholomews."

"Howdy," he nodded. His palm was rough, but his grip was gentle.

When he stood up to unpack his bag, I saw he wore stained old cowboy boots, the light brown kind with the suede finish and squared-off toes. His bluejeans were faded to sky blue, worn down to white spots at the knees, with more white strands at the cuffs. They were so thin and snug I could make out the muscles of his butt moving under the cloth as he carried some clothes to the locker at the foot of my bed.

He walked back over and reached for more of his things from above me. His belt buckle was right at my eye level. It was a brass horse, rearing back on its hind legs, pawing at the air. The buckle was huge, easily three inches high. It looked like it weighed half a pound, and the horse's nose and ears stuck up over the top of his jeans and touched his shirt. I'd never seen anything like it, but that wasn't what really got my attention.

Below the prancing horse, below his fly, there was a long, curving line, tucked down the inside of his right pants leg. It was the obvious outline of his sex, showing through under his jeans for all the world to see. He was practically letting his dick hang right out in public, like it was just any old part of his body.

I stared at it. Back home, guys just don't do that. Most guys couldn't if they wanted to, but even if the could, they wouldn't.

Damn. I could even see the ridge at the end of the thick tube, and the heart shape of the head on it.

He leaned forward and fiddled with something on his bunk above me. I couldn't take my eyes off the bulging lump inside his jeans. After a minute he startled me by touching his finger to his belt buckle. I looked up, and saw that he was watching me stare at his pants.

He glanced down at his belt buckle and ran his finger along the brass horse's back, very slowly, and then petted its head with his fingertip.

Softly, he asked me, "You like my pony?"

"Uh, yeah," I stammered, "it's, um. . .very interesting. I've, uh, never seen one so. . . big."

I looked up again. Donnie had a long, narrow face with a straight nose and a thick chin that had a dimple in the center. In the light, I could see his eyes were brown with tiny wrinkles at the edges, wrinkles that grew into creases as a big smile spread over his face. His mustache was thick with straggly hairs that curled into his mouth and entirely covered his upper lip. His mustache grew down either side of his mouth all the way to his jawline.

He nodded and said, "Yup. Big horses turn me on." As his smile turned into a broad grin, his teeth showed under his mustache, and the corners of his eyelids crinkled up even more.

The door banged open. Steve barged into the cabin.

"Hey hey hey," he yelled, grabbing Donnie from behind in a bear hug. "Look who dragged his scroungy ass into camp three days late."

Donnie's arms were pinned to his sides, but he twisted and swung Steve around and into the empty locker at the foot of my bed. Metal boomed and Donnie cackled, breaking free and scrambling up onto his bunk above me.

Steve tried to follow, saying, "Huh, cowboy? Huh, Donnie the stud? Whatcha been doing, out fucking the cows again?"

His stubby bare legs dangled over the rail, but Donnie pushed him back with his boot and then jumped down after him. The blond boy fell into a chair, laughing, and Donnie grabbed his neck in an arm-lock. The two panted and giggled at each other.

Stanley drifted into the cabin and sat on his bed.

Standing up, Steve bellowed, "Hey, you guys, I want you to meet the biggest fuck-off in the history of Camp North Fork. This is Donnie Powers, and he's the only dude besides me who ever made it through a whole summer here without doing a lick of work. Last year, we stayed drunk the whole first two months."

Donnie chuckled. Leaning on the bed, he pulled off his boots and dropped them on the floor, then returned to unpacking his bag. The horse on his belt pranced two feet from my face.

Steve said, "I thought you weren't coming back here this summer. What happened to working on your daddy's ranch?"

Donnie gathered the rest of his clothes in his arms and tossed them into the bottom of his locker. He stood at my feet, popping open his shirt. It was western cut, with embroidered shoulders and pearl snaps on the cuffs and down the front.

"Ain't no future to it," he said, tugging his shirttail out. "Place is too small to make any money these days. Soon as my sister gets out of high school, my old man's likely gonna sell it and buy a trailer. Him and my mom want to move to Arizona."

His baggy teeshirt draped in folds at the waist but pulled tight across his shoulders. When he hung up his shirt and closed the metal doors, the tendons stood out on his forearm.

"Would you believe, I'm going to college this year?" he asked

Steve, lifting his teeshirt to rub his belly. He couldn't see me, and
I stared at the mat of hair above his belt.

Steve laughed and rocked forward in his chair. "Shit, you?
Where, reform school?"

"Naw, asshole, for real. Missoula." Donnie shifted his weight
and tilted his hips, framed by the metal bedposts at my feet. I
could see from his chin to his knees. Still holding his shirt up,
he sucked in his stomach and slipped a hand inside his pants to
scratch and adjust himself. When he let go, his dick showed
through his jeans even longer than before.

He took a breath and stretched, locking his fingers behind his
head. "'Course, we got to have a good fire season so I can save
up the bucks for tuition."

With his elbows up, curly brown hair, long strands of it,
protruded from the sagging armholes of his teeshirt. He twisted
his torso, slowly to the right, then to the left, groaning slightly.
When his pants pulled tight, the head of his cock showed in
outline, and his balls. He let his breath out in a rush and dropped
his arms.

I sighed with him.

Suddenly ducking his head under the rail again, he asked me,
"How about you, Bill? You in school?"

His friendly brown eyes made me picture him riding a horse
and squinting into the sun. His muttonchop sideburns bristled
out on both sides of his cheeks, and untrimmed whiskers curled
into his mouth at the corners. Donnie wasn't pretty. His face was
too thin, and his nose too long and straight. But, damn, he sure
was all male.

What had he said to me?

"Uh, yeah," I mumbled. "I'm going to Carolina. North
Carolina. The university, I mean. This fall." Dummy, I thought.
Of course it's this fall. When else?

Donnie didn't seem to notice. Standing up, he turned to
Stanley and asked, "How about you?"

I had forgotten he was there. Stanley shrugged. "I don't
know. I just got this job. I don't know what I'll do after that."

Donnie unbuckled his belt. His jeans were button-fly Levi's,
and he unfastened them slowly. "You from around here?"

"No," Stanley said. "Iowa. Near Des Moines." Steve snickered.

Stanley glared at him. "Don't start giving me shit."

Donnie interrupted, "Nothing wrong with Iowa. I hear it's real pretty there." Turning his back to me, he dropped his pants, and I saw why his privates showed through so plainly. He wore boxer shorts, big baggy ones.

Somebody outside yelled, "Hey, that's Powers' car. Hey, fucker, where are you?"

Guys I didn't know yet thundered into the room, slapping backs and jabbing at Donnie's arm. Donnie grinned and hopped around in front of his locker, off balance with his pants around his ankles.

"Come on down to our place," one of them said.

Pulling up his pants with a wiggle of his butt, Donnie buttoned up and went outside with them.

Steve followed, grinning and strutting, nodding his head to anything anybody said.

Stanley and I were left in silence. He shook his head. "I wish Steve would move down there with all those other loudmouths." He went to his locker and took off his shirt.

"So," I said. "How long did it take to get here from Iowa? I was on the bus three days coming out."

He shrugged. "Couple of days. I was hitchhiking."

My eyes widened. "Really? All by yourself? Isn't that dangerous?"

He smiled grimly. "Not as dangerous as staying home. My dad hates my guts. He tried to kill me a couple of weeks ago."

Still wearing his pants, he took his towel and toilet kit to go wash up in the now-deserted shower room.

Donnie was the last one to go to bed, coming in after Steve had flipped the light off. I listened to him undress at the foot of my bed.

Thump, he dropped his boot. *Thump*, the other one. His belt buckle tinkled, then clanked on the floor as he stripped off his pants. Leaving his clothes in a pile where they dropped, he stepped onto the rail by my feet. The bed bumped against the wall as he climbed into the upper bunk.

In my mind I saw the brass horse, prancing over his snug jeans, pawing at his hairy bellybutton. The horse became an erect penis. How big would his be, in action? I saw him in the back seat of his convertible, top down, with a girl. I could see his white behind, pants down to his thighs, putting it to her. In the dark, I wondered, why does he stick in my mind? He's not even that good-looking. Nose is too long. Big feet, too. You know what they say about guys with big feet. Bet he's really hung, under those droopy drawers he wears. Hick underwear. But, something about the way he moves is sexy, the way he swivels his hips, chewing that toothpick and squinting.

A cowboy, I thought as I drifted off to sleep, listening to Steve's snoring. My bunkmate is a cowboy.

The bed swayed. Tired as I was, I sort of surfaced for a minute and then sank back into sleep. The bed moved again. I wasn't used to anyone in the bunk above me. I turned over and nestled against my pillow. The bed jostled some more. My eyes popped open.

I knew that movement. Every boy knows that movement.

Donnie was jacking off.

My heart skipped a beat. There was no mistaking that rhythm. He wasn't being at all shy about it. The bed began to jiggle rapidly. My dick thickened under my belly, sprouting out against the mattress.

It was too much for Billy Beat-off. I rolled over onto my back. I wiggled my shorts down and tugged on my boner. The bed was going *bump-bump-bump* as Donnie pumped away on himself. What the hell, I kicked my briefs all the way off, crossed my legs and started pumping with him.

I tried to imagine an older guy like Donnie masturbating. Did he have his boxer shorts down around his knees? Or all the way off, like me? Or was his cock sticking up out of the fly? These things are important.

I pulled at my nuts. My hand moved faster. I was getting close, breathing hard, when Donnie stopped.

I stopped too, holding my breath, listening to the silence. He must have heard me or felt the bed move from my own hand job. I waited in the dark, frozen, my dick in my hand. Was he playing some sort of game?

Sheets rustled above me. God, what if big Donnie was getting up, like Stanley had done, and was going to climb down to my bed?

But then the bunks began to rock again. He must have thrown back the covers, because I could hear the slight slapping sound as he resumed his steady beating off.

The sound of his fist on his cock electrified me. What a ballsy fucker. I pushed my own blanket down. I grabbed my dick in both hands and felt my right palm get slick around my cockhead as the base of my prick throbbed between my left fingers.

BONK BONK BONK the bedframe thumped against the wall, and then the springs above me squeaked as Donnie stiffened in his bunk.

"*G-h-h. . .NUH!*" he went. Right out loud! The shaking stopped, but the bed swayed from side to side as Donnie twisted above me in his orgasm. "*NUH!*" he grunted again. "*UH! UH! Uhhh UH!*"

I shot off so hard my wad sailed all the way up and hit my cheek. I turned my head and felt another wet blob land in my ear. I was rigid in my bunk, still spurting out onto my teeshirt, when Donnie took a deep breath and sighed.

Stanley giggled from across the room, and then Steve went, "Hyah!"

Bastard. He didn't laugh when I did it.

"Sorry about that, guys," Donnie said. "Every now and then I have to see if it still works."

We all laughed, and then Donnie rolled over. By the time I found my Jockey shorts and cleaned out my ear, he was starting to snore.

I dabbed lines of cum off my belly, marvelling at how openly he had gotten himself off. He hadn't tried to be quiet, hadn't even cleaned himself up afterwards, just flopped over and went to sleep.

Shit almighty, it was only his first night in the cabin with us!

I listened to his snoring, lying awake half naked, holding my sticky briefs over a hard-on that would not go away.

4

The horse was huge, its shoulder as high as my face, covered with coarse bristles of reddish-brown hair, a giant animal standing right in front of me, so big and wild and muscular that I edged back away from it until my butt pressed against the fence, and the beast stood there going *FWAH*! through its nostrils, dripping mucus and puffing steam, with one brown eye fixed on me, staring me up against the fence.

Nervous as I was, I just had to find out something — had to know for sure about something that made my face burn with shame just for thinking about it, but I had to look anyway, down underneath the monster's belly, to see if it was true what they say about horses, down there. No one would see. No one would know if I was careful and just peeked.

Slowly, slowly, I turned my head and peered underneath, trying not to make any sudden movements that would startle the horse, because he was so big he could stomp me like a bug, but I got my head down, moving like I was stuck inside a bottle of glue, and then I saw it, and yes, it was true what they say, the horse's dick was big as my leg, and it was growing as I watched it, lengthening, sticky-wet red at the tip, uncurling from inside his belly, and then it came up at me, poked up at my face, and then suddenly the cowboy yelled, "Hey!"

Oh shit! I'm in trouble now, he caught me molesting his horse!

"Hey, man!"

Oh, shit, I didn't touch it, I just looked. Backing up, I tried to scramble over the fence backwards, and then with horror I felt the fence collapse behind me, and I was falling, and I couldn't grab anything to stop from going backwards, over backwards, and the cowboy yelled at me again, "Hey!"

"Hey, Bartholomew! You still in the sack?"

Donnie was shaking my leg. "Hey, Bartholomew, wake up, man."

I groaned and rubbed my eyes. "Mews," I said groggily. "My

name is Bartholomews." I realized I'd skittered backwards into the corner of my bunkbed, out from under my covers. Donnie grinned down at me. I looked down and saw my dick sticking straight up below the edge of my teeshirt. I was sitting bare-assed on my pillow. Where was my underwear? Where was I? Where was that horse? I covered my naked hard-on and tried to get my eyes to work right.

Donnie stood up and started making his bunk. His boxer shorts and hairy legs were right in my face, and I began to remember about the cowboy, and the brass belt buckle.

"Better get your ass in gear, man," he said from above. "Breakfast is in ten minutes. Everybody else is down at the head already."

He raised up on tiptoe to tuck in his blanket. His shorts were inches from my nose, and underneath the folds of thin, white cloth, a hefty weight swung back and forth with every movement of his hips. When he fluffed his pillow, his dick bounced around right in front of my face. He reached out to plop his pillow into place and his teeshirt hitched up, exposing the thick tangle of curly hairs just above his shorts, dark and kinky against the white skin of his belly. I was so close I could see the individual bristles spiralling down over his waistband. When he leaned forward again, his boxers got a fold in them right at the base of his dick, and the cloth tightened around the fat tube until the tip of it dangled out from the lower edge of his shorts.

I put my hand under my blanket and played with my hard-on as I watched him sleepily.

He stepped back to judge his bed-making, idly tugging his boxers down to cover his big dick again. He yawned, slipping one hand inside his underwear. His wrist pushed the waistband down as he reached back under his nuts to scratch himself. I saw more hair, an even thicker bush of it, sprouting and growing and curling out at me. For a second I glimpsed the base of his dick, a section of white skin buried in dark brown. The hairs around it were at least two inches long, radiating out in all directions from the root of his sex. I swallowed hard and squeezed myself as I heard his fingernail go "scritch, scritch, scritch" between his legs.

Then he snapped the waistband back up and said, "Good enough for government work."

He leaned over me again and pointed at my chest. "Looks like fresh pecker tracks."

"What?" I looked down at my front. There were big yellow spots on the white teeshirt, lines of dried semen reaching all the way up to my neck. So that part hadn't been a dream, at least.

Donnie reached out and touched my undershirt by the collar. "You must'a been holding that one in for a while, sport," he said. He ran the tip of his finger down my front, tracing the cum stains all the way down to where my teeshirt disappeared under the blanket. Another inch and he would have touched my dick, which was rock hard in my fist. I couldn't move. His finger stopped at my bellybutton. He poked me and then bent over suddenly.

"Want your shorts back?" he grinned, picking my Jockeys from the floor with two fingers. I remembered wiping up with them in the middle of the night, and now they were a stiff wad of white cloth and dried semen.

"Actually, I thought I'd put on some clean ones," I said.

Donnie held my briefs up in the light and slowly peeled them apart where the cum stuck the fabric together. "Why don't you wear these? I do it all the time. See here? See my drawers?"

He stepped up closer and pointed at the fly of his boxers, at his own dried yellow spots. "Pecker tracks," he said again. He hooked a thumb in the waistband, pulling his underwear down again to expose his hairy belly. Up close, I could see that his bushy pubic hair was matted with flakes of white, dried cum. "See all that? I'm full'a spunk, huh? I like it like that."

I couldn't breathe.

He rubbed his fingers over it. "Makes me feel real healthy, you know? Working all day with my britches full'a cum." He snapped the waistband and held out my Jockeys. "Here, put these back on. Come on, trust me. You'll get a big charge out of it."

He dropped them on my middle. I let go of myself and picked up my shorts. I couldn't stall any longer. I elbowed back my blanket and got up. I stood on the cold linoleum floor with nothing on but my teeshirt, and felt my hard-on swinging around in the chilly morning air.

Donnie watched me pull up my underwear. My erection stretched the front out of shape. Donnie just grinned, toying with himself through his boxers. "I know how it is," he said. "I tried to get mine to go down last night, but it don't last very long."

He looked down and put his fingers around his dick, and this time the whole head of it hung out from underneath his boxers. He turned around to step into his jeans, and I went to my own locker. I could barely zip my pants.

I sat across from him at breakfast. He had on a blue workshirt with the sleeves rolled up above his elbows, and I watched the muscles move under the brown hairs on his forearms as he ate. The rolled-up sleeve tightened around his biceps muscle when he lifted his fork. For a while he had some strawberry jam on his mustache, but then as he laughed he licked it off.

Checking out tools inside the barn, I got in line behind him, close enough to read the Levi's label on the back of his jeans: waist 32, length 34. I could wear his pants, but they wouldn't fill out on me the way they did on him, and they'd be a little short. He had a habit of casually tugging his crotch as he talked and joked with the other guys, but no one else seemed to see it. I hoped he would be working with my crew.

We waited at the end of the line in the musty dimness. Donnie pointed at the row of pale green trucks. "Used to keep mules in here, until they put the logging road through to the North Fork. I'd like to have been here back then. Everything would have been two notches slower. Mule speed. That's my speed."

The line moved up as boys checked out shovels and sling-blades. Something tickled my crotch. Donnie had his hands behind his back, wiggling his fingers at me.

I peered around. Everyone was in front of us, looking ahead. I stepped closer to his butt, and he found my dick with his fingertips and pinched the head of it through my pants, right there in front of everybody. Well, really behind everybody. No one else knew.

The last boy ahead ordered a pick and a hoe, then turned to joke with us. Donnie nodded, "Uh-huh," still fiddling with the front of my pants. I was starting to get hard, enough for him to get his fingers around my dick right through the cloth. When it was his turn to face the stern old man who passed out equipment, he looked up at the pudgy face. "Uh, sir?" he boomed. "I'd like to check out a tool, sir."

Donnie wasn't just working with us, it turned out. He was in charge. I followed him outside, staring at the way his butt moved under his Levi's. He had a slow, deliberate walk that was so sexy I couldn't take my eyes away.

We chomped into the gravelly soil. As the sun got higher and hotter, guys began pulling off shirts and tying them around their waists, then stripping off their teeshirts. Donnie had blots of sweat under his arms, but didn't seem to notice the heat.

At break time the others made a semicircle around him to talk, and my eyes wandered along his arms where he had rolled up his sleeves. His veins stood out, long blue lines that showed under the skin even high up on his arm muscles, not just down on his forearms like everyone else.

When the break was over he squinted at the sun and turned his back to me and unbuttoned his shirt. I fiddled with my buttons. He dropped his blue workshirt on the grass, then lifted his teeshirt over his head and dropped that, too. Hitching up his pants, he turned and walked toward me. The sun seemed to flare hotter.

With his shirt off, Donnie was as beautiful as a wild animal. His chest wasn't huge like Steve's, but it seemed perfectly shaped, with sharply defined muscles that threw slight shadows underneath his nipples, big brown nipples that stood out to points wide apart under broad, sloping shoulders. His chest was marked like an animal's, with fine brown hairs, a dark river of hair that streamed into the hollow between his nipples and flowed down, then fanned out over his belly. From the sides of his body, each hair pointed toward the center of his torso, as though neatly combed inward and then down, to form a line, a dark ridge of body hair. The ridge ran down the center of his slender waist, spread around his navel, and then grew to a flood of curls that disappeared underneath his jeans at his belt buckle. The bronco was poised over the rest of it, rearing up over what I knew he had packed inside his pants. No man had ever looked so magnificent to me as Donnie with his shirt off in the sun that day.

After break, it was much rougher work than before. We had to pry out the biggest rocks and carry them away in a wheelbarrow to make a border around the parking lot. We hacked at the big stones with picks and crowbars, clawing them up and shovelling out the dirt.

I went into a daze, watching the crew struggle around me, stooping and lifting, their bare shoulders and mud-splattered backs glistening with sweat. I wondered if any of them could smell my cum, if anyone beside Donnie and me secretly had sex drippings plastered to his body, hidden in the hair inside his pants. Boy, did I feel healthy.

We sweated and ached, and I had more strength in me that day than I'd ever known. By noon we cut through to the puddle. When the water finally started draining into our little canal we all cheered and stomped in it like kids, scooping the soupy mud along with our shovels.

After lunch, an older guy came by and told Donnie he was wanted in the office.

I said, "I'll wash off your shovel for you."

He handed it to me and said, "See you tonight after work." He winked, picked up his shirt, and left me standing there, watching his lean butt twitch as he walked away.

That afternoon we started hauling gravel and spreading it in the hole where the puddle had drained. I felt full of spunk, horsing around and sliding in the mud. We started racing with the wheelbarrows full of gravel, and I got blindsided and sent sprawling. It split the seam in my old pants, but I was so covered with mud it didn't show.

At quitting time we had to hose down all the tools, and then we took turns spraying each other. Somebody stuck the nozzle in the tear in my rear end, so we wrestled and shouted and splashed in the sunlight. When we ended up in a panting heap on the lawn, I was on bottom. When we tugged off our boots and stripped to our shorts, I held up the hose to rinse off all the bodies, because I was the tallest. It was easy to flush off a few pairs of underwear along with the mud, and see their cold little cocks all shrivelled up tight. Mine wasn't. Ice cubes couldn't have done that with the way their wet underwear was clinging to their butts and sagging in front.

In the cabin, Donnie wasn't back yet but Steve was undressing in his corner. He pointed at me and laughed as I stood in the door, dripping. "Get in a good workout today?" he asked.

"Busted my ass," I said, holding the torn pants so he could see the hole. I tossed them into the corner and peeled off my soggy briefs.

"See, they'll put some weight on that skinny bod of yours yet, man," he said, slapping my bare behind as he walked out.

I stood there a moment, staring at the empty doorway. It stung where he had popped me, and I liked it. Cool drafts touched between my legs. Guys walking by could see me naked, so I stepped back from the door, partly hidden, partly exposed. The evening air was thick with male sexuality, deep voices and dirty talk. This week everybody was saying "Fuckin'-A, man, fuckin'-A," whatever that meant. I was at half-mast without even touching myself. Moving back into my corner by the door, I leaned against my locker and tensed the muscles inside me that make my dick bounce when it's hard. I wanted to go running across the lawn, to jump up and down with my balls flapping between my legs. I wanted to run into the shower room and slap all the boys' butts, play with their dicks, feel their slippery bodies.

"You're like a crab." Stanley's voice came from the shadow behind the half-open door. I jumped back, startled. "When crabs get too big for their shells," he continued, "they split them open and crawl out of them and grow new ones."

"Damn, you scared me. What are you doing over there?"

He moved out into the light. "I live here, remember?" His eyes were on my midsection.

"I don't know what you're talking about."

"Crustaceans. And your pants that you split open. Obviously, you're, ah, growing."

The creep was making me wilt. He had a prissy way about him that turned me off. I turned my back to him and wrapped up in my towel.

I was half-through washing when Donnie came in and took the shower across from me. As he stood with his face into the spray, I got a good look at him, seeing him buck naked for the first time.

The tan on his back stopped at his belt line, and below that his skin was white all the way down to his feet. He was slightly bowlegged, and the backs of his calves were rubbed almost hairless. His thighs were shaggier, and the leg hairs grew halfway up the cheeks of his butt like a permanent pair of furry pants always partly lowered. Between the cheeks a tuft of darker, coarser hair sprouted out from the crevice, right about where the hole of his ass would be. More long strands of pubic hair hung between his legs.

When he turned to rinse his back, he didn't seem to have

much more of a nozzle than anyone else. It was the standard three inches or so, soft. But the ones on the other boys hung straight down. Donnie's seemed to arch out from the base of his belly, curving over his big balls before it drooped toward the floor. When he soaped it up, his pubic hair protruded between his fingers in thick, sudsy bunches.

I stood beside him as we towelled ourselves off, and just being that close to him, both of us nude, made my mind spin.

When Donnie and I got back to the cabin to dress for dinner, Stanley was sitting on his bunk with his toilet kit. When Steve came back, Stanley got up to go out in his towel, but first he stopped in the door and looked at me.

"Just remember, Bill," he said softly. "When crabs change their shells, it takes a while for the new one to harden." He touched my stomach very lightly. "Between shells, a lot of them get eaten." A smile crossed his face before he left.

"What was all that about?" Steve asked.

"I dunno," I said. "Stanley's weird."

Donnie said, "Sounds to me like you might have something going tonight."

I turned to him. "Are you kidding? With Stanley? Bleah."

Steve made a jerking-off motion with his fist by his fly. "Hey man, go for it, you know?"

"Aw, forget it." I sat on my bed. This was not what I wanted to hear, and I certainly didn't want either of them to know I had already gone for it with Stanley.

Steve wouldn't let up. "Shit, he's got a real dick-face, you know what I mean? Can't you tell? Look at his mouth. Can't you just see a dick in it? I mean, that guy has a cocksucker look if I ever saw one. Where'd he go, anyway? It's almost dinner. Is he just now hitting the showers?"

Donnie said, "He told me you called him a donkey dick. He says he's going to wait until after you finish before he goes to the showers from now on."

Steve grinned. "Now isn't that real sweet. I embarrassed the poor kid."

"You embarrass everybody, you turkey," Donnie said. "You're an embarrassment to the whole camp. To the whole Forest Service. To all of fucking America."

"Hey hey hey, that good, huh? Let's go eat."

We walked across the lawn to stand in front of the mess hall. Steve and Donnie hung out with the older guys, so I stood with them, and when the cook rang the triangle and the rush for tables started, I stayed right on Donnie's tail and sat with them.

Later, I sat on the steps of our cabin, only half listening to Steve and Donnie talking inside.

"Gotta get dressed before the queer gets back," Steve said, pulling up his gym shorts and grabbing his volleyball. He collected his socks and sneakers and darted out the door beside me as Stanley plodded across the lawn toward us.

Donnie turned to his locker and took out a leather jacket. It was brown sheepskin, worn and stained on the outside, furry white inside. He walked back to the door and stood there, gazing outside, over my head.

After a minute, he shifted his weight. Without looking directly at me, he asked, "You want to go drink a beer?"

"Out here? Where can you get a beer?"

"I got some in my cooler. Out in the car. Don't tell anybody."

I grabbed a jacket and followed him to the parking lot just as Stanley was going into the cabin. Stanley was still standing in the doorway watching us as I got into the car.

Donnie fished out two cans of beer from the trunk and tossed one to me as he got behind the wheel. The convertible top was up. The fabric inside was ragged and split.

"They fire you for drinking in camp," he warned me, cracking open the beer. "Keep an eye out." We drank in silence for a while. I kept an eye out, not sure for what, but glad to feel the glow of the beer. Donnie looked straight ahead most of the time, with his hand on his crotch. As he drank he rubbed himself absently with his thumb.

I took a pull of beer and asked, "How come you're in the cabin with us? I thought they put all the second and third year guys together at the other end."

"I checked in too late. I don't know why Steve's in this end. Maybe nobody else wanted his mouth around. Anyway, I don't mind him in the cabin. Stanley's all right. You're all right. We've got a pretty good crew, everything considered." He crumpled his beer can and dropped it over his shoulder into the back. It clanked against other cans on the floorboard. He leaned back and looked at the pile.

"Guess I ought to toss that shit out before some cop stops me. I never been much for keeping a car clean." He blew a puff of dust off the dash. "Never washed it in three years. Once you start, you just have to keep doing it. This way I don't have to worry about where I take it, 'cause it's already dirty. And it's too fucked up to steal. Like me, too goddam grubby to fuck around with. Life's a lot simpler that way." He winked at me. "Let's drink us one more, okay?"

While he was out getting the beer from the trunk, I looked around the car, Donnie's own little world. An old sleeping bag was flopped loosely on the back seat, with a fishing rod sticking out from under it. Lifting a corner of the bag, I found a flashlight, a hunting knife, and an old Playboy. One worn-out sneaker was under my feet in the front, with a hole in it where his little toe would be. I didn't see the other one anywhere.

I wondered if he'd been camping and fishing on his way to Idaho. That was probably why he had been late. "Shit," I whispered to myself, making a mark in the dust with my finger.

I leaned back and sighed. He'd said I was all right. I rubbed the too-clean sleeve of my jacket in the dust and then groped myself between the legs, feeling sexy. But when he got back in the car, I moved my hand.

Across the lawn, the night's volleyball game was still going. Their shouts sounded like birdcalls in the dusk. I could make out Steve's blond hair and stocky figure, swatting the ball, jumping and clapping.

"*AHRP!*" Donnie burped. "It'll be too dark to play pretty soon," he said, settling back in his seat. "Your buddy Steve will be looking for you."

"Shit," I protested. "He's not my buddy. He's a pain in the ass. I wish he'd move to another cabin."

Donnie took a gulp of beer. "Steve's just a tad uptight. You'll get used to him."

"Well," I said, shifting in my seat, "I wish he wouldn't keep calling everybody. . ." I hesitated, but the beer made me feel reckless, and I said it. ". . .queer."

There was a silence, a skip in the conversation that lasted too long, and I thought, oh fuck. I didn't have the nerve to look at Donnie. I stared straight ahead, waiting to find out if I had blown it completely.

Donnie held his beer up and scratched his mustache with his index finger. "Well, we're all queer for somebody or another," he said, and took a drink. "Difference with Steve is, he's just queer for himself, and don't know it."

I relaxed a bit. From the corner of my eye I could see Donnie fiddling with his lap again, petting himself, and I wondered if he could hear my heart thumping.

"Y'know," he said, "I got a buddy back home, works at the ranch, and he just loves that word. He'll say stuff like, 'It got real queer out today,' and he knows it gets me turned on, because I know he's horny to fool around some. He'll say, 'Let's go in the shower and turn queer,' and then he'll watch me get a boner and just laugh and laugh. Big dick on him, too. Big ol' knobby thing, 'bout that long." He held his fingers up a foot apart and grinned at me. "You got a jack-off buddy back home?"

I cleared my throat. "Uh, no. Well, I used to do it with my best friend, but, uh, well we haven't done it for a long time." After a silence, I had to giggle. "He said it was too queer for him."

Donnie burped again. "Probably means he liked it too much. That's what everybody's afraid of, that they'll like it better doing it with their buddies than doing it with their girlfriends."

"What about you?" I asked him. "Don't you go for girls?"

Donnie shrugged. "Girls are okay. But they seem to like me a whole lot more than I like them. They want something else, you know what I mean? They want shit I never even think about."

I nodded, although I didn't have any idea what he meant.

Donnie tugged at the bump in his jeans again. "Guys are so much more practical about sex. Like tonight, for instance. I'm horny, and I plan to get my rocks off out here in the car before I go back inside."

"Oh yeah?" I cleared my throat again. "Want some company?"

"See what I mean? If I was with most any girl I know, there'd be all sorts of complications. But I expected you'd just either stay or go, and not make much of a fuss about it."

I stayed, and I didn't make any fuss at all.

He got two more beers from the trunk and we took off our coats and tossed them on the back seat. "You keep your arms up on the window and on the back of the seat," he told me. "We don't want to upset any of the bozos if they look over here. I'll see if I can get you turned on."

Still sitting on his side of the seat, he put his hand on my lap. I took a deep breath as I felt his fingers poke between my legs, exploring my crotch. He lowered my zipper, reached inside my pants, and cupped his hand around my Jockey shorts. "Mmm, pretty quick trigger on you, big guy," he said. "I like that."

Dropping my empty in back, I reached for Donnie's lap. He was already hard under the denim. I felt the length of it, the long rod of his dick running down the inside of his thigh.

Donnie put his hand on top of mine, and moved my fingers up to his belt buckle. "Pull on it," he whispered. I tugged it open. He stroked the back of my hand. "Now," he said, "unbutton my pants, buddy."

My hand was trembling, and it took me a few minutes to get the hang of unbuttoning another guy's pants, with my left hand, too. The buttons popped open, one by one, and Donnie pushed my hand inside his jeans. "Get my dick out for me," he said quietly.

My own cock was stretching my briefs. He got one finger under the side of the pouch, and slowly pulled the head out. Fumbling inside the fly of his boxers, I felt strands of hair, and then soft skin. Following it with my fingertips, I tugged until the rubbery thing popped out into my hand, warm and smooth. I thought my heart would burst as I closed my fingers around Donnie's big dick. He twisted his hand, and then he was holding me in his fist, too, all of me.

"Ah-h-h-h," he sighed, settling back. "Ain't dicks great? Everybody ought'a have at least two."

We got comfortable, slouching down and playing with each other, keeping our eyes straight ahead. It excited me when guys looked over at the car, but I knew they could only see our heads and shoulders.

His dick jutted up from the slot in his jeans, long enough that I could thump it against the steering wheel. It was broad and flat on the upper side. As my hand moved down over it, the width of it forced my fingers apart.

The head was stubby, and then it flared out as though it had shoulders. It was like a toy soldier, only he had his helmet pulled all the way down over his head. No face, just a helmet and shoulders, standing up at attention in my fist.

"I haven't done this since about the tenth grade," I told him. "My friend and I used to double date, and the girls always had to be home before we did. We'd go park somewhere after that, and jack off."

"Before he spooked on you, huh?"

Donnie made everything sound so simple. I said, "His girlfriend started putting out."

"Well, I got news for you. Your partner was crazy to give up this thing. Look how straight your dick is." He leaned toward me and put both hands around it. "You tall guys always pack eight or nine inches."

"Naw," I said. "It's not that big." I hesitated, then blurted out, "Six and a half."

"Measure it?" he asked.

Damn, is nothing sacred? I nodded.

Donnie just smiled at me. "Feels like eight to me," he said, and my cock grew an inch and a half in his hands.

One of Donnie's buddies waved as he passed by on the way to the toilets and I froze in nervousness, but Donnie waved back with one hand and pulled on my boner with the other. Then he lifted his hips, and before his friend was through the door of the shower building, Donnie had his jeans and his underwear down to his knees. "Time to beat off," he said quietly. "Get your britches down and grab hold of my nuts for me."

It was completely dark in the front seat of his battered car. I did as he told me, sliding closer to him and reaching between his legs as he jacked off, cupping his balls in my left hand, jerking myself with my right.

"Yeah, that's what I like," he muttered. "Uh-huh, play with 'em, buddy. Play with my nuts for me."

He grabbed my teeshirt and pulled it up to my armpits with his free hand, and then he rubbed my chest roughly. "You like having your tits pinched?" he growled, and my cock just about exploded in my hand.

He leaned toward me, feeling my chest until he found one of my nipples, and then he tugged at it, rolling it between his fingers. I felt a jolt in my crotch and tried to tell him I did like it, indeed, but I could only manage to croak. I looked down and saw my nipple stretched out, and it was like he'd turned up the volume on a radio, the way my dick swelled with pleasure as he pulled on me.

Our bare arms crossed and our hands bounced in our laps. As it got better and better, I propped against him and put my head on his shoulder and rolled-up sleeve, watching him work on his cock as I fondled his nuts.

He stared down at himself intently, pounding it. His body was steamy hot. The smell of sweat welled up from his armpit, right under my nose. I pressed my cheek on his shoulder, handling his hairy meatballs and jerking off in rhythm with him.

His deep voice rumbled in my ear. "Uh-huh, feels like I got a quart of cum down there, just bustin' to come out. Oh, yeah, do that, that feels good. Pull on 'em. A-h-h. Fuck. Do that again. Harder. Twist my nuts. Twist 'em around. All the way, that's right. O-h-h-h, yeah . . . god . . . fuckin'. . . damn . . . I'm gonna shoot—"

His back stiffened and his fingers tightened on my nipple. I felt his balls pull up between his legs. "*HNYUH!*" he grunted. His head went back, and I saw the first foot-long streak of cum spurt up from his fist, a long white strand that looped up high in the air and then dropped back down and went *SPLAT* on my arm. In a second he laid two more quick squirts across the steering wheel. He pumped out shot after shot of cum, grunting and hosing it out onto the dashboard, wetting the windshield, slinging long ropes of jism all over the speedometer and the gearshift and the car door.

Forgetting about being seen by the other guys, I lifted my hips and leaned against his shoulder as my own dick started spouting off, too, and then I was moaning, "Oh fuck, oh fuck," twisting around and beating my meat and creaming and hanging onto Donnie's balls as we both fired cum all over the inside of the Oldsmobile. I went spinning out of control, laughing and gasping for air, and then we slumped against each other, leaking our last dribbles of sperm onto the front seat between us. Panting, I felt his big balls sag back down into my palm.

"Hey, guy," Donnie said, "you're fun."

I looked up as he turned his face to mine. He leaned toward me. I leaned closer. He smiled. I thought, this is it. He knows how I feel about him. If he kisses me, it means he knows I'm a fruit. I tilted my face up toward his bushy mustache. Well, it's pretty hard to keep pretending you're straight while you're holding another guy's balls in your hand. I took a breath and waited to enter total fruithood.

But he held up his wrist between our faces. Cum blobs were spattered all over the back of his hand. Grinning, he raised his hand to his mouth, stuck out his tongue, and slowly slurped at the shiny spots, still staring into my eyes.

I drew back. "You really eat that stuff?"

"Mmmmm, yeah," he said, licking his lips. "Told you I'm a dirty fucker. It's just gonna recycle. Means all that more will shoot out of me the next time. I love jism."

A string of it hung from the steering wheel. Donnie caught it on his finger and held it up.

"Looks like a booger, don't it?" he said, then lifted it up high and lowered the swinging drop into his mouth.

"You don't want yours?" he asked. I couldn't answer. "Gimme your hand."

He took my arm and licked the cum off the back of my hand, lapping at me like a dog, sliding his tongue across my skin, then around between my fingers. He put his mouth over my thumb, sucking it, wet and warm.

My dick started to thicken again. "Damn," I said, "you're the horniest guy I ever met."

"You ain't seen nothing yet." Donnie put his hand on my dick. I was still swollen, and he squeezed my cum-sticky cock until the last drops oozed out at the tip. "I wanna get a taste of the virgin cum you got in there."

"I'm not a virgin," I said.

Donnie caught the last glob on his fingertip and held it up. He stuck his tongue out and licked it off. "Yes, you are," he said. "I can tell."

"How can you tell?"

"'Cause of the way you taste. After you stick your pecker in a pussy, you never taste the same again. You get your juices mixed up with cunt juice, and it changes your flavor from then on."

"Really?"

"Uh-huh. Next time, I want all of your cum. I want you to shoot off in my mouth, Billy-boy, shoot that virgin juice in my mouth. I wanna use your big ol' dick like a straw, and suck your jism right out of your nuts. Nothin' I like better than fresh cum, and I'm gonna get me some of yours."

"Damn," I said as we were pulling up our pants. "I didn't think regular guys did stuff like that."

"One thing I never been much good at," Donnie told me, pausing to lick the last drop of cum off his mustache, "is bein' a regular guy."

5

"EE-MO!" Steve bellowed. "Bartholomew has an Ee-mo! Hyah!"

I groaned. I was sprawled on my back with my blanket twisted half off me and onto the floor, and idiot Steve was pointing at me and laughing. I didn't have to look down to know what he was pointing at. I could feel it in my hand. At least this time I had my undershorts on.

"Early Morning Hard-On," the big jerk sang out. "E.M.H.O."

He pounded on the bunk above me. "Wake up, Powers, they're ringing the breakfast bell."

He was gone before I could stumble out of bed. My legs ached, my back hurt, and I was sure it couldn't be 7 AM so soon. I stood up right under Donnie at the moment he lumbered down from above me.

We staggered together a few seconds with our arms thrown around each other's shoulders, like we were dancing. Underneath his warm and droopy teeshirt he felt bigger than me, and his arm muscles were hard as rocks. I held onto him with my eyes closed, and for many long seconds he didn't pull away. It was not helping me lose my E.M.H.O. at all, because I could feel Donnie's big one pressing against my thigh, through his boxers.

Then he patted my back and we separated. "Fuck," he said hoarsely, "how long were we out there last night?"

"Not long enough for me," I said, reaching down and batting at his dick. Donnie smiled, but pulled away.

He went to the foot of the bunk and stepped into the jeans on the floor. "Shit, I have to get some breakfast, or I won't eat all day. We're gonna skip dinner tonight and leave for town right after work." Hopping on one foot, he jerked his pants up and crashed against his locker.

In the head, we went around to the urinals first, and I could see Donnie's cock sticking out from his jeans beside me. Mine was so stiff it was hard to pee, and I tried to hide it from the other guys milling around.

Not Donnie. He put his knuckles on his hips and let fly. The boy next to him said, "Hey, pretty good, man, no hands."

Donnie stepped back to show it off, going "Heh heh," as his piss shot out and hit the urinal almost at the top.

Walking quickly toward the mess hall, he asked me, "You going into town for the weekend?"

"I guess so," I shrugged. "Maybe I'll get a ride with somebody Saturday."

He shook his head. "Won't be anybody left here with a car by Saturday. Everybody's going in tonight. I'd take you in mine, but I'm already full up."

Shit, I thought, but I just shrugged again.

"If you do get a ride in," he said, "maybe we'll get together and have a few beers or something."

I could hear the clink of forks on plates inside. Just before the steps I pointed to the back of his left hand. Some white spots were stuck to the hairs on his wrist, leftover dried cum from our jack-off party. "Pecker tracks," I said.

Grinning, he raised his arm to his mouth and licked his wrist, staring straight into my eyes as his tongue lapped across the cum spots.

At the door he smacked his lips and winked at me. "Think that must'a been some'a yours, sport," he said as we walked into the mess hall for breakfast.

Visions of Donnie stayed with me all morning. The crew leader put me out on the edge of camp, chopping weeds along the creek with a slingblade, and it was good, sweaty, swooshing work. My painful muscles needed the stretching, so I whacked at the brush until perspiration stung my eyes and I had to make a sweatband for my head with my red neckerchief.

I kept spacing out and imagining him, seeing him sitting in his car with a beer in one hand and his dick in the other, or standing by my bed in his underwear, scratching his belly fur.

All day I worked by myself. *Whack. Chop.* The sun burned on my back. Weed scraps floated in the heat and stuck to my arms. I wondered if I looked good or foolish with the headband on.

Steve could pull it off, I thought, with his muscles and his blond hair. Or Donnie could, just because he's so. . .

Whoosh, whoosh, I swung the blade. So, what?

So sexy, dammit, so fucking sexy.

Donnie Powers, Donnie Powers, Donnie Powers, his name went 'round and 'round in my mind. I remembered the feel of his arms around my shoulders only hours earlier. He'd actually hugged me, and patted my back. *We'd just bumped our hard-ons together this morning!* AGH!

At the lunch bell, Donnie came by and said he knew a good place to sit. He led me to a trail behind the cabins and I hoped no one would see us, but some of the other guys straggled along behind us with their lunch sacks. We stopped at a bluff overlooking camp and sat on a log.

I looked down at our little plot of civilization in the wilderness. The row of cabins stretched to the right, with the barn on the left, and the parking lot in the middle. The square lawn was a smooth, even green, and the mess hall put up a thin wisp of smoke on the other side. All the buildings were painted the same chocolate color, and they all huddled inside neat borders of white rocks. Beyond that boundary, the forest was a tangle of dark greens and earthy browns. I could make out the sparkling trace of the creek winding behind the mess hall. From the bank on its far side the woods rose steeply, all the way to a ridge a thousand feet above.

"Looks like a hundred years ago," one of the others said. Smoke curled up from the mess hall stove, and if our cars had been hidden out of sight directly below us, it could have been a pioneer camp.

Donnie stretched out, propped his head against the trunk, and covered his face with his hat, a floppy old felt thing he pulled from his back pocket. I listened to the boys' chatter, four voices at once.

"Yeah," someone agreed. "Can you believe they came out here on pack mules? With nothing but what they could carry in, food and tents and everything?"

"And hand saws. Don't forget, those fuckers worked their asses off."

"Maybe so, but they were away from everything, just working out in the woods all the time. I'd like that, nobody to give you any shit and tell you what to do. Just you and the fucking bears, nobody else for a hundred miles."

"You'd have to fuck a bear. No pussy for a hundred miles, either. And no cars to get into town on weekends to party. I wouldn't want to be stuck out here like that, no sex, no booze to drink."

Donnie chuckled under his hat. I slid down beside him and pretended to nap, but I looked at him as the other boys talked about going into town for the weekend. Donnie had put on his workshirt without buttoning it. His hands were clasped over his hairy belly, and I watched his chest rise and fall.

Our legs were almost touching. I studied the way his big thigh muscles filled his worn jeans. I stretched. My own shirt was splitting at the seams. I tensed my chest muscles, and felt some stitches rip at the shoulders. Was I really getting bigger so quickly? Maybe I would get new work clothes in town, if I had any money left. Donnie began to snore.

I touched the sole of my brown construction boots to his black ones. My boots were at the end of those dumb corduroy jeans — schoolkid pants. His Levi's were frayed at the cuff. Looking closer, I saw that he had unstitched the cuff and rolled it down a few inches, leaving bands of light and dark denim that ended in white fringe. Pants must have shrunk, I thought, longing for jeans like that; cowboy pants, worn out, thin, clinging to his legs, cupping his soft peter, so damn sexy.

The cook's triangle tinkled up from camp. I had to wake up Donnie. "You're supposed to order us back to work now," I told him, squashing his hat onto his face.

He pushed it back and stretched, then fixed his crotch. "Whatever's right," he said through a yawn.

More chopping. My hands blistered through my work gloves. I slipped down a bank beside the road, ripping my pants from the knee up and putting a foot-long scratch on my leg, but I kept going, and pretty soon I had turned a wild place into a respectable entrance to camp.

No one seemed to notice.

Late in the afternoon I took a break, sitting under a tree for half an hour. Forty-five minutes.

No one looked, no one told me to get back to work.

Just before quitting time, a green Forest Service truck rattled in, and as it passed in a swirl of gritty dust, Steve leaned out, banging on the side and yelling, "Get back to work, Bill. Half an hour to go."

But the truck stopped, and Steve held the door open. I tossed my tools in back and jumped in.

The driver was an older man I had seen in the office. "I'm Peterson," he said, leaning forward and smiling at me. "You look like my old tomcat after a night on the prowl. He comes in with his ears half torn off and sleeps for a week."

Steve said, "Phew. You may look like a tomcat but you smell like a horse."

I looked down at my scratched, dusty arms. My pants leg hung open at the thigh.

Steve was clean, not even sweaty. He was wearing shorts, but there weren't any marks on his bare legs, and his boots weren't muddy.

"What did you guys do today?" I asked.

"Snow check," Steve said, winking at me. "Real rough duty."

The driver guided us into the old barn. "We were up looking at some roads to see where the snow has melted," he explained. "We'll be sending some crews out Monday. Have to know which roads are open." He parked and we all got out. He waved and headed back to the office.

When he was out of hearing, Steve laughed and poked me in the arm. "Biggest bunch of fucking-off you ever saw, man. We drove around all day. He showed me where he's shot elk, and where all the big fires have been. Most of the time we sat in the truck and drank coffee out of his Thermos bottle. He's got this huge stainless steel one that must hold a gallon. I sure feel sorry for you poor dudes that have to work for a living."

"I don't mind the work too much," I told him as we walked back to the cabin. "I'm just so sick of being around camp all the time. You got to ride around some."

"Maybe you'll get out on a crew Monday. But you know what? It'll still be shit-work, only at least it'll be shit-work out where they can't watch you all the time." He laughed and slapped my back.

"Are you going into town tonight?" I asked.

"Sure. Everybody is."

"Could I get a ride in with you?"

"Can't do it, man. I got five guys in the car already. That's all it'll hold."

Back in the cabin he started packing a small suitcase. I watched him toss it into the trunk of his bright red Firebird. Preston sat in the front with him and three other guys were crammed into the back seat. At least he waved at me when he pulled out.

Then Donnie and his buddies took off in his convertible, leaving a cloud of dust drifting across the parking lot. I sighed and went back to the cabin. I was alone for the weekend.

Not quite alone, actually. Stanley the dick-face was staying in camp, too.

"Going into town tonight?" I asked Stanley as we undressed to clean up after work. It would be a long weekend. Camp was deserted, and I figured we might as well talk to each other.

"No," he said. "I like to be alone. Are you?"

"Nah. I'm staying here. No money."

Only five of us washed up together that afternoon, and the place had six showers. It was so quiet in there that even Stanley and his dick joined us, and nobody ragged him. There were glances as he soaped it up, though. Everybody else was circumcised. His hung down like a sausage in a deli, a fat white tube of bockwurst with a pucker of skin at the end. It sure got everybody's attention.

We were all being pretty respectful in the presence of a natural wonder, I thought. In fact, the guys were slackjawed with admiration. But he took offense and turned his back to us. Of all the naked kids, he was the only one without some kind of tan line. He was white all over, and the only hair on his little body was in his crotch and on his head.

Later in the cabin I tried putting a safety pin on the tear in my pants leg. He came over to my locker and said, "Why don't you just cut them off? Make shorts out of them. That looks dumb."

Of course, he had some nail scissors, and when he knelt in front of me, he turned his face up with that odd, blank expression. As he snipped in a ring around my thigh, the cloth fell away, and he deliberately touched my skin, lightly, smiling up at me with his hands between my legs.

"You made them too short," I told him, backing away from his hands and looking in Steve's mirror. He had cut them right

up to the pockets. "Damn, Stanley. When I sit down my balls
will come out of them."

"Oh, really?" He batted his eyelashes at me. "Let's try it."

"Don't be such a flit, man. I have to wear these to dinner."

He stiffened and looked annoyed. "Oh, well, God forbid you
should show any balls." He held up the scissors and snipped the
air. "Want a trim?"

He followed me to dinner. It was embarrassing, but with so
few of us there, we all sat at one table anyway, so it wasn't as
though we were actually together. He kept doing little things that
bothered me, things that guys don't do. When I asked for the
roast beef, he picked it up and served some on my plate for me.

"Next time just pass it," I told him. "You're not my mother."

Later, he stared at me while I was reading in my bunk. He
was looking at my crotch. "You look sexy in your cutoffs," he said.
I didn't look up.

He pursued it. "And I ought to know. I'm a flit, right? I know
sexy legs when I see them."

I looked up. He licked his lips at me. I put down my book.
"Aw, look, Stanley, I wish you wouldn't do shit like that. I mean,
I'm sorry, but you don't turn me on at all, okay? Don't do that."

"Gee, thanks a lot. What charm school did you learn that line
from?" He went to his locker and undressed with his back to me.
When he turned around, he had on his headphones, and for the
rest of the evening we didn't speak.

We looked, though. Leaning back in his underwear, he put
one skinny leg up with his knee against the wall, so that huge
thing shifted inside his Jockey shorts, rolling toward me. The guys
at the Jockey company didn't allow for what hangs below some
28-inch waists, and the tip peeked out, twitching at me. Stanley
kept touching his briefs, running his fingertips along the bulge,
so I could see it over my book. Sometimes when I looked up, our
eyes met, again with him giving me that blank look.

When I got up to turn out the lights, he smiled up and licked
his lips again, slowly.

I lay down on my bunk and waited. For a while the only
sound was the tinny whisper of his headphones. Then even that
stopped, and I heard the tape player clunk on the floor.

I waited. Stanley didn't move. I threw back my blanket. Still
nothing from across the room. I sat up and watched him in the

darkness. My feet were cold on the floor. After my eyes adjusted to the dark, I got up and walked across the cabin.

He was lying on his back with his eyes closed. I reached down and took his hand and pressed it to the pouch of my briefs.

His hand was limp. He cupped my genitals for a moment, then pulled his hand away.

"C'mon, Stanley," I said, surprising myself with how gruff I sounded.

"Leave me alone," he said, very softly.

"Come on," I said. "You did it the other night."

"So what?'

"Dammit, you've been making eyes at me all night," I said, taking his hand again and putting it on my bulge. My dick was getting a life of its own, stiffening in my Jockeys even though I wasn't even feeling sexy. "Come on," I said again, "I want a blowjob," and saying it out loud turned me on even more.

Again he jerked his hand away. "You had your chance, and you blew it, stupid. Get away from me."

"Damn you, you little prick teaser." I put my hand behind his neck, and he didn't resist. I pulled him toward me, lifting his scrawny neck until his face touched my briefs. I pressed his mouth against my dick, felt his breath hot through the cloth, and my cock surged up hard against his face. My heart pounded. His body was like a toy in my hands. I snagged my shorts and jerked them down. I had his lips to the head of my cock when he reached up and grabbed my balls and gave them a twist that made me howl.

He snarled up at me, "You stick that goddam thing in my mouth and I'll bite it off right down at the root. I swear, I'll castrate you, you fucked-up, redneck asshole."

I let go of his neck and jumped back. "You little shit!" I pulled my underwear all the way up to my navel, back-pedalling across the cabin, holding my balls with both hands until I bumped into my own bed, and sat down fast. "You little shit!" I said again, my voice cracking. "You, you *faggot*!"

"*TCHHH*!" he spit out. "Now I'm a faggot! Oh, right, right, hit me where it hurts."

He flipped over onto his side with his back to me, and jerked up his blanket. After a moment he turned his head and glared at me. "Get something straight, asshole, right now. Nobody is ever, *ever*, going to make me do anything I don't want to do. Never again."

"I thought you did want it," I snapped back. "You sure acted like it all night. You don't know what you want. Don't worry, you won't get anything from me, ever. I don't even want to *see* your fucking dick-face again."

I turned my back to him, and for a while there was silence. Then I heard a sound from across the room. My heart jumped. He could be coming after me. No telling what the creep had in his mind. I rolled over and listened. When I heard the sound again, it was a sniff. I think he was crying.

I lay awake, staring into the darkness, holding my crotch. For the first time since I'd left home, I wished I was back in my own bedroom, all alone.

When I opened my eyes Saturday morning, Stanley was kneeling a few feet from my bed, staring at me. I jumped and took a quick breath, and then relaxed. How could I have been afraid of such a puny little fart? He was nude except for his briefs, just waiting there on his knees, skinny and pale white, with his hands crossed over his crotch.

As I stared at him, he moved his hands to his sides. Inside his Jockey shorts, his dick towered up between his legs, stretching his underwear out until the leg holes pulled open and showed his balls hanging underneath.

When I looked up again, Stanley's head tilted back and his little body shifted toward me; he got such a painful look on his face that I couldn't help feeling sorry for him. In the thin early light, I could see his eyes begging for it, and I sighed and pushed my blanket back a bit. He moved closer and slipped his hands under the cover. He reached under my teeshirt and his hands were cold on my belly. I just lay there without moving, as Stanley lifted my blanket and put his head under it. He sort of melted into bed with me, burrowing under the cover and wrapping himself around my midsection. I let him take my underwear off completely and get down between my legs, nuzzling me and licking my crotch while I was still half asleep.

His fingers touched me all over, feathery light on the inside of my thighs. He licked under my nuts, until I had to cross my legs to keep his tongue out of my ass. He lapped all over my balls and then teased me up and down my dick. I grabbed his head and forced his mouth down over it.

He jerked back. "Don't fucking push," he said, his voice muffled under the blanket. "I know what I'm doing."

He sure did. He pointed my hard-on up and put his mouth over the first inch of it, licking and sucking on the tip until I couldn't stand it any more.

"Go all the way," I groaned. "Suck my cock." His lips went around the shaft, taking the whole thing inside his mouth, enveloping me with warmth, sliding down and down and down until I felt my cockhead stop at the back of his throat. "A-h-h," I sighed, getting what I wanted at last. He made little movements with his mouth, little laps with his tongue that made me swell up, made me feel huge under the blanket, and then damn if he didn't open up somehow and swallow even more. His lips sank down into my cockhairs and I felt myself slide all the way into his gullet. His throat tightened around the head of my dick, and I was so deep inside him the pressure made me groan out loud.

I got a little crazy and reached over the side of the bed to feel between Stanley's legs. There was more inside his briefs than I could cup in my hand. He reached down and flipped it out, and when the big thing fell into my palm, I almost started creaming right into his mouth. His dick was huge, hard, right in my hand, and oh-h-h, shit, was it big.

"Wait," I said, pushing his head back, with my load ready to shoot. I found his donkey and pulled on it, and his little body followed my hand. I grabbed one skinny leg and pulled him into bed with me.

Something about handling his body turned me on. He was shaped like a little girl, I realized. He should have a girl's sex between his legs, a hole that I could put my finger in, instead of a big fat cock sticking up alongside his belly, bulging out from under the waistband of his briefs. Stanley should have a twat, I thought. A slit, a cunt, a pussy. The words seemed so crude. I put my hand inside the pouch of his Jockey shorts and felt the balls of a man between the hairless legs of a girl. I pushed his briefs down with the back of my hand and bounced his nuts in my palm. My heart thumped. I tugged his shorts all the way down his legs and tossed them on the floor. When I put my hand on his huge cock again, I felt my own erection stiffen inside

Stanley's mouth.

Then he reached behind my neck and started pushing my face toward it. I pulled back.

"Hey, don't think I'm gonna suck that for you," I told him. "No telling where it's been."

He took his mouth off my dick and looked up between us. "Oh, come on, Bill. Loosen up. You're such a tight-ass."

"You're the dick-face, not me."

He grimaced at me. "I know what they call me. You don't have to remind me. I have feelings, too, you know."

"I'll jack you off, but I won't suck it," I told him, and he went back to doing me while I played with his giant dong.

It was even more incredible up close, almost as big as my wrist down at the root, and so long that it extended inches above his bellybutton. A tuft of kinky black hair grew in a fringe above the base, and the sack holding his balls drooped out from underneath, wrinkled like a bulldog's jowls.

The foreskin fascinated me, the way the loose sleeve of the very thinnest skin could pull up to envelope the whole thing, easily a foot long if you counted the base underneath his balls.

"Suck it," he hissed. "Come on, Bill. Be a fag. Go ahead and do it for once."

"No!" I told him. "I don't want your cum in my mouth."

"You're such a jerk," he said. His lips went around me again. He wrapped his arms around my butt, and let me face-fuck him, right down to the hilt.

His dick was already seeping that slippery, clear fluid that you get before you cum, and I made the whole fat thing glisten with it, stroking the loose skin, twisting it around, tugging it up and down. I bunched the foreskin around the head of it, and I could see the ridge of the head of his dick showing through under the skin. His juice oozed out from the folded-up pucker.

When I moved my hand down again, the big torpedo inside there made my fingers spread apart. I could feel it moving through my palm until the pink head spread the circle of skin open at the tip, wider and wider, tightening around his cockhead, and then as my fist moved down to the base the skin rolled all the way back and the big red head popped out and stood up, drooling from the slit at the tip.

I could feel my own cum building inside my belly as I stroked his dick, and then his balls began pulling up tight, and I knew he was as close as I was. I gave him another long, slow pump with my hand, and he stiffened and went down over me all the way again, sucking hard. With the next pump on his big dick, I made his first shot of cum pop out and dribble down over my knuckles.

He went "*MMMH!*" and raised his hips, trembling. I wrapped both my fists around the donkey dick and pumped faster. His second dollop of cum jumped higher, two inches of white cream that plopped onto my wrist and stuck there in a thick, pearly blob. The next shot splattered against my chest. Stanley started squealing through his nose, spurting his load at me, thrashing in my hands, sucking at me like mad, and then I felt myself coming too, and I groaned and pulled him to me, pressing my face into his big balls, rubbing my nose against his nuts as my own load churned out of me and into Stanley's hot, sucking mouth.

"Mmmmm-Hmmmm," I heard him going, between swallows and choking noises, "Mmmmmm-HMMMMMM!"

I hugged his butt and moved my face back and forth, glorying in the feel of his balls rolling against my lips, inside the hairy pouch between his legs, as I gave him lots and lots to choke on down at the other end.

I wanted to stay like that forever, but Stanley's hands were too tight on my leg, pinching my skin, harder and harder as he gulped at my cum.

"Ouch!" I said. "That hurts." He kept milking the cum out of me, gripping my legs, and I then I felt his teeth grazing my privates, and remembered last night. I jerked away and pushed his hand off my thigh. Stanley popped loose and fell back out of the bed, sprawling onto the floor.

He glared up at me for a moment, then wiped his mouth with the back of his hand.

Staring up at the mattress above me, I suddenly felt sordid and sleazy.

"Don't you tell the guys when they get back," I warned him.

"'The guys,'" he repeated. "I like that. Not 'the other guys,' just, 'the guys.' What does that make me?" He got to his feet, went to his locker, and started to dress.

"You know what I mean. The straight guys."

"Oh, dream on. Those two aren't any straighter than you are, and you just sucked my cock."

"I did not," I said. "That was my hand."

"Felt like your mouth to me."

"Prick," I snapped. He had made me turn red all over. As I dressed, I realized he had power over me, now. There were thirty guys in camp for me to get to know, and if talk linked me to Stanley, I'd hear about it all summer.

I was bored all day. After Stanley left for his hike, I visited a few cabins but nobody wanted to do anything. I talked to some guys playing cards, but I hate card games. I went back to the cabin to write a letter home, and every paragraph seemed to take half an hour.

While I was staring into space, I noticed two patches of cum that had dried on my arm, and wiping that off made me even more restless. The letter went unfinished on the table as I paced the cabin.

Donnie had left his locker door open. Inside, his clothes were a jumble of faded blue denim, brown workshirts, plaid flannel shirts, and white underwear. A dirty sock hung from the top of his black boots, and a pair of his shorts. I picked up the used boxers, and found spots of dried semen around the fly.

I was curious about something. I had never seen Donnie putting deodorant under his arms. He didn't seem to smell bad, but I couldn't find any in his toilet kit or on the locker shelf. I don't think he used it.

There was a little jar there, however. It was Vaseline petroleum jelly. I picked it up, and it was greasy all over. The lid was on crooked. *Damn.* The stuff inside had pubic hairs stuck in it. I put it back.

He had left his bed unmade for the weekend. I pushed back his sheets, finding spots all around the middle, evidence that he was busy at night while I slept. "Pecker tracks," I muttered.

Steve's bed was made and he had closed his locker. I walked over and peeked inside. His clothes were all folded neatly, with his colored briefs in one stack and his tank tops in another. He had almost a dozen bright gym shorts. On the shelf he had some medical anti-perspirant, "For Extra-Sensitive Skin," and a bottle of Old Spice aftershave. The only dirty clothes were one pair of shorts and a twisted jockstrap down at the bottom. I stretched the supporter open and looked in the pouch, but it was bleached white.

Stanley's locker was closed. Inside, everything he owned was either black or white or gray. His bed was unmade, and it was easy to see how he solved every boy's secret problem. His pecker tracks were all over by the wall, so I figured he must roll over and drop his load on the side where he didn't have to sleep in it. Hell, I thought, his hose would reach without rolling to his side.

But what about squeaky-clean Steve? Muscles had to masturbate sometime. I checked through the window in the cabin door to see that no one was around, and then I turned back his bedcover. His sheets were immaculate. I reached over into the crevice between his mattress and the wall. Aha! I pulled out another jockstrap. Steve and I shared at least one secret. He had shot off into it.

I sniffed it. Right away I thought, holy shit, what am I doing? I stuffed it back. I had to get outside. Banging the door behind me, I took off for a hike, up the trail to the bluff above camp.

I sat there for hours. The ridge behind the cookhouse baked in the afternoon sun. I wished I had gone up there, even if it had to be with Stanley.

That night we managed to avoid crossing paths. When I went back to the cabin I found a topographic map of the district spread on the table. He'd drawn lines on some of the trails leading from camp up into the hills around us. I guessed they must have been the ones he had hiked since he'd been in camp. But I didn't want him to catch me acting interested, so I took my book to the mess hall and read there until lights out.

Back in the cabin, I undressed in the dark and went to bed without speaking to him.

After breakfast Sunday, I followed him back to the cabin and tried again.

"Look," I told him, "we can fool around, but I just don't want everybody in camp to know, okay?"

He made it difficult. "I don't care if they know."

"Well, I do. You can act like a fag if you want to, but don't blow my cover, okay? Don't get all buddy-buddy with me around the guys. Okay, man?"

After a moment, he said, "Stop calling me 'man' all the time.

You're as bad as Steve. And don't worry, I won't hold your hand in front of them. I don't even like you, anyway. I just like to suck dick. Don't take it personally."

"Good," I said. "I'm going for a walk."

As I left, he called out, "Better a fag than a fake."

6

Rats, I thought, hiking back up the trail behind the cabin. Why did I ever get started fooling around with a fruit like Stanley? Damn, damn, damn. I couldn't even tell if we had a deal or not.

Kicking rotten stumps to splinters, I followed the trail through beds of pine needles and then up higher to an area that must have been hit by wind, because three trees were down across the path. I got under one and over the others, but a little farther along a fence with a locked gate stopped me.

RESERVOIR, a sign read. **No Trespassing, No Fishing, No Swimming.** Under that, someone had scrawled *NO PEEING IN THE POND.*

I farted around by the spillway for a few hours, making a little dam and tearing it down. But I was bored. Giving it up, I hiked back down to the overlook and stretched out against the log to nap. My mind drifted to Donnie, and my fingers drifted down to the cut-off pants that Stanley had made so short. My balls bulged out from under the ragged edge of the corduroy. I tickled myself through my underwear, and waited.

I heard the crunch of tires scattering gravel down below. When Donnie's blue convertible pulled into the lot, I scrambled to my feet and trotted down the trail.

It didn't do me a bit of good to run. In the cabin, Donnie was all wrapped up in maps with Stanley. He wanted to hear about the hike, and how the trails had been, and what Stanley had seen from the top of some mountain. I listened for a while, and then I went to my locker to do my laundry. I had only two pairs of pants left, and one pair had the hole in the seat. I tossed it on the stack anyway.

"I'm doing half a load of wash," I called out. "Anybody want to add anything to it?"

Donnie said, "Oh yeah, I got some," and handed me a paper sack containing his dirty clothes from the weekend.

In the laundry room, I pawed through the bag for his underwear. Sure enough, his boxer shorts were stiff in front, damn, even crusty with white dried cum. There was something else on them, too. I held some blue and white striped ones up to the light. The fly had a big dark stain on both sides of the opening, as though they were wet. But they weren't wet, they were greasy. Donnie had gotten Vaseline jelly on them, playing around over the weekend.

Where? I wondered. Where had he stayed? In a motel? In a tent? In his car, I bet. Jacked off under a blanket in the back seat.

Could it be something else? Maybe it was what they call lubrication, from a girl. Had he fucked a girl this weekend? With his underwear still on?

No, no, no, I thought. Donnie beats off, maybe as much as I do even. It was Vaseline. I could almost see his greasy cock jutting out through the fly.

Dumping the rest into the machine, I stuck the striped pair into my back pocket and headed for the woodshed. Inside, I closed the door behind me and felt myself getting a hard-on as I dropped my cut-offs and stripped down my briefs, kicking them to one side. With my dick rising in front of me, I stepped into Donnie's underwear and pulled them up and over my erection, hitching his boxers up over my butt, running my hands over the thin material. I held my dick through the cloth, feeling my cock pressing out stiffly against the greasy fly, right where Donnie's dick had been hanging this weekend, right where he'd jacked off. I pulled my cut-offs back on and tucked my own briefs away behind a log, up high where no one else could reach. I don't know what makes me do stuff like that.

The two of them were still at the table, hunched over the map, when I got back. Steve had come in, undressed, and started pumping his weights, so I sat on my bunk and watched his back muscles for a while, and then I folded the hot laundry. I made a stack of Donnie's underwear on top of his bluejeans and took them over to him.

"Just throw them in my locker," he said, without looking up from Stanley's map. There wasn't a clear place to put them, so after a moment I did exactly that, just tossed them inside. He probably never even noticed how they were scattered around.

I went to the door and put my hands up on the ledge above it, hanging there and watching the boys walk by. I did a few quick pull-ups, trying to tell if I had gotten any stronger in a week. It seemed easier than I remembered. A breeze brushed my exposed stomach and swirled around the hairs on my legs, and I did more pull-ups, feeling my muscles flex.

Dropping down, I walked over by Steve. He seemed hypnotized by his own image, standing in front of his mirror, lifting the dumbbells up and down. His arms bulged. He was wearing a faded blue pair of gym shorts that made his buttocks look huge.

There were more weights in his locker, so I picked up some small ones and imitated his movements. It was easy. I pulled my teeshirt over my head and switched to some heavier weights. Throwing them around felt good, and I pumped my arms beside his until I grunted and sweat formed on my upper lip.

"Aw, would you look at this," Steve grinned. "The string bean here is gonna make some muscles." He held out a dumbbell that looked bigger than I could hold with both hands, easily straightening his arm and touching me with it.

"Here's one," he said, brushing the cold metal on my skin. "Here's a muscle, right there. Can anybody see it?"

"You're hogging the mirror," I told him, bumping my hip against his. He pushed back, of course, and I jostled with him, trying to take the spot in front of the glass. Steve set his weights on the floor and crouched, holding his arms out. All I had to say was "Gorilla" and he jumped me immediately, kicking my legs out from under me. I laughed as his big arms encircled me, and as I went down I bumped Donnie's chair with my shoulder, hard. It scooted out from under him and the cowboy fell backwards on top of us.

We thrashed around, and I rolled us over to the table, halfway turning it over. Donnie yelled, "Sit on him, Stan!" and then the kid piled on top of us all in nothing but his white shorts, his tiny body perched on top of Steve's big, hairy bulk. I pulled him into the struggle. Donnie was the only one dressed in pants, and with all those bare legs and chests rubbing each other, I wasn't surprised when Steve sang out, "Stanley's got a hard-on, Stanley's got a hard-on." I found the little guy's briefs and jerked them down, and for a moment we all stared as it waved in the air. I grabbed it and wiggled it for everybody to see.

"Shit," Steve said, pulling back. "This is too queer for me."
He dumped Stanley on the floor and went to his locker.

Stanley tried to pull his briefs up, but with the Empire State
Building growing between his legs he couldn't get the elastic band
high enough. He wrapped a towel around his waist and darted
out the door.

I heard Steve mutter, "Fucking faggots," with his head still in
his locker, and I wasn't sure if he was including me for waving
it around, or if he was just making a general position statement.

Donnie set a chair upright. "Don't start calling names," he told
Steve. "You know how it is out here in the boondocks.
Everybody's a walking hard-on."

He gave me a wink and a nod toward the door, and I followed
him outside toward the parking lot. His teeshirt had hiked up
above his waist. He pulled it down as he walked, then rolled each
short sleeve up to his armpits, sauntering across the gravel, with
his lean, muscular arms bared to the evening air.

"If you've been cooped up here all weekend you need a little
antidote for cabin fever," he said, tossing me a cold beer from the
trunk of the Oldsmobile. We sat in his car and sneaked sips from
the cans as guys sauntered in and out of cabins and walked across
the square.

Stanley came back from the showers, and seconds after he
disappeared into our cabin, Steve popped out and walked across
the lawn to the volleyball game over by the mess hall.

"David and Goliath," I said.

"Tinkerbell and the jock," he said. "You knew Steve was a
wrestler at school, didn't you?"

"No, I didn't. You mean, he's like, on a team?"

"Oh, yeah, he goes to matches and all that silly shit. That's
the only reason he's out here, for the workout he gets. The way
he talks about his parents, he doesn't need the money. I thought
you ought to know before you get your arm broke fucking around
with him."

"Thanks. I didn't know. He's huge, isn't he?"

"Yeah. And dumb as they come. Did you hear him tonight?
'Oooh, this is too queer for me!' Shit, soon as we leave he
probably jacks off in his fucking mirror."

"He jacks off into his jockstrap," I said. "I found one this weekend, all stuck together." Donnie and I grinned at each other, and said together, "Pecker tracks," and laughed.

"Damn," Donnie said, "it's good to be back with you. Those guys this weekend were such jerks, talking about pussy all the time. I was hoping you'd show up, so we could have us a little session."

"A session?"

"Yeah, you know. Fuck around for like an hour or two. I get so bored with quickies and pussy talk. I like to see how long I can go without coming. Soon as it gets dark, let's get a little action going."

"What if somebody comes out here?"

Donnie twisted around in his seat, looking behind us, then jammed his hand into his pocket and pulled out his keys. "I'll fix that," he said, starting the car. The old heap took a minute to fire up, then Donnie hit reverse and backed up to the barn, swerving into a space between a double-cab pickup and a tank truck that was used to carry water to fires. They both sat so high that no one could see us from the sides, and the barn protected our rear. Ahead were the cabins, but with another row of cars parked in front of us, we knew we wouldn't be seen.

"Somebody still might come out to their car," he said, so we sipped beer and waited for the dark. While we sat we grinned and fiddled with our crotches. I adjusted my pants so my cock pointed down my leg inside them, and then scratched it with my fingernail until it lengthened.

"You got a nice one," he told me. "Make it good and hard."

I made it hard for him. I made it a steel spike under my thin, worn corduroys.

"Yeah," he said. "I can see the head of it through your pants."

"I put on some of your underwear," I said. "Tonight, while I was washing your stuff. It's still greasy."

"Oh yeah? You got my drawers on? Hey, I like that. No shit?" He slid over to me. "Let me feel it." Donnie's big arm went around my shoulders and his other hand went to my lap. My breath wheezed through my nose as he squeezed the lump on my leg, making it stiffen until I thought it would rip through and stick up in his hand. I put my hand on his shoulder and his head dropped down into my lap. He worked the tip of my dick out from under my cut-offs, and licked at the head of it. He pulled at it with his lips, nibbling on it until he got the whole thing out, and then when he went down on it, taking my whole cock into his mouth, it felt so hot and tight in there I lifted my hips up and thrust myself into his throat, moaning at the sexy, slippery feel of his mouth and tongue and throat all wrapped around me at once.

Donnie was like a madman, sucking my dick, pulling my balls out, tugging at them with his fingers, licking at my cut-offs, then suddenly lapping at my bellybutton, rubbing his rough cheeks on my belly, kissing and licking his way up under my teeshirt until his lips circled around my nipple and sucked it hard, going "*GROWF!*" and chewing at my chest until I thought I'd explode in his hands.

The bathroom door banged and some guys came out of the building, shouting and laughing. Donnie raised his face to mine, looked me in the eye, and slowly licked his lips. "I'm gonna eat you alive tonight, big guy," he whispered, and I just twisted in my seat.

"Beer break," he said, and sat back, leaving me with my hard-on stuck straight up. We both took long pulls on our cans. Donnie gave a big stretch, lifting his teeshirt to scratch underneath.

"Mmmh!" I said. "You're so *goddam* sexy."

He smiled at me slyly, then grinned down at his exposed stomach. "You like that? Come over here and rub it for me. Hell, they can't see us back here." He lifted his teeshirt up to his armpits. "Time to start your basic training. Number one lesson for Billy, How To Get A Buddy Off."

"God," I said. "I didn't think this was allowed." My heart banged in my chest as I slid across the seat and put my hand on his belly. His skin was warm, and the hairs were soft there.

"First of all," he said, "start out slow. Play with my tits some. Yeah, like that. How about you suck on 'em a little bit."

I bent down and touched my lips to him, right on his nipple. I licked his hairy chest, slurped at both the smooth, hairless little knobs. He put his hand behind my neck and held me tight against his muscles. "Suck on 'em," he whispered. "Take my nipples and rub your tongue all over 'em, yeah, get your teeth on 'em, just a little bit, and pull on 'em, aw, yeah, like that, just chew on 'em some." He shoved my head from one side of his chest to the other, rubbing my face against his hairy skin.

"Get 'em both, suck 'em hard. Yeah, tits get hard, you know that, Billy Boy? They get hard when you play with 'em, just like dicks. Make my nipples hard, ol' buddy. Make my nipples get boners. Suck on me, buddy. Aw-w-w-w, ye-ah-h-h-h-h."

Donnie made a peculiar noise in his throat. He whispered, "Now work your way down my belly, lick all around my stomach. Run your tongue up my bellybutton, and rub my crotch some while you're licking me. Feel my dick, buddy. Fool around until it's real hard. Get it hard, y'know, tease me some, then unhook my pants and take my dick out."

My cheek brushed his stomach. I could feel his heart thumping inside. I kissed his navel, licking at the tiny knot in the center of his hairy belly, and then when he raised his hips up, I went lower, and kissed all over the lump in his jeans.

"Go real slow," he said. "I want this to last an hour, okay?" He let me open his pants and turn back the flaps to show the white pockets inside. Then he lifted his butt so I could see-saw his underwear down over his thighs. His dick popped up in my face.

It bulged out powerfully from the hairy darkness between his legs, even fatter than I remembered. Slipping a finger under his nuts, I flipped them out so they hung down from the vee-shaped notch of his open pants. I moved my hand up and closed it around his dick, noticing that it curved up slightly, rigidly, toward the swirls of hair on his belly. Even in the fading light, I could see how his pubic hair ran down a line from his navel, then thickened around the base of his tall, white centerpiece.

"Damn," I groaned. "You're so fucking beautiful, man."

"Play with my nuts next," he said, shoving his pants below his knees, and I lifted his big balls with my fingertips. The skin was soft, the hairs much coarser than on my own. He put his hand on the back of my neck and pushed my face closer.

The pouch smelled musty, like garlic or salami.

"Lick 'em," he whispered, and I did. Donnie pushed my head into his crotch firmly, and I put the man's left testicle into my mouth. It took some prodding, but I got them both in and rolled them around with my tongue, sucking on them until he let me back off for air. I rested my cheek on his leg.

He pried his dick away from his stomach and squeezed on

it. "I think you got a natural talent for this, sport," he said. "See?"
A clear drop of fluid formed at the tip of his cock.

"Oh, no," I blurted out. "Did you do it already?"

Donnie laughed. "Naw, that's just pre-cum. Don't you know
what pre-cum is?"

I made a face. "I know what it is, I just never heard it called
that before. 'Pre-cum.' It sounds like medicine."

"Best medicine you'll ever get. Yeah, this is Doc Donnie's
Special Formula. Home-made. It's the medicine your momma
never told you about." Holding his big log in front of my nose,
he milked out another blob and spread the stuff around with a
finger until his cockhead glistened. "Here. Take a dose." He
touched his fingertip to my lips. "Put some hair on your chest."
He painted his pre-cum over my lips, made them slippery with
it.

I licked his finger, tasting the sticky juice from his balls. He
pushed his thumb against his cock and pointed it at my mouth.
The head of it flared, and more pre-cum seeped out through the
little slit.

"Now be a good buddy," he whispered, "and suck on that some
for me."

Well, that did it. Your guy Bartholomews finally caved in.
With the taste of sex painted on my lips I closed my eyes and put
my mouth around Donnie's hard-on.

He grunted, holding the back of my neck, pressing me down.
My jaws wouldn't seem to go wide enough to get it in, but Donnie
was very encouraging.

"Aw, yeah, eat it," he said. "Eat my dick, buddy. Can you take
all of it? Huh? Can you swallow it? All of it? Huh? Can you
eat me all the way?"

I knew what I had to do. What I didn't realize is that you
can't breathe while you're doing it. His big chunk of meat choked
me, but I opened my throat the way Stanley had done on me,
forcing my mouth down until my lips were stretched wide and
my nose was buried in his pubic hair. It made my jaws ache, but
I took the whole damn thing inside me and held it there.

"Yeah," Donnie said. "Oh, yeah. Oh-h-h, ye-a-a-h. *Fuck!*"

Then I gagged and came up snorting and dripping tears and
saliva and god knows what from my nose.

Donnie laughed and handed me a beer.

"Damn, that's fun," I told him, and took a couple of long, cold slugs. Donnie slipped his arm around my shoulders.

I put the beer on the dash, and he guided my head back into his lap. I have to admit, I liked it a lot when he did that, pushing me around like that. He wasn't rough, but he knew exactly what he wanted, and he didn't hesitate to get it from me.

No place had ever seemed so comfortable as the floor of Donnie's blue Oldsmobile, me down on my knees between his legs, beating my meat and sucking him off, him guiding me with his hands, going fast, then slowing down, sometimes holding my head completely still for long minutes as his dick throbbed in my mouth, then sometimes raising his hips and fucking my face with fast, hard jabs that went all the way down my sore gullet. I gave him whatever he wanted, scratching his nuts for him, ruffling the fur on his belly, taking his cock as far down my throat as I could, holding the man's sex in my mouth, feeling him tremble with pleasure.

"You got me now, man," he said between gasps. "You got me in your hands. If you go any faster, or suck any harder, or especially if you put both your hands on my dick, and jack me off while you suck at the same time, then I'm gonna go totally out of control."

I did exactly what he said, all of it at once. I grabbed his meat and balls and pubic hairs and everything, and tried to stuff it all down my throat. Donnie held me by my shoulders, thrusting up, fucking my fist, penetrating through my hand and deep into my mouth and up against the back of my throat, and then he arched his back and groaned, "FUCK! YEAH!" He rammed his dick all the way into my face, and suddenly between the long stabs his hot cum flooded into my mouth, jets of it coming so rapidly I couldn't keep it all in. Sucking hard on his squirting dick, I gulped down the essence of masculinity right from his nuts, hanging onto his big hard cock with both hands, pulling and slurping and swallowing like a madman, getting what I wanted at last, Donnie Powers shooting his load in my face, Donnie Powers coming in my hands, big Donnie Powers letting me jack him off, creaming and creaming and creaming in my mouth, putting out his cum between my lips and stuffing his cock all the way down my throat.

Donnie had to pull me up by the collar to get my mouth off

his cock, even after it went soft. He put a beer can to my lips and poured. We took a break, and this time we sat together, pants still down at our ankles, with our hairy thighs pressed tight. I was dazed. He lifted my teeshirt and wiped my chin.

The night's volleyball game broke up at dark and we watched Steve walk to our cabin. The beefy guy stood in the door looking into the light, then turned and looked around outside.

"Uh-oh," I said. "Bet he's looking for us."

We both fumbled with our pants. Steve waved and started across the parking lot.

I got my pants up and hooked, trying to make the zipper work as Steve loomed at the window. I got it closed just in time, but Donnie had to leave his jeans unbuttoned. He covered his open fly with his beer can just as Steve stuck his face in the driver's side window.

"Hey, you guys aren't gonna sit out here all night, are you? I don't want dick-face making passes at me."

"You're not that good-looking, hoss," Donnie told him. "Anyway, what do you pump up like that for, if you don't want to turn us all on?"

"Not the fruits, man, not the fruits," he said, flexing for us, filling the window. "This is for the pussies. Gimme a hit of that." Donnie gave him the beer, uncovering the white of his underwear, but Steve threw back his head to guzzle it all down, so I didn't think he could see. Donnie put his hand in his lap.

When Muscles handed the can back empty, Donnie told him, "I don't want it back if you chugged it all, asshole."

Steve said, "Hyuk," and tossed it in back with the others.

"Now go on back in there like a man," Donnie ordered him, "and you keep your hands off of Stanley's dick from now on, understand? No fooling around in our cabin."

"Shit," Steve said. "Did you see the size of it just now? What a humongous damn schlong he's got on him. I don't know how a little guy like him can stand up straight, with all that weight pulling him down in front. You'd think he'd tilt when he walked."

He backed up and staggered in circles, both hands on his crotch. We hooted, and he pounded on the hood of the car a few times.

"Hey, you guys, don't get too drunk out here. We got work to do in the morning." He put his chin down on his chest, forced out a big burp, and strutted off.

Donnie and I got out to pee. He went to a tire under the tank of the water truck parked beside us, and I stood by him.

I was worried. "Think he knows what we're doing?"

"Nah. Steve's doesn't get it. He's too hung up on muscles to know what his dick is for."

While I was shaking off, Donnie put his hand on my cock. "Let me get that for you," he said. "Lemme show you what buddies can do for each other."

He dropped to his knees, and before I could laugh, he was sucking out the last drops for me.

I fell back against the tank. "Donnie, that's so gross," I said.

He looked up at me and unbuckled my belt. "Heh, heh," he chortled. "I can get a lot grosser than that." He pulled my pants down to my knees and reached between my legs, behind my nuts.

"I can get re-e-a-al dirty," he said, feeling my fanny with his hand. As I stood against the water truck, looking at the lights of camp behind him, Donnie sucked my dick and tugged my balls and rubbed my rear end all at once. It worked. I put my hands on his shoulders and felt my cock stiffen in his mouth.

Then I found out what he meant by dirty. He poked up between the cheeks of my behind and touched my asshole with his fingertip. Right there under the stars, he stuck his finger up inside me.

I yelped out loud. Closing my eyes, all I could think about was Donnie's finger sliding up the wrong way on what I always thought was a one-way street. I squirmed over his finger. When I opened my eyes, I could hardly focus. A figure appeared in a cabin door and started walking toward the parking lot. "Shit," I whispered to Donnie. "Stand up, quick."

He pulled his hand away and got to his feet. Turning around, he pulled the old water truck's door open. It squeaked, and I went "SHHH!" and it squeaked again. Holding my trousers, I hopped up on the running board. Donnie pushed me inside with his hard-on bumping against my bare butt.

We fell onto the seat, trying not to giggle. He got on top of me and yanked my pants down to my ankles. I leaned back on the cold vinyl, holding the gearshift knob, as he pulled off one of my sneakers and tossed it over his shoulder. He drew my foot out of my pants and spread my legs apart.

Now, when people talk about their private parts, they usually mean their genitals, but I think we keep our backsides even more private than our fronts. They're harder to reach, and then of course they smell pretty bad. And in the showers, for instance, you see everything a guy's got up front, but nothing in back, because what's there is hidden.

It's really the most secret place on your body. I had checked mine out on my own a few times, but then I'd never bothered playing with it much after that, until Donnie got between my legs.

He leaned forward. I raised myself toward him, closing my eyes, opening my body. His mouth went down over my dick, and everything got slippery and sexual down there, all licking and nuzzling and sucking and poking.

Then Donnie spit on his finger, and very slowly, with a gentle twist, he plugged it all the way into my asshole.

I gasped. I looked down and saw my hard-on wedged under his bushy moustache, and felt his finger probing my innards. He took my dick in his fist, nodding deliberately, moving his hand up and down with his mouth, so my cockhead slipped up through his fingers, between his lips, along his tongue, and then inches deep into his tight throat. My cum swelled up in me and started to rise. Just as I stiffened to shoot off, Donnie twisted his finger around hard inside my butt.

That triggered something I'd never felt before, a sexual explosion, a blast of sensation that racked my whole body. I bucked and flopped. I saw colors. I think I must have yelled out loud, too. Donnie's finger felt enormous inside my butt. I seemed to open up and spread around his hand. I couldn't believe the pleasure of the sensations between my legs, the feeling of my hard-on sticking up through his fist and into his mouth, and the opposite feeling of taking his finger inside me, and then I just opened up and felt my cum spilling out like a waterfall, a rush of hot pumping sexual flooding that doubled and re-doubled with every plunge of his finger into my asshole as I shot my load inside his mouth.

Donnie sucked out my cum like a little kid slurping up spaghetti, pulling the stuff out of me, jacking me off with one hand, and using the other hand to push it out of me with his finger up my butt as I flopped from side to side on the seat. My wailing and heaving hit a peak of glory, and then gave way to hoarse grunts and muscle spasms that gradually became spaced further and further apart. I gripped his shoulder for one final, wonderful arch of my back that squeezed the last drop of cum out through my cock, and then I slumped back slowly, panting hard.

Donnie leaned forward and jammed his mouth down over my dick. I could hear the slapping sound of his fist as he started beating himself off. His body jiggled between my knees. I reached down my belly and touched my hairy root where it speared up between his lips. I was still hard as steel, and there were two inches of my cock left for him to take. I put my other hand behind his neck and pulled his face tighter against my crotch. He whimpered, and I pulled harder. Slowly, his mouth slipped down the shaft of my hard-on until his lips kissed my fingertips, right at the base of my belly. He choked. I put both hands behind his head and forced it all the way down, wedged it tightly between my legs.

Donnie's body stiffened. I wrapped my legs around his shoulders, felt his arm muscles tighten up hard, and heard the slapping of his hand on his dick go faster and faster. His whole body shuddered under me and then the pounding of his fist turned to the sticky smacking sounds of a hand full of fresh, hot, gooey cum. It's a sound I know real well, and I smiled in the dark as Donnie twitched between my legs, shooting his load all over the floorboard of the truck, with my dick crammed deep inside his throat.

When the old tank truck stopped rocking and Donnie had unplugged his mouth from me long enough to catch his breath, he slowly struggled up and stretched out on the seat beside me.

I thought we'd fall asleep that way, all tangled up together with our pants still down to our knees. All I could think about was how I'd just had the greatest orgasm any man has ever known, but Donnie had other ideas.

He put his mouth to my ear and asked softly, "Did you like that, Billy boy? Did you like getting your dick sucked?"

"Oh, man," I started to answer, but then Donnie stuck his tongue in my ear—damn, stuck his big, warm, wet tongue right inside my ear. "Oh!" I gasped, and then Donnie reached between my legs and poked his index finger up against my asshole again.

"Heh, heh," he chuckled. "I'm just getting started with you, big boy," he whispered. "Next time, I'm gonna fuck you, you know. Not tonight, but sometime soon. I'm gonna fuck you, big guy. Yeah. I'm gonna fuck you with my dick, instead of my finger."

His tongue was lapping at my ear and his finger was searching for the hole in my rump. Hell, I was just getting my eyes uncrossed, and he was wanting more already. "Uh, I dunno if I'm ready for that," I said. "My rear end hurts."

Donnie raised his hand to his face, right between our noses, and took a long sniff at his index finger. He grinned at me.

"Oh, yeah," he said, his eyes twinkling in the darkness. "You're ready. We're butthole buddies now. I'm gonna get a lot more than my finger up that pretty ass of yours, and you're gonna love every long, hard inch of it. You're ready. You're my fuck-buddy now. It's just a matter of time until I get what I want."

7

Some of the guys lucked out that Monday and got assignments riding in the back of a pickup truck "out into the field," as everyone called it. I got stuck painting an empty cabin. Donnie was working in the office.

"What color are we painting it?" I asked, as the kid in charge repeated our orders to us. The other guys all laughed.

"There are only two colors in the Forest Service," he answered. "Shit brown and puke green. All you have to remember is put the shit outside and the puke inside. Other than that, nobody gives a fuck how you do it."

Stanley and I painted together that day, and I tried to stay on the other side of the room from him. At the morning break he followed me into the toilets. While I was taking a leak, he stood beside me, looking over at my business, and then up at my face. I ignored him, and he moved away.

But when I finished peeing and turned to zip up, he was sitting in the toilet stall behind me with the door open, playing with his donkey dick and motioning for me to come over to him.

I told him, "Stanley, you don't do a thing for me. I mean, if I wanted a girl, I'd go get one."

He slammed the plywood door shut in my face.

I went outside to look for Donnie, but he was nowhere in camp.

Back at work with Stanley, I tried to soften it up. "Hey, we had some fun this weekend," I told him, "but I've got something else going right now, okay?"

He made a prissy face. "Oh, don't worry, I understand. It's perfectly obvious. Now that Donnie's back, you want to be the girl, that's all."

"Oh, fuck you, man," I said. "This has nothing to do with anybody wanting to be a girl, believe me." I added, "Man."

"I told you to stop calling me 'man.' You ought to be glad I'm around. I'm the only one in camp who's a bigger sissy than you are. I make you look good, stupid."

I didn't see Donnie until lunch break, and then, as I was sitting under the tree with my crew, he came walking across the parking lot, moving toward us with that slow, sexy, deliberate, give-a-shit attitude he had at work. Even that far off, I could make out the line of his dick down his right pants leg. Nobody else in camp showed it off like Donnie. He came over and nodded to everyone, but it was me he sat beside to open his lunch sack.

We couldn't talk much with everyone around. "How's it going in the office?" I asked.

"Pretty boring," he said with his mouth full. "Rather be out here." After he finished his sandwich, Donnie leaned toward me. Very casually, he threw his elbow around my neck, just horsing around in front of the guys. He held his hand beside my cheek and lifted his index finger like he was shooting me a bird.

"Sniff it," he said under his breath. I turned my nose to it, and his finger still smelled of my butt. Donnie laughed and slapped my back.

Walking back to work I asked him, "Isn't anything too gross for you?"

"Aw, it's not so gross. It's just your crapper. You wash it out in the shower every night, don't you? I'm just playing a little stinkfinger with you. You liked it plenty last night."

"Well," I said, "it's unsanitary. You might get some disease or something."

He shook his head. "Not me. I never catch anything. Anyway, I don't do it with just any old body, you know."

Looking behind us quickly, Donnie took my arm and guided me off between two buildings. I backed up against a wall, and Donnie got up so close to me I could feel heat from his body. He put his mouth to my ear and whispered, "Buddies got to take care of each other's, uh, special needs, you know what I mean?"

He looked around. Putting his hand on the front of my pants, he said, "I mean the need to get raunchy, real raunchy." He fingered my crotch. We both looked down our fronts, and Donnie's cock was jutting at an angle under his pocket instead of hanging down like before. "First interesting thing that's happened to me all day," he said.

Then he looked me in the eye. "I ain't your little girlfriend back home," he growled. "We'll take the car out someplace tonight where we won't get interrupted this time." My dick was curled up tight and hard inside my Jockeys, and his fingers were moving all around between my legs. "Are you with me, sport?"

I squirmed against the wall, nodding "Uh-huh."

He gave the pouch of my underwear a squeeze. "You save that for me, okay, big fella? Work up a good load of spunk down there, and save it for me. I already got some ready for you. This time, I want us to have a real hot session. I wanna go all the way tonight."

He sniffed his index finger again, still staring directly at me without blinking. The corners of his brown eyes wrinkled up as he gave me one of his slow grins. It made my asshole tighten and my dick lift up in his hand when he looked at me like that.

Back on the walkway, he patted my butt as we separated, and I had half a hard-on the rest of the afternoon.

After dinner we didn't even wait for dark. We walked back to the cabin quickly, grabbed jackets, and headed for the car.

Donnie had brought his little jar of Vaseline jelly from his locker. He set it on the dashboard and started the motor.

"I know a place where we can have us some privacy," he said.

"Put the top down," I suggested. He unhooked the clamps and we both lowered the ragged top into the well behind the back seat. It wouldn't go all the way, so we just left it there without putting the cover over it.

I listened to the tires crunch on gravel as we pulled out of camp and followed the dirt road into the woods, the first time I'd gotten away since I arrived. I tried to find some music on the radio, but got only static. I stared at the blue Vaseline label and imagined what he wanted to do with that stuff.

This must be what it's like to be the girl on a date, I thought, and the guy shows you he has a rubber. Stanley had said that about me, that I wanted to be Donnie's girl. I squirmed in my seat. Was it true? I'd never thought about being a girl before.

No, actually this was more like going for a ride after school with one of the kids my mother didn't want me to hang around with. It was like sneaking off with one of the bad boys for the afternoon. My mother wouldn't approve of Donnie's looks for one hot minute. Not with those sideburns. Especially not with that mustache running all the way from the corners of his mouth to down below his chin. He didn't have anything on under his shirt, and I could see chest hair at his neck. He whistled, steering with one hand, stroking his pants leg with the other. I watched him until our eyes met, and he grinned at me.

"How do you like being a cocksucker, now that you've had a day to think about it?" he asked me.

"I like it," I said. "With you."

"Me too. We're gonna have us some fun."

The wind blew our hair the wrong way and I threw my head back and laughed, watching the tall trees pinwheel above us. He turned off onto a freshly-scraped side road, following a creek. We bounced into the shade under a grove of cedars. Around the bend it got so dark he switched on the headlights, and then beyond the next bend a muddy, yellow bulldozer glowed in the headlight beams. We circled it and parked, headed back the way we came in.

"If anybody pulls in behind us, we'll see their lights before they see us," he said, killing the motor. "Won't be anybody, though."

We finished our beers in the silence of the big woods, breathing cedar scents as night air drifted through the open car. Wordlessly, we got out together and stood side-by-side to pee on the treads of the giant dirt-moving machine, making two dark streaks in the caked mud, and then crossing streams to make one big streak together.

Donnie climbed up to the seat. "*Brmm, brmm, brmm,*" he said, pulling control levers and stomping pedals. I clambered up behind him and watched him play and make motor noises. When he bent his head back to smile up at me upside-down, I leaned over him, and this time when our eyes met I kissed him quickly, just barely touching my lips to his and then backing off.

"Hey, I didn't think you'd want to do that," he said.

"Why not?" I asked, looking away, then back at him. "Actually, I wanted to last night."

"Some guys just don't kiss," he said. "You act sort of straight, you know. Sometimes I can't tell exactly what it is you are."

I shrugged. "I don't know what I am yet, either. Until I met you, I thought I was straight."

He swivelled the seat around to face me. "Well," he said with smile, "if we're gonna make out, let's do it like this." He reached up and pulled me down onto him. I stretched myself over his body, and put my hands on his shoulders, feeling the solid muscles even through the thick, rough leather. This time he raised up and kissed back, and I got a mouthful of mustache. My heart thumped. My dick surged. I tried to lean all of myself against him, and the chair squeaked as it rocked back under the weight of two men.

Donnie was as eager for it as I was. He wrapped his arms around me and licked at my mouth, sucking at my lips, wetting my whole face. I put my arms around his big shoulders and chewed at the hairs on his upper lip. His beard scratched my cheek, giving me the shivers as he kissed his way down my neck. He pulled my butt to him, pressing our hips together.

When we looked at each other again, I was breathing so hard I could barely speak. "Damn," I said, "you sure aren't."

"Aren't what?" he asked, licking my chin.

"My little girlfriend back home," I panted. I put my hand up underneath his coat and felt the curve of his chest muscles under my palm. The white woolly fur inside rubbed on the back of my hand, and smelled like a mixture of male sweat and leather and wet dog hair. "Damn," I whispered again. "It was sure never like this with her." I was so excited my voice trembled, but I didn't care.

Donnie gripped the cheeks of my butt and rubbed my crotch against his. My hard-on bumped against his through our pants. "Let's go get in the car," he said. "We can run the heater and get nekked. Come on."

We grabbed the top and flipped it forward. Inside, he took off his jacket and made a wad against the door on his side. Leaning back, he pulled me on top of him again. I popped open the pearl snaps on his shirt, kissing the hairy nipples underneath, nuzzling my way down his belly, all the way to the rearing horse on his belt. The thick lump underneath it went halfway to his knee.

He held a beer in one hand on the back of the seat, and draped his other arm across the steering wheel.

"Go for it, cowboy," he whispered, grinning down at me. "Ride your buddy's pony some."

I unhooked the brass buckle on his belt and opened the buttons on his frayed Levis. I snuggled my face against his warm underwear, feeling the bristly hairs curling out of his fly. When I reached inside his boxer shorts with my fingers, his dick was so hard I couldn't bend it. He moved his hips so I could get it out, and then the proud, stiff cock I'd wanted so long stood up like an Idaho tree, tall and straight in front of my crossed eyes.

He made it bounce in my face, going "*BRMM, BRMM, BRMM,*" and then I went for it, went all the way down over it. "Ye-a-a-h," he breathed, settling back. "Show your buddy how good a cocksucker's mouth can feel." Dusk came while I sighted up his belly and watched him drink his beer and smile down at me, at me sucking his cock. "Watch the teeth," he instructed me. "Little wider." I loved it. "Play with my nuts some." I was in heaven, giving my guy what he wanted.

There's this funny sort of reversal that happens when you suck another man's dick. You get a wonderful sexual rush of your own from giving him what he likes so much. He goes, "Yeah, feels good," and your dick tingles. His cockhead hardens up, and you think you're about to come. His juices start to flow, and you wet your pants. How come, if I'm the one blowing him, I feel like my whole body is one giant orgasm? I mean, I didn't even have my dick out yet.

He groaned and put his hand on the back of my head, stopping me for a moment. "Go slow," he said. "Don't make me come. Make it last. I'm so full of spunk I can't hardly hold it in." I found I could keep his entire erection in my throat for minutes at a time without gagging, just holding my breath, suspended in time, wrapped around his sex.

He whimpered with pleasure. I felt the head of his cock throb against my tongue, and then he grabbed my hair and pulled me back until only the tip was between my lips. "Hold up," he whispered. "Don't move, oh, oh, shit, yeah, I got to let some out, UNH-H-H. . ."

A burst of cum spewed around my teeth and dripped from my lower lip. Donnie moaned, still holding my head motionless, as my mouth filled with his thick juice, not in spurts, but in a quick flow that lasted for two or three seconds, then stopped.

"Don't swallow, or I'll shoot off all the way," Donnie told me, and I held the slightly salty wad of his semen in my mouth. "Don't move," he said. "Don't do anything." I waited and felt another short squirt against my tongue. Donnie shuddered, then began to relax back against the seat.

"Uh-huh. Right there, that's right," Donnie said at last, and took a deep breath. "That's right where I want to be. I love it when I can stop in the middle of shooting my load, and hold it half in and half out."

He moved my head with his hands, up and down over his dick, slowly masturbating himself with my mouth. "Ah-h-h, yeah, that's what I call ridin' the high trail, yeah, just clip-clopping along on my pony, up there on the top of the ridge. I can go forever now without actually shooting off. I just have to leak some out now and then, sorta let the pressure off. Wups, here comes one more." He pulled my lips away, and I could see a new dribble of milky jism drooling from the tip of dick. His hard-on twitched once, then held stiff.

"Don't swallow it, buddy." He took my arms and raised me up. "Bring it up here for me. I wanna lick it out of your mouth. Come here, sport. I wanna eat my own jism."

I was limp in his hands as he lifted my face to his. I opened my mouth and Donnie kissed me hard, running his tongue in between my lips, licking at my teeth, sucking his own cum out of my mouth and swallowing it. He ran his hand up under my shirt, pinching both my nipples, and then worked his hand inside my zipper, rolling my hard-on around inside my Jockey shorts. I could feel sticky wetness, and when Donnie put his hand inside my shorts and pulled on my dick, it was already slick and dripping.

"Uh-h-HUH," he said, cranking me around. "Pretty juicy down there, fella. You really like this queer shit, don't you?"

"God, Donnie, you turn me on so much," I moaned, "I'm just crazy for your dick." My voice was husky and hoarse. "You stretched my vocal cords," I told him as we sat up for a while and ran the motor for heat. We giggled as I tried to clear my throat and couldn't. "Next thing, I'll be losing my voice. Or maybe it will just get higher," I said, coughing. "I'll be swishing around in a dress, like Stanley."

"Ah, Stanley doesn't wear a dress."

"Not yet. Give him time. He'll be our maid."

Donnie didn't laugh. After a moment, he said, "You put him down too much. Ought to keep in mind that he's one of our brothers."

"Sisters."

"Whatever. We're all faggots, Bill."

"Don't say that."

"Better get used to it."

"You're not. You're a man. That's why you turn me on."

He sat back and stared ahead without saying anything, and I thought he was mad about something, but then he started a story.

"My buddy back home, my jack-off buddy, he used to mail-order sexy underwear, girls' stuff, you know, with the hole in front so you can fuck your girlfriend while she's got them on. From L.A., Hollywood.

"He had boxes of them, and he'd take them with him on weekends and give them to girls and come back and tell me how it looked to stick his dick into them, with the girl's cunt inside all that red lace.

"I wasn't even in high school then, and I just ate that shit up. He lived out back in a bunkhouse, by himself most of the year. I'd go back and hang out with him.

"I woke him up one day, and he had 'em on in bed. Turns out he liked to see his dick sticking out of them better than he liked to see it go into them. He wore girls' panties all the time, under his jeans, and this is an ugly fucker who never shaves and wears chaps when he's herding cattle and all that good shit."

He paused, and I told him, "I don't quite get it."

"It's just that you shouldn't, you know, judge people. Especially about their sex habits. Some rough-tough cowboys wear lace panties. And some real pansies are tigers in the sack. That's what being queer is all about, being different from the bozos. All the pussy hounds know about is how to make babies in the dark. Nothing wrong with guys who act a little bit like girls. They're just being what they are. Nothing wrong with that. Turns me on, in fact. They're even queerer than me, and I like that."

He took a long pull on his beer, swallowed hard, and let out a long burp. "'Course, I like anything with a dick hung on it," he said. "Including Stanley."

I didn't want to talk about Stanley. Sliding back next to him, I ran my fingers under his open shirt, feeling the hard muscles of his chest, plucking at the hairs. He turned up his beer can, gulped, and crumpled it. I leaned over to rub my cheek against his sideburns, and he hooked his elbow behind my neck.

When I turned my face up to him, he kissed me, gently, and I closed my eyes and leaned toward him. I was beginning to get the hang of making out with another guy. I chewed at his mustache, and then opened my mouth for him, but this time instead of his tongue he gave me a mouthful of cold beer that leaked out and dribbled down our chins.

"Heh," he chuckled, wiping his neck. "Guess I ain't much good at being romantic. Whyn't you take your clothes off for me? Let me watch you strip."

He tugged my teeshirt up over my arms and then used it to dry my chin as I took off my sneakers.

"Socks, too," he told me. "Get buck nekked. And help me get my boots off, okay?" I did it all, pulling his cowboy boots loose, then balancing on my knees on the seat as I dropped my pants. "Keep your shorts on for a minute," he told me. I pulled my pants down and tossed them onto the floor.

He pulled his cock out and put his hand on my Jockey shorts, feeling my behind. "You got a sexy butt. Anybody ever tell you that? No? Hmm, yeah, cute ass." Donnie ran one hand all over my backside, squeezing the cheeks of my ass and calling me "Sexy Billy," over and over. Me, he called me that! I was dizzy with excitement as he rubbed my bare back and felt my legs and wrapped his fingers around my arm and pressed his thumb against the muscles.

His dick waved from his pants as he peeled off his shirt and moved over on the seat. Still on my knees, I could feel my erection pushing my Jockeys out in front. Donnie stuck his fingers in under the leg holes and tickled my nuts.

"Lemme get a good look at this thing," he whispered, hooking my hard-on with a finger and tugging it out so the head of it was aimed down beside my leg, sticking half out. "Nothing I like better than a big ol' dick pokin' out like that, pokin' out from the side of a guy's undershorts."

"Aw, mine's not nearly as big as yours."

"Don't matter, when two guys are fucking around with each other, big dick is one word."

He worked it all the way out, and it was so hard it ached. When he let go, it flipped straight up. "Big ol' ball bag you got on you, man," he said, pulling those out, too.

He tugged down on my nuts until it made my dick drop down

level to his face, and then Donnie leaned forward and spread his lips around it, and my dick glided easily into his mouth. It seemed like such a natural place for it to go, like it belonged right there. He made a long, slow slide all the way down to the hilt, twisting my briefs all out of shape as he sucked my cock. I had to hold onto the seat back as he worked me over with his tongue and his lips and his throat, swallowing and sucking and fingering my balls until I had to warn him I was close to coming. When Donnie moved back, a thin string of my pre-cum stretched from me to his mouth.

He licked it off and looked up at me with his eyes narrowed. "Now, pull your shorts off, big guy," he said, still jacking off as he watched me. I sat down and kicked my underwear off. I was totally naked. Kneeling on the floorboard, pushing my legs apart, Donnie had complete control of me, and I closed my eyes and let him handle me like a toy. He licked my thighs. He kissed all around the base of my cock. He sucked my balls. I put one foot on the steering wheel column and braced the other on the dash. I was wide open, utterly open to him.

Donnie pushed my knees up and spread the cheeks of my ass. I expected his finger again, but this time I felt the rough scrape of his beard instead. He was licking me back there, Donnie was licking my ass! Yielding to the obscene and the sublime, I closed my eyes and groaned at the maddeningly sweet, warm slide of his tongue over the slot of my butt. He pushed my knees up higher, and spread my crotch open wider, and then I felt the tip of his tongue press against the hole.

Gasping, whimpering, rocking my head from side to side, I let go down there, let myself go completely loose. Donnie never lost an advantage when he was close to getting what he wanted. Pressing up, higher still, he wedged his tongue in and darted it all the way up inside me, right up inside my asshole. My reflex was to bear down, and I squeezed him back out of me, but it had been too good, what I'd felt. I got control of myself and relaxed my ass again, and sure enough, I felt Donnie's tongue push up, and up, and then he held it there, held his hard, wet tongue right in the center of my butt, right up inside the hole between my legs.

Hanging there in ecstasy, I made a little squeak in my throat. He swirled his tongue around inside my asshole. My dick swelled up, throbbed, and dripped pre-cum onto my stomach.

Donnie backed off. I went limp. He wiped his mouth and burped.

"Find that Vaseline for me," he ordered from between my knees.

I held it while he dipped a finger into the goo and then prodded under my legs, back up between the cheeks of my ass, and once again he fingered me where I'd never been touched before, except by a few doctors.

Well, okay, my mom got a thermometer up there a few times when I was a kid. But Donnie was whispering, "How'd you like to feel this end get stretched like your throat did?" and I knew he wasn't thinking about taking my temperature.

He stuck his finger up my asshole. It made me squinch my eyes shut and gasp out loud, "Ah! Donnie! Oh! Mmmh!"

It stung at first. Donnie purred in my ear. "Can you remember back when you were real little? Back to when you were in diapers? I can," he said.

He put more goo on his finger, and I squirmed when it went back in me. "I can remember crapping in my diapers, and feeling the hot turd back there sliding out of my asshole. I'd squeeze my butt on it, and it felt real good. That's why babies cry when you change their diapers. They're pissed off. They don't know it's shit, they just know it feels good, having something big and warm back there. Very sensitive spot."

He twisted his finger, and it felt slick, and delicious. I groaned.

He whispered, "Open it up, Billy. Make like you're gonna shit in my hand. Nothing will come out. I already checked. Maybe one little old fart up there, that's all."

Dirty talk, shitty talk, floated up from the floorboard. I thrashed and slumped down over his hand, feeling my cock thump stiffly against his arm, and Donnie whispered, "That's one." Then he did something with his fingers that made me gasp for breath. "That's two," he said. His fingers moved up, and then popped out. The next time, the pressure brought tears to my eyes, but I took it, and Donnie said, "That's three, old buddy."

I heard a high squeal and realized it was coming from my nose, but all I could think about was the feeling of his three fingers wedged up my rear end, and I was sure he was going to force his whole hand up my ass. It hurt and it felt so good all at once, and I threw back my head and went "GAH-H-H-H-H-AH!"

Then he was out of me again. I was straddling him as he kneeled on the floor. He leaned forward, looming over me like a bear. "You're gonna like this," he said, and chuckled. I felt the real thing, Donnie's hard dick, slick with Vaseline jelly, sliding up between my legs, between my cheeks, poking at my butt, tunneling up my asshole, and I wasn't ready for what I felt then.

He jabbed upward but my ass didn't want to stretch that far. I pulled back, "Ouch, wait."

But he didn't stop. He reached under us to aim it, feeding the big tube through his fist and up my ass. The pain made my jaw drop. When it popped inside, I tried to part myself for him, but he was splitting me open.

"Wait, you're so big." I put my hand on his chest. He backed off, trembling.

My big mistake was reaching for him, wrapping my arms around his muscular body. Chest hair rubbed between us, and his beard rasped on my neck. I felt his urgency, his male potency, and I couldn't help telling him, "Fuck me, Donnie. I want to take it inside me."

He leaned forward and pushed, and the next time it got halfway in he went wild, lunging at me, growling, kissing my mouth, and then he raised his hips hard and just impaled me all the way down on his dick. The pain made me dizzy, but there's no stopping a man halfway through a fuck. As it sank into me, my guts seemed to turn inside out. I let him do it as long as I could, hanging onto his neck, but when he started to thrust at me, roaring in my ear, it hurt so much I had to twist away. I reached down and pulled his cock out and pointed it up under my balls instead.

"Oh-h-h, shi-i-i-it," he groaned, and slippery warmth shot up between my legs as Donnie fucked my fist, pumping his load out into my hand instead of my ass. His dick stabbed at me, squirting cum up under my nuts, flooding my crotch. I hugged him and rubbed him, trying to make it good for him while he got off, even if it was only between my legs.

The big guy was crazy on top of me, grabbing and humping and shoving his hips at me, and when he laid a line of his cum up between us, his hairy belly was scratchy and slippery against my dick at the same time, and I felt myself unloading with him, coming at last, making a big messy glop of cum between our bellies that trickled down my side as we lay there panting together.

Mopping up with my teeshirt, I told him, "You stretched it, all right. It feels like you drove that Cat through me."

Donnie petted me, stroking my hair. "Sorry, buddy. I got carried away. I should have gone easier for your first time. I forgot I was busting your cherry. You're an awful good fuck for such a virgin. I'll get us another beer."

The pain was so bad that while he was gone I checked behind myself with a finger to see if any of the wetness was blood. I held my finger up in the darkness, and it didn't look red.

"It'll be easier the next time," he assured me when he returned.

"Right, right. My dentist says the same thing." I hugged myself. I was cold, but I didn't want to get dressed. "Can I wear your jacket?" I asked.

"Sure." He handed it to me. When I put it on, it was instantly warm. I slid over beside Donnie. He had no top on, and his pants were still open. I had no bottoms on, and I liked it. He put his arm around my shoulder and things seemed better, but my butthole still hurt.

I asked him, "Do you do it to your friend like that?"

"Yup. Then he does me. We fuck around a lot, every which way we can think of."

"Doesn't it hurt?"

"You sort of learn to like it."

Maybe I would learn to take it, but I couldn't imagine learning to like it. "So, are you guys. . ." I hesitated. "In love?" I blurted out.

"Nah, we hardly even talk, much less kiss." He cleared his throat. "Actually," he said, glancing over at me quickly, then looking down, "I never kissed a guy before tonight."

Donnie shifted in his seat. "Me and Monty, we're just, well, fuck-buddies. I don't know any other way to put it.

"I started out watching him in the shower through a knothole after school, out back in the bunkhouse. He had orange hair around his dick, and a big knob at the end of it. Then he caught me beating off like that and told me to strip down and jump in with him. Shower drain got clogged up a lot after that.

"But we didn't start fucking until one night he caught me

looking at his jerk-off magazines. Blew my mind that they were half gay and half straight.

"I thought he'd be gone all night, 'cause it was a weekend, so I jumped in his bed and greased up. All those pictures of men fucking men in the ass got me so turned on that I reached under the bed and got his whiskey bottle and stuck the neck of it up there to see what it felt like."

I shifted my weight and drained my beer. "Did it hurt?"

"I got used to it. Actually, it's dumb as hell to stick glass up your ass, but you know how it is when you're thirteen, when you first find out how good it feels, you go around putting any fool thing up it. I lost a cucumber for two days that way once."

"Aw, now you're bullshitting me."

"Well, anyway, there I was, one leg in the air, and by the way I'd put his chaps on bare-assed, and I'm looking at his book and whacking off and stuffing my butt with this whiskey bottle, and in walks my buddy with a drunk broad on his arm.

"I was so fucking embarrassed. But she cracks up, and old Monty walks over to me, cool as ice, and pulls the bottle out of my ass, *THOOMP*! He unscrews the cap, takes a slug, and offers some to his girl. She's rolling in a chair laughing by then.

"Then he says, 'Donnie?' and passes me the bottle.

"Well, I didn't want him to think he could gross me out, so I took that whiskey bottle and I sucked that fucker dry. Ha!

"But he got me back," Donnie continued. "He screws the cap back on, lifts my leg up, and sticks it back up where it was. Then he just says, 'Don't mind us.'"

I shook my head. "Ah, that never really happened, did it?"

He chuckled, but didn't answer.

"Come on," I said. "You don't know anybody with a name like 'Monty.'"

"In Montana, lots of guys call themselves Monty."

I stared. "And after that, you guys started fucking each other?"

"I moved out back with him. Gave my room to my sister. 'Course, I was jailbait then, so we kept it quiet. But at night we reamed each other out good. He brought his girls home for me, too."

"Which do you like better?"

"Oh, I like guys. I like dick. I like butt-fucking with a buddy. After that, girls are okay." He shrugged. "Every now and then."

Maybe butt-fucking was fine for him, but by Tuesday morning, I felt as though I had a red peppercorn lodged in my anus. Sitting hurt. Standing was a little better. We had classes in fire fighting, so when I had to sit at a desk, I tried leaning far to one side in my chair. When we walked to some demonstration, I had to lag behind the others so they couldn't see me walking bow-legged as a duck.

Stanley watched me eat my lunch sandwich standing up, and began to smile at me. The smile became a smirk, a knowing, superior look. "What's the matter, Bill?" he sneered. "Fool around with something you couldn't handle?"

"Fuck you," I answered cleverly with food in my mouth, which I never do, but he pissed me off. He narrowed his eyes and licked his lips at me. I hoped nobody saw him do that stuff.

That night Donnie told me, "You just got a bad case of the piles, that's all. No big deal. There's a first aid kit in the kitchen. Cookie keeps it locked up, so just go ask him for some Preparation H or something."

"I can't do that," I said. "Everybody in camp will find out."

Wednesday, we had to dig some firebreaks using what they call pulaskis. The last thing I needed to do was swing an ax, and a pulaski is like an ax, but worse. It's a weird thing with a double-sided head. The back side is a sharp hoe, designed for chopping up roots and clawing them out of the ground. Every time I swung it, my ass clenched around that peppercorn.

"Pry it up, chop it up, dig it clean," they yelled. Every chop sent a stab of fire up my sore behind.

"Line up," they hollered at us. "Bellybutton to asshole, make a line."

We each bent down to scrape away leaves, roots, and soil, until the patch of ground in front of us was clear of anything that would burn. When the last guy was done, he'd yell, "Bump up," and each of us would move forward.

I only got my patch half cleared before I heard, "Bump up," and moved ahead, letting the others behind me finish. Soon it was "bump up, bump up, bump up," faster and faster, until the line started to move like a caterpillar. I'd make two chops and move up to the next guy's butt. We snaked through the woods like a dirt-eating monster, leaving a line behind us that a fire couldn't cross.

By dinnertime, my peppercorn had grown to the size of a hot chestnut, and I worried about being able to take a crap.

Donnie went down to the other end and played cards that night. I sat on somebody's bunk and watched for a while, just to be with Donnie, but somebody in the cabin smoked, and the radio had some boring talk show from San Francisco droning and crackling. My ass hurt. I went to bed early and worried. How would I explain this to a doctor?

Then, whee, I woke up Thursday with my first erection in days. I could tighten my ass without any pain. Steve and Stanley were gone when Donnie climbed down, so I swiped at the lump swinging inside his shorts and told him, "I'm all better now."

He patted my head, and I sat on the edge of my mattress and hugged his middle. His underwear was still warm from bed. He was half-hard, and I nuzzled my cheek against the rubbery cock under his boxers.

Maybe I had been too crabby about my sore ass, I thought. With my fingers, I toyed inside his fly, and then flipped him into my mouth.

"Ummmm," he said, "a quickie." He put his palms on my cheeks and pressed my face closer. I was just getting into it when I saw a shadow, and peered around Donnie's shorts to see Stanley in the doorway.

I froze with my mouth full. I felt Donnie turn to look, too. Stanley was a blank. I looked for shock, or disgust, hoping for a grin, but he gave me no sign. His eyes went up to Donnie's face, then back down to me, and then he grabbed the toilet kit he had come back for, and walked out.

Rats, I thought. First I wouldn't blow him, now he sees me blowing Donnie. He's going to get me in trouble, I know it. To Donnie I said, "Do you think he'll tell on us?"

Donnie laughed. "He's in no position to talk, believe me. He won't say anything."

"You don't know what he thinks."

He bent down and gave me an amused smile. "Don't I?" Pinching my nipple, he gave it a few tugs, then wiggled his eyebrows, and went over to dress.

I grabbed my pants and followed him outside, calling out, "Donnie, wait up. What's going on?"

Inside the washroom, Stanley was alone, staring into the

mirror. Donnie walked to him and said, "Hey, sport, it's okay."

Stanley tilted his head, and softly asked, "Is it?"

"Yeah, everything's fine," Donnie said, giving the boy a tug on his nipple.

It was just the way he pinched my nipples, and he'd called Stanley 'sport.' I knew in an instant they were fucking. They had to be.

Stanley looked at me with his eyes narrowed down to slits. "Okay," he said in a low voice. "We'll share him."

"Share him!" I repeated.

I turned to Donnie. "Share him?" My voice faltered. I searched his eyes for some explanation.

He sighed and looked down at the floor.

It was true. My heart sank into the pit of my stomach.

I looked at Stanley and saw a smirk of triumph twist his lips.

That hurt more than I wanted either of them to know. I turned my back to them and walked outside, fast.

8

Morning sunlight sparkled in the creek, flashing between clumps of stalky new grass and dancing on my face. I sat on a rock behind the mess hall and stared into the bubbling water. Donnie and Stanley had come back into the cabin together just as I had pulled on my shirt and run for the breakfast line. Moving into the crowd, I had turned my back on them and waited for the bell, but then I had let everyone else file inside ahead of me and walked around back to be alone.

Donnie and I had never made any sort of promises to each other. Hell, I'd only known him a week. Why shouldn't he be having sex with the camp slut? I was. Hell. I kicked a rock into the creek. Oh, but Donnie, I thought, how could you? Dammit, I just kissed you.

The vision of Donnie kissing Stanley made me clench my fists and hold my breath in, and then I let out a long groan. It had been too good out in his car. It was special, it was Donnie's own little world. God, I had let him put his hand inside me, almost. I had let him fuck me.

Wasn't it special for him, too? Or did he play sex games like that with just anybody? Maybe he really got off on having two of us after him. I gathered some pebbles and tossed them, plink, plink. What could he see in Stanley? His big dick? Bigger than mine, certainly. Was that what Donnie really wanted, a swish with a big dick?

"Bill?"

It was Donnie, standing in the weeds behind me. "They've closed the kitchen already." He held out a paper bag. "I made your sack lunch for you."

"Thanks," I said, taking the bag.

He reached to give me a pull-up as I stood up on the rock, but I didn't want his help.

We walked together toward the office. "Hope you like ham and cheese," he said.

Stopping, I looked at him. "Why didn't you tell me about

Stanley and you? You're doing it with him, aren't you?"

He shrugged. "It only happened a couple of times."

"I never see you together."

"He gets busy at night. Last week sometime, I got up to take a leak in the middle of the night and he followed me outside. I was peeing in the bushes, and he did me. It doesn't mean a thing, Bill. He just likes to give head."

I sighed, and we walked across the parking lot.

"You know," Donnie continued, "If you'd give him a wink every now and then, instead of treating him like a cockroach, you'd get a little, too. He's good."

"I know he's good," I wailed. "I found out this weekend."

"You did? Great. So what's all the fuss about?"

I clenched my teeth and moaned. "I feel so mixed up, Donnie. You have this real powerful effect on me. I don't know what the hell's going on. And I know they've got me down to work with him all day. I don't think I can stand it."

"No problem. I work in the office, remember? I've got some pull, at least on the assignment sheet. They've got seeders going out into the field today. Want to do that? You work all day by yourself. Give you some time to get your head cleared out, how about that?"

When they posted the duty list my name had been scratched off the paint crew and penciled in on the seeding crew. I lined up in the barn and checked out a red mechanical gadget with straps and a crank, and jumped into the back of a pickup with four boys I was glad not to know.

We didn't get into the woods, though. They dropped us on a hillside that had been clearcut the summer before. Dead stumps and ashes from the burn-off stretched for acres. The only trees left standing were the ones that had already been dead when the loggers came through, ghostly gray snags that tilted with motionless alarm, branches raised in defense like skeletons after a war.

Crude dirt roads laced between the tree stumps, and the melting snow and the spring rains were cutting gullies through them, wounds on wounds.

We bounced along the logging roads, dropping sacks of wildflower seed. At the top of the hill, I was told to fill my seeder and walk back and forth, zig-zagging down and refilling at each sack. The pickup lurched over a washout and disappeared, and I was alone.

The seeder buzzed as I turned the crank. Chaff flew into my eyes. I wondered how much would wash all the way down to the river before the forest healed its scars, but I did my job, pacing off the hours.

Since I was on my own, I ate lunch early, sitting on a blackened log in the ashes. I was amazed to see a chipmunk scamper up. "You and me against the world, fella," I told him, opening my sandwich and tossing him some bread. Maybe the forest would grow back, if a chipmunk could find enough to live on in all this desolation. Then again, maybe he was eating all the seeds we were trying to plant. "Don't trust anybody with your nuts," I advised him.

I spread the waxed paper and laughed. Donnie had put a slice of cheese on top of the sandwich, and he had used a spoon or something to cut it into the shape of a penis and two testicles. I ate it first.

I'll eat you like that tonight, I thought. I'll get it down my throat so far I can't breathe, and I'll hold it there and make it throb. I'll eat it all, dick and balls and your smelly asshole too, and I'll eat your cum, and your hair and muscles and all of you, dammit. I'll make you scream, it'll be so fucking good.

Strapping the machine on my shoulders, I returned to playing Johnny Appleseed.

It wouldn't work. I was kidding myself. No matter how good a blowjob I gave him, Stanley would probably do better. And when it came to offering something for Donnie to suck on, well, I just didn't measure up.

My silly spray of seeds seemed futile. The thunder-showers of summer were coming. I felt the cold stares of forest spirits, resentful of the intruder with the noisy gadget, come to make ineffective restitution for the damage done by other men with louder machines.

BUZZZZZZZZ. I thought of the real cold looks I had been getting, the glares from Stanley. Well, I wouldn't give him the satisfaction of seeing how I felt. I'd be cool. My move would be with Donnie. Tonight, I'd give him what he wanted, no matter how much it hurt. Share him, like hell we would. I'd give Donnie the best fuck of his life, and leave the twit eating our dust. I stomped off in a roaring flurry of scattering seeds.

When the truck parked for lunch on a loop of road a few hundred feet below me, they waved and honked the horn, but I yelled, "I already ate on my morning break. I'm gonna take a nap. Blow the horn when you go back to work."

Dropping the seeder, I hiked off the clearcut and into the living forest, looking for a place. I found it in a patch of sun, a log with purple wildflowers and bright green grass around it. Draping my shirt over the bark, I sat down and leaned back against the cloth, letting the sun sting my chest. I closed my eyes and unzipped my pants to give myself some comfort.

Already, I knew how I would do it. I would put blankets in the car tonight, and make sure the Vaseline jar was in the glove box. I would even take a crap first, just to be sure I was ready for him. I would drink coffee at dinner, because that always made me go to the bathroom. After that, I'd even wash my fanny out at the sink, to show him I wasn't naive.

I'd say, "Let's take the blankets and go somewhere and fuck." He'd like that, real direct. Then we'd do it, and it would be him down there instead of my hand, on a blanket in the woods. He'd turn me over and fuck me. I wanted that, but I'd make him kiss me first, this time. Maybe I wouldn't be so tense, making out with him first. I imagined him on top of me, hot skin on my back, his hairy loins pressing my buttocks, so strong and manly, prodding inside of me with that grand tool of his, maybe kissing my neck. Maybe he would bite my neck when he shot off. "Damn," I whispered, feeling myself start to come. "You big sexy man. I want you to fuck me again, fuck me, fuck me."

Crossing my legs tightly, I rolled onto my side as my cum blossomed in my hand and dripped onto the purple flowers beside me. My semen oozed down the petals and stretched from them to the earth, leaving behind long, silky threads.

Good, I thought. I'm fertilizing the hillside. Somebody needs to. My cum would seep into the dirt and feed other life. Nothing is wasted in nature. In time, all seed goes to more seed, even if it means letting the tiny beasties of the soil chomp on your chromosomes.

"Lunchtime, you guys," I said aloud. "Pure protein." I squeezed myself empty and stretched out to watch a black and red caterpillar ripple its way up a stem. Closing my eyes in the warm sun, I dreamed of spinning a cocoon around myself and willing my body to change into a butterfly. For a moment I was afraid to open my eyes, for fear I'd see great yellow wings lifting my body high above the trees.

Trudging along later that afternoon, tired, I said out loud, "I want to get fucked." Nothing happened. I proclaimed to an assortment of birds, "I suck dick, and I love it." They continued to chirp. God did not strike me dead. There wasn't even thunder.

Giggling, I began to dance along, grinding out seeds and singing, "I'm a cock sucker and I take it up the ass," kick. "I'm a cock sucker and I take it up the ass," kick. I chanted with my footsteps, and the spirits around me seemed to be smiling. Watch out, Stanley, I'm taking him back.

Just before the dinner bell that night, Donnie signaled to me to follow him outside. To hell with that, I thought. Let Stanley run after him like a puppy. But when Stanley started to get up from his bed, I jumped ahead of him and went after Donnie.

"What if I'd opened my sandwich in the truck with everybody looking?" I asked him, pretending to be annoyed. "Talk about ruining a guy's reputation."

"I knew you'd be off moping by yourself," he said, poking me. "Still pissed off?"

"I'm not pissed, I'm just surprised. I thought it was only us." We walked slowly toward the mess hall.

"It is only us," he said. "Hey, come on, I see the way you watch Steve, for instance. If he gave you the chance, you'd go down on him, wouldn't you? You wouldn't stop to think, 'Oh, what's Donnie gonna say,' you'd just go for it. That's the way guys are. None of us are gonna get pregnant, you know. That's the way it should be with men. You get turned on, you get your rocks off, and then you shake hands and split. Go for all the fun you can get. Shit, that's the best part about being gay."

We held back from the others. The word 'gay' seemed to echo. He continued quietly, "Bill, lots of guys, soon as you start fucking, they start this 'I love you' stuff, right away. Then as soon as they come, they forget your name. I hate insincere shit. I'm just not that way. I'm used to lots of space around me, and not much talk. Don't rush things, okay? I mean, I like you a lot, but I've got to be able to fool around with other guys, too."

"I just want to know you're not playing games with me."

"But, I am playing games," Donnie said, throwing his hands up. "And you love it. Sitting in the car and pretending to be talking, but really jacking off in front of everybody's noses? That's sex games. And you get off on it, just as much as I do."

He frowned and kicked at the ground. "Come on," he growled softly.

I had to ask, "Do you play games with Stanley like that?"

Donnie stuck his hands in his pockets. "No. Stanley and I play a whole 'nother game, entirely."

"Like what?"

Donnie shook his head. "The rule is, I don't tell you about what I do with him, just like I don't tell him about what I do with you." He shrugged. "You wouldn't be turned on by it, anyway."

"Don't be such a wise-ass. Give me a clue."

Donnie stared at the ground a moment, then glanced over at me. His eyes narrowed, then softened. "Okay, Boy Scout," he said, looking me up and down. "You wanna know so bad, I'll tell you." He leaned toward me, raising his eyebrows. "Did you ever go into the can late at night to piss, and notice somebody is in one of the stalls?"

"Yeah, so?"

"So," he repeated, nodding his head from side to side, "think about it, man. Nobody takes a crap in the middle of the night." He grinned at me, slyly. "Huh?" He elbowed my arm. "If you really want to know what goes on, next time, open the toilet door."

Maybe there were some things I didn't really want to find out about, I decided. All I wanted was to go someplace private with Donnie for another chance at his dick. At dinner, I drank a cup of coffee, and had seconds. Sneaking into the supply room without turning on the lights, I found a spare army blanket and took it to his car, and checked for the Vaseline jar. Then the coffee worked, and I hurried for the head.

When I was empty, I peeked over the stalls to see if anyone was there, then tiptoed around to the sinks, clutching my unzipped pants and backing up to the faucet. The warm water felt good splashing back there, but I liked it better when Donnie did it. Not wanting to get caught with my pants down, I dried off and went outside to find Donnie.

He was standing with his friends in front of the far cabin, so I went to his car and sat on the fender, hoping he would see me and come over. He didn't, and they all went inside together. I walked over and looked in, catching his eye. I nodded toward his car. He said, "Give me ten minutes and I'll meet you," so I went back to our cabin, tugging between my legs on the way. It was all set.

Steve was pumping weights. Ignoring Stanley on the bed, I told him, "Shit, Steve, you're still getting bigger."

He pulled off his shirt and flexed for me, looking serious. "Yeah, but you have to work at it every day to put on the inches." He held his arms together at the wrists and made the muscles jump and knot up.

Stanley snorted. "Why, Steve? Do you need a few more inches? Wonder where."

"You ought to know, Stan baby. You watch me close enough over that book." His face reddened as he picked up his weights. "After I work out, I'm gonna take a shower. You want to watch that, too?"

"Only if you wear your jockstrap and promise to pose like you do in here."

Donnie came in and looked annoyed. "Are you two bitching at each other again?"

"Nah," Steve said. "Stanley just wants me to pose for him so he can get another hard-on, that's all. You ready, Stanley? Ready for the big show?" He stepped toward the boy and struck a body-builder's pose, holding the dumbbells high over his shoulders, "Hah!"

Veins popped up on his arms. When he took another step and changed position, I moved out of his way.

"Hah!" he barked. Then again, "Hah!" He stalked toward the bunk, freezing like a Greek statue with each step, holding the two dumbbells out over Stanley's face. Nobody moved.

"Hah HAH!" He fell on top of the boy, plopping the weights into his pillow beside each ear.

Stanley squirmed under him, yelling, "Get off of me, you big shit."

Steve scooped him up in one big arm, reaching between his legs with the other hand, groping him. "Stanley's got a hard-on, Stanley's got a hard-on," he sang out.

Stanley scrambled loose, muttering, "Pick on somebody your own size."

Steve laughed at him. "I'm not so much bigger than you. Only, you're half dick."

"Jealous?" Stanley's hand jabbed at the gym shorts. "Is that the only muscle you can't get pumped up? You probably don't even know how." He walked out.

Donnie flashed a look of disgust. "Why can't you two knock it off?" He went out after the kid.

"Aw, did I hurt the poor little fruit's feelings?" Steve asked.

Through the door I could see Donnie say something to Stanley on the walk, then they went toward his car. "Ah, shit," I said, thumping the doorjamb.

Steve was doing pushups. I grabbed some weights, telling him, "You've got to get off Stanley's case, man. We all have to live together in this dump for two more months."

"Forty-nine, fifty," Steve gasped. "He started it."

Pressing the dumbbells in front of the mirror, I was surprised at how easy it had gotten. Steve jumped up and flapped his arms, stretching. After watching me a moment, he touched my elbows and guided them to my sides. "Slower coming down," he said. "Don't bounce at the bottom. It's supposed to be hard. Feel the resistance, don't swing them." He dropped over and held his ankles.

I smoothed out my movements, feeling for the pull on my tendons. "I wanted to talk to Donnie about something, and now they'll be out there all night."

"If Donnie's smart, he'll get a blowjob out of it." He squawked lewdly, bending down to touch his toes. I joined in. He counted us up to fifty and we stopped for breath. "I see guys like him around the gym. They have these big, sad eyes, and they look at you like, 'You're so big and I'm so puny, please let me suck you off.' Pisses me off. If they'd just work out a little instead of feeling sorry for themselves, they wouldn't be puny."

He switched to heavier weights, and I took the ones he dropped. I followed his lead, and he gave me tips. I wondered if they really were doing it in the car. They'd been out there long enough.

Working out in unison, side by side, neither of us could see his own body in the mirror. He watched me, and I watched him,

108

eyes locked, pump, pump, pump. It was like dancing. We even
breathed together. I fought the urge to blow him a kiss, but it
seemed very queer all the same.

Then we did push-ups, then we ran in place. I was dripping.
"Hey Steve, did Stanley really have a hard-on?"

"I was just goosing him. I didn't put my hand around it like
you did the other night. Hold my ankles for sit-ups."

"Looked like a good wrestler's hold to me. You guys do that
a lot, I hear."

"Don't need to grab guys," he said, rising and falling before
me. I watched the way his muscles slid under his skin. "Got all
the girls I want," he puffed, "grabbing for me." He stopped to pat
his hairy chest. "Girls just love this stuff, you know? I mean, they
can't get enough of what I've got."

"Bullshit. You're muscle-bound. Hold my ankles." He held
my legs down as I struggled to sit up. "I bet you practice together
naked." He let my ankles go up in the air. I flailed for balance.

"A thousand cunts can prove you wrong, pal," he smirked.
"I'm a hundred-percent red-blooded male. I'll leave that shit for
you and Stanley."

"You're a meathead. Hold my legs."

I wondered what was taking them so long. Damn, I'd set
everything up for them. They were probably using the blanket.
I concentrated on following Steve's sweaty ritual.

"Cool down," he said, as we tapered off. Then, "That's it."
He stripped his shorts and jockstrap down to his ankles and
stepped out of the rings of twisted cloth.

"That's the twenty-two exercises I do every night," he said,
kicking the wadded-up shorts and jockstrap into his locker.
"Works out every muscle you got."

He looked for a towel in his locker, and I looked at him, at
the white triangle where his butt was untanned. The curly blond
hairs were slicked to it with sweat. When I dropped my
underwear I was at about half mast. I covered it with my towel,
and when I turned I saw that Steve was poking out under his, too.
As he walked by, I snatched the terrycloth from his waist and
bolted out the door.

He chased me down the walk, dick flapping in the night air.
At the door to the head we grappled under the light, and I hoped
the other two were getting a good look. Steve pulled off my

towel, saying, "This one's mine, then." We wrestled over it, nude and giggling, tugging each other off balance until we went sprawling through the door into the bathroom.

"Steve's got a hard-on," I bellowed. He hooted, waving it at me. We rolled our towels into rattails, snapping at each other's bouncing cocks, ending up in a panting heap on the floor.

He was hard, but it almost didn't show. Not that it wasn't a normal cock, but it was overwhelmed by the muscles around it. He put his hand on it, and the head didn't extend beyond his fist. "Time for my twenty-third exercise," he said, sheepishly, getting up. "Only, I can't do it with another guy around." He went into a toilet stall and clicked the lock.

I sighed, and went into the shower room to lather up. Steve's voice echoed around the corner. "You want to go into town with me this weekend? Look for some action?"

"I dunno," I said, jerking off quickly in the soapsuds. "Maybe." Deliberately, I arched my hips and squirted my load all over the floor slats, slinging cum left and right.

We passed in the doorway, and from outside I heard Steve slip in my cum and laugh. "Hey hey hey," he said behind me as I dried myself. "Guess we did number twenty-three together after all, huh pal?"

Walking to the cabin, I scanned the parking lot for Donnie's car, but didn't see it anywhere.

9

I woke up after midnight. From the way the bunk moved I could sense there was no weight above me. I reached up and pushed on the mattress. Donnie wasn't there.

Steve was snoring. I sat up and peered across the room. It was dark, but Stanley's white sheets were obviously empty. I flopped back. They were still outside. In the car? In my blanket together? Or were they playing their games in the toilet? I took a full breath, released it, and got out of bed. At the door I peered into the darkness around the corner. Donnie's car was out there again.

In just my underwear I slipped out into the cool night air. When I stepped off the boardwalk, the grass was dry under my feet. Back home in North Carolina, on a summer night like this, the dew would be drenching wet. Insects would be buzzing in the trees, too, but here in the Rocky Mountains there were no insects and no dew.

I looked around. Shadowy mountains hovered in the moonless sky. My nostrils flared at the odor of spruce that drifted down from the hill behind camp. Maybe I could find them like an animal, by smelling and listening.

I crept up to the car. Nobody there. I turned, sniffing. The bathroom door was closed. I tiptoed over to it and listened. Nothing. I pushed it, gently. It was locked, and my heart pounded loudly enough for anyone to hear. What balls he had, locking the door. What if somebody had to take a leak? I looked around, wondering if anyone could see me standing there in my underwear.

The bunkhouses were yards away. It was a long walk, and I was sure at night they all went in the bushes behind their cabins. Some guys just hung their hoses out the back window, just to show how gross they could be. No one would come here.

It occurred to me that the porch light was off. Were they playing in the dark inside? Tiptoeing around the building, I saw the lights were out in the side window, too. I peered in from the edge of the glass. I didn't really expect to see them, and when a light gleamed at me, I jumped back.

I peeked around again. It was Donnie. He was standing at the door of one of the toilet stalls with a flashlight.

He was still in his jeans and teeshirt and cowboy boots, leaning on the stall door to prop it open. One hand held the flashlight, and from the other hand a cluster of beer cans dangled by the plastic loops. I heard him laugh through the windowpane, and then he turned and shone the light right in my face.

I dropped to the ground, heart thumping, certain he'd seen me. There was a clunk at the window, and then silence. I looked up. The window was still closed, but now the bathroom ceiling was lighted. Rising slowly, I saw the back end of the flashlight braced on the ledge. He had set it on the windowsill.

Inside, it lit up the row of urinals on the left wall, opposite the stalls. The white ceramic bowls and their chrome fixtures gleamed in the light. At the middle one Donnie was leaning back with his ankles crossed, tilting up a beer.

He threw his head back and poured beer into his mouth, spilling foam down the front of his shirt. He dropped the can into the next urinal, rubbing his dripping chest and saying something I couldn't hear. Slowly, he peeled the soaked teeshirt from his body and pulled it over his head. Lifting one arm he used the soggy wad to clean out his armpit. He wiped his mouth with the undershirt and then held it out dripping.

The bait worked. Stanley appeared from a stall, ghostly white, wearing only his undershorts. Moving slowly with his head down, he knelt in front of Donnie and turned his face up to suck at the sopping teeshirt.

Donnie bent over and grabbed Stanley's arm. The boy flopped like a rag doll, off-balance, as Donnie hauled him to his feet and spun him around, towering over the little guy. Donnie wrapped his muscular arms around both of the naked, narrow shoulders in front of him and pinched Stanley's nipples. The insistent way Donnie pawed at Stanley and pushed him around made me frown, but Stanley's dick jutted out under his shorts, stretching them into a tent, as Donnie held him from behind.

Letting go of the boy, Donnie popped open another can and guzzled it sloppily, letting beer splash down his neck and drip through the hairs on his chest. Stanley turned around to face

Donnie, lapping at the beer dribbling down his chest.

As Stanley licked the wet fur, Donnie put his hands on his hips, smiling down at him. The sides of his torso swelled upward from his narrow hips to the solid, lean muscles of his shoulders. He flexed his muscles, and Stanley chewed at the big guy's nipples hungrily.

I rested my arm on the windowsill and reached into my shorts, toying with my own rubbery half-erection.

Stanley's briefs were clinging to his cheeks in back, almost transparent. I could see the slot of his ass through the cloth, and his hairless legs looked shiny. I wondered if he had been wallowing in beer, too.

Donnie belched like a frog. Stanley looked like a plucked chicken. The tall cowboy leaned forward and snatched down the kid's underpants, jerking them roughly off as Stanley danced to kick them free. Lifting him in the air, Donnie turned around and plopped his naked butt into a urinal. Stanley's arms were limp, and Donnie hooked his elbows over the chrome flush handles on either side, so that the kid sat in the pisser, spread-eagled, with his skinny legs dangling down a foot above the floor. The ceramic rim must have been cold under his bare ass, but his exposed hard-on angled out rigidly horizontal between his legs.

My dick got slick in my palm, and my breath fogged the windowpane.

Donnie unbuttoned his jeans and flipped out his dick. He pointed it at Stanley, moving his mouth, but I couldn't hear what he said. He stepped closer, tugging the skin on his erection. Stanley's big one swelled up even bigger, throwing a huge bobbing shadow on the far wall in the flashlight beam. He seemed to shrink back into the bowl as Donnie stepped closer, pinning him to the wall with the force of his male sexuality.

Donnie said something. Stanley nodded eagerly. Donnie held his dick down and aimed it at Stanley's dick. For a moment they both were motionless. Then a short arc of piss spurted from Donnie's cock and landed between Stanley's legs.

Stanley's huge dork throbbed and raised up at an angle. Donnie aimed higher and hit Stanley's hard-on with a second squirt. Stanley's erection stiffened until it reared up and touched his belly. Donnie put one hand on his hip and let a long stream splatter over Stanley's hard-on.

The boy writhed inside the urinal. Donnie waved his cock up and down, splattering piss over the length of the boy's dick, onto his balls, his legs, up to his belly. Stanley scooped at the stuff with his hands and splashed it up to his skinny chest, slathering it over his skin. He pulled his cock down and held it under the stream of piss, then let it snap back up against his dripping stomach.

Smirking wickedly, Donnie cut off the stream and slowly raised his dick up until it was aimed at Stanley's mouth. Stanley focussed his eyes directly on it and licked his lips. Donnie fired a short shot that hit him right in the face. Stanley jerked as though he'd been slapped, and so did I.

But then the boy leaned forward, closed his eyes, and opened wide. Donnie let go full blast, pissing steadily right between the kid's lips. Stanley put a hand on Donnie's hip and pulled the cowboy closer, until Donnie's pissing cock plunged into Stanley's mouth. The little guy's throat worked, gulping it all down, only this time it wasn't cum he was swallowing.

I looked away and drew a long breath of night air. The ancient evergreens above camp were black silhouettes against a startling spray of bright stars. I couldn't tell how long I'd been watching. My stomach was queasy, and I thought I should leave, get away from all of this. But my hard-on was tenting out my shorts just the way Stanley's had been. The light in the window drew me back.

Donnie had his head back again, pouring yet another beer into his mouth with one hand, aiming his piss at Stanley with the other. Stanley leaned out of the urinal and buried his face in the cowboy's hairy belly, hugging Donnie's butt with one arm, beating his meat with the other, sucking Donnie's dick madly as piss dribbled down his chin.

Donnie pulled him to his feet, turned him around, and plugged his thumb into the wet boy's butt. Stanley cringed against the wall, clinging to the pipes, but Donnie's hand followed. Stanley lifted up on tiptoe, almost climbing the wall. Donnie jabbed relentlessly with his thumb. He grabbed Stanley by the hair, and this time I could hear him growl, "Stick your ass out for me, boy. Come on, open it up for me."

Stanley raised his backside. He reached behind his butt and spread his cheeks with both hands. Donnie bent his knees, aiming one last stream of piss into the crevice. Still pushing Stanley's head against the wall with one straight arm, he hosed out the boy's ass and then shoved his hard-on up the dripping hole.

My knees trembled. Stanley grimaced, his mouth pushed out of shape against the wall, but he took it. Donnie clasped his big arms around the boy and humped him hard, and I heard myself groan out loud. Startled by my own noise, I realized I was propped on the windowsill with my butt sticking out just like Stanley's, and my cock was slick and hard in my hand.

Donnie reached around Stanley's waist and, still butt-fucking him steadily, started jerking the boy off. He rammed his dick hard up Stanley's ass, once, twice, three times. Hanging onto the chrome flush handle, Stanley lifted one knee and bent his back, raising his butt even higher for Donnie to ream him out. Stanley's face twisted up, he shuddered, and then the boy howled out loud as he started shooting his load all over the urinals. As Donnie pounded it for him, Stanley's big dick laid out ropes of cum, hanging loops of the stuff on the wall inside, and right at the same time I moaned and stiffened and shot my wad all over the wall outside.

I rested my face on my forearm, panting. When I looked up, Stanley was letting go of the pipes and slumping down the wall. Just before he hit the floor, Donnie picked him up. As he hefted the kid into his bare arms, I saw that Stanley was releasing all that he'd drunk. He trailed a steady stream of piss as Donnie cradled him in his arms. The scrawny boy put his arms around the big guy's neck, still shooting a sparkling line of water that would do justice to a fire truck, while Donnie carried him around the corner to the showers.

I heard water running, and a clatter. Donnie reappeared with a bucket, filled it at the utility sink, and sloshed it over the wall and floor. He filled it several times, heaving some into the stall they had used, and then went back to the showers to join his fuck-buddy.

They sat beside me at breakfast Friday morning, and I couldn't look them in the face. At least Stanley had the courtesy to sit on the other side of Donnie.

"We're thinking about going camping this weekend," Donnie said. "Want to come with us?"

"No." I poked at my bacon, pushing it around my plate.

"Something wrong, Bill?"

We were at a table by ourselves, so I told him. "I watched you guys in the toilet last night."

Stanley leaned forward and looked across Donnie's plate, staring at me expectantly.

"Well," I said, "I got up to take a leak, and y'all had the door locked. I watched through the window."

As I expected, Stanley began to grin.

Donnie said, "You should have knocked. You could have joined us."

"No, thanks," I said, picking at my food. "I don't think I'm your kind of guy. Go ahead and laugh, Stanley. You win."

Donnie frowned. "Well, we saw you getting it on with Steve. That wasn't soapsuds you guys left in the showers. All around, seems like it was a good night for the boys in Cabin 8."

I put down my fork. "I didn't 'get it on' with Steve," I snapped. "In fact, we're going into town together tonight to do something normal, like maybe meet some girls."

As soon as the words left my mouth, I regretted them.

Donnie only smiled, but Stanley spit food all over his plate, laughing at me.

I hunched down over my plate for the rest of breakfast, and we didn't talk any more.

10

"Over there, the pointy one?" Steve was saying.

I had been daydreaming, staring at the road whizzing under the red nose of the Firebird.

"That's The Snaggletooth. See, the one with a rock on top like a tooth? It's only about 8,000 feet, but you can recognize it from anywhere in the district. The round one over there is Turtle Mountain. You get sight of that, and either The Snaggletooth or Twin Buttes, and you can pretty much tell where you are without getting out the map and triangulating. Learn to tell those three mountains, and you can't get lost, even out here.

"Jesus F. Christ, man, look at that view. Nothing prettier than Idaho, man, nothing in the world. I just love this fucking road, don't you?"

My throat was dry from not talking. I had to swallow a few times before I could agree, "Yeah, it's a good road."

Donnie betrayed me, I kept thinking. It doesn't matter what he says about being free to play around. If he felt what I felt, he wouldn't have taken Stanley to his car in the first place.

But then, I had been griping for days about being too sore to do anything. I slumped in my seat. Of course he went with Stanley. Stanley's a good fuck. I'm not. Simple as that.

God, how could he take it like that? Without any grease or anything, except, damn, all that piss.

Well, Donnie had told me he liked it dirty. Now I understood. He was out of my league. I couldn't compete. He's all yours, you creepy little urine-faced fruit.

"You don't have that in North Carolina, do you?" Steve was saying.

I sighed. "Have what, Steve?"

"Open range like this. See, there aren't any fences. Cows go everywhere. If you hit one, you have to pay for it."

We were driving through a huge green meadow. Cattle grazed by the road and some wandered across it. Steve slowed and tooted the horn, but they turned and walked in front of us. We inched along behind the big stupid animals, with Steve banging on the car door and hollering out the window.

"Why don't you stop the car and be quiet?" I suggested. "Maybe they'll forget we're behind them. They think you're herding them."

He stopped the car and tapped his head. "You're a smart kid. I like guys with brains."

I looked at him. "What would you say," I asked abruptly, "if I told you I wanted you to pee on me while I jacked off?"

His eyes widened.

"What would you think of that, Steve, my man? What do you think about kinky sex?"

His mouth twitched. He smiled, and then he grinned broadly.

"Hyah!" he laughed, slapping the dashboard. "Hyah! You crazy fucker! I don't fucking believe you said that!" He bounced in his seat, pounding the steering wheel and laughing.

The cows had wandered back to the grass, and he was still grinning as we picked up speed.

I said, "You haven't answered my question. Would you do it?"

He looked at the road, moving his mouth, suppressing a grin. "Well, shit, I'd pull over and do it, I guess. I dunno. Is that what you're into? God damn." He wrinkled his nose. After another few minutes, he said, "Aw, man, that's so gross. You want me to? I'll watch, I guess."

"No. I don't really want to do it. Just asking."

He slapped my leg. "You crazy fucker. Hey, store's coming up. Let's get some beer. Let's get drunk tonight. *Whoo-eee!*" We swerved into a parking lot and he jumped out of the car to get the beer.

After a beer, I relaxed and sighed. Steve looked at me seriously. "Something's bugging you, huh, Bill?" We were on the paved highway by then, and the car hummed. "Did you and Donnie have a fight or something?"

"Sort of."

"I thought so. You guys were getting real tight, and then today you didn't have two words to say to each other. I know what you're thinking. You think he's turning gay on you, huh? With Stanley, I mean."

I looked out the window. "I don't know what he's doing with

Stanley, or care."

"He's going camping with him."

"I know, I know."

"Kinda makes you sick to your stomach, doesn't it. Big hunk of man like him. But, you know, when I think about it, he never does talk much about girls. I dunno, I can't figure out what gets into guys, to get hooked on that queer shit."

I reached for a second beer. "Tell me about L.A., Steve. You like living there?"

"Oh, wow, shit, yeah. Nothing prettier than the beaches there. You ever been surfing?"

I half listened as Steve told me his story, about growing up in Santa Monica only three blocks from the ocean, surfing every day after high school. His parents had given him the car when he was sixteen, and then they had rented an apartment for him when he started classes at UCLA, even though it was only a few miles across town.

To me, California had always seemed an impossible illusion, but, listening to him, I realized there are people who have everything easy. Santa Monica sounded like paradise. Steve was beautiful, muscular, tanned. A gold chain necklace made of thick, square links showed at his collar. He had put it on just for the weekend. It was just one more advertisement to the world of what a hotshot he was, along with the beefy arms with the half-inch thick blond fur on them, and the red car with the California license plates.

The necklace glinted through the yellow curls peeking out at the top button of his shirt, as though even his chest hairs were made of fine metal. The shirt fabric seemed to drape perfectly across his muscles. Big as he was, the buttons weren't even pulled tight. "How do you find shirts that fit like that?" I asked him.

He looked down. "Find 'em? I don't find 'em. I have 'em made." He smiled at me. "Store-bought stuff is too tight at the top. My pecs are too big. If I get a shirt that fits my chest, then it's all baggy at the waist. I just have my tailor knock off a dozen at a time."

His tailor. Of course.

The highway snaked through the rocky canyon, following the river until we turned a bend and saw the town ahead on the far side of the water. A sawmill further downstream looked like the only reason the place existed. I hoped something would happen that night, but didn't know what. As we turned off the highway and crossed the bridge, I hid the beer cans under the seat.

Skipping dinner, we pulled up at the only flashing neon sign in town, the Starlite Lounge. Steve wanted to hear the music, and I wanted him to shut up and let me get drunk.

We seemed to be the only two in the bar not dressed for a rodeo. A local band in matching red shirts shuffled through a country song. We walked through scattered peanut shells and bought two beers in long-necked bottles, leaning on the bar and looking around the big room.

The place had a mixture of ages, everyone in pairs. Settling onto a barstool, I pulled on my beer until I began to feel comfortable. I watched the boys in tight jeans, stomping and strutting in front of their girlfriends. We chugged our bottles empty and Steve signalled for two more Lucky Lagers.

After half an hour, the blaring music was beginning to sound good. Lights flashed. Steve told me to get us a table, and I walked over to an empty one. On the way I accidentally knocked a purse off a table. I retrieved it and handed it to a blonde girl sitting alone. She had blue eyes and a pretty smile.

"Thanks," she said.

I noticed her blouse was unbuttoned at the top, and pink underthings showed inside her bosom.

Her eyes crinkled. "Bet you're a good dancer," she teased.

I stared at the edge of one breast and nodded. Then I shook my head. "No, uh. . ."

She smiled up at me for a few more seconds. I wondered if she would dance with me.

"Why don't you sit down?" she asked.

"Well, I'm with somebody," I said, and then I thought, no, dummy, Steve doesn't count.

I straightened up, ready to ask, but Steve was lumbering toward us with two beers. When he saw the blonde, he grinned, and I was glad I couldn't hear the "Hey hey."

He stopped at the table, glancing to me for a cue. We both looked down. There were three beer bottles, and three purses. He bent down and said something to her, and she shifted her weight toward him, listening. She laughed. With his eyes still on her, he put one of the beers in front of her and patted around behind him for a chair, drawing it underneath him and squatting on it with his legs apart, cocky. She leaned closer and they laughed again. Steve turned up his bottle, sucked half of it down, banged it on the table, and led the girl off to dance.

I went back to the bar. In the mirror, I watched Steve and the three girls talk and laugh. He waved me back over, and I went to the table to be introduced. The blonde's name was Deena, and her friends were Patsy and somebody else I never got around to talking with. Patsy was as quiet as me, and after another drink we danced together.

When they played a slow number, she seemed to fold up to the size of a bird in my arms. The lights changed. I looked up at a mirrored ball that had started to turn and flash on its wire in the spot lights. I remember noticing the motor beside it, and the reduction gears clogged with dust, and the wires stapled to the ceiling.

Steve and Deena were dancing with their eyes closed, Deena with her cheek against his chest where she had unbuttoned his shirt to show the fuzzy blond hair. I wondered, where do girls learn to do all that, as my partner easily followed my steps.

I tried to imagine dancing with Donnie. Who would lead? I didn't know how to follow, and I was sure he wouldn't. We'd look funny, both being about the same height, almost. Our cheeks would touch. I remembered the scratch of his beard, and bumped us into another couple.

Stanley would know how. It could be Stanley in my arms right then, and he'd dance exactly like Patsy. When the lights came up, I was seeing double. I took Patsy back to the table, excused myself and went outside.

Pickup trucks full of teenagers paraded down the main drag. I went around the side of the building in the dark and threw up. Feeling better, I wiped my mouth and went back into the noise.

The Starlite shared a hallway and bathrooms with a cafe. Just outside the barroom door, a boy who looked too young to get in was standing by the cigarette machine. He wore a silver jacket and a ball cap embroidered with the name of a Dodge dealer in Lewiston. The kid stared in at the band, playing air guitar with the music. I propped against a wall for support and watched him move his fingers, hands down by his crotch, wiggling sexually.

I had to find the bathroom. When I got back, he was talking

to a handsome man in a red plaid shirt and tight jeans. The older guy put his head down to listen to something the kid was saying, then straightened up and glanced around the room. After a moment, they went outside together. I followed them.

On the sidewalk I glimpsed the silver jacket going around the corner where I had been sick. When I peeked around, they were disappearing behind some stacked lumber. I crept up to the lumber and looked through the cracks.

The older one had his back to the wall, and the boy was on his knees, giving him a blowjob. I could see the cock sticking into his mouth. After a few minutes the man grabbed his head and pulled it tight to his hips. The boy choked twice, then stood up.

I flattened against the wall in the darkness as they passed close to me. The big guy stopped, shaking off the last drops of cum before he stuffed it back into his pants, and I heard him telling the kid, "Wait a sec and I'll give you the keys. But if you get stopped by the cops it's your ass, not mine."

He handed over the keys and headed back to the bar. The kid got into a big pickup truck with oversized tires and a light rack, cranked it up, and pulled out of the parking lot, tires screeching.

I went back inside the lounge and had another beer. I danced with all three girls, and drank until things were spinning.

Then I was outside again, sweat drying cold under my clothes. I vomited again beside the bar and stumbled across the parking lot to Steve's car. My ears were roaring as I crawled into the rear seat and fell asleep.

"It's Billy," a girl's voice said. The interior light was in my eyes. Deena leaned over me. "Are you all right?"

I sat up. Steve was outside the car, taking a leak on the parking meter, weaving back and forth. "'S passed out," he slurred.

Deena looked at him in annoyance. "Ste-eve! Somebody will see you!"

"So what?" Steve finished peeing and tucked himself away, but couldn't get his pants zipped up. "Time for you to take a walk, ol' buddy," he said. "Me and Deena are going for a li'l drive." He lurched against the car, still fumbling with his zipper.

Deena said, "Steve, I don't think you should drive."

Steve's eyelids drooped. "I can drive."

"Let's have Billy drive us," she said. "We can get in the back seat, okay?"

Steve hesitated. Deena looked at me. "He'll get arrested. Please?"

I took a breath and got out of the back seat. My head hurt, but I wasn't cross-eyed any more. It was two in the morning. I had slept for hours. Steve gave me the keys and started for the back seat. Deena said, "Not yet," and pushed him into the bucket seat in front next to me. She sat on his lap.

We cruised the main strip, up to the single stop light, around behind the school, back down the main street. Deena and Steve were kissing like those fish that keep aquariums clean.

"Ouch," Steve said. "You're sitting on my nuts."

Deena moved to the console between us. "Better now?"

Steve took her hand and put it on his pants, which were still unzipped. "Better now," he said. Then I heard, "Hey hey hey!" Deena was playing with his dick, right there on Main Street.

I cut a glance to the side to see it, almost bumping the car in front of me. She went down on him, right before my eyes. She just scooted her butt toward me, leaned over, and went down on him, just like that.

Steve looked at his lap with his mouth hanging open. "Drive somewhere," he said hoarsely.

At the stoplight I turned for the bridge, thinking to cross it and get onto the highway that ran along the river on the far side. But once we were beyond the streetlights, Deena raised her head and whispered, "Turn left on that dirt road."

I followed the bumpy ruts down past a baseball field to a parking lot by the river, with Steve breathing harder by the minute. There were other cars there, all with their windows steamed up. Killing my lights, I found a spot, set the brake and opened the door to go for my walk.

The interior lights flashed on. Steve was pushing her blouse down over her shoulders. "Oooh, close the door," she said, so I did.

In the dark again, she murmured, "Unhook my bra, Bill." I did and Steve didn't object. He slid her bra down her arms and kissed her breasts. As he nuzzled, she twisted around and kissed me, her fingers tugging at my zipper. With a little giggle, she ducked her head under the steering wheel. Before I could clear my throat, I was getting my dick sucked by a girl for the first time in my young life.

Steve dropped down onto the front floorboard and buried his face between her legs, trying to push her skirt up and get his pants down at the same time. Deena's head got caught under the steering wheel. I fixed that by moving my hips closer, but then the gearshift jabbed my thigh.

"Shit," I said, raising up.

"Mmm-hmm," Deena answered, approvingly.

Steve said from below, "Hey, I can't breathe when you guys do that."

Deena laughed and wiggled past me and into the back seat, shedding clothes as she went. Steve got his shoes off but fumbled with his shirt buttons. "Oh, fuck," he muttered, and then I heard them pop and ricochet off the windshield as he ripped his shirt off. He had to turn sideways to squeeze his big chest between the front seats, telling me, "You get sloppy seconds," as he passed, stripping his pants down with one hand. He got caught halfway, and I grabbed his cuffs and pulled his pants loose. I snagged his bikini shorts with my finger, and felt his stiff dick thump my wrist as I tugged them off, too.

Snickering, Steve fell all the way into the back seat with his feet waving in the air, naked as a fuzzy baby bear except for his socks.

I turned around and stared toward the river to give them some privacy, but in a few minutes Deena started making such astonishing noises that I had to look around. Steve was licking between her legs, and she seemed to like it as much as guys do. He lapped at it frantically, like an excited puppy, and then crawled up higher and pointed his dick up to it.

"You have to use a rubber," she said.

"I don't have one. I'll pull it out before I come."

"No way. Bill, find my purse for me, please."

Steve went back down to business while I patted around on the floor, found her purse, and handed it to her. She made snapping noises with it, and then gave me the condom. "I'll break a nail. You open it," she said to me, and then told Steve, "Hold it out for me, baby, I'll put it on for you."

Steve reared up on his knees and stuck his dick out, but

instead of taking the rubber, Deena guided my hand to him in the dark. While she held his hard-on steady, I rolled the rubber down over his stiff, short pecker.

Steve said, "Feels good already," and Deena giggled. I tugged on it a few times, and then leaned forward and reached underneath to feel his furry little balls. My own cock stiffened in my shorts as I played with them, and big Steve began purring like a cat.

"Put it in for me," he whispered, and we did. Deena spread herself open, and I pointed Steve's cock in the right direction as he dropped himself down on top of her.

"Yeah," he gasped. "Touchdown!"

"Ooh-h-h," she murmured.

My heart jerked in my chest. They were fucking! Right through my fingers! Nobody complained, so I didn't move my hand. My cock got rigid. I could feel her soft skin and his hairy stomach pressing on both sides of my hand. As he squirmed against her, I circled my thumb and fingers around his dick, holding it as it squished in and out of her cunt. Oddly, her pubic hair was coarser than Steve's. I could even feel the ridge of the rubber top when he thrust in deep enough.

She whimpered, he groaned. He pushed harder, then went "MMH!" and held his belly tight against her for a moment, trembling. I felt his dick throb in my hand three times, and then he slumped back.

"Aw, Steve, not already," she said. "I was just getting going!"

Steve rocked back on his knees and turned to me as I pulled my hand back between the front seats. "Okay, pal, I got her started for you," he said, and then he asked Deena, "You got another rubber?"

"No, just the one. Why don't you guys ever have any?"

"Never mind. Here." He peeled off the used condom and held it out to me. "Already juicy, like her. Hyuh!"

When I pulled out my dick, the inside of my shorts already felt as sticky as if I'd shot off in them. I stretched the rubber open and pulled it over my cock. It was wet inside, slippery with Steve's cum. The feeling of sliding my dick into his fresh load while it was still warm got me so aroused that I didn't think I could last even three minutes. My hard-on raised up another notch as I gave myself a few pumps inside the tight rubber, swirling Steve's gooey jism around my cockhead.

We clambered past each other again, trading places. When I got my pants and underwear down to my ankles in the back seat, I wasn't sure what to do next. I couldn't very well ask Steve to do for me what I'd done for him, but it would have helped a lot. Then Deena made it easy, pulling me on top of her, reaching between us, guiding me in, enveloping me in the warmth of her pussy.

She felt strange under me, like a guy with padding. I couldn't feel much through the rubber, and she didn't seem very tight. I humped against her, but it was like fucking a marshmallow. I kissed a breast, also soft. She was having a great time, it seemed, but I worried about losing my erection.

Deena said, "Oooh, lookee," and reached toward the front with one hand.

It was Steve, straddling the console on his knees and jacking off. Deena rubbed his belly, and after a moment I twisted around, reached up between the fork of his legs and found his nuts.

"Yeah, yeah," he said as I fondled the hairy pouch. He had to know there were two hands down there, and they couldn't both be hers. I played with his nuts, fingering them back and forth until they began to pull up too tight to hold, and then I flicked them with my fingertips.

"Oh, shit, yeah," he gasped.

I ran my finger behind his furry little nuts and found the puckered hole in back. He jerked harder on his cock. I made circles around his asshole. He whimpered, but he didn't stop me. I worked my fingertip into his ass. "Oh, *sh-e-e-IT*!" he whispered, rocking to one side and lifting his knee a bit, just enough to give me a good shot at his tight little hole. I stuck my finger all the way inside his ass. He threw his head back and howled. Once again I felt his ejaculation throbs, but this time it was from inside him as his butthole spasmed around my finger. I forgot all about losing my hard-on.

Hot cum droplets spattered onto my arm and my back. Deena's tits got slippery under me as Steve shot off all over us. I let go of him and grabbed Deena, fucking faster and harder, and she put her arms around me, smearing Steve's cum over my back. I felt myself wallowing in the muscle-boy's semen.

Deena cried "Oh! Oh! Oh!" in my ear, writhing under me.

I got rock hard inside her, and pushed my dick up so high she squealed and dug her fingernails into my back.

"Yeah, man," Steve said. "Fuck her, man." He slapped my butt.

The sting of his hand on my bare ass put me over the edge. I hunched up hard against Deena's belly, groaning and driving it all home, shooting my load deep inside her as she squealed and humped back at me, hugging my shoulders and meeting every thrust I made.

"I'm coming," she squealed breathlessly. "I'm coming!"

Steve slapped my ass again and hooted, "Yeah, pal! Go, buddy!"

"Yeah, buddy!" I gasped, making one last, hard shove into her and then holding it there. Deena trembled, her cunt clutching at my dick, milking the last spurts of my load out of me.

"Yeah, pal!" Steve said again, smacking my ass and laughing. "We did it, buddy!"

My hard-on throbbed once more, mixing my last spurt of cum with Steve's inside the rubber, and then I collapsed slowly onto Deena.

"Yeah, buddy," I sighed. "Fu-u-u-ck."

"Hey, guys," Deena said. "I had a little bit to do with it, y'know."

11

"*Uurrrrp,*" I heard. Splash.

I squinted painfully into the glare of sunlight. My eyes watered, my head ached, and I was filled with a profound sense of remorse.

"*Uurrrrp.*" Splash. Steve was sitting at my feet with his elbows on his knees and his head bowed between them. A string of saliva hung from his lower lip. He heaved forward and went "Uurp" again, working his mouth, but this time there wasn't any splash.

I had to look away, swallowing hard to keep my own stomach down.

We were on the wooden benches of a shabby old grandstand. "Idaho River Stomp and Rodeo," the flaking paint advertised on the wall above me. Sleeping bags were scattered on the bleachers, some empty, some with sleeping boys still in them. Shoes and clothes and beer cans dotted the seats.

I had slept in my clothes. Struggling to my feet, I walked stiffly to the railing to piss. The river parking lot was below us. Somewhere down there, I realized, I had at last triumphed with a girl. After years of hearing stories about sweaty sex in the back seat, I had done it, too. At least I thought I had. I tried to remember what had happened. When I pulled out my dick to piss, I saw lipstick on my Jockey shorts, and smiled weakly.

Steve came over and stood beside me, his eyes puffy and his hair sticking out uncombed. As he unzipped his pants, he turned slightly away from me and grinned over his shoulder at me, aiming his morning leak over the rail. I remembered how Donnie and I always crossed streams when we pissed, and wondered why Steve had gotten next to me if he was just going to turn his back. My head hurt too much to think, so I just grinned back at him.

Back at our bench, Steve pulled a warm beer from a paper bag and popped it open, holding it out until the foam stopped spewing from it. "Breakfast," he said, and slurped some down.

"Oh, god," I said. "How can you do that?"

Steve let out a long burp and wiped his mouth. "Settles your stomach. Here, try one." He pulled another can from the bag and handed it to me.

It tasted bland, but the bubbles cleaned the paste off my tongue. Once I burped it was better. We finished both cans.

We both moved very slowly getting down the steps. "Not a bad place to crash," Steve said. "It's free, and you're up off the ground. And if you're drunk, you can't roll off."

Behind the grandstand, we found the Firebird parked with other cars I recognized from camp. "Everybody knows about it," he said. "Cops check us out, but what are they gonna do? We have to sleep somewhere. They only hassle you if you build a fire."

We found a faucet and washed our faces. Steve combed his hair in the car mirror and opened a leather suitcase in the trunk. He had brought enough clean underwear to lend me fresh socks and a skimpy blue bikini and a tanktop. Changing together under the bleachers, I kidded him about his tiny briefs. "Not much room in these shorts," I told him, stretching them in front, and for the first time I caught him staring openly at my crotch.

"You've got more to put in them than I do," he said, with a look I thought was admiring, but for once I was too sick to care.

Using his shirt with the buttons popped off, he went through the car front and back, wiping cum spots off the upholstery. "Guess I got kinda carried away," was all he said about it as he tossed the shirt into a trash can.

We went for food. "Grease is what you need," he said. "Coats your stomach. We'll get some fried eggs and sausage."

I almost had to open the door and lean out. "Tonight," I told him, "Let's just get a little drunk, and then stop."

"Uh-huh. Sure."

After breakfast, there wasn't much to do in town. "This is it," Steve told me, spreading his arms out wide as we left the cafe. "One general store, one drugstore, a phone booth, five churches, and eight bars." We found a few other buildings. We passed a steakhouse. We walked by the school, and there was a one-room library that wasn't open. In the block beyond that, the only building was boarded up.

"Then, of course, there's the Green House down there," Steve said, pointing toward the river. "It's a whorehouse."

"Really? Right here in town?"

"Yeah. All these horny dudes come here every weekend, looking, you know. People here lock up their daughters at sundown Friday night. I guess they figure it's better to have it going on down there than to have us scratching at their back doors and knocking up the girls."

We stopped at the general store to get a pair of boots. I wanted logging boots like Donnie's, the big, black kind with high tops for ankle support and thick Vibram cleats. The ancient store had an oiled wooden floor that sagged and creaked when we walked in. A tiny lady with white hair in a bun lead us to the back of the store, tiptoeing on the noisy boards as we passed shelves of heavy gloves and striped work clothes. "You want White's," Steve said. "The cheap ones won't last the summer."

They cost me most of my first paycheck, but I didn't mind a bit. They were exactly like the ones Donnie had in his locker.

I fumbled with the laces. The boots had regular holes over the foot, but above the ankle they had brass hooks. Steve knelt in front of me. "Lemme show you how to speedlace," he said. "Hold both laces in one hand, like this, and go zip, zip, zip. Like that." He weaved them back and forth across the brass hooks. "One tie at the top, take the loose ends around back, thread them through the pull-up loop in back, bring them around front, tie them again." He snugged the laces down and stood up.

I did my other boot. When I got to my feet, I was two inches taller and had the beginning of a hard-on swelling in my borrowed bikini briefs.

Steve wanted to watch a baseball game at the Sportsman bar. I went in and had a beer with him, but then I got bored. In the men's room I propped my foot on the urinal and practiced speedlacing. When I thought I had the hang of it, I checked myself out in the mirror, standing up on tiptoe so I could see my boots. Not bad for a new guy, I decided. Not exactly a lumberjack yet, but pretty sexy.

I took a leak. On the wall over the urinal somebody had written, "I need a dick." Under that someone else had put, "You already have one." I stared at that a while, long after I'd finished peeing. My face flushed when I realized the first line could have been written by me. If Steve had been there, he would have added the second line.

The door opened behind me. I tucked myself away quickly and hurried out into the bar.

The TV set blared with that sing-song babble that sports announcers all use. My throat tightened at the thick cloud of cigarette smoke. I didn't belong in any bar called the Sportsman. Giving Steve a quick wave, I clomped outside to get some air and break in my boots.

The big black things put a swing in my walk that felt good, all male. I pulled off my shirt and tucked it into my back pocket, striding along in Steve's tanktop, feeling the shirt brush against my pants leg with each twitch of my butt. I felt sexy. The sun burned on my bare arms and shoulders.

Down the street the neon sign of the Starlite Lounge looked shabby in the daylight. With a shock I remembered Deena, and stopped dead still on the sidewalk.

Deena! The back seat! I fucked a girl last night!

Smiling, I straightened my back and started walking again, taking longer steps, holding my chest out proudly.

Turning off the main street, I passed a house where a man was pushing a lawn mower across his yard. His back was to me as he bent over the mower, struggling to force the blades to chop into the thick grass. He was short and beefy, and his buttocks trembled underneath his shorts as he leaned into the lawn mower handle. I slowed down to watch his hairy legs pump against the ground.

He turned the machine to start back toward me, then paused a moment to wipe his forehead. When he lifted his arm, his powerful chest muscles filled out a teeshirt that showed a big circle of sweat under his arm. My eyes dropped to his shorts. They bulged in front. He brought his arm down sharply, flinging the sweat off the back of his hand, and as his body moved I could see his cock swing under the cloth.

He gripped the handle and leaned forward, chugging along in my direction, and with every step the fat tube of his dick flopped from one side to the other inside his shorts.

Just as I passed, he stopped to catch his breath. Our eyes met for a second. I nodded. He smiled, then turned back to his work.

I kept walking, feeling a twitch inside my shorts. Steve's little underwear was suddenly way too tight.

"I need a dick." Who in a town this small could have written that over that urinal? The man with the lawn mower? Would he fool around? He probably had a real hairy chest. Had he winked at me just then? No, guys like that don't wink at other guys. I walked faster.

There is always a trail beside a river, and that's where I headed, following it along the banks, looking for a place. My dick strained in my pants. Nobody was under the bridge, so I ducked under the riveted struts and found a private spot, up by the concrete abutment. There were crude sketches of ejaculating penises all around me. Standing in a corner, I unzipped and touched myself, feeling the kinked-up curve of my erection straining inside Steve's blue bikini shorts.

I tried to think of Deena while I did it. It started out good, turning me on, but then I remembered Steve, naked over us, jacking off onto us. I almost shot off thinking of that, but I stopped myself.

My cock jutted out, jumping with my pulse inside my fist. I tried to remember sticking it into Deena. I closed my eyes and pictured it. That lasted about a minute, and then I was back in the Sportsman, back in the men's room, and the man with the lawn mower was beside me, pulling up his teeshirt to show me his hairy belly and his big dick. I got huge in my hand, big as a goddam telephone pole, and then my cum spurted out of me, hot and thin as though the sun had melted my sap. My load just poured out of my cock and dribbled down all over my new boots.

Dripping cum, I stared at the dirty pictures on the structure of the bridge, and admitted to myself that what I had just done turned me on a hell of a lot more than Deena had. In fact, I couldn't imagine getting that excited with a girl around. In fact, when I was doing it with Deena, having a girl there in my arms when I had my orgasm had seemed strange, kind of odd, out of place.

Ha! Queer! That was it. To me, doing it with a girl had seemed *queer*.

I said goodby to some things under the bridge that day. There would never be a girl for me, I realized. I cried a little bit over that. It seemed to me that girls care about you in a way that guys never do. In my experience guys never seem to care at all.

It was a cold and lonely world I was entering, but I had no choice. What I had done with Deena had been fraudulent. I couldn't even remember for certain what she looked like. All I could think of was Steve, or Donnie, or the man with the lawn mower. My butt muscles tightened. I remembered the excitement of having Donnie between my legs, thrusting at me so powerfully. My ass felt empty, unused. For the first time, jacking off hadn't satisfied me. There was a hollowness inside that only one thing could fill.

I wanted to get fucked again.

It was late in the afternoon when I left the river. I was tired of wondering, why me, what's wrong with me, why am I different, all that crap. Somebody in this burg was gay besides me, and I thought I knew where to find him. I needed a dick, and the one I had wouldn't do, not for what I had in mind.

First I found Steve and we went to the steakhouse for cheeseburgers. We both ordered two, with double fries each. "Two Lucky Lagers now," I told the waitress, "and two more when the burgers come."

"Saturday night in the big city," Steve said, jiggling his knee and tapping on the table. He was wearing a tight black muscle shirt, the kind with no sleeves, and he still smelled of cologne from the haircut he had gotten that afternoon. The combination of short hair and day-old stubble on his jaws made him look tough. When couples passed by, I noticed it was always the man who eyed him quickly.

We cruised the street some more. "Come on-n-n, nine o'clock," he said. That was when the band would start. At eight-thirty we hit the Starlite to watch the crowd gather.

My big boots bumped chairs as we looked for a table. They were work boots, and everybody else had his cowboy boots on for dancing, but I didn't care. They made me walk with a swing that I liked. I hoped people would think I was a logger.

The band started late. Steve was looking around for Deena, and I was looking around with him, scanning the crowd for the handsome face of the guy who had gotten the blowjob out back. If I could find him, I was going for a ride in his truck.

But, two hours later, Steve and I were back riding around in the Firebird.

"Bunch of trogs in there tonight, huh?" Steve said. "Can't believe it, man, not one single girl that wasn't a scag. Deena's girlfriends must not have given her a ride in tonight. They were pissed last night because they had to sit in the car until three AM waiting for us to finish fucking her. Hyah!"

He hooted and slapped my leg. "That was something, wasn't it, man? Best piece of ass I've had in a long time. You couldn't believe it when she started giving me head, could you? I'm getting a bone on just thinking about it."

We drove through a neighborhood of small houses. "You should have seen yourself, man," he said, parking on a side street and opening a half-pint bottle of whiskey. We both took sips and made faces.

"Ah. Damn, that's good shit," he said. "You know, Deena thought you were a real stud. She told me you really know how to fuck." He took another hit, grimacing. "Man, you put it to her good. I even got off, watching you."

I shifted in my seat, wondering how far this would go. If Steve couldn't have Deena, maybe he would go for second best. I told him, "I got off watching you, too. It was sexy. I kinda liked it when you — you know — got it all over me."

He made bubbles in the half-pint. "Whatcha think, man?" he asked. I didn't know what he meant. He nodded to his left. I looked past him. We were parked in front of a house with the porch light burning. The porch was painted green. The whole house was green. My heart skipped. It was the whorehouse.

"I always wanted to fuck a girl with another guy," he said. "Only, tonight, we could get a room and all three get in bed together. You know, you do her in the mouth while I do her in the pussy, good shit like that. Want to?"

"Aw, Steve," I protested. "I don't want a goddam whore."

"Hey, I hear they'll go around the world on you if you pay them extra, and you know what that means."

"No, what?"

He showed his teeth in the faint glow of the dash lights. "First they suck your cock, then they lick your balls, and then they get their tongue all the way back around to your—"

"Okay, okay, I know. I had that done to me once."

"No shit? You've been around more than I thought. You got girlfriends like that?"

I slumped even lower in the seat. "Never mind," I told him. "You ever really been in there?"

"No, not yet. But I'm going in tonight. No balls if you don't come with me." He took another drink.

"No. Look, Steve. I don't know how to say this, but I've got to tell you something." My palms were sweaty. I rubbed them on my pants. "I just don't like girls the way you do. You want to know the truth? I was getting off on you, not Deena."

"Aw, give me a break, Bill. I saw the way you went after her. You trying to tell me you didn't like it? You don't like feeling a pussy wrapped around the old peter? Feeling those titties jiggling under you? Come on."

I shook my head. "If you hadn't fucked her first, I wouldn't have even been interested." We stared at each other. "The truth is," I said quietly, "I got a hard-on watching you."

He leaned back and looked at the roof. "Shee-it," he muttered. He sighed. "And here I was thinking you were gonna be my main man this summer, and now you're going queer on me, too. What's the matter with all you guys out here?"

"Don't call me queer. You liked it plenty when I stuck my finger up your butt last night."

He straightened up and glared at me. "That was Deena."

"Deena's got fingernails an inch long. You know damn well that wasn't what you felt. It was my finger, and you liked it."

He whirled and slammed his fist into my chest, grabbing my shirt. "Don't you say that. Don't you ever tell anybody that, you hear me? I'll kill you, dammit." He glared, and I glared back.

Slowly, he let go, and we settled into the bucket seats. He stared at the porch light, and without turning he said in a low voice, "If we go in there together, and you want to, um, fool around some, you know, with me, well, I won't stop you."

"I can't do it in there," I told him. "I'd be too nervous. Why don't we pick up some beers to chase that whiskey with, and go back down to the river. If you're horny, I'll get you off."

Steve turned the steering wheel listlessly. He shook his head. "I can't get it up for a guy. I don't want to. I want a girl."

"You can pretend I'm—"

"God damn it, Bill!" He hit the steering wheel. "Don't say shit like that. I don't want to pretend anything. I want some pussy!"

"Well, I want some dick!"

His head snapped around. He stared at me. I braced myself for his fist. But after a moment, he got out and slammed the car door behind him.

Under the porch light, Steve pushed his hands into his back pockets and waited. The door opened a crack, then wider. He spoke briefly to someone and then looked back and nodded for me to join him. I reached for the door handle, but then I dropped my hand and watched him go in alone.

The dashboard clock ticked. Eleven-thirty.

I'd said it. I'd said it out loud. I'd said it to Steve. Nothing would ever be the same. Now I had to finish what I'd started. The whiskey bottle was in the glove compartment. I tilted it up and drained it. I got out of the Firebird and walked, very slowly, back to the Starlite Lounge.

There were so many men. I leaned on the bar, watching them pass through the bright hallway to the bathroom. When they stopped at the machine to buy cigarettes, each made a dip to reach for them, showing his butt muscles under his jeans.

The boy in the silver jacket was back. With his sleeves pushed up above his elbows, he was leaning on the machine and chewing gum. When a group of four men came into the bar, he walked behind them and melted into a dark corner. An alert waitress moved toward him, pointing at the door, and he went back to the hallway.

I finished my beer and went to the doorway. He hooked his thumbs in his pants pockets, and we eyed each other. I put some quarters in the machine, bending over the buttons and looking at his crotch. He rubbed himself.

"What kind you want?" he asked me. I told him Marlboros. The kid pushed a button and handed the pack to me. "Can I have one?"

"Sure." I gave him a cigarette. He dug in his pants for a lighter and lit his and then mine.

I tried not to cough. "Won't let you in, huh?"

He shrugged and grimaced.

I blew smoke.

He blew smoke.

"You got a truck?" he asked.

"No. I might could borrow a car, if you want to go for a ride."

He shook his head, leaning back and looking over my shoulder at the crowd. "Nah. I want to ride in a truck, you know? Wisht I had one."

He wasn't even aware of me any more. No truck, no fuck. I shrugged my shoulders and went outside. For a few minutes I waited beside the lumber where he'd gone with the other guy, but he didn't follow.

I took a leak on the wall and started walking.

Swell Saturday night, Bill, I told myself. Steve's in a whorehouse. Donnie and Stanley are up on a mountain fucking their brains out in a tent. Me, I'm getting turned down by the local high school cocksucker. I'd probably have to walk back to camp after propositioning Steve.

I zig-zagged through the dark back streets, wandering drunkenly, stumbling on a rock when the pavement ended. How could I have said that to him, to pretend I was a girl? Damn, how fucking humiliating. Some stud. I realized nobody in the cabin would be talking to me by the time I got back.

For a while I was lost, and then the bridge loomed ahead. I walked out onto it.

You're an all-around flop, I told myself, gripping the railing. I could hear water swirling in the blackness below me.

It's going to follow you everywhere, all your life. You're not normal. You can never change that. You fuck up every friendship you ever have, because you're queer.

One quick vault, that's all it would take. Into the darkness, then cold water, then nothing. It would be so easy, and then the pain would be gone.

What's one more dead faggot to anybody?

My folks would never have to know why. No note, like an accident. All those kids you read about in the papers, offing themselves without warning, and then nobody can figure out why, afterward. How many do it because they don't want to face the one big, bad, really dirty secret?

I tightened my hands on the cold metal. My eyes filled with tears.

Off to my right I saw a movement. Someone was coming toward me.

I wiped my face and waited for him to pass.

12

The shadowy figure hesitated at the beginning of the bridge. Even in the darkness I could tell it was a kid about my age, in shorts and a white teeshirt. He walked toward me, then stopped six feet away. He leaned back against the railing and looked off in the other direction.

He had long, gangling legs that made him almost as tall as me, and I was still wearing my new boots with soles an inch thick. He was in sneakers with no socks. I was too miserable to be shy. I stared at his exposed calf muscles, and wondered if he was waiting for someone.

He looked right at me. I got that automatic tightening inside my butt that happens when I see a sexy guy. After a minute he moved over next to me, turning around to face the river. His face was a blur as he pretended to look down at the water with me.

"Got a cigarette?" he asked in a husky voice. Either it was still changing, or maybe he was nervous. I sure was.

I cleared my throat. "Yeah," I said, shaking one out of the pack. "Um, I don't have a light."

"Me neither."

"Actually, I don't smoke," I admitted.

He grinned at me, a big, lopsided grin that showed lots of white teeth. "Me neither, actually," he said.

I dropped the pack over the rail, and he tossed the cigarette after it. They disappeared into the blackness.

We put our elbows on the bridge and stared down for a few more minutes. We couldn't see a thing below. He crossed his ankles. I peeked down at the slender bare legs beside me. He moved one hand down slowly, and tugged at his shorts.

My heart jumped. I edged closer. Slowly, he reached around and touched the front of my pants. He pressed his leg against mine. My throat went dry. He rubbed his hip against me. Under his hand, I felt a hard stump growing inside my briefs.

Car lights appeared behind us, and we moved apart.

As the headlights approached the bridge he said, "Shit. I know the people in that car. Don't let them see me." He ducked his head and stepped in front of me.

When the lights swept the kid, I saw that his shorts were shaggy cutoff jeans. They may have fit him last summer, but he was a growing boy, and the worn fabric was stretched tight over a very obviously hard lump under the right front pocket.

After the car passed and the blare of its radio faded, he turned to face me, breathing shakily, only inches away. I touched his hip.

We were still blinded from the lights. He took my hand and guided it down to feel his excitement. As I held the outline of it, he peeled up the frayed cloth and his bare, warm cock popped out and into my palm.

His breath whistled, a long 'whew' sound, as I explored his private parts with my fingertips. He was straining with sex. If I had pulled his dick too hard, I think it would have spurted like a stepped-on tube of toothpaste.

So I'm really not the only one in town, I thought.

Urgently, he hissed, "Let's go into the woods over there," and I followed. At the end of the sidewalk he took my hand and led me into the darkness.

We stopped at a tree. I leaned back against the trunk, and he knelt before me without a word and unzipped my pants. He was frantic for me, and I was astonished at how good it was. He gobbled at my cock, with his own sticking out from under his cutoffs.

It seemed a marvel. We'd just met. I didn't even know his name. We could hardly see each other, but he knew how to give me exactly what I wanted. His mouth was hot, his movements just right. He made my knees wobble. I put my hands on his shoulders, threw back my head, and closed my eyes. Grinning with happiness in the dark, I let a total, perfect stranger suck me off.

He hugged my butt with one arm, swallowing around my pleasure as I shot my load. His arm tightened behind me, forcing my cock deep into his throat at the end, and I could feel his body shaking and twitching as he jacked himself off with his other hand.

It was all over in two minutes. As I helped him to his feet, I couldn't think what to say. "Thanks," I whispered. "I mean, I really needed that." His dick was still sticking out from under his cutoffs, and mine was still hanging out of my fly. I straightened his teeshirt. "Gee, aren't you cold?"

"Nah, I'm okay." He sniffed and wiped his nose. "But I think I just messed up your boots."

"That's all right," I told him, scuffing them on the ground. "I already got them messed up, right after I bought them. It's kind of a turn-on."

"I know what you mean," he said, squeezing out his last drops of cum. "I always have to put my mark on boots when they're new. And jockstraps. My mom is always throwing my old ones away, and then I have to break in the new ones all over again, you know?" He had a sexy chuckle.

"Uh-huh," I nodded. "I beat off into my Jockey shorts, and then save them for the next time."

"Me, too." I saw his big white grin again, and he added, shyly, "I beat off into everything. I think I was born with a permanent hard-on."

"Me, too."

A car approached from town, and we both tucked our dicks away still half-stiff. As the car lights threw moving shadows of trees around us, I realized we hadn't made it very far into the bushes. We had done it right beside the road. Any passing car could have seen us, and this one was slowing down.

With a shock, I spotted a man sitting on the end of the bridge, across the pavement, looking right at us in the light. The headlights glared in his frowning face. It was the guy I had seen pushing the lawn mower. The car stopped in front of him.

"It's the cops!" I whispered, zipping my pants. "He saw us and called the cops! Run!"

My partner in illicit sex held my elbow calmly. The bridge guy leaned into the car window, said something, and got in. The car moved across the bridge. Music blared suddenly. At the stop sign, they squealed out onto the highway. I could see that I definitely wasn't the only one in town.

"Want to go down by the river and watch people parking?" he asked. "I can find my way in the dark. I grew up here."

He led me along the riverbank trail to the parking lot where we'd taken Deena the night before. Approaching the dark automobiles with the steamy windows, my new pal whispered, "My boyfriend and I come here on rubber hunts. One time he snuck up to a car and snagged one right after they threw it out, still warm, you know? We both jacked off with it. Greg's the only guy I ever met who's hornier than me."

We stood behind a tree and listened to a female voice gasping in one of the cars. The car bounced in the darkness. I stood behind him, slowly reaching around his front, lightly tracing the outline of his dick under the thin cloth again. And again, he lifted the leg of his shorts for me to touch him. It stuck up straight in my hand.

He turned his head around to my ear. I thought he was getting passionate, but he whispered, "The girls always squeal, but the guys always try to be macho and not make a sound. Then at the end they let go."

We heard, "Oh, oh, oh," from her, on and off for a while, then higher, "MHHHH!" The car lurched and then there came a deep "*Mmmggrrhhh. . .!*" My friend's cock throbbed in my fist.

"Now, the rubber," he whispered, and sure enough, a hand protruded from the back window and dropped something long and white.

"Now the guy will have to get out and take a leak." Clothes rustled, the car bounced, and a door opened. He had turned off the interior light.

In the blackness, they both got out of the car. The girl went to the rear and squatted, holding the bumper. "Don't peek," she told him, and the guy obediently turned his back to her. While he twisted his hips and made long sweeps with his piss, we heard a trickle from under the girl. My new friend's dick got sticky at the tip as we watched them. They kissed and got back in the car.

We walked away from the lovers, and somehow I felt as comfortable with the kid as with an old friend. He led me to a tree that had a fork in it at just the right height. When he sat in it, I knelt between his legs without a word, rolled up his shorts, and pulled out his cock. It was already dripping as I popped it into my mouth.

It was long and thin, with a head that grew into a hard knob against my tongue as I sucked on it. He made helpless little noises through his nose, and he was dribbling out so much fluid that I had to swallow every minute or two to keep up with him. I thought he was already coming, but then he put his hand behind my neck and said, "Oh shit, oh shit, oh shit," real fast, and lifted up on one foot. One skinny leg bounced uncontrollably, and the boy let loose a flood of cum in my mouth. It didn't just squirt, it ran like a garden hose. I couldn't begin to swallow it all. I held it with my fist and pumped out his cream all over my face, and the kid went "Aw-w-w-waaaaaah-h-h-h *SHIT!*" and danced in my hands like his feet were on fire.

When he was empty I got up laughing, and he put his arm on my shoulder. He wiped my face with his teeshirt. I kissed him, and we propped against the tree, hugging and giggling at ourselves in the darkness.

Walking along the dirt road by the baseball field, he said, "I've got a game tomorrow afternoon, if you want to come watch."

"Nah, I have to get back to camp. I work for the Forest Service."

"Which camp?"

"North Fork."

"Long way to drive."

"Uh-huh. We've been sleeping over there." I pointed to the rodeo grandstand.

"Want to come spend the night at my place? My room's out in the garage, so my parents won't know. We just have to be quiet so they don't hear us. Can't talk or anything."

I said okay. We cut through the field and followed back streets. Outside his yard, he said quietly, "I never had anybody sleep over before but Greg. Sometimes he climbs out of his window at night and sneaks into bed with me, and then he has to go back home in the morning before his parents wake up."

"Hell," I said, "I've never slept over with anybody before."

"Oh, yeah? Neat." He took my hand and led me silently through his backyard, around a white metal chair, to a door at the side of the garage. We tiptoed into the blackness inside.

Carefully closing the door, he broke his own rule, putting his mouth to my ear and whispering, "By the way, my name is Ken."

"Hi, Ken," I whispered back. "My name is Billy." I grinned in the dark. "Billy Beat-off."

He snorted, and I giggled. He put his hand over my mouth, and it was the last we spoke that night, but we communicated a lot, in other ways. We held onto each other and undressed, dropping clothes on the floor, and then he pulled me into his bed and tugged the blanket over us.

Ken didn't use a top sheet. His bed cover was made of some thick fabric that was soft and rough at the same time as it slipped over my butt. We hugged each other, naked. I had never felt anything so wonderful as another boy's nude body in my arms.

We touched lips. He was shy. I held his cock. When his hand closed around mine, it was so beautiful I couldn't breathe. I guess no man with a hard-on is a stranger. Something about our having erections makes us all brothers. Kissing softly, stroking each other, feeling all that warm, bare skin, we must have made love for an hour or more.

Much later we turned end to end. He was smooth all over down there, with wisps of fine pubic hair around his balls, but not much on his belly at all. Every time I ran my hands across his buttocks, the rounded muscles tightened and raised his hips toward me. I wet my lips and ran my mouth along his dick.

There is a seam in the skin there, very fine, that goes along the under-side, from the hole in the tip down to the balls, and I could feel it with my lips. It becomes a ridge that divides the scrotum into two pouches, and when I licked him there, I heard "Mmmm" from Ken, through his nose. I followed the seam with my finger, tracing under his crotch, up between the cheeks, to where the line disappeared into his butthole.

Ken made a surprised "Mmmh!" when I touched him there. As I worked my finger in farther, his dick jumped in my mouth and left stickiness at the back of my throat when he drew it back. He reached between my legs, found the spot, and poked his finger inside me the same way. I just sort of melted around him.

We made delicate sounds, signalling back and forth, sucking and squeezing and finger-fucking each other. With his mouth on me and mine on him, I caught myself thinking I was sucking my own cock, touching my own ass, feeling my own butt. Late in the night, curled up tight with him like that, I got another mouthful of Ken's sweet cum, and gave him a mouthful of my own. In the blackness of his bedroom, I didn't know where I was or exactly who I was with, but one thing was for sure. Billy Beat-off had found home.

The smell of bacon frying filled the room when I woke up. A model airplane with four wings hung from a rafter over us. Ken's face rested on my chest and his arms were around me.

"*Snnx*," he snored lightly. His hair was spiky, probably hadn't been cut since school let out for summer vacation. In the daylight I could see he had freckles.

Slipping one arm around his cold shoulders, I felt between us and smiled when I touched a warm erection. I toyed with it.

"Greg?" he croaked.

I whispered, "No, it's me. Bill."

He said, "Mmmm," and snuggled closer.

I moved my hand around his hips to his bare fanny, drawing him tighter so our cocks bumped. He lifted his face and kissed me; then after a moment he took my hand and guided it back between us. He'd still never even opened his eyes.

So many mornings I had waked up and done it alone in the early hours. How many times had I dreamed of a pal to play with this way, just this way, lying side by side, kissing and diddling our dicks together? We settled into a steady tugging, jacking each other off under the covers, and it was so good I knew I wouldn't last long. Why is it so much better when somebody does it for you?

"Ken, breakfast," a woman's voice called from outside.

"Dang," he said. We both pulled faster. He hooked his elbow around my neck. I liked that a lot.

"Ken, you're going to make us late to church." The voice sounded closer.

"I'm not going to church," he muttered in my ear. We jerked each other harder, and I felt that familiar sting inside me.

"Ken-neth!"

"God dang it," he moaned. Loudly, he said, "In a *minute*, Momma!" his voice cracking at the end.

He threw back the blanket. "Beat me off, okay?" he whispered, and I concentrated on his skinny dick in my hand. The knob got knobbier, the veins stood out. "Go faster," he told me, and then he raised up his hips and groaned, "I'm gonna pop!"

His eyebrows met in a frown. "Don't stop," he pleaded under his breath, and he wrapped his long legs around mine. His back arched, he groaned, and the smacking sounds of my fist turned squishy-wet.

"Oh, wait," he whispered, grabbing my wrist, holding my hand still as his cock throbbed and his body jerked in spasms. I stopped, and then I did him the way I like to do myself when I'm coming, moving my hand slowly, milking out spoonful after spoonful. His face relaxed into a smile as he trembled in my arms, whimpering with pleasure as his pearly white juice spurted out and dribbled down over my knuckles.

Tilting his face to me, he touched his lips to my chest, to my nipple, ever so softly. I could feel puffs of his breath on my skin. Something came to me as I pulled him closer, something enormously significant, I think. Only, I've never been able to remember it, exactly. It was unreal, the way things seemed so clear, and for just a moment it seemed I really understood everything, everything. I had it, and then, it just sort of evaporated from my mind.

Ken looked so open, so serene. He was safe with me, and he knew it, and that just knocked me out. Maybe it was because I'd never slept with anyone before. I've always thought it's a specially stupid euphemism that adults use, to say people "sleep together" when we all know it's fucking they're talking about. But sex is like sleeping in a way, when you let go so completely with another person. You close your eyes and you go away to that place everybody wants to be, and for a while, everything is perfect. Why doesn't everybody do this?

"Kenneth, if you don't get in here this instant, I'm coming out there after you!"

He groaned and opened his eyes. "Get my cum rag, quick. Under the bed." I found it and swiped at his slippery stomach.

"I'll do you when I get back," he told me, lurching from the mattress and stepping into a faded pair of long sweatpants.

As he danced into them, he made a little fart, just a poot, and said, "'Scuse me."

He pulled the sweats up and flipped his dick inside, with another poot. "'Scuse me."

He knotted the drawstring, hesitated, and squinted one eye. *Poooo-OOT!* "'Scuse me."

His cock showed through the thick blue cloth, still hard. I could see the head on it, and a dark wet spot spread from the tip as he tried to push it down. I poked at it.

He said, "Don't worry, they see me like this every morning. They won't know it's 'cause you're out here."

Pulling a teeshirt over his head, he told me, "If you have to go to the bathroom, there's a jar in the corner I use when I don't want to go inside."

He ran to the door, barefoot, and then turned. "You won't leave on me, will you? I'm just gonna eat and get rid of them. Please stay here."

I said I'd stay, and he went outside. Through the window I saw him lope to the back door of a shabby little house, still with a tent in the front of his sweats.

For a minute or two I played with my own tent pole, but then I got up, naked, to close the curtains and investigate his room.

The walls were unfinished two-by-fours with insulation stuck between them. Over his bed he had tacked up a row of posters. Two were blond surfers, one was a body-builder posing with a trophy, and others were football players and rock stars. Most were stripped to the waist, and all were men.

In the corner behind his dresser I found the mason jar and filled it halfway, thinking it would get rid of my hard-on if I peed, but it didn't help. I screwed the lid on and put it back on the floor.

On his dresser stood a tiny basketball trophy and a framed team photograph. Ken was in front on one knee, holding the basketball. His wallet had three dollars in it, and a school picture of a handsome boy who I figured was Greg.

At the foot of the bed a baseball uniform lay in a heap, with a frayed jockstrap on top of a leather glove. It was a real athletic supporter, the kind with a pocket in the pouch for a plastic guard to protect his balls. I picked it up and sniffed it. It smelled sweaty. I wrapped the straps around my dick. My erection was so stiff it held the jock in midair. I squeezed my last drops of pee into the pouch, and then arranged the supporter on top of the glove again.

His jeans were on the floor. I tried to pull them on, but they were two sizes too small. They were button-fly Levis, just like Donnie's. Sucking in my guts to try to get the top buttoned, I realized I hadn't thought of Donnie since — when? Since I'd met Ken. Why had I been so upset about him and Stanley? That night seemed like a bad dream.

Ken didn't have a closet. In one corner, a pipe was mounted between the unfinished walls with clothes hangers on it. He did have a block letter jacket. I pulled it down and slipped it over my bare chest, fingering the masculine maroon letters of his school. He'd gotten them in basketball, baseball, and track. I was impressed. The only letters I had ever won were English letters, for clubs. They didn't rate in our school, and I'd never worn them.

A man's voice came from outside. "Well, then you could at least clean up your room," he said, and I heard noises behind the wall, and then a car started.

That worked. My hard-on wilted. I got back into bed, still wearing his sexy jacket.

Out in the yard Ken's mother said, "You can go in there and pray to God, if you remember who He is."

The blankets were loose at the foot of the bed. They had cartoon pictures on them of cowboys and Indians chasing each other on horses. The car left, but still Ken didn't return. Reaching under the mattress, I found a body-building magazine, leafed through it, and put it back. I stretched to the floor for the ratty old towel he kept under the bed. The damp part had that funny smell of fresh cum, almost like ammonia. The rest of it was dried stiff, probably from Greg's nighttime visits.

Gawky Ken opened the door. His hair still stuck up and he still showed a wet spot on his sweats. He held out a glass of milk and a peanut butter and jelly sandwich for me.

"I grabbed this from my mom's dresser, too," he said with a grin, pulling a bottle of Jergens lotion from under his arm.

He kicked off his pants and settled onto the bed to watch me eat, crossing his legs with only his teeshirt for warmth. His dick flopped on top of the blanket.

"You have to excuse my mom," he said, ducking his head. "She's O.D.'ed on Jesus. She's one of those people who all of a sudden thinks every word in the Bible is true, straight from God. It's all she ever talks about. It gives me the willies when she starts all that 'thee' and 'thou' and 'thy' stuff. She gets like a robot.

"I tell her it's just an old book, and they didn't know any more back then than we do now, and boy, does it tee her off. She says I'm on the road straight to hell." He chuckled. "Shit, I can barely make it to school and back on my bike. I couldn't find the road to hell if I wanted it."

We nodded and laughed.

"Anyway," he continued, pushing his hair out of his eyes, "the Bible doesn't tell you what to do about sex. It's got that part about not spilling your seed, but hell, mine spills out all the time.

I can't help it. I mean, Jesus never got a hard-on in front of everybody in class. Even if he did, they wouldn't put it in the Bible.

"I like ol' Jesus. He's a pretty cool dude. But the rest of the Bible is just a lot of hooey, if you ask me. It's just a bunch of made-up stories and I don't think anybody really knows for sure what it says.

"All they give you is stuff like, 'Thou shalt not commit adultery.' Heck, I'm not even sure what adultery means. And what's fornication? Exactly, I mean?"

I said, "I know what sodomy is."

"Me, too," he grinned. In his deepest voice, he said sternly, "'Thou shalt not make it with another dude's bohunkus. For a man to get his rocks off with another man is an abdomination.' Hey, we're like Bigfoot, huh? Like the abdominal snowman?" He raised his arms up like a gorilla. "I'm gonna abdominate you, you cheesy little faggot. GRRR!"

"I think it's abominal," I said. "I mean, a-bom-in-a, tal? Nation, a-ble?"

He waved his hand. "Shit, it's just fun, that's what it is. Give me a break. I'd go out of my tree if I didn't have sex with Greg. Can you imagine waiting until you get fucking married to do it? MARRIED? That's, like, for-EV-er-r-r."

After a moment, he asked, "Do you believe in God?"

I shrugged my shoulders, chewing peanut butter and mumbling, "I dunno. Maybe it's all made up, even God, like you said." I shook my head. "I dunno."

"Me neither. They want me to be confirmed at church, and I don't want to. I think they're hypocrites. My dad's a deacon, and I've smelled booze on his breath right in church, Sunday nights."

I put a piece of the sandwich in his mouth. Talking as he chewed, he said, "I do think UFO's are for real, though. I think I saw one once, right from the yard." He pointed a finger and moved it in front of his face. "It went along in a straight line, not blinking or anything, and then, ERK! It went the other way, just like that. Couldn't have been a plane, or anything human. It was all over before I could call anybody, so nobody believes me."

"I believe you," I said.

We finished eating, and Ken leaned across my bare lap to put the dishes on the floor. I tugged his teeshirt over his head to look at his slender body in the dim morning light. I had touched him all over, and been so intimate sexually, yet I'd never really seen him. His shoulders were covered with freckles, and his muscles were still boyish, undefined. As I ran my hands over his arms and chest, his dick lengthened on the blanket. I cupped my fingers under it and stroked the fine, loose skin with my thumb.

"Only thing I'm really sure about," he said, "is that I sure like sex. It's the best thing there is. I mean, why should God care if we fuck our brains out? We're not hurting anybody. He's the one who gave us our cocks. Did you ever stop to wonder if God has a cock? That's something else they never put in the Bible. If we're made in the image of God, then he must have a cock, right? But if he does, what's it for?"

I laughed. "Is there a Mrs. God?"

He giggled. "Do they fuck?"

"Does he just use it to pee?"

"Why would God have to pee?"

We grinned at each other, and said together, "Does God jack off?"

Holding his dick, I told him, "I worry about myself sometimes, though. I jack off SO much. It's all I think about. I don't think I'm normal."

He nodded. "I do it everywhere, man, just everywhere. In the toilets at school, in the bathtub, in the bushes. All the time. I even did it in the back row at church one time. Not during a service, I mean. Nobody else was around. I was just sitting there and did it. Sometimes I think I'm crazy." The tube of his penis thickened in my hand as we both looked down at it.

I asked him, "How many guys do you think do it?"

He laughed. "Jack off? Everybody."

"No, I know that. I mean, how many guys really fuck with each other?"

"Aw, I think most every guy probably practices fucking with his best friend. Just nobody admits it. I mean, Greg and I go out in the woods and screw around for hours sometimes. The guys who put it down so much probably aren't getting anything from anybody, girls or guys."

"Yeah. So, who's crazy, them or us?"

"You got me." We watched his hard-on lift up from my fingers.

When I let go, it twitched and stuck out straight. He grinned at me. "Ruled by my dick!"

Pulling him up by it, I towed him to the mirror, me in only his varsity jacket, him in nothing but skin.

We compared erections. His curved to the left as it stiffened. "Mine is crooked," he said, "did you notice? Too much whacking off with my right hand. I try to remember to do it with my left hand, so it will even out, but I forget."

He got the Jergens lotion and pumped a white line of it along the top of both dicks. "Do like this," he told me, flipping his fingers around on my cock until it felt so good it hurt. Watching ourselves in the mirror, we showed each other our favorite grips.

"Do you think I'm sexy?" he asked, looking at his reflection over his shoulder. "I think my butt sticks out too much."

Patting his ass, I told him, "I like it just fine, just the way it is." My peter pointed straight out, touching the soft curve of his bare behind.

"You want to cornhole me?" he asked. "Greg always does." He bent over the bed and spread his cheeks for me. "Greg says just looking up it gives him a bone on." He got into a position on his elbows and knees that showed his balls dangling between his legs, and I thought his boyfriend was a pretty lucky guy.

I felt all over his rear end, tracing the tanline of his cutoffs with my fingers around his thighs and then along his back. "Put your jockstrap on for me," I urged him.

He brought a frayed old one, the regular kind with the soft pouch. When he stepped into it, his hard-on poked out on one side. The label was coming loose. It read, **THE BIKE. MEDIUM.** Three faded red stripes ran around the wrinkled waistband. When he stuck his bottom in the air again, framed by the thick, white elastic bands, my cock swelled up in my hand until it turned purple.

Kneeling on the bed, I took a good long look at his pink hole, spreading the puckered skin open with my thumbs. He was almost hairless in back. The muscle ring tightened at my touch, then loosened. "Put some jerkin' lotion on your finger," he said. I dabbed the slippery cream around the hole, and he made it squeeze tight around my fingertip. "Stings a little," he said.

Ken moved his knees further apart, pulling his ass wider with both hands. The accordion pleats of his butthole opened up around my fingertip. I poked inside him, up to the first knuckle. The circle widened, and I slipped my finger all the way in.

"Oh-h-h," he whimpered, squirming under my hand. "Do it now. Dog-fuck me."

I put the head of my dick up between the cheeks of Ken's butt, and he reached for it and pushed it up a little higher. He closed his eyes and grimaced, cheek on the blanket, as my red tip disappeared, enveloped by his tight muscles. He stopped me with a hand on my leg, and I pumped a few squirts of lotion between us. With a groan, he let my cock slide all the way up his asshole.

"Oh, god," Ken breathed. "You're pretty big. Oh, go slow. Mmmmh." My heart raced, seeing myself inside him, the way his cheeks held me tightly, like a sideways smile with a cigar in its lips. The farther in I got, the more Ken flattened himself against the bed and at the same time raised his rump to me.

After a minute, I moved my hips, fucking him slowly, tugging the elastic bands of his jockstrap, staring in fascination as the hard rod of my cock slid in and out of his white fanny.

He chuckled, pressing his soft, warm behind against my groin for more. Still on his knees, he reached back under his legs and pulled on my nuts. I fell on top of him and pressed him down flat, humping him the way dogs fuck, just as he'd said.

His shoulders were narrow under me, dusky brown from the summer sun, spotted with freckles, and covered with downy white hairs. I kissed his neck. His shoulder blades poked up under the skin looking like the buds of angel wings.

"Mmh!" he grunted, lifting his butt for me, eagerly squirming under my fucking. "Mmh, mmh, mmh!" I folded the block-letter jacket around both of us, cradling my skinny angel in my arms as I pumped his ass.

He turned his head, his adam's apple protruding from under his chin, and stared into my eyes, smiling. "Like Greg always says," he told me over his shoulder, "if it's so wrong, how come it fits so good?"

Oh, it fit. I reached under his belly for the pouch of his jockstrap, and the fit was just perfect. Tightening my arms around his chest and belly, cupping his dick in my hand, I found out how really good fucking can get. I could tell he was liking it too, because by the time I was starting to sweat, the pouch of his jockstrap was sopping wet in my hand. He must have creamed a cupful of juice just from the fun of getting fucked. I held his dick tight in my fist and whispered in his ear, "I'm gonna cum."

He tugged my nuts so hard it hurt, and then turned his head and kissed me over his shoulder as I went absolutely crazy on top of my buddy's back, crazy with the pleasure of fucking my buddy's ass, fucking my skinny angel with a hard-on.

Then I rolled over for him, but it didn't work out so good. I liked it when he finger-fucked me with the lotion, but it hurt when the knob on his dick popped inside me, and I flinched. "Wait a minute," I said. "Give me a minute to get used to it."

Ken hugged me from behind for a few seconds, then he whispered, "I can't," and shuddered. His leg jerked two or three times, kicking at the bed, then his weight sagged onto my back. He sighed, and rolled off me. I wasn't even sure if he'd come or not until I saw a creamy white spoonful of cum ooze from his cock and run down his thigh in a shiny silver trickle.

"Sorry about that," he said. "I can never last very long that way. It happens with Greg, too."

"It's okay," I said. "I get sore anyway. Can I wash up?"

Still sprawled in only his jockstrap, Ken nodded, "Uh-huh. Twenty minutes till my folks get home."

I pulled on his sweats. When I opened the door and sunlight filled the room, Ken raised his hands and covered his eyes in mock horror. "A-h-h-h, help, I'm blinded by reality!"

I hated being in his house alone. I saw a tiny living room with white lace curtains and an oil heater, and ugly brown, worn furniture. Ducking into the bathroom for my morning dump, I found out Ken had indeed gotten off inside me. The stuff makes a natural laxative. I splashed cold water on my face and armpits, and hurried back out to the garage.

Pulling on my clothes, I didn't know what to say. "You're sure a nice guy," I told him. "If I didn't have to get back to North Fork, I'd say let's hang around some, but. . ." I shrugged.

"Yeah," he said, "I've got a game today, anyway." He got up from the bed and hugged me from behind. "If you can get back into town next weekend, I work at the drugstore Saturdays."

I nodded but I still hesitated to leave. Blinded by reality, I guess.

Shifting his weight, Ken asked, "Uh, you want to keep this?" He stripped off his athletic supporter and held it out to me. "It's my best one," he said. We smiled at each other.

I had to unlace my boots again, but I undressed and put on Ken's old jockstrap. The stringy pouch was soft, stretched loose, and still sticky inside when I tucked my dick into it. I stuffed Steve's bikini shorts into my back pocket and kissed my new fuck-buddy goodbye.

As I crossed his back yard, Ken yelled from the garage door, "Hey, remember, man, it's them that's crazy, not us."

I waved and went to look for Muscles, wondering if the big jerk would still give me a ride back to camp.

13

Steve was in the Sportsman, hulking over a table, staring at a baseball game on the television above the bar. I ordered two Lucky Lagers and took a deep breath. Be Joe College, I instructed myself, and walked over to his table.

When I sat down I sprawled in the chair. I slid a bottle under his nose, hoping it wouldn't tip over into his lap and blow my act. "Drink up, my man," I said, heartily. "Time to celebrate."

He eyed me and returned his attention to his ball game. "Celebrate what?" he asked, without interest.

"Well, we both got what we wanted last night, didn't we?" I pulled on my beer. "I did, anyway."

"I don't think I want to hear about it," he said, but he drank some of his beer.

"How was it at the Green House? Did she make a man out of you?"

He shrugged. "It was okay. I've fucked uglier broads." After a pause and cheers from the television, he grinned at me. "Not many though. Actually, she was pretty scuzzy." He picked at the red Lucky label. "So, you scored, huh?"

"Yup." I propped my elbow on the chair next to mine.

"Just picked up some dude, huh? Just like that?" He snapped his finger.

I nodded. "A young guy, too." I was beginning to enjoy needling him.

He shook his head. "Man, I still can't believe you're into that shit." He peeled the label from his bottle, tearing strips and dropping them on the table. "I guess you've been getting it from Stanley, too. Shit. Is everybody in camp getting head from him but me?"

I just smiled.

"That's really why you and Donnie are pissed at each other, am I right? He's taking your pussy-face away from you, and you don't like it, right?"

"Um, well, not exactly. Well, something like that."

"You gonna fight him? I'd shit a brick laughing at that. You and Donnie, duking it out over a goddam fag. Hyah!"

In my imagination I saw myself in a boxing ring with Donnie, both of us stripped naked, with Stanley's little body tied up and gagged in a corner. I decided to let him think what he wanted to think. It sounded ballsier than the truth.

Somebody scored, and then commercials jabbered about trucks and beer brands. With nothing inside me but peanut butter, the beer made me glow quickly.

Steve leaned to me and asked, "Something I've always wondered about. Is a guy really better at giving blowjobs than a girl? Because, you know, they have one, so they know how to treat it right. Who gives better head, Deena or Stanley?"

"Well, Steve, I'll tell you," I began, trying to remember how Donnie had put it. "I'm not saying to you what I've done with Stanley, just like I'm not saying to Stanley what I've done with you, so—"

Banging his bottle on the table, he stiffened and glared. "You better not, man," he said gruffly. He looked over his shoulder and then leaned even closer and narrowed his eyes.

"No goddam guy ever got anywhere close to getting to me before," he said in measured time, poking my shoulder with his finger. "Not ever. And plenty of fruits have tried, too. Now, I was drunk, understand? I don't remember anything that happened, and neither do you, or I'll make you sorry."

He faced the television and scowled, but with such a pretty face, he only looked like a pouting little boy. I finished my beer and burped as loudly as I could. Scraping my chair noisily, I stood up and stretched. "You still giving me a ride back to camp?"

He looked up blankly. "Sure. Why not?"

Baseball scores droned from the set as I left. I smiled to myself. Bill - 1, Steve - 0.

That afternoon, on the twisting dirt road home, I kept losing myself in memory, thinking about sex with Ken. I watched trees go by, and stared at mountains, and listened to Steve's talk, but I kept remembering the endless long minutes of holding Ken's dick in my mouth, at first so hard and prodding, then afterward so soft, defenseless, dripping on my tongue as we embraced in bed, six to nine. My jaws still ached from it. And the fucking, how it excited me to think of doing it inside a guy's butt. My pulse raced, and when I imagined yet again how his dick felt going up my ass, the muscles in my seat tightened and my cock stiffened inside Ken's jockstrap. Getting off with another guy seemed a million times more intense than by myself.

God, I wondered, does everyone else spend so much time thinking about sex? Dick, dick, dick, that's all I ever have on my mind. I tugged at my crotch, and Steve looked over, grinning.

"Ooo-oooo," he said. "Somebody's gonna get a blowjob when we get back to camp, I bet. Hyah!" He looked at me slyly. "What's Stanley do for you guys, anyway?"

I shook my head. "Look, Steve, I don't like the guy. I only let him do me because I was horny last weekend, and we were alone."

"I mean," he persisted, "did you ever, you know, use him like a girl?"

"You mean did I butt-fuck him? No." Later I said, "Ken and I did that, last night."

We rode in silence for a while. I wanted to forget things and look at the mountains, but Steve brought it up again. "Bill, if I hadn't gone in the Green House, you'd have wanted to do that to me, wouldn't you? Put it up the old bung-hole?"

I shrugged. "Or, you could have done it to me. Or we both could do it. That's what I did with Ken. We took turns."

"Oh, no." He covered his ear. "I don't want to hear it. You mean you pitch and you catch, too?"

"Why not? If you think a finger feels good, well, think about it."

That stopped him. "Whoa, man. We're getting into some deep shit here. Let's just watch the pretty moo-cows for a while."

But he pondered it as we drove. I could see his jaws working and his eyes squinting as he argued with himself silently.

"Nope," he announced, shaking his head. "Can't see it. I think, with two guys, one would have to dominate the other. It's only natural. Guys test each other out, look for weaknesses. You have to find out who's the boss. If I was with a guy and he got on top of me, I'd be ashamed. And if I got on top of him, then I wouldn't have any respect for him."

I shook my head. "Hell, everything between men doesn't have to be like wrestling. Ken and I took turns, and he's a regular guy.

He's on the baseball team, and basketball too. I saw his block letter jacket."

"I don't want any dude messing with me back there. It's too — personal."

"Hey, Steve. There's nobody in the car but us. Now don't get pissed, but think about it and be honest. You got off on it. It feels good."

Steve's mouth worked. His fingers drummed on the console as he drove with one hand.

"Steve, let's tell the truth to each other, just for once. I dare you. The rest of the way to camp, no bullshit. No pretending we were too drunk. We were sober enough to fuck. If you'll come clean with me, I'll answer any question you ask."

"Okay," he said. "Deal. I admit it. I remember every goddam detail, because I never shot my wad that good in all my life. It was like my jizz was under pressure. I coulda knocked a jaybird out of a tree with it."

I smiled. "Okay, my turn. I can't tell you if guys are better than girls, because Deena's the only girl I ever had. I was too nervous. She made me nervous. You got me excited."

He grinned. "God, it was hot stuff, wasn't it?" He whistled. "You think I could ever get a girl to reach back and do that to me while we're fucking? I think a girl could reach it, don't you? If she had long arms?"

"Have to find the right girl. Deena would, I bet. Maybe you should have asked if they do that at the Green House. Do they have a menu to pick from, or something?"

"I don't think I'll be going back there. As long as we're being so honest, I'll tell you, I couldn't get it up in there. God, man, it was awful. She was squatting over a pot, douching herself, when I got in the room. Tits like leather.

"She tried everything to get me going, but I was sick to my stomach. She kept saying, 'You can do it, tiger, come on, tiger.' I mean, she worked hard for the money, I'll give her that much. She licked it, she sat on it, she tried to push it in soft. Worst night I ever had, oh, Jesus.

"Then somebody knocked on the door, and said, 'Your fifteen minutes are up, come on out.' Next thing I knew, I was in the car, puking my guts out, and wondering where the hell you went."

I laughed. "Fifteen minutes! I thought you got an hour at

least. No pink curtains and satin sheets either, I guess. What did you pay?"

In a small voice, he said, "Forty bucks."

"Aw, Steve. You got robbed, man. Forty bucks? For that? I would have done you for nothing, and I would have made it last a hell of a lot longer than fifteen minutes!"

He held up his hand. "Bill, please. I'm trying real hard not to put you down about all this. You can turn into a green Martian if you want to, I don't care but—"

He rubbed his forehead and frowned. "I'm straight, pal, I really am. Let's just be friends. Normal, healthy relationship. I like you but that's all. Get it?"

I sat for a few moments, but I had to say it. "No, I don't get it. I never have. If you like a guy, you should be able to show it. I've always felt cut off from other guys, because there are so many things you can't do with them. Don't you ever get lonely? Don't you ever feel cut off from your buddies?"

"No, man, no way. That's why guys play sports with each other, you know, yuk it up, get physical, blow off some steam. If you fags. . . if you gay dudes would play ball, you'd see how much fun it is."

We watched the road switch back and forth under us going up the last hill. "Something I always wondered," I said. "You're a jock. Don't you guys ever get turned on, patting each other on the fanny all the time, and taking showers together? Don't you ever have circle jerks with the team, or something?"

"Hell, no, man. Well, I've heard it happens, but I was never in on one. That's the god's honest truth."

"Then, what? You all go your separate ways, and jerk off alone? Why?"

Steve sighed. "There are some things men just can't do and still call themselves men."

"I'm a man," I said quietly. "Just as much as you are."

Coming down the hill, I asked him what had been his best experience with a girl. "Honest answer, now."

He gave me a shy smile. "I haven't had as many chicks as you think I have. Being good-looking can be a doggone burden. Ordinary girls think you're stuck up. Everybody expects me to take out the beauty queens, but most of them aren't impressed because they want to be the pretty ones. And the truth is, girls don't look at muscles much." He flexed his beefy arm. "This is mostly between me and the other guys. Girls think it's dumb. They don't understand."

He shrugged. "I dunno. When I was a kid in Santa Monica, I spent all my time surfing. Now, I'm working out in the gym after class every day. I like for the guys to think I'm a stud, but the truth is I really don't have much time for it."

"But, what was the best?"

He made an exasperated noise in his throat. "Friday night with Deena."

"Really? You didn't last very long."

"I know. I never can. I always get so excited I lose it as soon as I get it in." He struck his forehead with his palm. "God, I don't believe I'm telling you this shit. I could never in a million years talk to a straight guy like this."

"Why not?"

"You can't let down your guard with other dudes, man. They'll take advantage. That's the way guys are. You never give them the ammunition to attack you with."

"Damn, Steve, we're not fighting a war."

"Yeah, I trust you. For one thing, I really appreciate your not ragging me about, uh, my size. Down there. I know you had your hand on it while I was fucking Deena. And, okay, since we're being so goddam honest, I got off on it. I guess I thought I was proving something to you. I dunno."

He shook his head. "You know all my secrets now." He grinned at me. "You really got me by the balls, fucker. More ways than one. Hyah!"

I grinned back at him. "Don't worry. Handling other guys' balls is something I know all about. I've had experience."

We both laughed, and Steve pounded the steering wheel, and then we slapped palms and shook hands once, the way they do in beer commercials.

The drive through the tall trees was quiet after that, and I was riding high. Pulling into camp, Steve said, "Didn't we have fun, though? You wanna do it again next weekend?"

Everybody was in the cabin. Donnie sat at the table, chair tilted back against the wall, with his poker buddies laughing and smoking around him. Stanley curled on his bed, pretending to read but watching his master like a dog, like a house mutt who moves only his eyes yet sees everything in the room.

Then Steve's volleyball buddies followed him inside to hear about his weekend. They piled onto my bed, chanting "Poon-tang, poon-tang." One of them yelled, "We heard about the whore-house. Tell us what happened."

He gave them a good story. About the Green House, it was, "I've fucked uglier broads. Good thing I'd just chugged a half a pint of Wild Turkey. Leather tits, man. But she did everything I told her to do. Took it both ways, you know what I mean? She called me, get this, she called me, 'Ti-gerrrr,' ah hah, hah, hah!"

They screamed. I started sorting my dirty clothes, making a pile on the floor since my bed was the cheering section.

He left me out of the part about picking up Deena, not even bringing me into things until, "I was so fucking drunk, Bill over there had to drive. I was shit-faced, I tell you, but soon as we got out of town I told her, 'Go to it,' and man, did she ever. I told Bill to get us down to the river, fast, and you know what? He wasn't even parked before she was in the back seat, begging for both of us to fuck her, man, both of us."

I put my hands on my hips and shot him a disapproving look.

"But the best part," he said, pointing at me, "was the big stud over there. After I finished with her, you know what he did? He says to the chick, 'You got another rubber?' She says she doesn't, and he says, 'Give me that thing.' The man jerks the rubber right off my little old peter, slaps it on that big tool he's got, and puts it to her, hey hey hey!

"Now, I heard of sloppy seconds, but this dude is an animal. I mean, he made her moan for like a half an hour, and she'd already come twice with me! I do a pretty good job on girls, but Billy here, our man Billy, he's a primo, fucking, stud!"

He ran over and messed up my hair, just as I was pulling my pants off.

"Aw right!" somebody hollered. "Speech, speech, speech!" they chanted.

I stood there, confused and naked except for Ken's ratty old cum-stained jockstrap.

Somebody yelled, "He's the only guy in camp who has to wear a supporter when he goes out on dates. Hea-vy du-ty."

"Ah, come on, y'all," I stammered, feeling my face redden in the silence.

Donnie leaned forward in his chair with a big smile on his face, signalling with his hand for me to talk.

I cleared my throat. "It was pretty good. Yeah, hell, we both fucked her good. I mean, I was so fucking drunk, I can't even remember it all. Guess we'll just have to do it all over again next weekend, huh." I made a manly swipe at my dick, at least at the part that hadn't shrivelled up inside me.

They all laughed and went back to talking. Steve whispered, "See, man? That's how it's done."

Turning my back to the crowd and fiddling in my locker, I protested, "But that's not the way it happened."

"So what? All their stories are complete lies. At least ours is ninety percent true. This is what sex is all about, man." He thumped my chest. "Stud."

When I looked at Stanley, he rolled up his eyes and shook his head. I made a face at him.

The crowd was getting too rowdy for me. I had to wash my only good pants for work tomorrow anyway, so I stuffed my things into a pillowcase and interrupted Steve to get his dirty clothes from the weekend to make a full load. The jockstrap stayed on me. I put on my cut-offs and sneakers, carefully arranging my new boots in my locker so I could see them from bed later, and got out of the noise.

Sitting on the steps by the laundry room, I listened to the machine chug and swish behind me and proudly counted the pecker tracks that were getting soaked out of my clothes: mine, Steve's, Ken's. And now I knew it was true what they say, girls do get wet when they do it. Pussy tracks. Imagine me with pussy tracks on my clothes. And lipstick, too. I had spilled beer on them, and barfed on myself, and I had choked on Steve's whiskey and gotten that on me, and maybe some peanut butter.

I smiled up at the dipping sun, pleased with my weekend. Rubbing my chin, I realized I hadn't shaved for two days. Or had it been since last, what, Thursday? I put my hand to my neck to feel my coarseness. I liked it.

Donnie appeared with his own pillowcase full of clothes. "Hi, Stud." He looked all the way up and down my body, and smirked, "Your balls are showing."

I peered between my legs and adjusted my cut-offs. He

stepped over my shoulder, and I turned to watch as he went inside, telling him, "I thought I'd have to take a number in there to talk to you."

He dumped his things into a second washer. When it filled and started, he pulled the shirt off his back and added it to the water. When that disappeared, he peeled off his teeshirt and dropped it in. Kicking off his loafers, he put his dirty socks in, and then pushed his jeans and underwear down to his knees, mooning me and the whole camp through the door.

I laughed and he pulled up his pants. He got a little box of detergent flakes from the vendor, held open the lid of the washer, and tossed the box up to the ceiling, unopened. It arched beautifully, end over end, and plunked into the mouth of the sloshing machine.

"You can't do that," I told him. "You have to open the box first, you big goof."

He dropped the lid closed and sat beside me on the steps. "I do lots of things I can't do."

Wispy clouds were fading from white to yellow as we leaned back on our elbows. The late afternoon sun was half gone behind the trees on the ridge. I looked at the lanky fellow beside me as he watched the sky. Flecks of light gleamed from each hair decorating his chest, and I followed the swirling patterns with my eyes. He was marked like a wild animal. His nipples were big as quarters.

After a weekend looking at Steve's tanned, over-built torso, Donnie seemed pale and vulnerable. He was muscular, but the arms were leaner and the bulges looked softer. "You need some sun," I told him. "Didn't you run around naked in the woods this weekend? Or was that only at night?"

He wouldn't answer. I said, "Oh, I forgot. The Code," and leaned back again. "Well, I don't believe in The Code. Sometimes I think I don't believe in anything. I'll tell you what happened to me, I met an angel. A boy with a permanent hard-on."

"Mmh," he said. "My kind of angel."

"He was such a sweet guy. All that stuff with Steve and that girl, well, it wasn't like he told it at all. It was all screwed up. But then I met this kid, and even in the dark I could tell he was one of us. And we did it, right away, and we kept doing it all night. It's so strange. I don't know anything about him, except his name is Ken. But, we made love. Perfect strangers. And, it was beautiful."

Donnie nodded, staring silently up at the sunset.

"I think I know what you mean, now," I continued, "about how you can make it with another guy and it's not necessarily anything special. I mean, it was special. It was very special. Maybe that's what makes it okay. God, just think, any two guys in the world can fuck if they want to."

He grinned at me. "Yeah, we're all kinda like dogs, you know. Every time we meet somebody new, we have to sniff each other's butts and lift up our legs and piss on trees together." He tugged at his crotch and laughed. "Ain't nature grand?"

We didn't mention Stanley. But I think he understood me, and I was glad we didn't have to talk about it any more.

Following his gaze to the sky, I turned my face up and we watched a hawk circle high at the tip of a fir that had green tufts and almost no limbs. The last of the sunlight moved up the skinny trunk as the shadow of the mountain flooded camp. The hawk glowed, tan against the blue. Our heads tilted back together as we watched the golden creature loop around, effortlessly sailing up into the cold sky.

Donnie said, "He's catching the last updraft from that hill and hoping it's enough to get him home without having to flap." We lost him behind the roof of the laundry building.

It had turned dark on the old wooden steps. Donnie shivered and sat up. "I have to go get a shirt on for dinner. Here, I brought you something." He handed me a rock, smooth and round on one side and covered with quartz crystals on the other.

"It's a geode," he told me. "Or part of one, anyway. I found it up on the mountain today. There was some more, but I covered it back up. You're the only person on the whole planet who will ever have a piece of that particular one. At least, in our lifetimes."

The colors of the sunset sparkled in my hand.

When he walked away, I called out, "I'll put your clothes in the dryer for you." In the laundry room, I opened the lid on his washer. The box had unfolded into a single piece of cardboard, spread like a flower, and spun dry with everything else. It was damp but still in one piece, and Donnie's clothes smelled as clean as mine did.

In the cabin, I put the pillowcase full of Donnie's dry clothes into his locker. Shooing guys off my bed, and making sure Stanley could see, I folded Steve's laundry just the way he did it himself. I even rotated his stock when I put it away.

"Hey, thanks," he called. "You're hired."

"Better find out what the price is first," I said. Instantly, I regretted that. It sounded as though I had propositioned him, offered to do him other services.

They all laughed, and someone hooted and said, "Watch out, Bill, he might take you up on it. You know what they say about the guys in this cabin. You might get you some ass again tonight."

It was a miracle. They were taking it as a threat from me, rather than an offer.

"Yeah," another kid said. "Bill will collect for it after lights out. Better not roll over on your stomach in your sleep tonight, Steve. He's bigger than you, down where it counts." Steve roared with laughter, nodding and banging on the table.

Monday morning, I skipped shaving. I was growing a beard.

Later, checking the assignment sheet at the office, I saw that Donnie had moved my name again. This time he'd taken me off the seeder crew and added me to a trail crew.

Out into the real woods at last! And he'd even spelled my name right.

I looked closer. The top name had been scratched out, too. "D. Powers" was penciled in above it. Donnie had put himself in charge of my crew.

The game was on again.

14

"Thought we'd get us some sun," Donnie said in the toolroom
line. "You look a tad pale. Too much night prowling is bad for
your complexion, y'know."

He touched my forehead. "Nookie zit."

"Beer gut," I said, poking his belly, but it wasn't really soft at
all.

At the tool window he pointed at a crosscut saw hanging on
the back wall. It was four feet long with wooden handles on each
end. A slit length of worn fire hose was wired on to cover the
jagged, two-inch teeth. "We'll take that guy today," he said.

The old man behind the counter frowned, but he took it down
from the wall and passed it over carefully. "Thing's dangerous,
you know, Donnie," he said.

Outside, we positioned the handles on our shoulders and
carried it up the reservoir trail, following the rest of the crew.
We were last, but he just whistled and took his time.

The saw blade bounced between us, boing, boing, boing, as
I matched my stride to his, staring at the red Levis tag on his back
pocket. His behind twitched back and forth with each step, and
the black leather sheath of his Buck knife hung from his belt,
swinging left to right, left to right, as his butt muscles moved
under his thin jeans. Why is that faded blue color so sexy? Why
do frayed seams look so right?

Boing, boing, twitch, twitch, swing, swing, *BAM*. I tripped
on a root and stumbled down on one knee. *Thunk*, the saw
handle caught my neck from behind and sent me sprawling into
the dirt. If the blade hadn't been covered, I'd have probably killed
myself on it. I think my brain is in my dick.

After that I watched the trail, keeping in step with him but
trying not to look at his rear end. We hiked up a few hundred
feet and caught up with the rest of the crew at the fallen trees
I'd climbed over one Sunday before.

"Here we go," Donnie said, dropping the crosscut and pulling
his work gloves from under his belt. We gathered around him.

First he used an ax to lop off all the limbs, showing us how to do it from below, close to the trunk, so the blade wouldn't bite into the bark.

"There's an easy way to do everything," he said. "You just have to know the trick." Doing it the right way, he could swing the ax with one hand, very casually, and the branches popped off and fell at his boots.

"You guys scatter those limbs, and then do the same to the next one," he ordered the rest of the crew. Squatting down, he unwired the fire hose and pulled it off the blade. We lifted the saw into place and faced each other across the log.

Wood splintered as we dragged the rough teeth through the bark, chewing a slot into the trunk. "The trick is, you only pull, don't push," he told me. "If you push, the blade will bend and bind up."

He squinted at the sun and adjusted his gloves. "Blister city if you work too hard at it. Just pull when it's your turn, then relax and let me pull it back."

He winked at me. "You remember how to relax and pull on things, don't you?"

"Ain't you just Smokey the Bear," I said, matching his steady gaze. We drew the ugly blade back and forth, first straight across, then putting a second movement into it, dipping down with each stroke to get a better bite on the wood. We got smooth at it, pulling to and down, lifting up and back, pumping our arms, dropping into a steady rhythm.

He called a break so we could catch our breaths and wipe the sweat out of our eyes. We stripped off our shirts, and that beautiful hairy chest of his did it to me again. Back at work, I stared at the swirling pattern, the brown ridge that ran down to his bellybutton, and the sawing became hypnotic. Raw sawdust drifted in the thin mountain air, smelling like turpentine as we cut deeper into the tree. The sun burned on my shoulders.

We grinned, we leaned into it, we began to twist and gasp, *rip, rip, rip, rip*. Sweat drops flew. His muscles bulged up. We turned white with sawdust. I smelled burning wood and my lungs ached, and then it was a sudden thrill when the saw dropped through and the tree shifted in two directions.

"Aw right," the straight boys shouted. We put the blade on its side and leaned over the tree, pulling off our gloves and grabbing hands. We were gasping too much to speak, but we nodded and laughed. As he gripped my hand, I felt him tickle inside my palm with his index finger.

An hour later, we had three big drum-shaped sections rolled out of the trail. He got the other guys started on the next cut and said to me, "Let's go wash off."

The two of us crashed down through some brush to the creek and kneeled on the rocks beside it, splashing icy water on our faces and arms. Donnie leaned into the creek, dipping his head under and blowing bubbles. He drew back and shook his head, slinging water on me from his hair.

"Whoo, that's good. Wash off my back." He stuck his head under again, to his shoulders, and I scooped creek water onto his broad back, rinsing away the sawdust and wiping his skin clean with my hands. His shoulder blades felt muscular, and he had a slot running along both sides of his backbone that I traced with my fingers. I held him down, until he twisted up with another *whoosh.*

"Damn, that's cold!" he exploded, doing his wet dog imitation again.

He pushed my face into the creek. I jerked back and yelped at the cold, but he dunked my head back under the freezing water. It was a shock, and then it felt wonderful. Ice water sloshed onto my back, and then he reached under me and churned the fiery cold up against my chest. I felt two pinpoints of pain as he tweaked my nipples, and I pulled out of the water hooting and grabbing at him. We wrestled onto the rocks, giggling.

Donnie pinned me down. He held my arms back and slid his bare chest over mine, dripping and cold. He covered my mouth with his in a wet, sucking, sexual kiss, humping my leg.

I struggled, laughing and telling him, "Donnie, they can see us," but he paid no mind. He got my wrists around behind my back and wedged his leg up under my crotch. I couldn't help it. I kissed him back. He squeezed me tighter. Through our pants I could feel his hard-on against my leg.

The creek gurgled beside us; the guys up at the trail sawed wood, and Donnie rubbed his chest on mine, whispering against my neck, "Let me fuck you. Come on, let me fuck you."

"Donnie, wait a minute," I said.

"Go under that bush," he said.

I crawled under a limb out of sight from above and Donnie followed, flopping down beside me. His jeans jutted out in front. He popped open the buttons, and I could see the curve of his dick, just part of it, bulging out from his underwear. I slipped a finger into his fly and touched skin inside, curled up tight and hard.

He whimpered, but I didn't pull it out. I knew once I felt it in my hand I wouldn't be able to stop myself, or him either.

I told him, "I can't do it just like that, boom. We don't have any grease or anything. And they're right up there."

"Uhhhh! Please!"

"You'll put me in the hospital. Remember last time?"

He put his arm behind his head and took a deep breath. We didn't say anything for a while.

Donnie sat up. "I gotta take a leak," he said, and we slid out from under the bush.

We peed on a tree together, crossing streams. He was still half turned on, and when I looked down at the broad, flat back of it, with a crooked vein down the middle, I was glad I'd said no. Still, I couldn't take my eyes off it.

He tugged the skin down, shaking off the last drops, and then he turned to me and tapped it against mine. He put his arm around my neck and kissed me very gently, getting his fingers inside my fly. I felt him poking his cock through my zipper, tucking it up underneath Ken's jockstrap, right against my belly. He put his other arm around me and held me tighter.

We kissed, standing there dick to dick in the bushes. Just when I was thinking, "How sweet," there was suddenly an unusual warmth down there, and it was spreading way too fast for cum.

"Gotcha!" Donnie laughed, pulling away from me.

"*Aack*!" I said, looking down. "You pissed on me!" My pants were blotchy wet. He just laughed some more.

"They're all gonna see it," I said, watching the dark stain run down my leg.

"No problem," Donnie said. He grabbed his old hat and scooped cold water at me, splashing me right in the crotch. "All gone."

I pushed him into the creek on his ass.

He sat back in the water grinning up at me, his big schlong still hanging out, and said, "I missed you, Billy."

Climbing back up to the others, he scrambled like a monkey

in his cleated logging boots, and I was right on his tail in mine.

"Let's go, you shitheads," he said. "It's gonna cloud up this afternoon. Let's get it finished before it rains."

One of them asked, "Why don't we just get a chain saw?"

Donnie said, "You guys want to be pioneers so bad. This is what it's like."

Walking back to the trees, I asked him, "Well, why didn't we use power saws?"

He grinned. "I'm not qualified to run one. The guy I bumped off the crew was. The only way I could see your ugly mug was like this."

He made a slow-motion punch at my cheek. "I'm trying to tell you something, sport."

My pants seemed to dry in five minutes in the high mountain air, but the pouch of my jockstrap stayed damp all day. Sometimes if I bent over quickly I could smell his piss on my balls. Every time I did, I thought of his cock stuck up inside my underwear and felt his arms around me again, and my dick thickened inside my jockstrap.

Clearing trail after lunch that afternoon, I was full of energy. I was his puppydog, running ahead of him, circling around him. When he chopped at brush, I got beside him and hacked madly. When he dug at a root, I made the dirt fly.

We bumped each other every few minutes, staggering against one another deliberately. I would heave something with him, and feel his hard arms against mine, hot and sweaty and dirty. We would strain together, then get our legs mixed up and tumble into the branches, skin to skin, twigs scratching and stabbing our backs. He'd slap my butt and we'd climb up through the brush and start all over. We itched and sweat stung in our cuts and it was all glorious. By afternoon break we had opened the path all the way to the reservoir.

Last job was to carry the cut-out sections of the fallen trees down to the woodshed. Donnie balled up his shirt for a pad and told me to hold it beside his neck. Taking a deep breath, he wrestled the biggest chunk up into the air and balanced it on his shoulder. His butt muscles trembled under the weight.

I hefted the next one and tottered down the path behind him.

The slope made us stagger. His back arched, his tendons were taut at his elbows, and his exposed armpits trailed some really pungent fumes. I walked close enough to see his underarm hairs drip sweat.

We dropped the blocks of wood onto the stack inside the shed. The others took a breather, but Donnie charged back up the trail, and I ran after him.

"Stick with me," he said, throwing an arm around my bare shoulders. I hooked my elbow around his neck and we walked in step through the big trees. Far above us, their tops swayed. Clouds had covered the sun and a cold wind dried our sweat, but Donnie's body was my heater.

We lifted the last two sections and got them halfway down the trail before we met the others coming up.

"We've got forty-five minutes to kill until quitting time," he told them without stopping. "You guys go back up to the tools and take an unofficial break. Fart around for twenty minutes, then go wash off the tools." They all cheered.

"Make it last until five, but don't get caught in the rain," he warned.

We dumped the wood inside the shed and stood with our chests heaving in the cold air.

"Tired?" he gasped.

"Not a bit," I wheezed.

When our breathing slowed, he got in front of me, looking directly into my eyes. "I was kinda dense last week, huh? Going camping with Stan. I didn't mean it to hurt you. I missed you like hell when you took off with Steve. I thought about it a lot on the hike."

He scuffed mud off his boot. "It wasn't much fun without you. Stan spent the whole time up on the peak with his topo maps. He's teaching himself to read them. I think he's memorizing the whole damn district. Funny guy. I pointed out some stuff, but he doesn't want any help. So, I just messed around down by a spring most of the weekend. That's where I found your geode."

He moved over beside me and propped his behind on the stack of firewood. "And, um, about the water sports," he began.

I laughed. "Water sports?"

"Yeah," he nodded. "You know, when I pissed on you this morning. I don't know what gets into me sometimes. I just get off on playing around with my piss. Like the other night when

I was making it with Stan, in the toilets? That was mostly his idea. He told me about this fantasy he's always had, about getting hosed down and pushed around and all that. Well, hell, you know me." He shrugged. "I'll do about anything that involves drinking beer and fucking."

He laughed and tugged at his pants. Looking into my eyes again, he said, "But, I don't want to lose you over something like that. If it turns you off, we don't have to do it. I mean, I think it's kinda fun, but it's not real necessary."

Donnie's body radiated heat. A warm current of air drifted from his bare chest, carrying odors from under his arms, mixing with my own sweaty smell. I breathed in and thought I still could catch a trace of the scent he'd left in my underwear. It all made me so horny I twitched. "Actually," I said, "it turns me on, in a way. I guess I like anything you do."

He squinted at me. "What do you see in me, anyway? I'm nothing to look at, I know that. I can't hardly talk. I've always got dirt under my fingernails. Why'd you pick me?"

"I dunno," I said. Leaning toward him, I put my hand on his stomach and felt his body. I ruffled his chest hairs the wrong way, making them stand out, twirling strands together. "All I know is, whenever you're around, you're all I can think about. What do you see in me?"

Donnie stared into my eyes, then took my hand in his and moved my fingers down to his jeans. His right leg had a hard rod down it. He grinned at me.

I said, "You ought to have antlers on your belt buckle, instead of a horse."

He grinned. "Wanna pet my pony? He'll stand up and whinny for you."

Wind flowed through the slat walls, smelling of rain. Suddenly, fat drops pelted the roof. I asked him, "How did you know about that rain?"

"Cirrus clouds last night at sunset. Weather always changes a day later."

"Ah," I said, nodding wisely.

He laughed, ducking his head. "Shit, I'm trying too hard to impress you. They post a weather bulletin in the office every morning."

Outside, our crew ran past the shed and around the barn,

holding their tools and shirts over their heads against the rain.

Donnie moved closer. As the rain pattered on the shingles above us, we unfastened each other's pants. I pulled his dick out, surprised again at the stiff, hard curve of it in my hand.

He rubbed inside my zipper fly. "I like the jockstrap," he said, slowly working the head of my cock out from the pouch.

"There's a hundred ways to do it," he said, stretching the skin up and down. "I'll do it your way, my way, any way you want. I don't care. But I want to fuck with you, man."

He stepped in front of me. "Look at you. Look how you're filling out," he said, running his hands over my bare sides.

I looked down at my scrawny body. "Am I really?"

He moved between my legs and held his palms to my chest. "You don't know how sexy you are, do you? So smooth, such nice soft skin. I love to touch you. When I'm jacking off at night now, it's you I think about while I'm creaming. See, I've got a fantasy, too. You're it, big guy."

He bent down and kissed my nipples, sucking at each one, catching the tips with his teeth, making them stand up hard and erect like tiny penises. Then he moved lower, down to the real thing, and enveloped me in his mouth. I gripped his shoulders and stiffened against the woodpile, thrusting myself deep into his throat.

After a minute he raised his face to mine, and I just had to grab his neck and kiss that big bushy mustache. He squeezed our dicks together in his hands, slowly masturbating us both at once.

I reached behind him, slipping my hands under his jeans, inside his warm underwear, feeling the roundness of his butt. I plucked at the tufts of kinky hair that sprouted from the center. He kissed me harder. I pulled him closer, pointing one finger up between his ass cheeks.

"Oh, yeah," he breathed into my ear. "Right there."

Pushing up, I touched the hairless hole in his backside. He groaned and kissed my neck. I worked my finger into his ass.

"Wanna fuck me?" he whispered. "I'd really like that." He tightened his butt around my fingertip.

I blurted out, "Me, fuck you? I thought it would be the other way around."

But he nodded yes, and I nodded back.

"Wait," he said. "I'll go get the grease from the car." He

hurried out into the rain.

Lightning flashed in the distance. My heart thumped at the thought of getting into Donnie's butt.

He ducked back into the shed, dripping rainwater off the fur on his bare chest. "Heh, heh," he chuckled, scooping into the Vaseline jar with his index finger. He twisted his fist around my hard-on, slowly smearing it with warm goo, and then he took my fingers in a sexy, greasy handshake. Turning his back to me, he put his hands on the woodpile and spread his legs.

I lowered his jeans and his shorts, exposing his white behind. Hair down there gets me so turned on, and the slot of his butt was dark with the stuff. I poked my finger between the cheeks, probing. When I found the hole and put some grease on it, my hard-on lifted in front of me.

I gave Donnie the old finger, shot him a bird straight up his backside. "MUH!" he grunted. I twisted my finger inside him. He looked over his shoulder. "Stick your dick in it, buddy," he whispered, moving his hips, pulling on my finger with his butthole. "Come on, give me something big to think about."

My chest vibrated with excitement. He reached back and aimed it for me. The head of my cock pushed against coarse hair. He moved it down an inch, and then suddenly I went up into the spreading, satin softness inside his ass.

His body jerked. "Gah! Damn!" he choked out, going up onto his tiptoes.

Then, "Mh-h-h," he lowered himself onto me. "That's it," he said. "Right there. MMH! Yeah, let me feel it."

Holding his hips, I prodded my dick deep into the sticky, hot cave of Donnie's butt, and my balls seemed to get huge with cum as I slipped all the way into him.

Lightning flashed outside, glaring through the wide slots in the shed wall. *BLAM!* I saw the white shaft of my cock, drawn halfway out of him, plastered with clinging butthairs. It was frozen in my eyes, enormous, veins bulging, and, *damn*, it was beautiful. Next flash, my belly was pressed against his cheeks, with my dick solidly plugged into his guts.

Thunder smashed through us. He raised one leg. He reached back and grabbed my butt, pulling me closer. "All the way," he panted, "put it all the way up my ass." I shoved harder. He dropped his head and moaned softly, "Oh-h-h, fuck, man, you touch bottom. Oh-h-h, fuck, that's good. Big old dick, yeah, right up my fuckin' asshole, oh-h-h, fuck, you're good, you big stud, fuck me."

When I heard that dirty talk I became an animal, and so did he. Donnie hooked a leg around behind mine. He rotated his ass against my stomach, squeezing on me, then letting me dip back in, then clamping my cock tight between the muscles of his butt. I never knew a man could get so turned on by getting screwed, squirming his rear end around in my hands, and I jammed it into him as hard as I could.

"Oh shit, oh shit, oh shit," he gasped into the rumbling dark air, and if he had any up there inside him, I sure as hell must have been touching it.

The rain roared, blowing a rush of cold drops through the cracks in the shed, sprinkling the skin on my back. I hugged his body to me, reaching around in front to rub his furry belly. Feeling lower, I touched a goddam rhinoceros horn stabbing up between his legs, and he wasn't even jerking on it. I hunched over his broad shoulders, pumping inches into him that made his head snap back, and we both growled and cursed in the storm.

God, how I love fucking a guy! Donnie's deep voice kept rising and falling as I surged in and out of him from behind, "Uhh, UHH, uhh, UHH, uhh, UHH!" His back glistened with sweat. He hooked his elbow behind my neck, twisting around to look at me.

His eyelids were down to slits. Each time I poked up into his ass it pushed a moan of ecstasy out of his throat. He rolled his head back against the stacked wood, lifting one arm straight up, exposing the sweaty tangle of hairs underneath. I took a long sniff, and then buried my face in Donnie's armpit.

Underarm perspiration must have something in it straight from the testicles. He was hot and wet under there, musky, sour, slightly salty, all male. I was slurping up the sweat of a man getting fucked, and it turned my own cock to steel. I sucked at his armpit, licking the hairs, nuzzling my lips in the hollow between the muscles, steadily dicking the grip of his greasy butt, until my cum burned inside me and I couldn't hold it back.

I tightened my arms around him and let myself go.

It was wonderful, easily the best fuck I'd ever had, which was all of three by then. Straining up against his hard body, I hugged his chest, snorted his sweat, caught hairs in my teeth, and shot my wad into his guts, pumping burst after burst of sweet liquid pleasure up his asshole. I groaned into his armpit as my cum streamed out of me, coursing through my cock, shooting way, way up inside him, right where it seemed I'd wanted to put it all my life, right up my best buddy's butt.

We slumped against the woodpile, laughing and gasping for air. Donnie slipped loose and turned around. His dick stuck straight up to his belly button. I put one arm around his slick back and pulled him closer. We touched foreheads, looking down our chests as he started jerking himself off between us.

"I'm real close," he whispered. He caught his breath. His hand stopped. A blob of white oozed from his fist. I reached between his legs and tickled his big, soft nuts for him. He moaned, "Oh, fuck, yeah man," and wet my arm. I tugged at him. More cum splashed up onto my belly. I twisted his balls around, the way I know he likes it, and another hot line squirted all the way to my chest. He bucked in my hands, hitting me with shot after shot, until his cream trickled down through my pubic hair and dripped along the inside of my leg.

He hugged me, kissing me hard on the mouth, squirming his hairy body against mine, smearing his cum between us. We staggered together, pants and belts and underwear down around our ankles, doing the dirty dance only two guys can do, chests heaving, laughing at our gloppy mess.

All I could think was, he knows! He understands! And he wants to do it with me!

When we pulled apart, the smell of cum and sweat mixed with the sharp odor of shit.

"Wups," he said. "Think I browned you out some, sport."

Looking down, I could see dark streaks on my dick.

Donnie reached into the woodpile and pulled out the Jockey shorts I had tucked away there the week before. He cleaned me off very carefully, saying "Sorry about that," as he tugged at my sagging little sausage. He handled it like his own, lifting it to dab underneath and all around the hairy base. He even milked out the last drops of cum for me and wiped them off.

Then he swiped at his ass a few times and tossed the shorts back onto the woodpile. "The next guy in here's gonna get a big charge out of sniffing on those," he chuckled.

"You go ahead," a voice called out. "I'll meet you at the office.

I want to close that shed before the wood gets wet."

We locked eyes, then jerked at our pants, getting them up to our knees and over our dicks just as a yellow slicker appeared in the doorway, with Mr. Peterson's rather startled-looking face peering out.

"Oh, hello," he said. His eyes darted up and down our naked, wet stomachs, as Donnie finished buttoning his jeans and slowly buckled his belt.

"Oh," Peterson repeated. He frowned. "Oh!" He cleared his throat. "Aren't you men a little old for pee-pee games?"

Donnie reached for his shirt. "Don't worry about it," he growled. White drips of cum were still showing on his hairy belly as he fastened the snaps without looking up.

Donnie gave him the finger as the yellow slicker disappeared around the barn. "Fuck the old fart," he said. "Don't worry, he's not such a big honcho around here. And we're not the only ones they'll catch fooling around. Just because his balls dried up ten years ago don't mean ours have to."

When we undressed for the showers I saw we both had dried cum matted in our pubic hairs. Nobody seemed to notice, but then when I was drying off I saw my neck in the mirror, and there was a big red hickey on it. I was just waiting for somebody to rag me about it. I decided to say it was from the weekend if anybody got on my case.

Nobody did, but I put my towel around my neck instead of around my waist for the walk back to the cabin. For a minute there I went buck-ass naked in front of the whole camp. Loping along beside Donnie made me feel like such a man.

Standing beside his locker, I watched him search for a clean teeshirt. He pulled each one from the pile, held it to his nose, and tossed it aside.

"Don't you ever use deodorant?" I asked.

He made a face. "That stuff works for a while, but then when it wears off it really makes me stink. Fuck it," he drawled, raising one elbow straight up and sniffing himself. "I like the way I smell." He turned his armpit to my face. "Don't you?"

The fine brown hairs radiated from his underarm, glowing in the afternoon light. I took a deep whiff and my knees felt weak.

Donnie pulled his teeshirt over his head and down his sides. Giving me a wink, he tugged at his dick and went outside.

At my locker I put on a shirt with a high collar that barely hid my hickey. On the way out I dropped my roll-on deodorant into the trash can.

He was waiting outside. Nodding toward the Olds, he said, "I'm dying. I have to get something to eat before dinner."

I followed him to the car. He lifted the trunk lid and rummaged for a can-opener. Along with the cold beer, he had half a case of tuna back there. He opened a can and wolfed it down straight, with a fork that he first wiped clean on his pants.

"I can go forever on tuna and beer," he mumbled.

I opened a can for myself, and we took turns with the fork.

Next to the box of tuna was the biggest Vaseline jar I'd ever seen. I laughed and pointed at it. He grinned. "Some things you never want to run out of."

The crowd was gathering for dinner and I was nervous. As we walked across the lawn, I turned up my shirt collar so Donnie's bite mark didn't show. Couldn't they smell it on us, the sex and the shit and all? Couldn't they tell what we'd been doing? But they had saved his usual good spot on the steps of the mess hall that night, and they made room for me, too. The other first-time kids all stood as we waited for the bell.

When the door opened, Stanley followed and sat with us. Donnie tried polite conversation. "You guys should talk about books, sometime. Stanley is reading all of the one hundred greatest books, to educate himself. Me, I never get any heavier than Isaac Asimov."

Stanley bit. "Don't say that. He's good. Science fiction is some of the most intelligent stuff being written."

"Well," Donnie said, "I like Westerns, but they don't make them as good as they used to. What do you read, Bill?"

I clenched my teeth. "Why, gosh, Donnie," I chirped, "I read dirty books. Anything that's been banned, I read it."

Our conversation died.

The thunderstorms returned that night. Steve and Donnie played cards at the table while Stanley and I each got in bed with a paperback. It was cozy, hearing the downpour outside our little home. At least nobody played a radio all night, the way they did next door. We had a good cabin. I decided to make peace and asked the creep what he was reading.

"Chaucer," he answered, not looking up.

"Oh, yeah? *Canterbury Tales*?"

"What else did he write?"

"How is it?"

"Boring." He turned a page. "But anything's better than *Beowulf*."

I held up my *Tropic of Cancer*. "What do you think of Henry Miller?"

He took a breath. "Overrated."

"It's a modern classic. It deals with things that people never even dreamed about in the old days."

He dropped his book and looked at me. "The only thing that keeps you reading Miller is to see how smutty he'll actually get. It's his only trick. I don't care about his characters."

"Well," I said, "he writes for adults. You wouldn't understand. Anyway, don't you like a little smut when you read?" I smiled at him. "You seem to like it in real life."

Stanley smiled back, blinking. "Hey, Bill. Eat shit and die." He raised his Chaucer.

It was cool that night, and I slept deeply until the door banged open and the overhead light glared in my eyes. Somebody was pounding on the wall.

"Okay, you guys, everybody up!" a man shouted.

"Let go of your cocks and grab your socks, we got some fires to fight. Everybody, now, up up up!"

"Aw, fuck," Steve moaned.

Donnie said, "Hot damn! Overtime pay!" and jumped down on top of me as I hit the floor in confusion.

15

"Let's go, let's go, let's go!" the man yelled. He moved to the next cabin and started banging on their door.

We scrambled to our lockers and pulled on whatever clothes we grabbed first. I couldn't think. Fires weren't supposed to happen until the end of summer. I put on my watch—damn, four AM—took it off, couldn't wear that, reached for my wallet, put it back, reached for it again, took out a five-dollar bill and stuck it in my shirt pocket. What else would I need? My coat, my coat.

As I rubbed my eyes and wondered what to do next, Mr. Peterson walked in carrying a clipboard, with Preston right behind him. The two of them talked to Donnie about leading a fire crew. I heard, "Grizzly Creek, just a smoke. . . Cedar Ridge is the big one. . . dozers cutting a road up to it right now. . . calling Missoula for retardant drops as soon as it gets light. . . want us out there ASAP. . . ."

Donnie said, "I was just up the Grizzly Creek trail this weekend."

"No, we need you at Cedar Ridge. Grizzly's just one smoke."

Stanley said, "I've been up to Grizzly Creek twice. I can find it."

"Okay, good," Mr. Peterson said. "I want you to take care of a spot fire up there. Take Steve with you. You know the way, so you be crew leader."

"Him?" Preston said, wide-eyed. "You're making him a crew leader?" He looked at Stanley. "You gotta be shitting me."

Mr. Peterson hesitated. He looked at his clipboard. "It's only a snag that took a lightning hit. The rain has probably put it out by now anyway."

He eyed Stanley. "You just have to go and check it, make sure it's not smoldering. Steve knows what to do."

Preston looked up at the ceiling in disgust. I saw his mouth form the word "faggot."

Donnie interrupted. "I'll need Steve with me if I've got a big crew. Bill can go with Stanley. I've trained them both."

I could have killed him.

Mr. Peterson looked from Donnie to me to Stanley. "I'll bet you've trained them," he said under his breath with a smirk.

Writing on his clipboard, he nodded at Stanley and then at me. "Okay, you two are Fire Crew Three. You men come with me. Powers, you and Preston pick a crew of ten and meet me at the office. Let's go!"

Going out, I glared at Donnie over my shoulder, and he just smiled and waved goodby. I shot him a bird behind my back and followed Stanley to the office.

It was frantic inside. A woman's voice droned from a shortwave radio, "Tower Four has a definite strike at 278 degrees, flickering." Static crackled and drowned her out. Then her voice came back in, "Tower Two reports another flare-up at Cedar Ridge." One man copied the coordinates of the sightings. Others huddled over maps using clear plastic compasses, drawing red lines from lookout towers. Wherever the lines from two lookouts crossed, there was a fire.

"Grizzly Creek," Mr. Peterson said, and the guy at the desk shuffled through the maps and handed one to Stanley. He took it and we ran to the barn for our firepacks.

Steve and Donnie were pulling the orange backpacks from shelves and passing them out to their crew. Stanley and I pushed through the mob. Donnie shoved a pack at me, shouting, "You won't make it up there and back in one day, so I gave you guys some paper sleeping bags. They're pretty shitty but they're better than nothing, and they're light."

We went outside to wait for our pickup. Steady drizzle fell out of the darkness, so we put on our ponchos over the firepacks and leaned against the barn for balance. I didn't help him, and he didn't help me. We didn't speak on the bumpy ride to the trailhead.

They dropped us off at a fence. The truck pulled away and its lights faded around the next bend.

Stanley and I were alone in the wet, black woods.

He knelt down and unfolded the map, muttering, "Let's cooperate, okay? Shine your light for me." I held my flashlight over the map and he described the trail ahead. His voice trembled, and his hands shook so much he could barely point.

At first, in the dark, I had to follow his light. We tromped along in step through the mist. As the gray dawn seeped down through the trees, I let him get farther ahead. I resented having to follow him. Not only that, he'd gotten the radio, damn it.

When I saw him go off the trail as we cut through a stand of ponderosa pines, I let him disappear, hoping he would get lost. But soon the path I took went under a branch only a few feet above the ground and I realized I was following a game trail.

Doubling back, I searched in the pines for a glimpse of his light. It all looked the same in the fog, every direction a dim blur. All sounds were muffled, as though we were packed in cotton.

A snicker came from up above me. "Boo," he said, and switched on his flashlight. He was in some rocks. I scrabbled up them, but he turned off his light and was gone when I found the trail. I ran after the swish of his poncho against the branches, and he let a big wet one smack my face.

"Bastard," I said, wiping my eyes and following his giggle. "Stop being so damn silly," I told him.

"What's wrong with silly?"

With our ponchos over our backpacks, we looked like movie monsters, green humpbacked creatures, lumbering through the dripping trees. The rocky hillside tilted and looked out of focus in the fuzzy whiteness.

Stanley kept getting ahead of me, almost running on the level stretches. I would come up on him resting beside the path with his pack propped on a rock or a tree stump, and as soon as I stopped to rest, he would take off.

The third time he left me panting, I told him, "I might as well be hiking by myself if you keep charging ahead like that." He vanished around the bend.

Next he was sitting by a creek. I went past him and blocked the trail. "Break time," I puffed, dropping my behind on a log.

"Not yet. I'll call the breaks."

"Come on, Stanley, what are you trying to prove?"

"I'm only doing the job they sent us to do. Can't you keep up?"

"I can keep up. But that snag is dead out by now, in all this rain. They said it hadn't even flickered for an hour before we left. What's the rush?"

He shook his head inside his poncho hood. "It could be smoldering. Those old trees are all hollow inside. They can have

coals in them for days, and as soon as the wood on the outside
dries out, they light up again. That's why we have to check it
out."

"I know all that. But right now it's raining. We don't have
to kill ourselves to get there."

He stood up as tall as he could and glared at me. "Look, Bill,
I'm not going to have you go back and tell them I couldn't handle
this. We've got to get all the way to the top, and then down the
other side, and then out on a spur ridge. It's gonna take all day,
maybe until dark. I am going to find that goddam tree today.
We have to keep going." He struggled into his firepack and
pushed by me.

All morning it rained. The forest had been dry for weeks, so
dry that the sudden thundershowers couldn't soak into the soil.
The runoff had left sheets of mud on the bare slopes. By noon
we were above the last trees, slogging through muck. We took
a short break for lunch, then pushed on for the top.

My legs ached, but I wasn't going to give him the satisfaction
of hearing me complain. I was gasping in the thin air, following
him doggedly with my head down, when suddenly the trail
flattened out and Stanley stopped. I looked around, into white
mist everywhere. It was downhill in every direction. There was
no more mountain left to climb.

His eyes were fierce. "It's right down there, somewhere," he
said between gasps. Below us, the other side of the mountain
was exactly as gray and foggy as the side we had climbed.

"You sure you can find it in this weather?"

"I'm sure. I can remember everything down there from
Sunday."

"You went down there?"

"Well, no. But I studied it from up here. I know right where
to go."

It took him three false starts to find the trail. I was annoyed.
"You're gonna fuck up," I told him.

That afternoon I could tell he was starting to tire out. With
my long legs, I was faster going downhill, and I poked at his
backpack. "Man coming through," I said, elbowing past him. I
stepped across a muddy spring on rocks I knew his legs wouldn't
reach. When he tried to jump it, his black loafers scooted from

under him and he sat down hard in the water.

"Damn you," he wailed. "Now my pants are wet."

I didn't offer my hand. "You didn't mind getting wet in the head last week with Donnie," I sneered at him. "Looked like you enjoyed it. Of course, that was warmer water than this is."

"Pervert!" he snapped, sloshing out of the creek.

"Me?" I shoved his backpack. "You're the piss-drinker. You're the disgusting one."

He whirled and swung at me but missed, and I flipped a branch full of water into his face.

He screamed, "Well, you watched, didn't you? Pervert! I bet you jacked off, didn't you? You weren't disgusted—you loved it! You haven't got the balls to do what Donnie really wants to do, so you have to sneak around and watch me. Pervert! Peeping Tom!"

He stomped off, and after a moment I followed, but not closely.

As we slogged downhill late that afternoon the rain came back, changing quickly from a light sprinkle to drops and then to pelting splashes on our ponchos. My boots were beginning to leak.

"This is the spur ridge," Stanley announced. He left the trail and stepped carefully out onto a ridge that dropped steeply into fog on both sides.

I squished after him. There was no trail and the ridge grew narrower as we walked down it. It was just a wedge of rock a few feet wide, and the sides of it were sheer slopes of stone, left and right. My boot slipped on a wet patch of granite. I grabbed his backpack.

"Stanley, this is crazy," I said, holding my arms out to balance myself. We had to put one foot directly in front of the other. An outcropping of rock loomed up ahead through the fog. It was too steep to climb over, and there was no way to get around it.

"Swell," I said, backing up to it to lean my pack against it to rest. "Now what?"

Stanley stared at his map. "This is it," he said quietly.

"This is what?"

"The place on the map."

"Well, where's the fire?"

"I don't know where the damn fire is." He folded the wet map.

"I was told to get us to this spot, and we're here."

"Oh, bullshit. This isn't right. There aren't even any trees here. You fucked up."

His face turned red and his eyes bulged out. "I did not fuck up," he yelled. "That rock is on the map. The X is at the rock. Do you think I'm stupid? Do you think I can't read a map?"

"I think you're a goddam little pansy who shouldn't be out in the woods. They should have put me in charge. Give me the map."

"No!" he yelled, jerking the map back. I pulled at it. He began to whine, shaking. The noise in his throat rose to a squeal. This time when he swung his fist, it connected. My head popped to one side. I smacked his lip. He grabbed my arm and we toppled to the ground, tugging the map back and forth. The paper tore in half and I fell back. The weight of my backpack rolled me over. I felt myself sliding over the edge but I couldn't get a grip on anything but Stanley's arm.

We grabbed each other and screamed as we dropped off into the bottomless mist.

The flat sheet of granite was polished and wet. My heart went into my throat as we slid down the rock. We bounced twice on our bottoms, tumbled upside down, and crashed into some brush, thrashing around inside our plastic ponchos until we rolled to a stop. I couldn't see anything.

Stanley reached inside my hood and grabbed my hair.

"Damn you, damn you, damn you!" he hollered. "You think just because you're so big you're such a man. You're not, you're just a sissy, just like me, only you're a big sissy. Faggot! I know what you and Donnie do out in his car."

"Get off of me, dammit!" I pushed him away. "I never said I was straight."

"But you let everybody think you are, you phony." Stanley felt his mouth, and drew away a spot of blood. "You cut my lip, you big fruit."

"What do you know about me and Donnie? He doesn't tell shit like that."

Stanley made a mocking twist in his lips. "I've watched you from behind the barn. You two are so ga-ga for each other you don't see anything else. How do you like that?"

"Pervert."

He smiled. "Bet your ass I am. I've done stuff you've never dreamed about. Or maybe that's all you do. You just dream about it."

We got to our feet, holding onto roots and shrubs on the steep slope. Our ponchos were muddy and our pants were wet on our seats. The only way was down so I sat on the wet stone, lowering myself toward the creek below. Stanley slid after me.

"Here, you're bleeding, too," he said, pulling out a handkerchief and dipping it in the creek.

He dabbed at my mouth and I dabbed at his. He didn't have any beard at all. His upper lip had only a thin line of soft baby hairs.

"Some crew leader," I sneered.

"Some crew," he shot back. He paused and sniffed.

"Don't cry," I told him.

"No," he said. "I'm not crying. I smell smoke." He took a sudden breath, staring over my shoulder. His eyes went huge.

"Jesus!" he gasped.

I spun around.

The fog over us swirled, then parted. We both stared up to the next ridge. "Oh-h-h, shit," I breathed out.

Looming at the top of the ridge was a great, shadowy stub of a tree trunk, a giant snag, long dead, standing alone on the rocks. It towered over us, almost lost in the swirling rain clouds. We heard a crackle. A burst of sparks shot upward from the broken-off top.

It was huge. Alive and whole, it would have been a hundred feet tall. The upper branches had been gone for years, and all its bark had peeled away, leaving a bare silver trunk to dry in the sun. Now it was burning like a torch.

We struggled up to its base. The gnarly roots had a cavity of crumbling dirt under them. Stanley shuffled in the dead leaves to find a dry one and held it under the hole. When he let go, the leaf was sucked up inside.

"It's drawing like a chimney," he whispered.

We took off our packs. I tapped it with my pulaski, getting a hollow thunk. I gave it a hard whack. More sparkles of fire popped out at the top, but the snag didn't move.

"The coals must be fifteen feet up inside it," I said.

"We have to either get up to the fire or bring the fire down here," Stanley said.

I scratched my neck. "I dunno. How high can you piss?" I grinned.

He smiled for the first time all day and glanced at me quickly. "This is no time to get romantic," he muttered.

He pushed at the tree. It swayed, and he pushed harder. The snag creaked and moved, but not much. We both shoved, but it was too big.

Thunder rumbled, and a spray of big raindrops splattered our faces.

"Fuck it," he said. "I'm going to call camp on the radio and ask them what to do. It's their stupid tree."

"Okay, let's get off this hill in case the lightning comes back." I flipped up the back of his poncho and helped him get his firepack under it, and he did mine. We stepped carefully going back down to the creek. The wind gusted. A sheet of rain swept over us.

He used his deepest voice on the radio, "Uh, headquarters, I mean, uh, Camp North Fork, uh, this is—"

"Fire Crew Three," I prompted.

"Fire Crew Three," he repeated, blinking in seriousness, with rain dripping off his nose as he reported what we had found.

"Okay, Three," I made out through the static. "You guys hunker down for a few hours. When the storm passes, we'll see if we can get a chopper to run by there with some borate to dump on it. Get off the ridge for now. Did you find a motel for the night yet?"

"Yeah, sure," Stanley said. "A Holiday Inn, with a Burger King next to it."

We took off our packs again beside the creek, rummaging in them for food. Stanley said, "Army rations. Shit. Spam! Are they kidding? Look at this. Pork and beans. Cheese and crackers. God, what I'd give for a burger."

I felt some small, flat cans in my pack and pulled them out. They were Donnie's cans of tuna.

"Hey," Stanley said. "That's more like it."

While he opened it with a tiny folding can opener, I dug out the third object. It was Donnie's jar of Vaseline.

Stanley had the tuna can half open, wiggling the gadget around the rim, when a blast of wind hit us. We dropped everything and cowered together under the gusty sheets of rain and wind.

A crack like a gunshot went off over our heads. Creaking wood groaned above us.

I looked up. The giant snag leaned out slowly, hanging in space over us. CRACK! It broke loose from its roots and toppled quickly toward the creek where we were sitting.

Still clinging together, we scrambled to our feet and ran for the creek. Stanley made a flying leap for the other side but fell short and landed in the water. His shoe skidded on a rock, and Stanley went down. I grabbed his arm and pushed him up the far side as the snag crashed to the rocky slope behind us.

I looked back over my shoulder. The burning log hesitated, then rumbled downhill, pointed at my back.

I jumped, but my cuff caught on a branch. I fell back into the water.

I jumped again. "Augh!" I screamed. "I'm caught!" I looked over my shoulder again.

The tree was now a spear sliding fast downhill, bouncing and grinding on the rocky slope, throwing splinters and sparks and gravel as it stabbed through bushes toward me. I whimpered and jerked my leg, but my cuff was hooked on a branch. I couldn't straighten my leg.

I felt a hand on my ankle. Stanley tore at my pants cuff and ripped it loose. The little guy put his tiny shoulder to my butt and heaved up hard.

I shot up the bank. Clawing at the rocks, I grabbed a root with one hand and twisted around. I reached toward him. The log rumbled down and bounced into the air right over his back.

He grabbed my hand. I closed my eyes and jerked up with all my strength.

SMASH! The snag buried its pointed nose into the creek just below his feet as his little body sailed up into my arms. The monster log exploded into chunks of flaming wood that went spinning off into the creek.

We ducked our heads and clutched each other on the bank as splinters of wood and red embers showered down on us.

The thick base of the log balanced upright for a moment, then ponderously toppled into the creek, grinding into the gravel and spouting steam. It rolled to a stop. Hissing at us, the hollow core shot up a last tongue of yellow flames, then died at our feet.

I looked at Stanley's dripping, wide-eyed face.

"You saved my life," we said together.

16

Our pants were soaked. When the rain let up we were able to take off our ponchos, but then the wind was cold. We poked at the big pieces of the snag, shivering, and gathered some that still had glowing coals in them.

Stanley said, "Weren't there some tea bags in those rations?"

I rummaged through my pack while Stanley piled some splintered wood together and blew on the coals.

First we opened the tuna, finished it, washed out the can, and then he held it by the lid to boil water for the tea. We both raised our pinkies as we passed the hot, fishy-smelling stuff back and forth. There was powdered soup, and he even heated the spam, and then the pork and beans.

"You're a good Boy Scout," I told him.

"Shit. The Boy Scouts wouldn't have me. I was the class faggot, remember? We're not allowed in. I only went camping once in my life, and that was with a guy whose father was half Indian. He was a half-breed and he stuttered, too, so he had nothing to lose by being seen with me."

He grimaced. "We had something in common. We both had our hands slammed in our locker doors by the bullies. We had lockers next to each other, so they could get us both at once, very economical. We also both had to go outside to pee. If we went into the boys' room, they'd jump us. So we peed behind the bushes. One time a teacher saw us, and then we were suspended for masturbation. He pretended he was retarded, but he wasn't. It was just easier than fighting."

Stanley made a fake smile. "Isn't high school fun? Who are you taking to the prom?"

I shook my head. "Whew! Stanley, slow down. I think maybe I liked it better when you weren't speaking to me." We ate the beans.

He thought about his words. "I'm only trying to tell you, you don't have any idea what it's like to be me. You can pass for straight. People take one look at the way I walk, and then never give me a chance. It's not fair."

"Well, I know better now. You sure had a lot of balls, to help me out of the creek. I give you credit."

"Oh, bullshit. You've hated me ever since you met me. You're no different from the rest of them, only you're more polite about it. You all look at me like I'm a freak."

I couldn't meet his eyes. It was true.

He took a deep breath, letting it out slowly. "I know, I am a freak. Look at how skinny I am. Look at my legs. I'm almost eighteen, and I haven't got any hair anywhere. I feel like a chihuahua with a St. Bernard's dick."

"Almost 18? How did you get this job if you're not 18?"

"I showed them fake ID when I applied at the district office. Don't tell on me, okay? Anyway, I'll be eighteen this Friday."

"Where'd you get the ID?"

"From a truck driver who picked me up when I ran away from home. I had a fight with my dad."

"Yeah," I said. "I heard. What about?"

"I kicked my old man in the balls. He was trying to kill me. And my mom is having me excommunicated. Here, eat this."

The light was fading as we finished the food. "We'll have to make camp for the night before it gets dark," Stanley said.

There was a flat shelf of ground above the creek just in front of a hollow in the rock wall. "Okay, this is it," Stanley said. "Camp Grizzly Creek. Gather up as much of that dry wood as you can."

"Yes sir, boss," I said.

We gathered all the splintered pieces of the smashed snag and made a pile beside the rock. "If we make a new fire here," Stanley said, "and sleep between the fire and this rock, I think we'll be warm enough. If the rain comes back, we'll have to use the ponchos for tents."

We got the fire going and sat in the shallow cave, looking out over the creek. The paper sleeping bags Donnie had given me were so thin they seemed useless except as mats to sit on. My little runaway camper sat with his arms around his knees, staring at the fire.

"And I thought I had problems," I told him. "I mean, my folks are pretty regular people. My mom sort of fusses over me, and my dad and I don't talk much, but, well, I've never doubted that they loved me. They don't understand me, but they love me."

He looked sad. "Lucky you."

"Come on, now. Hasn't there ever been anything good in your life?"

Stanley stared into the fire, tracing the edges of his lips with two fingertips. "The library," he decided, with a faint smile. "The only place I'm really happy is in a library. I feel safe there, for one thing. And I have friends in my books. They're more interesting than real people. And, of course, some of the best bathrooms are in libraries. You can lock yourself in a toilet and, well, relax. I had my first good sex there."

"Ha! You were corrupted by the public library system, is that it?" We grinned at each other.

"Don't be dumb," he said. "Nobody corrupted me. I was always a pervert. It's my natural state. You know, it really is. I feel perfectly normal, doing what I do."

"Until you get busted by the vice squad," I said, poking the embers with a branch and sending red sparks up into the growing darkness.

He shrugged. "I dunno why people worry about it so much. It seems to me it's the rest of the world that's perverted. I have such a good time in toilets. I don't understand why everybody doesn't do it. It's, like, a fantasy world. I go in, and when I leave, hours have passed. It's a hobby. I'm not hurting anybody. I'm just giving blowjobs."

"Did you ever get caught?"

"Once I got in trouble in the showers in Phys Ed class. They sent me to my counsellor. Guess who the boys' counsellor was? The coach, of course. 'Hi coach, I'm a fag.' The whole conversation was a disaster.

"At least I got out of P. E. I told him they were torturing me in the showers, and he said I had to tough it out, and I told him that me being in the boys' showers was like him having to take showers with the girls. He got all flustered and ordered me to leave, but after that I had study hall instead of gym."

He turned his dark eyes to me, sad eyes. For a kid who was about to turn 18, his eyes looked old. "Why does everybody hate me, Bill? Why do they torture me?"

"People don't hate you," I said, trying to sound convincing. "They just—make fun of you. Sometimes, I don't know, guys have a way of kidding you to show they like you. Steve does that. I've figured him out. When he starts giving you a lot of shit, it's just his way of carrying on a conversation. It means he's decided you're OK."

"Oh, bull fucking shit. I feel like a walking dart board when he's around. Don't tell me he doesn't hate me. Donnie's the only one in the whole camp who's treated me nice, and he did right from the very start. He's about the only guy I've ever met in my whole life who doesn't give me any attitude. That's why I've been, you know, good to him."

He sighed. "He's all yours, I guess you know that by now. We didn't do anything when we were up here together. Smelly cowboys aren't my type, anyway.

"But Steve can't stand me. Macho pig. I hate him. That story he told was revolting, about you and him and that girl. He thinks he's so hot for women, but he talks about them like they're dirt. And you're no better, Bill. You're gay, and you're a bigot."

I straightened up. "I'm not either. Just because I'm from the South. Hey, I have black friends."

"Yeah, sure. Mom ever have them over for dinner?"

"Well—no."

He sneered. "Bet you're a Baptist. Did you meet all those black friends at the church social? Hmmm?"

Again, I couldn't answer him.

"TCH!" he spit out. "Phony. Bigot."

"I'm not. And I never joined any church."

"Well, that's something. But listen to the way you talk about girls sometime. 'We fucked her good.' Oh, please."

"Give me a break. I never had a chance to be a star like that before."

Stanley stood up suddenly and kicked the fire into an explosion of red streaks. He stared toward the creek with his back to me. "Yeah, that's exactly what pisses me off. You can pretend to be straight and get away with it. Oh, they love you, Billy. They're all pulling their peters right now, thinking about what you did with big Steve and Pussy Willow, or whatever her name was."

"Deena," I said.

He whirled and glared at me. "Don't you see, I can't do like that. If I ball up my fists and puff up and say, 'Hey, I'm a man, too,' they all just laugh."

His chin trembled. "When do I ever get to be a star?" he asked, his voice cracking. "In a sideshow? 'Step right up, folks, take a good look. Is he a boy? Is he a girl? No, ladies and gentlemen, he-e-e's the donkey dick.'"

He swallowed a couple of times and wiped his nose. "Of course, I can use my brain. I've got science project medals. Oh boy, do I star at shit like that. But—you do science projects all alone, you know, while the other guys are outside playing ball together."

He stood speaking into the dark, looking over my head, and I thought maybe he was crying. But when he looked down and pushed the fire back together with his shoetip, the flames caught up again and I saw his eyes were dry and hard and cold.

"That's okay, don't feel sorry for me," he said evenly. "See, I've found something out. My donkey dick is going to be my ticket out of all that shit. Out of school, out of my house, out of fucking Iowa. I don't need any of them any more."

He smiled slightly and raised his eyebrows. "There's a truck stop on the interstate near where I live—where I used to live. I used to ride my bike over and hang out in the bathroom. I started getting rides with truckers, to Chicago, and Denver, and even Dallas. All over. I've seen half the country since this winter. A trucker got me here, and a man in town told me about this job. I can go anywhere. I can support myself, even if I have to bag groceries for a living. After this job, I'm going to California. And I won't take shit from anybody, ever again."

"Damn," I said softly. "Stan, you've got more balls than anybody I ever met."

He grinned over the campfire. "You really think so?"

"Yeah. You know, I applied for this job almost a year ago. I even bought my bus ticket a month early, and then I found out bus tickets aren't dated. I couldn't do what you've done, honest, just taking off from home like that."

He put more wood into the flames and sat down beside me. We held our hands out close to the fire, but when the flames got too big the heat burned our palms, and our wet pants legs started to steam.

"Shit," I said. "It's either too hot or too cold. I'm burning up in front and freezing in back."

"We can't do this all night," he said. "I've got an idea." He rolled a chunk of the snag over to the campfire.

"Take off your pants," he told me. "We can drape them over this and dry them out."

We both took off our shoes and stripped down our soggy pants and socks, arranging them on the log so they caught the heat. I started to shiver, standing up in my underwear with my legs bare.

"These paper bags will be twice as warm if we put them together. We can conserve body heat if we sleep next to each other, and that way we won't have to feed the fire all night."

Shaking out the disposable sleeping bags, he stuffed one inside the other. We eased our bare legs into the cold bags side-by-side, still wearing our Jockey shorts and coats, padded above with clothes while our legs were naked, skin touching skin. I put my arm around the little guy and pulled his back against my chest. We rubbed our knees together to warm up.

We stretched out on our sides curled around the tiny campfire, with our pants drying on the other side of it. My back was to the rock wall. Within minutes I felt warm at last.

He propped up on one elbow and poked the campfire with a long branch. "Wish we were on a real fire," he said. "Bet Cedar Ridge is a good one. I bet it's like an army there. They use earth movers sometimes, and they build a road right through the woods in a day. I'd love to see all those dozers chugging away, everything all Caterpillar yellow, and airplanes dive-bombing with chemicals. They say that last year a guy stepped in a hole where a tree stump was smoldering, and it was full of hot coals, and it burned his leg off, right up to the knee."

I frowned. "Damn, don't say things like that. Donnie's out there."

"Oh, he can take care of himself. Bet you wish you were doing this with him instead of me, huh."

"Yeah," I nodded. "Don't you?"

He didn't answer.

I chuckled. "Aren't we a bunch of misfits in Cabin 8? I'm in love with Donnie. And Donnie's in love with dick."

"Any dick," he interrupted.

"Uh-huh," I agreed. "Steve's in love with himself. And Stanley—" I didn't know how to complete the joke.

After a moment, he said softly, "And Stanley's in love with Bill. Didn't you get that yet?"

I blinked at the fire. "No," I said in a whisper. "I'm — I'm sorry, man. No, I didn't get that. Not at all."

He shrugged and said, "I tried to let you know."

His head was turned away from me. I touched the curly dark hair on his neck and tried to think of something to say.

"Don't worry," he said, still looking at the campfire. "I know you don't love me back. And I won't interfere with you and Donnie any more. I'm sorry I did all that to you. I couldn't help it. I was so jealous. I hated you for falling for him instead of for me. And you're such an easy schmuck to get upset, so I was torturing you. Deliberately. Do you think I'm horrible, now?"

I swallowed. "How can I think you're horrible when you just told me you love me?"

He twisted around onto his back and gave me a questioning look. After a moment his face softened. He turned his face back toward the fire, but didn't roll over. I put my arm inside the paper sleeping bag and patted his chest. He said quietly, "Well, don't let it go to your head."

We stared into the fire after that, watching the growth and decay of the glowing red caverns that formed under the burning wood. Gently, distractedly, inside the paper sleeping bags, we fingered each other's underwear, and for a long time, we didn't talk. I held him close to me, but it wasn't like sex at all. It was comfort, one fellow to another.

Then, he started to tremble. He took my hand and squeezed it, tighter, until it hurt. "Bill, are we friends? I never had a friend. Can I tell you something? I have to tell somebody. It's something . . . bad."

I held his hand. "You can tell me, buddy. It can't be any worse than what I already know about your sordid past. God."

"It's about my father," he began, turning and staring into my eyes.

"Your fight with him?" I laughed. "Okay, why'd you kick him in the balls? I think that's funny. I think . . ."

His stare bored into me. His breathing got irregular. In a voice so small I could barely hear it he asked, "Are you sure you want to know about my father?"

I said, "Oh, no, Stanley. You don't mean what I think you

mean."

His grip got so tight I thought the bones in my hand would snap. He whispered, "I'm going to burn in hell for all eternity for what I've done."

I tried to meet his stare, but couldn't. I dropped my eyes.

He said, "I knew it. I shouldn't have told you. I really disgust you now, don't I?"

I looked him in the eye, and shook my head, and then I leaned over and kissed him.

He put his head against my chest, and for a while we listened to our hearts pound. Then he spoke into my coat in a distant voice.

"It started when I was about nine. It was my own fault, for being half boy and half girl. See, I had this even then," he said, putting my hand back on his crotch.

"I'd wake up in the middle of the night and he'd be getting into my bed with me in the dark. And I let him put his hand on me. I'm so sick and twisted, you just don't know what I'm really like."

He shook his head. "I've changed my mind," he said. "I don't want to talk about it." But after a few minutes he started rambling again, his voice muffled by my coat.

"Something about getting dirty turns me on. Toilets are always so filthy, like there are no women around to clean up. Nobody's mother ever goes in one. It's all male. I love it, and real men hate it. They all try to be so tough, but they all hate going into a vile public restroom and having to pull out their precious peters in front of the other guys, and then make it work. Ha! I see guys pretend to pee all the time, shake it off and flush, and I know they couldn't get a drop out. I know because I'm watching them real close, and it gets them all nervous. They have to go find another bathroom because of the piss on the floor and the pervert staring at them, and I just laugh, 'cause I know I've got the power over them. It's my turf, even if it is the urinal. I can go ZAP! You can't piss! Ha ha ha-ah!

"And then some guys, oh, god, how they can put it out. I think the guys who piss the hardest go in the toilets instead of the urinal, just to make it roar. They want to show it off to everybody. I mean, some men can unzip and turn it on like a faucet. After they leave I go in and watch the foam, and imagine how hard they can squirt."

He looked up from my chest. "Pretty gross, huh?"

I nodded and grinned.

Satisfied that I liked his story, he snuggled back against me.

"I always dreamed about meeting somebody who understood what I wanted, somebody who wouldn't really care, you know, a guy too manly to care about sick shit like me, but he's so cool, he sees the fag in the toilet with his pants down and a hard-on and instead of getting all flustered he just calmly walks up and hoses his piss into my mouth. What does he care, he's such a stud, one place is as good as another. He just wants to take a whiz. He'd do it on a tree if it weren't for the cops, but he gives it to me instead, and then he just winks at me and leaves."

"Donnie," I said.

He nodded. "Mr. Cool. That night in the toilet, that was the best night of my life."

"I think I understand now," I said.

He turned toward me and wrapped his arms around me underneath my coat and shirt. His cock was warm on my leg, and as he talked, he began to squirm against me. "I can't explain it," he said. "About the piss. It's just so intimate. It's alive, it comes out of his body, through his dick, into my mouth, down through me, and then out of my dick. It's so personal. And, you know, it really doesn't have much taste. First thing in the morning, oh pew, that's awful. But at night, after a guy's had a few beers, it's really only water. The fact that it's beer piss is part of what turns me on."

Stanley reached for the pouch of my briefs. We squeezed each other's half-hard dicks.

"I don't know why my parents ever had me. I think they just did it because everybody else does. It's natural, right? The priest goes 'Gobbledy gobbledy, in the name of God I pronounce it okay to fuck her.' But of course, no nookie unless you're making babies the way God intended. It's what they call 'holy wedlock.' Then you're stuck with me.

"I don't think my mother has given my father any at all since she had me. 'One is one too many for me,' she likes to say. And of course, the pope says no rubbers. I think she'd rather do without anyway. But, you know, a man's got to have it, and I was next in line."

I ran my hand through my hair, trying to understand. "Hey, Stan, don't blame yourself, just because your father is sick. He's the one who's raping his own kid. He's the one who's going to hell, if you're gonna get religious about it."

"You're right—of course. I'm so fucked up, Billy. I have feelings I don't understand."

"Yeah, I guess so. You must hate him."

"It's worse than that. You see . . ." He squirmed against me and groaned painfully, but what he said next still came out in a tiny whisper.

"Bill . . . I liked it. I liked getting fucked by my father. See, he never touched me any other time. It was the only thing we ever did together. He didn't read, and I didn't watch football, so we never had anything to talk about. Hell, it wasn't rape. He didn't hurt me. I got so I tried to make it good for him. I wanted it to last because it was the only time he ever held me. I didn't mind the sex so much. What hurt, what really hurt, was that he'd just get up and leave me alone afterwards. That's when I'd cry. He—he never even thanked me."

A little wailing sound escaped from his throat, and I gave him a quick squeeze.

"Then, you know, I went through puberty and all, and I made him stop or I'd tell it in confession. He left me alone until this spring. A few weeks ago, he tried to get me again, and I turned around and kneed the bastard in the nuts. I think I castrated him, and I'm glad. The next day he got all swollen up, and Mom took him to the doctor, and I knew he'd kill me when he got back home, so while they were gone I packed up and left."

"Oh, lordie," I sighed.

"Pretty fucked up, huh?"

"Well, at least you got away. You just took off hitchhiking? You must have been scared shitless."

"No, you don't understand, about hitchhiking," He turned in my arms, eyes twinkling again in the firelight. "That's the best part. People are so good to you. Men buy me food and let me sleep in the truck, and all they want is some company so they keep awake."

He smiled. "Oh, man, in the middle of the night, you should see it, the interstate is full of big rigs, there'll be ten of them behind you, lights flashing, and ten of them ahead of you, warning you on the CB about cops, and it's like a big brotherhood out there. I know it's out there, every night, a great big brotherhood of strangers, and when I really need it, they'll be there, to take care of me, better than my real family ever did. I don't need my old man any more. I hope he gets gangrene of the balls and dies."

He laughed, bouncing in my arms. "I love truckers, and I know how to take care of them. They've all got a wife and kids back home, but out on the road they can come out of disguise and pick up a boy. I think every man wants a boy, deep down in a secret place in his heart, and I'm a good one. I get in the toilet and see that wedding band, and I stretch my dick out at the pisser, and the trucker looks at what I've got, and then I lick my lips real slow, and I've got a ride.

"I get down between their legs and blow them while they drive. First I say it's hot, and unbutton my shirt. If I've figured them wrong, that's when they kick me out. But if they just watch, then I strip naked, and I get down on the floorboard, and I suck their dicks while they shift gears. I've seen guys cry, they like it so much. Big daddy trucker and little faggy me, VROOM! Pull that air horn, man." He pumped his arm. "HONNNK-A-HONNNK! God damn, I love trucks."

I hugged him and laughed.

He put his face close to mine, smiling. "You know what my re-e-e-al fantasy is? Some day I'm gonna find the right guy. Now, he's not going to be pretty. He's gonna have a big beer gut, and he'll smoke cigars. We'll have a house, and it won't be all dippy-shit nice like the straights do. It'll be shabby on the outside, and the lawn mower will be rusting out front in the weeds, and the neighbors will hate us and say, 'Yuck, stupid old trucker and his sissy friend,' but they won't really know.

"See, inside the house, it will be all light and clean. I'll keep it clean, and I'll have shelves of books and records everywhere.

"Now, Trucker will be stupid, but he'll love me. Every night when he parks his big rig out front, I'll say, 'Daddy's home,' and run to the door, and every night he'll bring me a book. He won't necessarily get the right books, but he'll always bring one for me, and eventually I'll have every book ever printed.

"And I'll cook him dinner, and serve it to him on the coffee table so he can watch ball games, and if he falls asleep I'll catch the cigar before it drops out of his hand. And if he has to take

a leak he'll never have to get up and miss a big play, because I'll
be like his personal urinal. He'll just snap his finger and point
at his cock, and I'll kneel down and unzip him and take it out so
carefully, and it'll be huge, of course. He has to be bigger than
me, that's important. I'll just put my mouth on it and look up,
and he'll let out a ton of piss for me, and I'll be a good boy and
drink every drop, and take it in the bathroom and piss it out for
him. Don't you think a guy would like that?

"And then, late at night when normal people are asleep, he'll
say, 'Put on some of that pretty music you always play,' and I'll
put on Mozart, the Twenty-ninth Symphony, and he'll pick me
up off my feet naked, and hold me to his big fat belly with the
beer stains on his underwear, and he'll spin me around the house,
'round and 'round and 'round, and I'll close my eyes and giggle,
and hang onto his neck, and we'll just dance. . . and dance . . .
and dance . . . ."

Stanley's voice trailed off. The fire crackled and sputtered.
In the flickering light his eyes seemed dreamy, lost in some vision
over my shoulder. As I watched his face, his eyelids drooped.
I pulled him closer. He closed his eyes and snuggled against my
chest.

I yawned. "I don't think the pope is gonna approve," I said,
putting my arm around his skinny shoulders.

"The pope won't know," he said against my teeshirt. "It will
be one of many, many things the pope will never know about.
God will know, and he'll like it, because he'll see we're happy.
We'll make God laugh."

He hugged me. "That's what I want to do," he said with a
little giggle. "I want to make God laugh. He must get bored.
I mean, why else did he make me like this, if not as some kind
of a joke?"

17

The campfire popped and sent up a shower of sparks. Stanley lifted his head and looked at the fire as yellow flames flared up and danced, making bright reflections in his eyes. I studied the features that people kidded him about, the way his eyes bulged, the full lips that used to make me think of overripe fruit. In the firelight he looked older. In his own way, Stanley was actually cute.

"The fires of Hell," he said softly.

I looked at the campfire. The last burst of flames flickered out and left caverns of glowing red coals.

"That's where faggots go," he whispered.

A shudder ran through me. "Don't say shit like that," I told him.

He twisted around to look at me and raised his eyebrows. "Scared?" he grinned.

"No, I'm just cold," I lied, and looked up at the sky. Without the flames to blind me, I could see black shadows moving swiftly across the sky as the storm clouds blocked the stars, then rushed on silently. The tip of a crescent moon peeped out from one side of the canyon.

Stanley opened my coat, unbuttoned my shirt, pushed up my teeshirt, and pressed his face to my bare chest. He held me for a moment, then murmured, "I want to be next to you." He sat up and took his jacket and shirt off, and tucked them under my head for a pillow. Shivering, he burrowed back against me wearing only his briefs. His arms went around me, inside my clothes, and his bare legs wrapped around mine. I closed my coat around his slender body and tugged the bags up as high as they'd go.

Stanley kissed my chest softly. I watched the thin, white curve of the moon slowly edge free from behind the canyon top and hang in space above us. Inside my coat, Stanley found a nipple with his lips and sucked on it, nursing at my tit like a baby. I thought he'd sleep in my pouch like a little kangaroo, but soon nature took its course. Stanley hunched down in the sleeping bag, curled up between my legs, and rubbed his cheek against the lump inside my underwear. He nuzzled at my cock through the cloth, rolling it back and forth until I felt myself stiffen and stretch the cotton fabric tight over a full-out erection.

Stanley kissed all over my dick through the cloth, then worked his way up to the waistband. The head of my dick swelled up so hard it popped out and stuck up against my belly. Stanley found it with his lips and licked at it.

Watching the stars above me, I gasped in the cold air as the warmth of his mouth surrounded my dick, just the head of it. He sucked on it softly for a while, then he removed his mouth and licked at it, exploring under the waistband with his tongue.

I reached inside the bag and touched his face. I traced the circle of his lips around the sensitive head of my cock. It still seemed so amazing that another guy would want to put his mouth on my sex, to suck on the hose I piss with, that he'd want to get his head down between my legs, in the darkness of a sleeping bag, not to just look at it, but to press his face into my smelly crotch and eat me, suck the juice out of me and swallow it.

Who was giving who the most pleasure? Reaching inside my shorts, I ran my fingers down the rubbery tube and pinched it at the hairy base, making it swell up in his mouth, and I heard a muffled whimper from him. I wiggled it with my thumb, pulling it out and slapping it against his face, and Stanley's fingers tightened on my butt. I pushed my Jockey shorts down to my knees. My dick swung out free and hard. He lapped at my nuts, licked between my legs, and then raised up to gobble at my cock again. He was hungry for my sex, crazy for my cock, and feeding it to him was turning me on as much as it was turning him on.

I pointed it straight out at his mouth. A puff of vapor drifted from my mouth in the moonlight as I groaned out loud, feeling Stanley's mouth sink all the way down over my hard-on, inside the rustling sleeping bag.

Stanley came up for air and rolled over. He tugged his own shorts down, backed his behind against my belly, and guided my cock to his ass. "Please," he whispered. "Fuck me. Please fuck me. I need it so bad."

Donnie's Vaseline jar was in my firepack. I scooped some out on one finger and reached for Stanley's butt. He sighed and lifted his leg for me as I spread the goo in the slot of his soft, hairless fanny, buttering up his hole and working my finger into it.

"MH!" he whimpered. His entire body spasmed as I pushed my index finger up inside him. He turned his head and brushed his cheek against mine. We hung suspended together. I could sense him allowing me total control of his body. I moved my finger just a quarter of an inch, and he trembled all over. I pushed it in and back out, and he writhed in my hands. Softly, he breathed out, "Fuck me. I need your dick so bad."

I removed my finger. He winced, and again sighed, "Fuck me, fuck me, fuck me."

His voice trailed off into a moan. My dick ached. I aimed it with my fingers, then slowly prodded the head of it into the tight ring at the center of his ass. The ring didn't stay tight very long. Stanley just raised his leg a bit higher, wiggled his butt against my stomach, and zup! My cockhead slipped right up inside him.

He tossed his head back and pursed his lips, sucking air through them with a long, delicate whooshing sound as I slowly plunged my hard-on all the way up his ass.

I kissed the boyfuzz on his cheek. He turned his face and pressed his lips to mine. I kissed little Stan right on the mouth, gently at first. He threw his arm around my shoulders, twisting around and kissing me back urgently. I got my tongue into his mouth, and then held him still, just like that, probing deep inside him at both ends.

There. I had what I wanted. He had what he wanted. Neither of us moved. It was all so perfect, our warm nest, the canyon around us, the creek trickling beyond our feet, the stars overhead. The world of others was another world, another planet. For that moment, we had perfection. I had wanted this as far back as my memory went, without understanding it. I had wanted this from another boy, this "yes" instead of "no," this "please" instead of "don't," this "fuck me" instead of "fuck you."

My peter was alive, swollen with sex, feeling huge inside him. I pushed it deeper into him, stroked it in and out. He whimpered and raised his butt for more.

"So good," he whispered into my mouth. "Dick is so good. Oh, dick in my ass. Feels so good." His lips brushed mine as he breathed out, "Fuck me. Oh, fuck me up my ass. Oh-h-h, feels so-o-o good."

"So good," I whispered back into his mouth. "Sweet little guy," I told him. "I want to fuck all that hurt out of you." I kissed his nose, and his cheeks, and his eyebrows. "It's not a sin," I said, touching my lips to his soft cheek. "Fucking is holy." He raised up and kissed me hard, as I plunged in and out, in and out, in and out of his ass.

"Billy," Stanley said, his eyes still closed, "when you finish, please, leave it in me, okay? Don't pull it out, please? I want to sleep with it in there. It's the only thing that makes me feel safe. You can use me as many times as you want to. Just don't pull it out. You can fuck me all night long. Just please, leave it all the way up inside me. I want to hold you in my ass, all night long."

He took my free hand in his and held it to his breast. His hand was so small and delicate on the back of my hand, and his skin was so soft and smooth, that I felt like I was making love to a little girl, too young to even have breasts. All I found on his chest was a little button of a nipple, so tiny I couldn't even pluck at it.

Then he guided my hand down to his cock, folding my fingers around the big meaty thing, and there was no doubt that his sex was male. I toyed with the foreskin, pulling it up in a bunch and twirling the loose skin with my fingertips. But when I tried to move my fist down over the head of his dick, he stopped me from jacking him off. He held my hand still, so I just caged my fingers around his fat cock without moving my hand up and down.

I tried to be good to my little boy-girl friend, fucking him gently, pausing for minutes, starting again, building my pleasure until I felt my cum almost shoot, then holding back. I felt his slippery pre-cum oozing into my palm, so I knew he was enjoying himself, too.

I reached down and dragged the ponchos over us in case it rained again in the night. He turned his back to me and fitted his body against mine. I adjusted my coat flap so he could breathe, hugging him to me and feeling cozy. He snuggled and tightened his butt on my dick, and sighed.

Cradling the kid, I put my hand back between his legs and fondled his big balls. His head sagged, and I realized he was already asleep in my arms, right in mid-fuck.

Exhausted as I was, I couldn't lose my hard-on. It was too sexy to be holding his naked little boy-body in my arms, both of us with our underwear down to our knees inside the bag. With his asshole wrapped tight around my cock, I drifted into a dream about deer running from a forest fire, then the fire caught me and I jerked awake. The moon had moved almost to the other side of the canyon, and an hour must have passed while we half fucked and half dozed. My erection had softened, but a few easy pumps inside Stanley's Vaseline–slickened asshole brought it back up.

It was strange, fucking in a dream, dreaming of a fuck. I heard a coyote yowl somewhere far away, and when I opened my eyes again the moon had passed beyond the canyon above us, and the fire was dead out.

When I woke up again we had the plastic poncho over our heads, and morning light peeked in under the edges. Stanley was still naked in my arms, and still conked out asleep. My left elbow tingled, cramped under his chest, and my back ached. We had been so tired that we had gone the whole night without turning, and he was still clenching my cock in his butt.

It was hot under the plastic, and the air was foul, but I didn't move, savoring the delicious sensation of getting my morning hard-on inside Stanley. It expanded on its own, stiffening into him. I ran my hand over his body, feeling the smooth skin of his ass, and touched myself where I was inserted between his cheeks. He began to squirm, with his eyelids still stuck together from deep sleep. I had never noticed what pretty black lashes he had, or the curving lines of his brows.

Holding his narrow hips, I moved him over my dick, using his body to jack myself off. He smiled and reached around to my bare behind, pulling me into him, and this time I went all the way, driving my cock deep into his ass and holding it there.

Still not opening his eyes, he took my hand and guided underneath his belly. His big dick was dripping wet and rock hard. When I put my fist around it and tugged on it, the boy shuddered and twisted under me. His asshole tightened up around my dick, his big cock swelled in my fist, and his cum flowed sticky and wet, spurting all over the inside of the sleeping bag as I jacked him off hard.

My own orgasm was rising inside me, spreading sexual warmth through me like rising of the sun, and I hunkered down over the helpless little kid, totally overpowering him, making him sprawl under me, fucking hard until that wonderful warm light flooded through my brain, and I pumped out all that cum I'd stored up overnight, groaning and jerking and heaving, shooting my load up Stanley's hot little asshole.

Sweating, I pushed back the rustling poncho for air, and saw bright blue sky above us. I pulled away.

He frowned and said, "No, don't. Not yet." With his eyes still shut tightly, he said, "When the light comes in it'll be all over. Keep it in me. Keep the fantasy going."

"We have to get up sometime," I said, pulling my dick out of him slowly. "Anyway, I have to take a leak."

When I popped loose, he groaned.

I stood up and stretched. My peter arched out from my belly, glistening with Vaseline. The air was warm. I walked over to a bush and pissed on it without holding my dick, just raising my arms high in the air and letting fly, feeling the sun on my back, on my bare ass, on my legs, all over my body, top to toe, shivering with pleasure as I drained myself empty.

"Hey, the sun's out," I told Stanley. "Come on, it's actually hot today."

"Are our pants dry yet?"

"Who cares? We don't need them out here. Let's go naked. Get some tan on your butt."

"Really? Can we?" He sat up, then stood and dragged the paper sleeping bags out into the sunlight.

"First things first," he said. We stirred the campfire, blowing the ashes to get it going again, and heated water for tea. After our breakfast can of tuna, Stanley said, "We have to burn the cans now. I read it somewhere. You burn the food out and then you have to carry everything out with you, cans and everything. You're not supposed to leave anything behind that you bring in."

"Well," I said, looking around, "I've got something I'm gonna leave behind. I have to take a crap."

"Me too. Get a shovel. I'll show you how to dig a latrine. I read how."

Stanley grabbed the little packs of tissues from our firepacks. "Go up the slope," he told me. "We should get fifty feet from the creek."

I took a shovel and headed uphill. Stanley stepped into my

boots and tromped along behind me. He dug a hole for me and another one for himself a few feet away. We squatted beside each other and looked out into the wilderness.

"Everybody's always so uptight about shit and piss," he said. "Always hiding in toilets and closing the doors. I don't know why. It's just a natural function. I think it's because it feels good to shit, and nobody wants to admit it. The truth is, your rectum is a sex organ, just like a woman's vagina. Your anus is a third sex organ. Why else would it feel so good? I mean, it's not like we need the encouragement to take a crap. You got to shit, you just shit. It feels good because you're supposed to use it for fucking, too. Just like your dick is for pissing and fucking, too."

I grunted. "Donnie says he can remember being in diapers, and how good that felt. Can you?"

"No. But I've read that the most concentration of nerve endings is in your dick, and after that your mouth, and after that your asshole. And another thing. You know the head of your dick, how it's super−sensitive? That's called erectile tissue. Your lips are made of the same thing, and so are your nipples, and so is your asshole. It's a sex organ, it really is. It's the male pussy. That's the thing that real men don't want to admit, that they have a pussy in back."

"Okay, I believe you. Toss me the toilet paper."

"I read that in Nepal everybody does this. They have communal latrines, and in the morning everybody goes and takes their dumps together. They think you're weird if you don't do it with them. Maybe that's where I should go. Maybe I'd fit in in Nepal. They're all little people, too, like me. I could go around from tent to tent in the morning and take care of all the men's piss-hards, and then we'd all go shit together and laugh at how stupid everybody else is." His face lit up as he talked.

"You're warped, you know that, Stan? Really warped."

"Yeah, I know. Thanks. You're pretty strange, yourself."

I grinned at him. "Yeah. Thanks."

We stood up and peered down at our two holes with the matching set of brown lumps sitting in them.

"You're supposed to burn the toilet paper," Stanley said, striking a match and holding it at the edge of his little pile of paper and poop.

"Why?" I asked.

"I dunno," he said. "You're just supposed to."

I shrugged and did the same, and we watched the smoke curl up from the holes in the ground. It was like a ritual, as though we were natives in some primitive world. We were exorcising the devil out of our own shit.

"See?" Stanley covered his hole with the shovel. "It's not dirty. It's not obscene. Why does everybody worry so much about their assholes? You know, I think obscenity is like looking at clouds. Do you know how clouds have shapes, and you can see animals and stuff in them? Well, do you know what you see if you look at clouds with binoculars? Nothing. Just fog. Clouds are just fog, and when you look at them too close, they vaporize. All white nothing. It's the same with sex and shit and piss and everything. If you look at it up close, it's not dirty or obscene. It's just there. People think they hide their sex because it's dirty, but, really, sex is only dirty because people hide it. The whole world is backwards, do you know?"

Stanley slipped and grabbed my hand. We walked back to the campfire holding hands. "This is fun," he giggled. His dick hung down, swinging like an elephant snout. I knelt in front of him on the mat, touching it, pushing it back and forth, hefting the fat thing in my palm.

"Oh, stop," he said, but he didn't push me away. I rolled the loose skin in my fingers. He had veins all the way down to the tip, and I could see the outline of the head underneath, only the round end with the slit peeking out. As I played around, it lengthened in my hand. When I peeled the thin foreskin back, it swelled more, and in a minute it lifted up horizontal.

My asshole twitched. My own hard-on bounced against my thighs as I knelt between his legs, playing with his dick. I could only get half of it into my mouth, but when I skinned it back and got the head wet, he touched my shoulders and moaned.

"There's just one more thing I'd like to try," I told him, "before we go back to reality. If you promise to go real slow, I'd like to know what it feels like to take something this big up my ass. But you have to stop when I say to, or I'll get hemorrhoids. I thought I was gonna die after Donnie fucked me last week."

He grinned. "I know a trick. Roll over on your stomach."

I stretched out nude on the mat and closed my eyes. I tingled all over as my buttocks absorbed the sun's heat.

Stanley ran his hand down my back and over the cheeks of my ass. "God, you're so long," he said, tracing his fingertips along the inside of my thighs.

He reached for a canteen and some toilet paper. "If we're gonna play doctor, let's do it right," he said. I felt him wipe my butt.

"Nobody's done that for me in a long time," I said. My cock stiffened against the paper mat.

"You only get hemorrhoids from lack of proper exercise back here," he said, slipping a greasy finger up my butt.

"Relax," he told me.

"This is your sphincter muscle. I've read about it in anatomy books." His finger twisted inside me. I moved my knees wider apart and closed my eyes. He got in farther. "This is your prostate. It's really where your cum comes from. Your testicles only produce the sperm. The seminal fluid squirts out of this thing here. Most people don't know that." I gasped as he rubbed it slowly from within, saying, "Anal sex stimulates it from inside." Indeed, his finger seemed to be touching the very source of my ejaculations, the base of my dick, from inside.

"See, men are 'specially designed to fuck each other," he said. "That's what pre-cum is for. Women make their own lubrication. If you're going to fuck a woman, you don't need for your dick to get slippery. She'll get slippery for you. Pre-cum is just there for jacking off and for ass fucking. And another thing, if the guy fucking you isn't circumcised, it doesn't make your asshole sore. Once I get the head of my dick in, then the foreskin is loose enough so that it doesn't have to slide back and forth any more. The skin stays in one place, and my cock slides in and out inside it. You'll see."

Into my elbows I muttered, "I feel like one of your science projects."

"Well, I've had a lot of practice at this," he said, casually. "Married men love it, but they don't have the faintest idea how to do it."

He knew. He seemed to be able to get most of his hand up my ass without hurting me. "Don't play with yourself while you're loosening up," he advised. "It makes your sphincter muscle tighten up. Stay soft until you get used to it, and then when you do start jacking off, after I'm inside you, oh boy, pow, it's gonna feel great."

The sun and the petroleum jelly and the smooth, sliding movements in my rear end lulled me into a dream of warmth and sex. My dick wasn't even half hard, and the pleasure, instead of being focussed there at a point six inches out in front of me, was diffused through my interior. Throbs of deep sensation spread from the base of my back, radiating through my body.

Then I felt the big, round head of Stanley's dick, pressing between the cheeks of my ass. He slid it up and down the slot of my butt, and it felt so good I moaned out loud. He moved it to the center and pressed harder.

"Just relax," he said. "You're tightening up again."

"Oh-h-h shit, Stan, how can I relax when I'm about to get screwed by an elephant?"

Stanley rolled onto his back and held his huge cock straight up for me. "Try it this way. It's easier if you sit on it."

I straddled his hips, and he pointed it at my rear end. When I gingerly lowered my most tender spot onto him, it was like sitting on a fire hydrant, but perseverance furthers, and I did it. An inch at a time, I slid down over him, with my asshole stretching like one of those wide rubber bands they put around a fat Sunday newspaper. Sweat beaded up on my forehead. The enormous thing plugged me full, but I took it, all the way down.

"Don't move, please," I begged him. Then I lifted myself up, and he was right. All that loose foreskin moved under me. There was none of the friction that had hurt, before. "Maybe you've got a point," I told him.

"See?" he said. "If they didn't go clipping the ends off boys' dicks while they're babies, guys could fuck each other a lot more easily. I think that's really why they do it, to keep us from having fun together."

Stanley raised his hips. My eyes crossed inside my eyelids at the feeling of being stuffed so full. He was fucking me from underneath, and it was ecstasy.

Lifting up on my knees, I started using my butthole like a mouth, sucking on Stanley's dick with it. I could raise up slowly and feel my asshole lips run along the entire length of his hard-on, sliding up from the hairy base, widening in a circle around the meaty middle of the shaft where it swelled out larger, then tightening around the head of it. I let it pop out, held myself there at the tip, sort of nibbling at his cockhead with my asshole, squeezing at it, letting more of his slippery juice dab at my hole. Then I went down over it again, sliding down every long, hard inch of his pole.

I groaned, pitching forward onto his body. I crouched over him, hugging him, kissing him, and he kissed me back, hard, sucking at my tongue, digging his fingernails into my back. He crammed his giant cock up into my ass, again and again, sending me spiralling, and then I heard him cry, "I'm coming. Oh Billy, I'm coming. Oh-h-h," he sighed. "This is my dream come true." He heaved up, and called out, "Billy, I love you!"

I grabbed my cock and beat myself off hard, and when I came I went off like a cannon, firing blasts of cum at our chins, thrashing around on top of his little body, streaking our chests with slickness. Squirting like mad, I held him tight and told him I loved him, too, and I meant it. Creaming all over the kid with that big dick of his stuck up my ass, I loved every man in the world, in all the universe.

Much later, when I managed to stand up and unplug myself, it was like taking a huge shit, those ten big fat inches of it sliding out of my asshole, hot and slick, baa-loop. Nothing that size had ever come out of me before, and no crap had ever felt so good.

Still nude, I laced up my black logging boots and clambered around on the rocks over the creek while Stanley splashed off in the water.

Stanley pointed at the flat rock where he had slipped. "If I'd had on boots like yours, I wouldn't have fallen yesterday," he said. "This weekend, I want to buy myself some logging boots. Could you maybe help me find the right kind? Could I maybe ride to town with you guys this weekend?"

"Sure," I said. "I'm getting some Levis like Donnie's, with buttons instead of zippers. We could all three dress alike. We'll be The Three Musketeers."

Stanley grimaced. "The Two-and-a-Half Musketeers."

"No no, I've got it. We're The Three Must-Be-Queers. You have to lisp when you say it."

We kicked at the remains of the tree trunk. The snag was dead out. We scuffed at anything burnable, checking it the way they had trained us, making certain there were no hot spots in the ashes, and then we climbed back up to the ridge to see if any roots were burning.

They weren't. Stanley shrugged. "There's nothing to do."

He called camp on the radio while I gathered up our things.

As we loaded our packs, he touched his dick and asked, "Think anybody will be around?" We decided not to dress until we were back to the main trail. I helped him with his pack, and then he stood there grinning, wearing only the orange firepack and his black loafers. They were getting so shabby I didn't think they would last the day, much less to the weekend.

"Okay, Donk," I said, slapping his bare little ass. "Lead the way."

"Okay, String Bean, follow me." He struck out upstream, map in hand. His slender white legs stuck out under the backpack, and with each step he took I could see his dick and balls swinging free between his legs.

"Don't scare the bears with that thing," I warned him.

"Ah, yours is so skinny I can only see it when you stand sideways."

As we worked our way along the creek the brush got too thick to stay beside the water, so Stanley led us up to the ridge. We hiked with blue sky all around, feeling the warm wind whipping through our crotches.

We stopped at a crest of rocks, big slabs of granite propped one against another, all angles and broken pieces, like parts in a game of pick-up-sticks tossed there by giants. Beyond the tumbled–together boulders the steep hillside was dotted with trees. The land dropped away at a forty-five degree angle, as steep as a hillside can get without breaking away in a landslide.

Far below us, thousands of feet down, the silver trickle of the North Fork threaded through the canyon. Camp was down there somewhere, out of sight. The next ridge was greenish-blue in the haze, so far away we could barely make out the individual tops of trees. The ridge beyond that was pure blue, a smooth line too distant to show treetops. Another ridge beyond that was so pale it almost faded into the sky.

"It's a million miles of mountains," Stanley said in a small voice.

"Yeah," I said. "And it's like we're the only two guys in the world."

Stanley slipped his arm around my bare waist, and looked up at me. He blinked. "We did it, huh?" he whispered.

I put my arm on his shoulder. "Yeah, crew leader, we did it," I said. "Now we've got to get all the way down to the river by dark."

We stood on the rocks a while, listening to the vast silence of the Rockies. Reluctantly, without a word, we stepped back slowly and started down the trail. We hiked naked as long as we dared. After half an hour the trail began to level out, and the lone trees turned into forest. Stanley radioed for a truck to meet us at the road, and then it was almost over.

When we put on our dirty jeans again, the sweaty cloth chaffed at my crotch. I tugged at myself and wondered if Donnie was back in camp yet.

18

When Stanley and I jumped down from the back of the pickup truck, Steve was standing outside the cabin in his underwear, drying his hair with a towel. "Hey hey hey, you guys aren't green any more, huh?" he called out, bowing to shake our hands, making a ceremony of it.

Stanley and I staggered into the cabin and collapsed onto our bunks.

Steve said, "Donnie's due back on another truck this afternoon. You know how it is, hurry up and wait. My crew got back early. First they needed us, but then the road was cut through and the dozers got a big firebreak dug in no time. We only got sent out to the line once, and then my crew got separated from Donnie's crew. Mostly we just sat around and ate smoke. 'Least you guys had rain. Down where we were, not a drop. Sat on our asses, looking like we'd been crawling around inside a bag of charcoal briquets.

"But, what the fuck, you know, on fires they still pay us day and night, whether we're working or not, so we racked up some bucks. When the eagle shits next payday, there's gonna be a big party."

Outside, a caravan of pale green trucks splashed through the puddles in the parking lot. Stanley and I bumped heads looking out the door.

"There he is," Stanley said. I saw Donnie's sooty face above the crowd around the pickups. His eyesockets were white from goggles, but ashes covered every other part of him. His hair was matted with the thick stuff, and his teeshirt was almost as black as his pants.

He sauntered toward us, dragging his shirt. He looked so sexy that I couldn't help letting a quick "Mhh!" escape from my throat.

Stanley smiled up at me. "Fix your hair, hon," he whispered, brushing at my forehead.

Steve put his fingers to his mouth and made a wolf whistle so loud my ears rang with the screech.

When Donnie got to the door he threw his grimy workshirt at Steve. "You turkey, what are you doing so goddam clean?"

Steve threw the shirt back at him. "Look at that suntan. What did you guys do, hide down at the river and kick back all day?"

Donnie came over and poked my arm. Instead of poking back at him, I grabbed his smoke—perfumed body and hugged it.

Steve was combing his hair and saw us in the mirror. "Hey," he called out. "You guys, don't do that in the door, okay? We're getting a reputation."

Cold beer had never tasted so good as that night in the Oldsmobile with Donnie. We watched Steve go down to the volleyball nets, but no one was playing. He walked over to the mess hall and went inside, probably to make a sandwich.

Stanley went to the showers to wash up alone.

Donnie scratched his chin. "So, you and Stanley finally got to liking each other, I guess?"

"Isn't that what you planned?"

"Sorta, sorta. I figure, the more fucking guys do with each other, the better it is. You two could have gone on forever hating each other. Just not worth it."

"Aren't you ever jealous?"

He sighed. "I guess I never understood what jealousy's all about."

"Maybe you never really loved anybody enough to get jealous."

He shook his head. "Now, that's not true. I kinda love you."

I laughed. "Kinda? That's all? Just, kinda? Thanks a lot."

Donnie slouched in his seat. "I hate conversations."

I poked his arm. "Aw, now you're gonna sing us a chorus of 'Don't Fence Me In.' You big goof."

A truck pulled into the parking lot. I moved over on the seat, away from Donnie. We both held our beers out of the light as the guys in the last fire crew jumped down and walked toward their cabins.

When the truck left I moved back over beside Donnie. I slipped his teeshirt up to his armpits, feeling his lean body between my palms again, pressing one hand on his smooth back and one on the patch of fur that covered his chest, measuring the thickness of the man, testing the firmness of him. "God," I said, "if anything had happened to you on that fire, I'd have just died."

Donnie unbuttoned my shirt and reached inside, brushing his hand across my chest. "Yeah, all I been thinking about is getting back here and getting it on with you."

He found a nipple and pinched it, and I leaned forward against his hand, wanting more. I rolled off the seat onto my knees in front of him, kissing his chest, working my way down his belly, following the hairy trail down toward its source. I pressed my mouth against the fly of his jeans, biting the lump under the denim, and then ran my cheek down his thigh, feeling the rough cloth, the thick seams, crouching down until I hit his cowboy boots, and then I bent all the way down and kissed the creases of leather on his boots. I hugged his legs, rubbing the toe of one boot against my crotch, and he lifted his foot so it dug against my hard-on inside my pants.

"Yeah, man," he growled. "Make your buddy happy. Your buddy needs his dick sucked. You know what to do."

Donnie spread his legs, and I crawled between them and unhooked his belt. Pop, pop, pop, I unfastened his Levis and folded back the flaps.

"He's been waiting for you," Donnie said, as he lifted his hips and let me see-saw his pants down. "He's been so lonely out there," he said, with his dick bulging up inside his boxer shorts. "He's been needing his dick sucked, out there in the woods." I hooked a finger under his waistband and pulled down. Donnie's hard cock bounced loose and swung up high before my face. "He's been dreaming about his buddy's mouth on his dick," Donnie breathed, as the big thing arched up toward his bellybutton. I opened my mouth and sank down over his hard cock, letting it stab all the way down my throat at the first plunge inside me.

"Aw, yeah!" Donnie called out. "Make your buddy happy. Show him you know what he likes."

I knew exactly what he liked, and I gave it to him. I pulled back, almost all the way back, until I was just kissing his dick at the tip. He whimpered for more. I went down on it urgently, getting his hard male sex all the way inside me again, holding my mouth around him until I could feel his pulse on my lips. He made a low growl that told me he was totally into getting his rocks off in my mouth. I pulled back, then went down on him, again and again, until his voice rose with each growl and I knew I had to stop or he'd blow his load right then.

I paused and listened to his panting. I cupped the potent swelling of his testicles in one hand and used the other hand on his dick, stroking him slowly as I held the head of his cock in my mouth and ran my tongue around it.

"Oh, yeah, suck it," he hissed. "You just don't know how much I've been needing this." He put his hand on my neck. I felt my own dick throb in my underwear.

He swelled up in my mouth. His first pre-cum oozed from the head of his dick. I put the tip of my tongue into the slit, tasting the seepage straight from his nuts, slippery on my tongue. I wanted to get all the way into that tube and down into his scrotum, to roll his balls around with my tongue and lick inside their bag of skin.

A hoot came from outside.

"Company's coming," Donnie said.

"Shit," I said, climbing back up to the seat.

The guys from the fire crew were headed for the showers. Some of them waved, but nobody came to the car.

I got out to pull two beers from the cooler. When I adjusted my hard-on I felt a cold spot on the front of my pants. I turned to the light and saw a dark wet circle right next to my fly, where my own sexual fluid had soaked through my underwear and my pants as well.

Donnie reached up to unlock the clamps on the canvas roof and pushed it back a few feet. "No more rain for a while, I guess," he said, shoving it farther back. I moved up beside him on the seat. There was a draft of cold air from above, and I snuggled against his body for warmth. He put his arm around my shoulders and I held his dick in my hand. We could see stars above us.

More boys headed for the showers, towels wrapped around their hips. "Uh-oh," Donnie said. "Stanley's nightmare. Is he still in there?"

"I think so," I said. "You know, Stanley's birthday is Friday," I told him. "He wants to go into town. With us. He wants to buy some boots."

"Fine with me," Donnie said. "He needs to loosen up some. Let's get him drunk. We'll give him a birthday party."

Laughter echoed from inside the shower building. Then the lights went out. Silence. The lights blinked on, and the guys inside howled. There was another silence, then wolf whistles and laughter.

Stanley popped out of the shower door and walked quickly from the building, holding his towel around his waist. His head was down and he swung his free arm stiffly, his hand balled into a fist.

"Damn," Donnie muttered. "Now what?"

Moments after the boy went into our cabin, Steve came out and looked around. There was continuous laughter from the shower. He strolled over to the car. As he approached he covered his eyes and said, "Get decent, you guys. I want to ask you something."

Donnie leaned over my lap and made slurping noises.

"Cut it out," Steve told him. "Hey, did you see what happened out here? Stan ran in and jumped in his rack naked and pulled the covers over his head. His hair's still wet. He won't talk to me."

"There's your answer," Donnie said, as four older boys came out of the shower door. When they passed our cabin, they whistled.

"Hey, fuck them," Steve said. "Are they picking on the runt?"

"Either that," Donnie said, "or he tried something with the wrong guy."

Steve scowled and thumped the fender with a fist. "Assholes," he muttered.

Donnie looked surprised. "Since when do you care so much about Stanley? You give him more shit than anybody."

"That's different," Muscles said. "He's in our cabin, he has to take our shit. But he doesn't have to take it from any of them. It makes us look bad, you know?"

The same four guys reappeared from one of the end cabins. We could hear them snickering as they went to our door and looked inside.

"Uh-oh," Steve said.

The four guys went inside our cabin, and I could tell by the broad shoulders and black hair that the last guy was Preston, an olive green army blanket slung over his shoulder.

"Shit!" Donnie said, opening his door and jumping out of the car.

"Blanket party!" Steve said.

"What's going on?" I asked, getting out to follow Donnie.

Steve yelled over his shoulder, "They're gonna beat Stanley up." Both of us ran for the cabin behind Donnie.

As I got through the door I saw Stanley's feet sticking out from under the blanket. They had him on the floor, holding him down and jabbing at him while his head and arms were covered.

"Leave him alone, you fucking bastards," Steve yelled. "He's the littlest guy in camp!"

Preston looked up, grinning. "He's not gonna be in camp much longer. We're giving him a little message that it's time for him to haul his queer ass out of here."

Donnie caught one raised fist and jerked the guy to his feet. The other three were laughing, and the one Donnie had his hand on was grinning, too, until Donnie spun him around and drew back his fist.

The guy's eyes widened in surprise. "Okay, okay," he said, holding his hands in front of him and backing off. "Since when is it such a big deal to kick a fag's ass?"

Steve grabbed another boy by the shirt collar and pulled him off Stanley. The boy yelled and tried to swing at Steve, but Steve blocked his fist. Muscles got his hand on the guy's belt in back, lifted him off the floor, and walked him out through the door.

I dragged the third one away from Stanley's crouched body. The guy jumped to his feet, whirled around and pushed me back with his hand. "Fuck off, kid!" he snarled, pushing me again. I shoved him back. He hesitated, then narrowed his eyes. "You're one, too!" he said, sneering at me. "You are, aren't you?" he repeated, jabbing at me again. "Faggot!" he yelled.

That got me mad. I went at him swinging, too angry to care that he easily blocked the blows I tried to land. I was fighting like a sissy, my arms going like a windmill, but I was a seriously pissed-off sissy and I pushed him back until his foot hit Stanley's body. He glanced down, off balance, and I connected, POW! right on his sneering mouth.

I was so surprised to have actually hit somebody that I hesitated. When he drew his fist back, Steve grabbed the guy's arm with one meaty hand, twisted it behind his back, walked him to the door, and shoved.

"All right, everybody, knock it off," Donnie said. "Everybody just calm down."

Preston was the last to get to his feet. He glared at Donnie, then at Steve, his dark eyebrows forming a sharp notch over his angry face. "Guess we all know where the homo house is now," he said with a smirk.

"Out of our cabin, Preston," Donnie said, pointing at the door.

Preston walked past them warily, going almost sideways so he wouldn't have his back to either of them. He pursed his lips and made smacking noises. "Kiss him and make him well, boys," he said, then darted out snickering.

We peeled back the blanket. Stanley was huddled on the floor, naked, with his arms over his head.

"I'm all right," he said quietly into his knees. "They weren't hitting me that hard."

"They were just trying to scare you," Steve said.

His voice trembled. "Well, it worked," he said, still not lifting his head. "Could you guys just leave me alone for a minute?"

But it was too late. Stanley's skinny shoulders jerked and he started sobbing. "They said, 'Let's have a jack-off contest,'" he whimpered. "They said they'd cut the lights off and see who could shoot off first. I thought, well, I can do that. And then, they turned the lights back on, and I was the only one jacking off. The rest of them were just slapping their legs to make it sound like they were beating off."

I put my hand on his shoulder. "It's okay, man. It's an old trick."

"Yeah," Donnie said. "They do that to somebody every year."

He looked up at us and sniffed. His eyes were wet and red.

"That's not all," he said. "I could see that Preston was getting a hard-on, too. He was trying to cover it up with his hand, but he's got a pretty big dick, and I could tell it was getting hard. I reached over and pulled his hand off it. I thought maybe"— he tilted his head to one side—"just maybe I could turn it all around, you know, get something going with them. But when the other guys saw it, they started laughing at him, too."

He held the back of his hand up. There was a red welt on it. "He got really pissed off. He slapped my hand away, really hard. He said he'd get me for that." Stanley's forehead bunched up in a worried frown. "He's gonna come after me now. I made them laugh at him. The way he looked at me . . . ."

"Don't worry," Steve said. "They won't be back, Stan."

Stanley looked up and shook his head slowly. "You shouldn't

be sticking up for me. They're just going to think you're gay, too."

Steve scowled. "So what?" He sucked at his bloody knuckles. "Hey, I don't give a flying fuck what they think." He stood looking down at little Stanley sitting naked on the blanket. I could tell he was staring right at Stanley's dick.

"What do you want for your birthday?" I asked Stanley as we lowered the top on the Oldsmobile Friday afternoon.

"I want in the middle," Stanley said, tossing his bag into the back seat.

"No, I mean for a present."

"I want in the middle," he said again. "I don't want any present. I just want to hang out with you guys."

Steve came out of his cabin with his suitcase.

Donnie asked him, "Sure you don't want to go with us?"

He shook his head. "I've got guys riding in with me. See you in town." He headed for his car.

Donnie started the Oldsmobile, then left the motor running while he ducked into the barn. He came out with three sleeping bags under his arms. He chucked them into the back seat, and then we were off.

The pointy trees of mountain country wheeled over our heads in the last sunlight of the day. We blasted down the washboard ruts of the logging road that took us to the nearest highway. With the wind in our faces we left a cloud of dust behind us, rattling and bouncing around blind curves, veering toward the edge of sheer drops on one side, sliding right up to rocky cuts on the other. The old car plowed along like a boat, but Donnie steered it around the rocks and managed to straddle most of the potholes.

"No shock absorbers left," he shouted to us as we went sideways over a hole that would have destroyed a sane driver. "Hang on."

Stanley put his hand in my lap, working it down between my legs, and grabbed Donnie's crotch as well, leaning from side to side as Donnie and I grinned at each other over his head.

We stopped to put the top up when it got too cold, and took a few beers from the trunk. Soon after that we hit paved road.

Donnie slowed down. "Pavement takes the fun out of it," he said with a yawn.

Stanley said, "I want to go to a bar. That's what I want for my birthday. I've never had a beer in a bar."

"Are you really eighteen?" Donnie asked. "They'll probably card you."

"I'm eighteen," he said. "I am. I am. I'm grown, okay?"

Donnie shrugged. "Worst they can do is say no."

"I don't care if they let me in or not," Stanley said. "Now that I'm eighteen, they'll just raise the drinking age to twenty-one pretty soon anyway. I'll always be an outlaw. Might as well stay used to it."

Donnie whistled as we swerved down the switchbacks, the fat tires squealing on the hairpins. It was dark when we crossed the river at the bottom of the grade and turned onto the highway.

Staring through the windshield, Stanley said, "I've always felt like I was some kind of alien, you know? Like I was dropped onto Earth from the planet Mars or something."

He lowered his voice and said in a monotone, "'Your mission is to observe the Earthlings and try to act like them. Pretend you are a human being'."

He shook his head, slowly. "It's like I'm always faking it. Around other guys. They all seem to know something I don't know. I'm always outside."

Donnie patted his leg. "We'll find a bar, don't worry. You go in one with the older guys, and they're all real friendly. I'll show you a good place."

"No," Stanley said. "It's not just getting into a bar. It's everything. When you're gay, it's like, there aren't any instructions to follow. Nobody tells you shit."

"Yeah," I said. "The rules straight people have sure don't seem to apply with us."

Donnie shrugged. "You just have to make your own rules up, as you go along."

We turned the last bend in the highway and saw the lights of town reflected in the river below. Just across the bridge, Donnie took the dirt road down to the rodeo grandstand.

"I'm already in trouble with Johnny Law here from last year," he told us. "They know my car, so I try not to drive much in town, 'specially after dark. I usually leave it down here all weekend. We can hoof it up to the street."

The Three Must-Be-Queers marched into town. It was still too quiet at the Starlite dance hall so we went into the cafe instead, to kill time eating hamburgers and playing the jukebox. We stretched it out until the band started playing next door. Outside, music rose and fell from passing car radios. The Friday night cruise had started. When a line formed in the hallway at the entrance to the bar, we joined in.

A hand stopped Stanley at the door. He showed his identification, but the bouncer made a face and shook his head, waving for the people behind us to go around.

Outside again, neon signs lit the dusk along Main Street. We paced the sidewalks and watched the cars.

"Swell," Stanley said. "Just swell. I'm finally legal, and nobody believes me."

A horn tooted beside us. Steve opened the door of the Firebird, motioning for us to get in. Stanley and I crouched in the cramped back seat while Donnie folded his lanky frame into the front bucket.

"I hope Deena's coming to the Starlite tonight," Steve told us over his shoulder. "I hope she shows up. I want all those assholes to see me with her. I want them to see me dating the best-looking blonde in town. Nobody would ride in with me tonight, and that really burns my ass. They think they can tell me who to be friends with. Fucking hicks."

Steve was too full of himself. He got to be a real nuisance, yelling out his window at cars with girls in them, following them around the blocks and flashing his lights.

Donnie said, "Hey Steve, give us a lift over to Two Jacks, okay?"

Steve looked at him. "Two Jacks? On the highway? What do you want to go out there for?"

"We want to get Stanley drunk."

Steve shrugged. "It's your funeral."

We drove back across the bridge and turned onto the highway. "You know that bear they had?" Steve asked. "In the cage out back last year? Well, he died."

Stanley whimpered and slumped in his seat.

Around a bend, Steve pulled off the pavement and turned back toward town. He stopped to let us out. Across the road, glowing in the headlights, a hand-painted sign announced 'Two Jacks' in red letters. Neon beer brands flashed in the windows of a square building made of unfinished plywood. Rusty cars and jacked-up pickups with dogs waiting in the back crowded the dirt parking lot. We could hear country music, clinking bottles, and laughter from inside.

Stanley wavered. "Maybe this isn't my kind of place after all."

"It's the best place in town to try," Donnie said. "It's all locals, so maybe they won't check ID." We headed for the bar. At the door Stanley stopped to turn up his jacket collar.

Inside the roaring crowd the guys were all dressed like Donnie, so I hoped we might blend in. Pinball machines dinged, video games beeped, and along one wall two men played at a miniature bowling alley, ten feet long, smashing hockey pucks into tiny plastic bowling pins. A bell rang each time the puck banged into the back wall, and lights flashed the score. The guy who was winning yelled and hopped around on one leg, slapping his thighs and hooting.

Donnie ordered three beers, but the sullen bartender looked once at Stanley and only opened two. He put them on the bar and waited for Donnie to pay without telling how much they cost.

Stanley held out his ID card. The bartender glanced at it, looked at Stanley's face, and said, "Dream on, kid."

Stanley cleared his throat and said, "I'll have a Coke."

The bartender filled a glass, still not offering any information, so Donnie paid with a twenty. The bartender slapped the change onto the bar and walked away.

We sat at a sticky table by a window with a humming neon Oly beer sign that made us red and then blue and then white.

"Gee, fun," Stanley said.

He glanced around. I hoped he wouldn't stare at anybody. The good old boys looked as though they wouldn't hesitate to throw their bottles at us if we did anything that made them decide we were fags.

We got one more round. When Donnie and I were down to the last inch of beer he said, "Shit, let's go," and I was glad.

"I have to take a leak first," I told them, and made my way through the smoke to the men's room. A dirty sink hung crookedly on one wall, and beyond an unpainted plywood door, a single toilet stood in a puddle on the concrete floor.

As I went in and unzipped, Donnie followed me. Stanley said, "I'm not staying out there alone," and crowded in between us. Donnie pushed the inside door closed behind Stanley, and we pulled out three dicks over the yellowed bowl.

We crossed streams. Stanley's cock began swelling faster than his bladder was emptying. In a minute, he was having to push it down to keep his piss from hitting the wall.

"I can't help it," he said. "This always happens." His donkey dick stuck straight out, and his stream of piss dribbled to a stop.

Erections are like yawns—they're contagious. Donnie and I stopped pissing and pointed our dicks at each other, with Stanley's little body squeezed between us. We touched our cockheads together, holding those three little slits against each other.

Donnie chuckled his dirty "Heh heh heh," and shot a short squirt onto both our hard-ons.

Stanley whimpered.

Donnie put his arm around Stanley's shoulders. "Want your birthday present now?" he asked, playing with himself slowly.

"I saved some beer for you. 'Course it's been used once already, and it's getting kind'a warm now, but you don't mind that, do you Stan? Drinking a little used beer? Huh? Sucking it out of my hose?"

Stanley moaned out loud as Donnie turned and laid a squirt of piss along the length of Stanley's big dick.

"Get down on your knees," Donnie told him.

"Yes, sir," Stanley said, dropping down immediately. His eyes locked on Donnie's dick.

Donnie unbuckled his belt and dropped his pants, leaning back against the door, waving his big hunk of meat in Stanley's face. The kid leaned forward, his mouth open, his hand already moving on his own cock.

Donnie fired a burst of piss from a foot away. Stanley snapped at it, caught it in his mouth and swallowed it, and growled for more. He got what he wanted.

Donnie could turn it on and off like a water pistol. Each streak shot from Donnie's dick right into Stanley's open mouth, and the kid caught each spurt neatly and swallowed it. Donnie leaned forward and aimed a long burst right down the boy's throat. I got my first piss out, but dribbled it on Stanley's chin.

"Practice makes perfect," Donnie said, expertly filling Stanley's mouth, stopping just before it ran over.

Stanley gulped it all down and gurgled, "Gimme some more. Please please please, oh-h-h please."

We both turned it on then, leaning forward together and making our white beer piss sizzle as it filled Stanley's open mouth, two heavy streams at once. He closed his eyes and started beating his big meat like mad.

Donnie took a breath and started singing, "Happy Birthday to you-u-u," as he got the head of his cock into Stanley's mouth. I joined in, "Happy Birthday to you-u-u," as I wedged my dick into his mouth next to Donnie's. "Happy Bir-r-rthday Dear Sta-a-a-n-le-e-ey," we sang, as Stanley stiffened, opening his mouth wider, vibrating as he whacked himself off.

"Happy Birthday to-o-o you-o-o-o-o," we finished together, as Stanley groaned through his nose, beating himself off so hard that we could see long white strands of his cum slinging from his fist onto our shoes and splattering all over the floor of what was already probably the grossest toilet in the whole state of Idaho.

We pulled him to his feet. He wiped his mouth and said, "You know, I'm getting to like this place after all."

The outside door banged open. Loud music and crowd noises blared in. I stuck my foot against the toilet door just as someone pushed on it. It bent on its flimsy hinges.

We stuffed ourselves back into our pants. A deep voice bellowed through the crack, "Hurry up, I got to piss."

When we opened the door and pushed our way out, we were blocked by a huge beer gut of a man. He frowned when he saw three of us coming out of the one small toilet. His mouth opened, but before he could speak, Stanley looked up at him and announced, "It's my birthday," as though that explained anything.

Donnie dropped his jaw and burped in the guy's face like a bullfrog, and the guy stepped back to let us by.

Outside Two Jacks Bar we looped our arms across each other's shoulders with Stanley in the middle.

"Let's go back to the car and get shit-faced drunk," Donnie said.

The Three Must-Be-Queers staggered off toward the bridge. I looked up at the stars and thought, let it be like this forever.

"I want my boots," Stanley said, unzipping his sleeping bag.

I squinted one eye at the sun. Three buzzards were circling over us. Not a good sign.

"I need a shower," Steve said, standing up beside me and stuffing in his shirttail.

If Steve was with us, maybe we were safe. I looked around. We were on the bleachers again. I checked inside my sleeping bag. I had my pants on. Good. I patted my butt. My wallet was still in my back pocket. Could have been worse.

Donnie's voice came from the next bench below me. "Fuck all that," he croaked out. "I want some food."

I remembered something from the night before, something about chugging beers with Donnie and Stanley in the Oldsmobile.

I unzipped my bag and stood up slowly.

Hazily, I could remember being on my knees in the front seat of the car. The top was down, and Donnie and I were facing each other on our knees. Stanley was in the back seat, saying "Go!"

Donnie and I were gulping down beers and then holding the cans down and pissing in them. We were racing to see who could drink a beer and then fill up the can again first, and it seemed I won.

I won quite a few times, it seemed.

Fat brown grasshoppers buzzed in the weeds as we cut across the field and followed the trail up to the dirt road. We hiked past back yards littered with junk and dead cars and stacks of firewood, and then we were on the main street, with pavement and a sidewalk and everything, and the one stoplight three blocks to our left.

We hit the cafe and killed an hour over sausage and eggs, feeding quarters into an old neon jukebox and getting free coffee refills. Steve started drumming his fingers on the table. "I'm going out to see who's in town," he said. "Catch you later."

"I want my boots," Stanley said again.

Donnie picked at his teeth. "In a minute, in a minute. Buying boots is serious business," he said. "Don't want to rush up on it."

At the general store it took a few tries to find a pair that fit, but the little white-haired lady winked and ducked behind a curtain and came out with a pair of the smallest size boots they make, and Stanley got his big black logger boots.

I climbed a ladder to pull a new pair of button-fly jeans off the shelf for each of us. We bought the same brown shirts, and white teeshirts, and grey bootsocks with red tops.

We left with armloads of boxes. Donnie led us out into the

light, then back into dimness, through the swinging doors of a bar.

"The Pronghorn Saloon," he announced, setting his clothes on a wooden table with four mismatched chairs.

The room was long, narrow, and high. Hanging fans rotated majestically, their motors thick with dust. I noticed brown water spots on the ceiling, and when my eyes adjusted to the dim light, I saw animal heads looming from the walls—antelope, deer, mountain sheep with thick curved horns. I turned and gawked at the stuffed heads. An elk lifted its nose elegantly over the door, and the flat rack of a moose seemed too huge to be real. All of them had cobwebs on their horns, and their eyes were dull glass.

"Only place in town with no goddam music," Donnie said. "Have a seat."

The bartender was bald and pear-shaped. He wore a white shirt with long sleeves, cufflinks, armbands, and a string bow tie. He was playing chess with an old man at a bar that was so long it extended through a crude plywood partition into a back room where the chairs were all stacked on the tables.

"Hello, Al," Donnie called to him, and Al nodded, seeming to float over to meet him at the center of the bar.

"Uh-h, pitcher of draft and three glasses, please," Donnie said casually.

A handmade sign taped to the mirror read, "You MUST be 18."

Al hesitated. He looked at Stanley. "Can I see some ID?"

Stanley handed it to him.

"Iowa." Al said flatly. He looked from the card to Stanley and back to the card. "Sorry," he said, shaking his head. "It looks phoney to me."

"Al, you can trust me," Donnie said.

"After last year? You guys try this every summer. Sorry."

Stanley took the card back. "Never mind," he muttered. "I'll have a cherry Coke."

Al flipped the tap with a flourish, tipping off the foam and running the beer up to the glass pitcher's rim. With great dignity he arranged our order on a tray for Donnie, then returned to his game. A cat stood up to stretch on the bar beside them, and then curled up again.

"Sorry about that," Donnie told Stanley, handing him the glass of Coke. "It's a real small town, and you can't get away with much. I got mixed up with some guys with fake ID's last year. At least he's letting you stay inside."

Drinking beer from glasses put foam on our mustaches. Donnie rocked back in his creaky chair, licking his lips and wiping his mouth on his rolled-up sleeve. He pulled a red pocketknife from his jeans.

"Have to doctor these a mite," he explained, unwrapping the jeans and nipping off the stitches that held the cardboard Levi labels attached.

"They only made one mistake when they designed these things, and that's when they sewed up the cuffs. That's why you got caught in the creek on that fire. You guys think I have my pants unrolled at the bottom just to be scuzzy, but there's a reason."

Donnie pricked loose all the stitches on the cuffs of his new pants, unravelling the threads, unrolling the thick seam down to the end of the cloth.

"You get that loop caught on something, and you can't tear it loose for hell. Anybody who goes stomping around in the woods knows about doing this. That's how you can tell a working man from a weekend cowboy. Take a look and see if his cuffs are rolled down. Don't know why they don't just make 'em this way."

He held up his leg with the fringe hanging over his cowboy boot, and grinned. "Anyway, I like the white shit on the ends."

Stanley and I unravelled the cuffs on our stiff new jeans, and then we pooled our quarters. Taking all the clothes on one arm, I hiked the main street until I found the coin laundry. I stuffed everything into one washer, setting it for hot water and adding two packages of bleach.

Back in the saloon, Donnie sat with his chair tilted against the wall, thumbs hooked in his belt loops. Stanley was listening to him tell some long story, but I was just watching Donnie. Even the way he pushed back his hair was sexy. Every move he made turned me on. When he sat forward, thunking his chair down on the floor, the soft, robin's-egg blue denim stretched around his thighs. I leaned forward to see the bump of his dick under the thin cloth, loving the way it bulged out below his rearing horse belt buckle.

When Stanley left for the bathroom, I put my hand on

Donnie's leg, glancing around the room. No one was looking at us. I slipped my fingers up to touch the lump under his jeans. "Tonight?" I whispered, "let's sleep together, okay? Just you and me?"

He put his hand between my legs. "Uh huh," he whispered, stroking my dick with his fingertip. "We'll take the sleeping bags out in the woods and find us a spot." He raised his eyebrows and gave me a knowing look. "Those bags zip together, y' know."

Back in the laundry, putting our clothes in the dryer, I muttered, "Shrink and fade, fuckers, shrink and fade."

I passed the next thirty minutes studying the mahogany bar. It had dull brass rails that formed corrals for the rows of upside-down glasses. Behind the glasses, three huge mirrors were framed in wooden scallops, swooping up to a carved crest at the top. Above that a painting of a reclining nude woman, gone brown with age, hung at a tilt. I stared at the painting, wondering why anybody would want to look at naked women when there are men like Donnie to watch.

"Same thing with the hat," Donnie was saying to Stanley. "I know it looks dumb. But when I go through brush, I duck my head down like this, and it folds down over my ears. You try to follow me through some alder bush, and you'll get your ears ripped off."

Next trip outside, Stanley and I went back to the general store and bought floppy hats. We collected everything from the dryer, and Stanley said, "Time to play dress-up."

Inside the Pronghorn Donnie was on a barstool talking to Al over another glass of draft. Stanley whispered in his ear.

"Say, Al," Donnie said. "Mind if we use the back room to put on some clean clothes?"

We crowded together behind the partition in our underwear, changing into our matching bluejeans and heavy brown shirts. I'd only brought my sneakers and Donnie had on his cowboy boots so we weren't exactly alike, but it was close.

The dark new denim was still warm from the dryer. Stanley got a hard-on that showed even under the thick fabric. He laced his boots and rolled up his sleeves, and we took him back out to the front to check himself out in the mirror.

"The pants are too baggy," he said out of the side of his mouth, not taking his eyes off his reflection.

Donnie told him, "They're supposed to be, at first."

The kid strutted out through the swinging doors and came back inside swaggering and grinning, two inches taller and four pounds heavier.

Al peered at us over his chessboard as we clomped back to our table and sat down, all decked out in our matching bluejeans and shirts. He poured a pitcher of draft for us, and this time when he set it on the table he put down three clean glasses.

"Perhaps I was wrong," he said. "On the house for the three gentlemen, on the house," he said with a slight bow.

"See," Donnie said to the kid as soon as Al left. "Nothin' to it."

Stanley rolled his eyes up. "Oh, sure. It only took twenty-four hours and three different bars."

I took a glass and successfully poured Stanley his first legitimate beer.

"Happy birthday," I said, " – man," and Stanley just grinned and grinned.

19

"He's drunk as a skunk," Donnie said as we stumbled across the rodeo field after midnight. Stanley kept dropping on his butt. Donnie hoisted the little guy over his shoulder and carried him the rest of the way to the car.

The top was down. Stanley was hiccuping and singing, "Hap Be Bird Day Doo Me, Hap Be Bird Day Doo Me," as Donnie laid him out in the back seat.

We pulled the sleeping bags from the trunk and tossed one over the kid. Donnie told him, "If Preston and those guys come by and give you any shit, just blow the car horn."

Stanley sat up and blinked at us. "You're leaving me?"

Donnie nodded. "We'll be right over there."

"Okay," he said, burrowing back down into his sleeping bag. We heard a muffled hiccup. "I know, you guys are on your honeymoon. I unnerstan."

We took our bags down closer to the river and hunted for a level spot, moving hesitantly in the pale light of a moon going on half full.

In a grove of trees we zipped the two square bags together into one, double sized, and spread it out on the grass. We pulled off each other's shirts and unbuttoned each other's pants, hurrying to get naked together. We stood barefoot on the bottom end of the bag to take one last beer leak, feeling each other's butts and swaying drunkenly as we pissed out into the darkness. Then at last we struggled into our new bed, nude and shivering.

He took my hand and put it on the sheath of his hunting knife, pressing my fingers around it. "I'll have this beside the sleeping bag, just in case," he said.

"Jesus, do you really think they might come after us?"

"Probably not. But you know how straight guys are. They get a little crazy about us sometimes, and dogs run in packs. If they do come looking for trouble, this is kind of an equalizer."

"Oh, shit," I groaned.

"Don't worry," he said. "Out in the woods, I always sleep with my knife. It's no big thing. Might be a bear out there to shoo away, that's all."

We folded our bodies together and got comfortable.

"Stanley's right," I said, nuzzling at his neck. "Why do they hate us so much?"

"Search me. But, you're a Southerner, you don't let anybody tell you what to do, right? Westerners neither. 'Specially not what to do in bed."

He put his face to mine so I could see the whites of his eyes in the light of the moon, and his arms tightened around my back. "I'd die before I'd give you up, do you understand that, Bill?"

"Oh, lordie."

"Man's got a right to privacy, and every man has to fight for what he believes in. I believe in us, Billy." He squeezed the breath out of me, kissing me hard as he rolled me onto my back and laid on top of me.

"Fourth of July is coming up next week," he said, reaching between us to guide his cock up under my nuts. "Doesn't it say in the Constitution, we all got the right to life, liberty, and the pursuit of happiness?"

"I think it's the Declaration of Independence," I said, running my finger up and down the crack of his ass, feeling his butt move as he pushed his dick in and out between my thighs.

"Well, I declare I'm a pretty independent guy," he said, "and this is how I like to pursue my happiness."

I put my arms around my All-American boyfriend as he humped at me quietly, touching his lips to mine.

Gravel crunched in the distance. Donnie lifted his head. An automobile moved toward us slowly. Donnie raised up on his elbows and reached for his knife. I wondered where my pants were.

"Could be them, could be the cops," Donnie whispered. "They check this place out sometimes. Could be just somebody else who wants to fuck."

Lights swept across us, then the car backed and turned. It pulled up right beside the Oldsmobile. When the headlights died, we could see the red nose of the Firebird beyond the bushes.

"It's just Steve," Donnie said. He relaxed, lowering himself back down onto me.

A car door opened. After a minute, we heard the piddle of

Steve taking a leak on a tree. "AHRRP," he burped.

Donnie and I lifted our heads, opened our jaws wide, and "AAHR-RRRUP!" we let out our last beer burps together.

Steve giggled, and called out, "'Night, you guys."

We heard his car door close, and Donnie and I settled back down together. The chrome grille of the Firebird gleamed on the far side of the tree. The radiator pinged as it cooled. We were at the end of the dirt road, hidden in bushes, close to the river, and now that we had both of the cars blocking the road, I felt safe enough to forget the rest of the world.

At last, at last, Donnie was in my arms for the whole night, warm and naked, hugging me, rubbing his knee between my legs, kissing me sloppily.

He turned and shifted his weight off of me, nestling his cheek against my chest. I put my hand around behind him and pulled his furry butt closer. He did the same to me, and when an owl hooted in the distance, he squeezed my behind and sighed. I felt a trickle run down the inside of my thigh as he sagged in my arms.

I loved the heft of his solid body, the skin-to-skin contact with a big, hairy man, reeking of beer, his dick dripping on my leg.

This is it, I thought. This is the finest thing in life, to fall asleep holding my best buddy in my arms.

Donnie's hips moved against me. I could feel his dick growing hard against my leg. Minutes passed, with only the steady thrust of his body keeping me awake. Slowly, my own cock thickened against him. He moved up higher on top of me, and I raised my body up to his.

We wouldn't be sleeping quite yet.

I reached between our stomachs and held both our dicks with one hand, shivering at the feel of double masculinity protruding into my fist. Donnie reached down lower, cupping our four balls in his palm, rolling them around together. He squeezed our bags and twisted the hairy pouches around, and I felt both our dicks bulge in my hand.

"Here," he whispered, "I'm starting to drool. Jack us off with this." He took a breath and tightened his belly muscles. "MHH!" he grunted, squeezing out a spoonful of warm pre-cum into my palm.

"Fuck!" I gasped. Our dicks melted together in my fist.

"Oh, Billy!" he gasped back, sliding his hard-on against mine. He put his arm around my neck and sighed.

The big guy and I had learned to go slowly when we made our cum together. We knew each other's slightest sounds, understood each other's tiniest trembles. With Steve sleeping just beyond the tree we held back, catching our breaths in the cold night air, whispering "Ah," and "Oh," in the darkness.

It made my heart leap to be twins like that, him on top of me, fucking in symmetry, mouth to mouth, chest to chest, hard-on pointed up by hard-on. I mixed our dicks in my hand, his thicker, mine longer, both stiff and ready. Donnie's weight and his energy pressed the air out of me, and he took it right into his lungs. We traded our very breaths, still holding back, not wanting to move too fast, waiting for that perfect second.

Our peters kissed in the slickness of my fist. "Yeah," he muttered into my lips. "Love feelin' my dick right up next to yours, man. Squeeze 'em together, Billy. Yeah, squeeze 'em together hard. Oh yeah, I just love goin' dick to dick with my buddy."

He pulled on our nuts, holding both pairs of them in his big hand, twisting them together. "Love goin' balls to balls with my buddy."

We tensed up, quietly straining against each other, thrusting up, pulling back. Both our dicks were oozing creamy pre-cum that spread over my palm like warm butter. He jammed his stiff tube up into my hand, then pulled it back. I jammed mine up, then pulled it back. The rigid knobs of our cockheads bumped against each other as they passed. I spread my slippery fingers around his hard-on, then mine, then his, then mine. They felt enormous, ready to explode, too swollen for me to get my fist around both of them at once.

"Oh yeah," he whispered. "Gonna go cum to cum with you, good buddy." Our twin cocks bulged, ready to pop. "Gonna pump my cum all over your dick, man," he groaned, gripping our nuts. "Gonna shoot my load all over you, Billy," he growled, and I couldn't hold it back.

"Donnie!" I gasped. "I'm gonna cum!" I hugged him tighter and moaned as I felt my own load rising up.

"Shoot it, Billy!" He groaned into my ear. "Shoot it, buddy! Shoot your cum all over my dick!"

We both let go and lunged at each other, grunting, fucking my fist faster and faster. I felt our rock-hard cocks throb in my hand, side by side, felt us explode between my fingers together, unloading our nuts at last, making those wonderful squirts through our dicks, right together, one two three quick ones, then a fourth, and a fifth, spurt after spurt of hot, sticky cum jetting into my palm, filling my fist full, dribbling out between my fingers and dripping onto my belly.

Kissing him madly, I got lost in Donnie's orgasm, got totally swept away shooting off in his arms, feeling him shudder and shoot off with me. For those precious moments, those sweet, head-spinning moments making love with my man, it seemed there wasn't any "him" any more, and there wasn't any "me". There was just "us", one guy, one sweaty guy, joined together in one muscular, heaving, man-to-man fuck.

One very noisy guy.

"Hey!" Steve called from the Firebird. "Hold it down, will ya? Some of us are trying to sleep."

"Shhh!" Stanley said from the Oldsmobile. "I wanna hear 'em."

"That you, Stan? I thought you were with them."

"Not any more."

Donnie and I slowed our fucking, still kissing, panting through our noses. I took my hand off our dicks and hugged him with both arms. He let go of our nuts and hugged me back, squirming over me. He moved his hips back and forth, bumping our softening dicks together in the squishy mess between us. As he stirred the slippery mixture of my cum and his cum, I wondered if even our tiny wiggling sperm cells could be queer for each other, too, little Donnies and little Billies finding each other in the puddle on my belly, wrapping their tails together in miniature orgasms.

You guys better get off on yourselves, I thought. You won't have any female stuff to go for, not while I can have this man in my arms.

His breathing slowed. I hugged him, and kissed his scratchy cheek. He began to snore in my ear. We fell asleep in each other's arms, with our cum still mixed in a puddle between us, gluing our bellies together inside the sleeping bag.

In the middle of the night he made a noise that woke me up, and I realized he was dreaming. He twitched and made another sound in his throat. I could feel his cock projecting against me, hard and virile, even in his dreams. We lay together in the dark, crossing our swords, all warm and hairy.

All night we touched, nude, sprawling loosely. Each time we turned I fought to stay awake, holding my breath to feel his chest move against me in his sleep. He groped between my legs and held onto my nuts. It all felt so right, so familiar, so safe, as I watched stars twinkle between the branches above us.

Early, when a mockingbird started twittering overhead in the first light of dawn, I woke up again to the feel of his warm hand still fondling me down there.

He kissed my ear and whispered, "Nice set of balls you got, fella," rolling them around between his thumb and fingers. "Big old low-hangers, just the way I like 'em. Think I'll eat these two for breakfast." He flicked at my nuts with his fingertips.

I smiled, my eyes still closed. My Donnie. My boyfriend.

He hunched closer, stretching the sensitive skin, popping my testicles back and forth inside their bag of skin.

"Scratch my nuts for me," I said groggily. "Mmmm. The left one." His fingernails did a little dance against the pouch. "Nuh-uh," I said, "the other one." He switched sides, making my left nut bounce with his fingertips, scratching the sensitive, hairy skin with just enough pressure to take care of the itch, handling my genitals with a touch that only another man could know about. "Mmm-hmmmmm," I murmured, "that's just right." I felt my dick stiffen out from my belly.

Moving slowly, I raised my arms over my head, took a deep breath, and stretched my body until my peter raised up and pointed at my bellybutton.

Donnie's warm hand closed around it. "Big old dick, too," he muttered, twisting my erection. "Man-sized dick," he said, flopping it around under the flannel lining, as I put my arms high, lifting my hips and wiggling my bare fanny in his hands.

I touched cold, wet leaves above me, and collapsed back into the warmth of our bag, shivering, "B-R-R-R-R."

"Definitely a male of the species," he said, poking his nose into my armpit and smelling me. "And a ripe one, too."

I sniffed myself. My underarm was dry, with a sour, masculine smell, not foul, but unwashed.

"I quit wearing deodorant for you," I said. "Do you like it?

I think it's kinda sexy."

He gave me a big lick under my arm, nuzzling me so hard it tickled. I shivered as his wet tongue lapped at the fine hairs in the hollow of my armpit. He burrowed into me, licking and kissing and darting his tongue. I got the giggles and wrestled with him, twisting our naked bodies around until I ended up on top.

His sideburn rasped against my beard. I propped on my elbows and toyed with the long wiry hairs, twisting them around and plucking at them to make them stand out. He rubbed my cheeks with his thumbs. Donnie's warm eyes crinkled at the edges. He spread his fingers over my ears and pulled my face down to his to give me a gentle, sweet kiss.

I stretched myself out over him, feeling his warm, hairy skin from my cheek to my shins. I wallowed over his body, smelling his armpits and his sour morning breath.

I kissed his hairy chest all the way down to his belly. When I licked the skin down there, my spit wet the dried cum and made it slick all over again. I rubbed my face in it, smelling his cum mixed with stale piss. I kissed all around the bush of his cock hairs, then I put my mouth around his hard dick and held it with my lips, sucking gently, pulling at his sex until I milked out his first drops of pre-cum.

Holding the slippery stuff in my mouth, I nuzzled down lower, getting my nose up under his nuts. I ran my tongue out and left a mouthful of spit and pre-cum there at his crotch. When I moved back up inside the sleeping bag and stretched out over his body again, my dick slipped right up between his thighs.

"Mmmmmm," I sighed. When he made the same sound it was deeper, and his chest vibrated underneath me. We lingered that way, not quite fucking, just holding onto each other in sleepy, sexual companionship.

Stretching out onto him made my insides gurgle, and I felt a bubble of gas working its way through my intestines. I was so relaxed I let it pass without thinking about it.

"Oops," I said. "Sorry about that."

I was glad he didn't make a joke, or fan the covers or anything like that. He just casually wrapped his big arms around me, enveloping me in his hard muscles along with the raunchy, masculine smells of our bodies. "I don't mind," he whispered. "You can fart in my sleeping bag any old time, big guy."

He raised his head and sniffed. "Guess we ate some cheeseburgers last night, huh?" he drawled. He sniffed again. "Extra onions."

I laughed. "You're so gross," I said, getting onto my elbows over him, with my dick still stabbing between his legs.

"Yeah," he said, his eyes twinkling. He ran a fingertip up and down the slot of my butt, stroking it gently. "And you just love it, don'cha?"

"Uh-huh," I said, closing my eyes as he worked his finger between my cheeks and poked gently at my asshole.

I rubbed my chest against his. "Where's the Vaseline?"

"In my coat pocket," he said. "Hey, yeah, let's get gross with the grease. Let's have us a session."

I searched the pockets of his sheepskin jacket and pulled out the little blue jar. He dipped his finger in the goo and reached for my ass again. I settled back onto his chest. This time he slipped his whole index finger all the way in again, easily, and then out, and then back in.

Donnie's dick throbbed under my belly, rearing up every few seconds as he slowly finger-fucked my butt. Holding his neck and rubbing against him, I could feel a slick spot starting to spread between us where our two cockheads touched.

He whispered against my cheek, "Whyn't you roll over and let me have some of that cute ass of yours?"

I moved over and stretched out on my stomach beside him.

Donnie got between my legs on his knees. I turned to look over my shoulder. His cock stood straight up between his thighs, curving toward his bellybutton. It was already glistening wet.

"Prettiest butt in camp, you know that, man?" he said, opening me up with his thumbs. "I just love watching your butt." Cold air touched me back there as he spread my asshole wider. "Squirm around some."

I moved my hips for him. "Stanley says it's the male pussy," I said.

"That's 'cause Stanley never had any real pussy. If he had, he'd know there's a mighty big difference." I felt a drop of warm spit hit my hole. "I like fucking ass because it's ass," he said, pushing his spit up inside me with his finger. "Male ass." He pulled his finger out and spit on my asshole again. "Pussy's the last thing I got on my mind right now." He inserted two fingers this time and explored inside me with them, stretching my asshole wider.

Donnie stroked his cock as he played with me. Pre-cum oozed out over his knuckles.

"Got a big load of cum building up inside my balls," he growled. "Yeah, big ol' load of hot juice just bustin' to shoot out of my dick." He twisted his fingers inside me. "And this is where I'm gonna shoot it, right here."

He pressed his hand against me so hard I gasped out loud, "Donnie! It feels like your whole fist is going up my ass!"

"Not my fist, buddy," he growled. "Only thing goin' up there is gonna be my hard dick. Gonna stick my dick up your ass, buddy. Gonna plant my load inside you. Uh-huh, gonna plant my hot cum right up inside your butt."

My cock got raging hard as Donnie finger-fucked my ass. I twisted against the sleeping bag, leaving sticky pecker tracks on the cloth.

"Yeah, squirm around some," Donnie said. He pulled his fingers out. "Show me you want what I got for you." He put his hands on my hips and lifted my midsection off the sleeping bag.

"Raise it up for me, buddy," he urged. "Give me a good look at that pretty ass of yours." I edged my knees forward and stuck my butt up for him with my cheek pressed against the sleeping bag.

"Uh-h-h-h hu-u-h. Wiggle your butt in my face. Show me those big ol' low hangers you got down there." I felt Donnie's hand between my legs, playing with my nuts. "Nothin' pussy about what I'm lookin' at." He fondled my nuts with one hand and finger-fucked me with the other. "That's a butthole, and that's a pair of balls hangin' down under it. That's a man's ass, and I'm gonna fuck it."

Donnie crouched over my butt. I felt the blunt head of his cock press against me, round and hard.

Taking a deep breath, I tried to remember what Stanley had showed me, tried to go limp and open up, but still it hurt. I flinched, and he drew back. He lowered himself onto my back. His breath was hot on my neck, his arm muscles trembled, but he held still, with his cockhead lodged just inside the cheeks of my butt. "Don't want to hurt you this time," he whispered. "Tell me when you're ready. Tell me when you want my dick."

I lifted one knee, spread my legs frog-wide, and wiggled my ass. I wanted to feel the damn thing. Gripping at the cloth under me, I closed my eyes and concentrated on the muscles of my asshole. I raised my butt for him, and then the angle was just right, my hole was lined up at just the right angle, and his dick was aimed straight into the tunnel back there. I lowered my head. Something about that position—chest down, butt up, knees apart—something about it all fit together, and seemed to trigger a natural response. Suddenly my asshole let go.

"Now, Donnie," I whispered. "Fuck me."

Donnie hugged me tighter. His cockhead popped into me. Slowly, he hunched forward. We both groaned at once as I felt my butthole spread open enough to allow every big, thick, hard inch of his dick to push right up inside me in seconds.

I dropped flat onto the cloth, and Donnie stretched out flat on my back.

"Oh yeah," he breathed into my ear.

He kissed my naked shoulders and settled on top of me, hugging me from behind, waiting for me to get used to being fucked. Male hardness projected into my core.

"Heh heh," he chuckled. "Bet'cha can't fart now."

I relaxed as much as I could with Donnie's big meat plugged solidly into my ass. It felt huge. I was stuffed so full of him I could barely breathe. Then he moved his hips, stuffing me even fuller. I stiffened, then relaxed again.

He hesitated, then pushed in deeper. I raised my head and gasped, "Ah." He pulled back, and my head dropped.

Donnie worked it in and out of me gently, with steady, slow, velvety strokes. The smooth, sliding sensation back there was starting to feel wonderful. I knew he wanted to go harder but he was holding off, dipping it in until I tensed up, then pulling it back and waiting a few seconds.

He whispered in my ear, "Is it all right?"

Oh, yes. I nodded my head. It was unspeakably good. I couldn't open my eyes.

He pushed it in, all the way in. "Uh-h-h, huh-h-h," he breathed. He took another stroke, harder this time. "Ridin' that ol' Hershey highway, up my buddy's ass."

"Yeah!" I grunted, raising my butt for him, meeting his thrusts. He pushed into me a dozen times, steadily increasing the pressure,

stirring me up until I howled. He held off. I whimpered for more.
He plunged into me with twenty or more hard strokes, fucking
me faster until it brought tears to my eyes. He held back. "Oh,
please," I whispered. "Don't stop." He came back with more,
dozens and dozens of sweet sexy plunges into my butt that left
me moaning and squirming under him.

"Gonna give you all you can take," he growled. "Gonna plant
my load up there inside you." I felt sweat forming on his legs as
they pressed against mine.

I dropped my head. "Oh, fuck, yes!" I groaned into the cloth.
"I love it! I love your dick, Donnie! Give me your dick!"

He jammed it.

"GAH! DAMN!" I gasped. "SHIT!" I went crazy, calling out
over and over "Yeah, man, fuck my ass! Fuck my ass! Fuck my
ass!"

He pounded it into me. I twisted my neck around to kiss him,
to kiss him hard as I could.

Donnie grabbed my wrists and crossed our forearms in front
of my chest, taking me into his muscles. I hooked my ankles
around his ankles. He shifted his hips sideways, and I felt that
big proud butt-poker of his moving back and forth, stirring me
around, deep inside me as we kissed.

His thrusting got urgent then, flattening my stomach against
the ground. Each push of his hips felt better, each pump up my
butt brought me closer.

I got that rising sensation inside the base of my dick, that
tingling of cum welling up that I get just before I shoot my load
when I'm jacking off. But I wasn't even touching my cock, and
my cum stung inside me without quite reaching the point of
release. My asshole throbbed from his butt-fucking, but I couldn't
quite get off.

"Harder," I grunted, "fuck me harder," and Donnie did,
ramming his stiff cock up my ass, pumping my butt so fast the
pleasure and the pain mixed together into a hot glow of sexual
sensation that overwhelmed me, overloaded my brain. Raising
my butt to meet every push, I reached for the invisible, trying to
merge our souls, trying to come with him, just from the
excitement of getting fucked.

Donnie locked his arms around my chest, whimpering through
his nose, "Mmh!" His voice went higher, "Mmh!" Higher still,

urgently now, "MMH! MMH!" I knew he was right on the edge and I was right there with him. With my cum bursting for release I tightened my butthole around the plunging of his big, hard, greasy dick.

Then, "HNK!" He kissed me harder. I clutched my ass tighter. "HNK!" He straightened his legs, trying to cram himself all the way into my guts. "MMGHH!" he groaned into my mouth. "MMGH-GRRHH!" I knew he was shooting off. The pressure of his butt-fucking made my eyes cross inside my skull. My asshole burned with pleasure. I was almost there.

"MMGH . . . GRRU-U-UH-H-H!" he roared, with that helpless tone of surrender, that growl of gutsy satisfaction that men can't help making when they get their nuts off, really get their nuts off right.

That did it. I arched my back and roared with him as he pounded his cock into me, fucking and fucking and fucking my ass, stuffing me full of his cum. I squeezed his hands to my chest, still kissing him over my shoulder, howling into his mouth as I shot off with him, shuddering in his arms, twisting from side to side under him, spewing out my cum at last as he pumped his load up my butt.

I wailed through my nose. Every thrust of his dick from behind sent a sexual jolt through me that forced another spurt out of me in front. I writhed under the power of his ass-fuck.

It was dreamy, it was ravishing, it was deeply intimate, and it was enormously, wrenchingly satisfying.

And oh, oh, oh, I wanted it to go on and on forever.

He made one last hard shove all the way up my ass. We tensed our muscles together and held our breaths, peaking with each other, suspended for a glorious moment all locked together with his big dick probing half a foot into me. We both shuddered, and then he pulled back slowly.

Donnie fucked me more gently then, nudging the last squirts of my cum out onto the sleeping bag, slowly massaging it out of me from behind with his dick.

I wallowed in the warm puddle of my own juice.

Donnie let out his breath and went limp, panting, heavy on my back. Perspiration dripped from his armpits and trickled into my underarms, mixing with my own sweat.

We made three wet spots on the sleeping bag, two under my

arms and a third big one under my belly. The spots were starting
to get cold, but I didn't want to move.

He sighed. "Perrrrr-fec-to."

His lips touched my ear. "Did you come?" he asked, softly.
Very slowly, I nodded.

"You sure? I'll suck you off if you didn't. Anything you want."

Was I sure! I moaned into the sleeping bag. With my eyes
still closed, I took his hand and guided it under my stomach to
feel the sticky spot I'd left. He went, "Ummmm," and cupped me
with his fingers. We dozed that way, his hand around my dick,
my ass like a sleeve around his dick, as the sky brightened with
the rising sun.

A gust of cold air shook the canopy of limbs over us, drying
our sweat. Donnie reached down for the cover we'd kicked off.
He pulled away from my back, and when he slipped out of me,
I winced at the sense of loss, the separation.

Rolling onto my back, I gathered our clothes on top of our
boots and leaned back on them. The sun was just clearing the
hilltop. Flickers of yellow glinted through the leaves over us.

Donnie crawled onto my chest, grinning up at me. "Don'cha
just love that fresh-fucked feeling?" he asked, nuzzling at my
nipples, tickling them with his mustache.

"God," I said. "I can't tell you how good that was." I shook
my head slowly. "God."

He nodded, switching his brown eyes from my left eye to my
right eye, down to my mouth, back up to my eyes. "If you could
see the look on your face right now . . ."

"I'm in heaven."

"Yeah," he said. "Good." He raised his face and kissed my
lips, then laid his head on my chest and reached around my back
to hold me.

I tugged the sleeping bag up over us, and rested my arms on
his cold shoulders.

"It don't get no better than this, buddy," he whispered.

His chest expanded in my arms as he took a deep breath and
held it. He squeezed out his morning fart under the blanket.
Twisting his hips against me, he let out his breath out in a long
sigh against my chest.

"Me 'n you, man," he said, snuggling closer to me. "Just me
'n you."

I hugged him as the wind swished around our nest in the grass. A million birds chirped madly in the bright golden sunrise. They called to their mates from high in the treetops, screeching back and forth to each other all up and down the river.

I gave Donnie another squeeze, thinking of the cum I was holding inside me, the cum Donnie had planted there, deep inside my still-glowing butt.

20

The Firebird and the Oldsmobile were parked side by side when we got back from the river. The top was still down on Donnie's car and Stanley's sleeping bag was crumpled in the rear seat. Donnie reached in and tugged at the bag. It fell open, empty.

"Shit!" Donnie said. "They got Stanley!"

"Who got Stanley?" I asked, looking around.

"Preston and those guys, I bet," Donnie said, turning to take a few steps up the dirt road. No other cars were in sight.

"Hey, what's happening, guys?" Steve called out through the open back window of his car. He rubbed his eyes sleepily.

"Stanley's gone," Donnie said.

"No, I'm not," Stanley's voice piped up from inside the red car.

Steve squinched his face up and covered his eyes with both hands, as Stanley peered out from behind him. Both of them had their shirts off.

Stanley beamed at us over the big blond's muscular shoulder, licking his lips. Steve slowly shook his head, still hiding his face.

"I figured I owed him a favor," Stanley said.

Muscles dropped his hands and grinned sheepishly. "Well, hell," he said, shrugging at Donnie and me. "What was I supposed to do? You guys woke me up over there sounding like two elephants fucking. I had a boner that wouldn't quit, and I sure as shit couldn't lose it listening to you two."

"Giving assistance with problem boners is something I specialize in," Stanley said, tracing the curve of Steve's bare arm with a fingertip. "All you have to do is whistle."

Steve tried to whistle but his mouth wouldn't work. He couldn't stop smiling long enough.

We went for breakfast at the Starlite Cafe, sitting in a corner booth by the window and watching people pass by on the sidewalk. Most of them were bleary-eyed guys who needed a shower and a shave, like us.

As we were finishing our third round of coffee I asked Steve,

"Remember what you wanted to know last weekend? About who gives the best blowjobs? Girls or guys?"

Steve flapped his hand and looked around quickly. "Don't say that so loud," he whispered, frowning.

"Nobody can hear us," I said.

The wall was behind Stanley and Steve and the booth behind Donnie and me was empty. Laughter and loud talk filled the cafe. Plates clattered, frying food hissed in the kitchen, and nobody was even looking our way.

We all leaned toward Steve.

"Well?" I said. "You tell us. Who gets the most points on the peter meter?"

Steve thought about it, working his mouth from side to side. He started to say something, hesitated, then raised his hands and shrugged. "Do I really have to make a choice?"

Stanley squeaked, "You ingrate! That was one of the best blowjobs I ever gave anybody. You ignorant pygmy-dick, you'll never get sucked off like that by a girl."

Steve flapped both hands this time. "SHHH!" he whispered. "All right, all right, it's true. You've got the timing down just right. And there's that thing you do with your hand, the way you twist it at the same time you . . . um, well . . . you could teach Deena a few tricks."

He drained his coffee cup and sat back. "But you'll never have titties, squirt. And you'll never have a pussy."

Stanley smiled slyly. "Titties, no," he said. "The pussy part is arguable."

"Hyah!" Steve laughed. "Hey, let's go for a swim. This town sucks. Let's get some beer and go party."

He reached for his wallet and tossed enough bills onto the table to pay for all of us. As we got up to leave he glanced at the waitress and added five dollars.

"Chick was cute," he said.

As we left the liquor store with two bags of beer and munchies, a car pulled up to the sidewalk. Deena was in the rider's seat. Patsy waved from the back.

"Steve!" Deena called out. "Billy!"

Steve's face lit up. "Hey hey hey, Deena, baby. Where you been?"

"Oh, here and there." She smiled at us, her eyes jumping from

Steve to me to Donnie to Stanley. I could just hear her thinking, four guys, three girls.

Steve put his elbow on the window. "We're going down to the river to party. You wanna come with us?"

"Just me?" She eyed me, cocking one eyebrow and smiling suspiciously. "What do you guys have in mind?"

Stanley said, "Don't worry. You're real safe with us. In fact," he added, stepping closer to Steve, "right now I'm your main competition." He shifted his paper bag to one arm and slipped his other arm around Steve's waist and dipped his knee.

Steve batted his hand away.

Donnie looped his arm over my shoulders. "So am I," he said.

Steve's face reddened. "Uh, my buddies are all gay," he muttered.

Patsy drew back from her window. "Maybe we should be going now," she said to the girl driving.

Steve's thick neck turned crimson. "Uh, I'm not into it, uh, myself, you know," he mumbled.

"Ha!" Stanley barked. He slipped his hand around Steve's waist again.

Muscles batted it away again.

Deena looked at me coyly. "Well, I've heard that guys who go both ways are always better in bed."

"Do tell," Donnie said, bumping his hip against mine.

Deena turned around to Patsy and told her, "Guess you get the front seat."

Grinning broadly, Steve opened the door for her. She got out and Patsy took her seat. The two girls drove off without looking back.

Steve pointed at Donnie. "This is Donnie, the cowboy," he said.

"Naw, I'm not a cowboy and you know it," Donnie said. "I just grew up on a ranch, that's all."

Deena looked down. "You've got on cowboy boots."

"Nope. They're actually saddle boots. There's a difference."

I bumped my hip against his hip. "You're a cowboy to me," I said.

He grinned at me. "All right. Whatever turns you on."

"And the runt here is Stanley," Steve said. "He's our mascot."

Deena laughed. "What is this, a boys' club?"

"Yeah," Steve nodded. "We're the boys from Cabin 8. We're a team, am I right, guys?"

"I'm not the athletic type," Stanley said.

Steve passed the bag of beer to Donnie. "Hey, I'll go get us a coupl'a more sixpacks."

We stood for an awkward minute. Deena checked out our matching brown workshirts and our dark new Levis, each with the cuffs unravelled over our boots. Even after Donnie dropped his arm off my shoulders, our outfits shouted "faggots."

Deena looked at me curiously, searching into my eyes. "Billy, I don't get it," she said, finally. "Didn't you, uh, enjoy . . . you know what I mean . . . wasn't I . . . ." She sighed.

"It's not that, Deena." I tried to think of a way to explain myself. "It's nothing personal, I mean."

"But, didn't you like what we did?"

"Yeah, but"—I glanced at Donnie—"not as much as what we do."

Donnie shrugged and shifted the paper bag. "Don't look at me. I haven't got a clue. I just am what I am."

She shook her head. "I don't understand."

I shook my head. "Neither do I."

Stanley raised his hands. "Hey, nobody gets to pick what they are. You think I picked being a sissy? A runt?"

"On, now, that's just Steve talking," Deena said. "I think you're cute."

Stanley backed off a couple of inches. "Uh, I don't like it when girls come on to me, okay?"

"Okay. Sorry. I'm not used to this. It makes me feel really weird. None of you guys think I'm sexy? I don't know how to act with guys when there isn't a little"—she made a frisky wiggle with her butt—"sizzle between me and a fella, you know?"

Donnie grinned. "Can't make any sizzle when you don't have any sausage."

I shut my eyes. "Donnie . . . ."

But Deena laughed. "It's all right, I'll get used to it."

I looked at her. "Can't we just be friends? And leave out the sex part?"

Deena nodded thoughtfully. "Okay. So, I'm supposed to just be one of the guys, right?"

Stanley said, "If I can get used to being one of the guys, hon, you can get used to being one of the guys."

"O-o-o-kay," Deena said as Steve walked up with another sack of beer. "This should be a real interesting afternoon."

"Hey hey hey, did you guys get acquainted? Let's hit the river." Steve paused to let Deena go ahead of him.

"Ladies first," he said with a little bow.

"Thank you," Deena and Stanley both said at once. They looked at each other and laughed, and started out first together.

"Um, pal," Steve said to Donnie. "Am I missing something here?"

Donnie nodded. "Same thing you been missing all your life."

"Hyah!" Muscles said, shifting his sack and strutting after Deena.

Following Stanley and Deena down the dirt road behind the grandstand, I watched the way her butt swivelled with that rotating swing that girls have and guys don't. Even Stanley's feminine steps weren't really like a girl's. Stanley was somewhere halfway between male and female, a boy lost in the clothes of a man. Sexy as Deena was in her shorts and blouse, it was the kid's movements that fascinated me. It was his butt that I wanted to get my nose into, not hers.

As we walked past our cars Donnie handed me the beer and unbuttoned his shirt down to his belt buckle. "Phew," he muttered, pulling at the pockets to pump fresh air under his armpits. "I could use a bath, huh?"

His bare chest showed under his open workshirt. I caught a glimpse of the swirl of brown hairs around his nipple. "I don't mind," I said, matching his step and putting my hand in his back pocket as we walked.

"I do," Steve said from behind us.

"I know where there's a good swimming hole up ahead," Donnie said. "We need to get far enough away so the straight guys don't see us with Deena."

We hiked along the riverbank trail, threading through trees until we rounded a bend and were out of sight from the cars. Donnie stopped at a huge boulder that sat half on dry ground and half out into the water. Stretching to grab a bush that sprouted from a crack in the granite, he hoisted himself up onto the flat top and walked out to the edge.

He faced the river and stood high above us with his feet apart and his fists on his hips. He had the sleeves of his workshirt rolled all the way up above his thick biceps muscles. A gust of wind blew his shaggy hair back and made the shirt billow out like a sail just above his tight, jean-covered butt.

We wedged the sixpacks between rocks in the cold river water and turned to look up at Donnie above us.

He raised his arms and spread them out wide, embracing the river, the rocks, the trees, all the wild and natural territory that was ours for the afternoon.

"I declare this land," he boomed out in measured phrases, "THE KINGDOM-M-M OF FREELANDIA-A-A."

"O-o-o-o-h look!" Stanley cooed. "It's Queen Elizabeth."

Donnie snickered but didn't look down.

"FREE-E-E LAHN-N-N-DIA-A-AH," he repeated, this time in a British accent. "A kingdom," he shouted out to the river, "without a king." He raised his arms up high. His shirttail pulled out and flapped in the breeze. He was so gorgeous that I stood looking up at him with my mouth hanging open as the brown cloth swirled around his lean, tanned torso, showing the sexy curve at the small of his back. For a second it lifted high enough to expose the patch of dark brown hairs under his arm.

My butthole twitched.

"A kingdom where everybody's free to do whatever they wanna do," he yelled. "A land where nobody gives anybody any shit. Because in my kingdom," he said, tossing his head back, "there ain't no fuckin' rules!"

"Yay!" Stanley cheered.

"Except for one," he added, raising a finger to the sky. He turned and swooped his hand down to point at us. "In the Kingdom of Freelandia," he said sternly, "the only rule is—" He made a goofy smile. "EVERYBODY HAS TO GO NEKKID!"

He threw his shirt into the bushes and shucked his pants down to his ankles, sticking his hairy butt out at us and laughing. Sitting down bare-assed on the rock, he pulled off his boots and pants together and tossed them onto the riverbank in front of us.

He took a running start and leaped out into the air with his arms flailing. "Hee-yah!" he yelled. His big schlong swung up free as he dropped naked into the river like a bomb.

Deena and I flinched when the cold splash hit our faces.

She was watching me watch Donnie. "You're in love with him, aren't you?" she asked with a slight smile.

"Yeah," I nodded, staring at the bubbles. "I'm crazy about him."

He bobbed to the surface and tossed his head to sling the water out of his hair. "Billy!" he yelled. "Come on out!"

I stripped naked quickly. I could feel my dick thickening as I folded my clothes and set them on a rock. I stood for a moment in front of Deena, looking directly at her eyes as she glanced down at my lengthening hard-on. When she looked back up, I raised my eyebrows, turned away from her, and sloshed out into the river after Donnie, following my hard-on.

I heard Stanley say from behind me, "Give it up, Deena. I know. I tried, too."

Steve waded out next leaving his bikini shorts on, but Donnie pointed at him and commanded, "You too, Meathead. Off with your drawers or out of my kingdom."

Steve pulled off his underwear and tossed it onto the bank.

Deena was already down to black lace panties and a skimpy bra when she stepped to the water's edge. She paused to look from Steve's face to mine to Donnie's, making sure she had everyone's eye. Reaching behind her back and pouting her lips, she unfastened her bra and stuck one shoulder forward.

KA-BOOM, she dropped the string to her elbow. KA-BOOM, she dropped the other string. Running her tongue over her lips, she shrugged out of her bra, KA-BOOM BOOM BOOM, and tossed the little strip of cloth behind her.

Steve threw his head back and howled like a basset hound, "AH-ROO-ROO-OOH!" with his dick starting to lift its head.

She giggled. "I've always wanted to do that," she said as she wiggled her panties down and tiptoed into the water. She covered most of her pubic hair with one hand, but the red polish on her nails and the fringes of blonde hair curling around her fingertips only made it sexier. Her breasts were just full enough to make the nipples point up slightly, and her slender body was tanned nut-brown all over, with no bathing suit lines, even on the smooth sloping cheeks of her behind.

It was obviously not the first time she had gone naked in the sun.

She tottered out to Steve, making tiny tinkling giggles and

waving her free hand for balance. His cock stuck straight out as he took her hand to steady her.

Stanley waded out last, with his elephant snout slapping between his pale legs every time he slipped on the mossy boulders underfoot.

Steve yelled, "Look who's not bashful any more!"

Stanley threw his hands out and thrust his hips forward. He grinned at us all. "Ta-dah-h-h!" he said, moving his hips to make his donkey dick swing with the famous double wiggle.

Deena's eyes widened.

"It's warm where the water isn't running," Steve told Deena. The two nude blondes lowered themselves gingerly into a bathtub-sized pool.

"You're so white," Deena said, scooping water onto his chest.

Steve turned his head and peered back at his shoulder. "Shit," he muttered. "Am I gonna get sunburned?"

Stanley found a shallow pool of his own and squatted with his elbows on his knees, seeming unaware that his giant genitals dangled into the water between his ankles.

"You're gonna make some big, hungry fish real happy," Steve called out.

Stanley ignored him, poking at the rocks between his feet. "Hey, I found a crawfish!" he announced.

Donnie took my hand. "Show you something neat," he said. Bracing each other, we waded unsteadily out past the shallow pools and into the swift, icy river. We hooted together when we dropped into a hole that got water up over our crotches. I found a submerged log and hooked my elbow around a limb, easing myself down to my armpits.

"Hold me," Donnie said, grabbing my wrist. I locked my fingers around his wrist so we held each other's forearms in a double grip. Donnie stepped out and slipped completely under the surface.

I could see the form of his body in the brown water, floating free in the rushing river, anchored only by my hand. Swirling eddies swept across him, and for a few seconds he was gone, completely submerged in the muddy river.

Then he bobbed up, spitting and spraying and laughing. It took all my strength to drag him back toward me. He paddled like mad with his free hand until he got close enough to get his footing. I put my arm around him and held him as he shook the water from his hair.

"You try it," he yelled over the hissing water.

I shook my head.

"Come on, try it. It's great."

He hooked his elbow around the log and held out his hand. I grabbed his wrist.

"Trust me," he yelled as we locked forearms. "I want you to hear the rocks."

I didn't know what he meant, but I closed my eyes and let go of the limb.

The current grabbed me immediately and sucked me off my feet. My legs shot out straight and my head went under into darkness. Ice-cold water rushed around me, waving me violently back and forth like a flag flapping in a hurricane. I felt powerful whirlpools surge across my nude body with a suction that would sweep me miles downstream in minutes if I slipped loose from Donnie's grip.

An awesome, deep rumble vibrated in my guts, like distant thunder. It mixed with sharp cracks and clicks and rattles. I understood then what Donnie meant. It was the sound of boulders tumbling along the bottom of the river, stones washing past underneath me. I was listening to the living earth. I was hearing rocks clattering down the river bed, grinding themselves into sand under the force of the spring flood.

Idaho is the continental divide, and the water rushing across my skin would flow west, through Oregon and Washington all the way to the Pacific Ocean. I was really a part of the Wild West instead of the Sleepy South. It was at that instant, hanging onto Donnie's hand in that river, that I realized I'd never want to go back to North Carolina. Maybe I'd go back to visit, but I could never again believe in that stifling old way of life after having found what freedom is like.

I couldn't hold my breath any longer. I squeezed Donnie's wrist. His grip tightened on my wrist, and then the water got brighter beyond my eyelids, and then my head broke the surface.

Gasping and coughing, I struggled to my feet and scrambled up into Donnie's arms. "Rivers back home sure aren't like this," I yelled, hugging my naked buddy.

We sloshed out of the water together. My feet were too numb

to feel the stony river bottom. With our arms on each other's shoulders we staggered to a flat rock and flopped back against it, grinning and panting together.

We sprawled out nude on two rounded places to drip dry in the sun, with the heat of the dusty rocks warming us from below.

When my chest stopped heaving I propped myself up on one elbow to look at him, at the way the water slicked down his body hairs.

"Maybe there's no king here," I told him, "but for sure there's a prince." I touched the sparkles of water drops on his chest. "You're the prince." I pulled at the long hairs around his nipple. "Prince Donald," I said, "of Freelandia."

"How about you," he said, rolling onto his side to face me. "Can there be two princes?"

"Okay," I said. "I'm Prince William of, uh, North Carolina. Doesn't sound as good."

Donnie reached out to toy with my nipple. He stared at me with his big brown eyes. "And these two princes," he said, "you think, maybe, someday these two guys might get to be, like, lovers?" He plucked at my chest. "'Cause that's what Prince Donald is thinking about."

We fingered each other's tits, making circles on each other's sensitive skin, making our little nubbins stand up hard.

I nodded. "Yeah, I think that might be what Prince William has in mind, too."

Steve called up, "Hey, you guys are giving each other pointers."

We looked down our chests, and it was true. Both our cocks were lifting up hard in the sun.

"Let's see if we can stay hard together all day," I said, tapping his big log and making it bounce.

He gripped my dick. "How about we stay hard together forever?" he asked softly.

Stanley warned us, "They can see you from the grandstand."

We sat up. I hadn't noticed that the top of the grandstand just cleared the treetops in the distance. I could make out the figure of a single man, leaning over the railing and staring in our direction.

"Let's go in the bushes," Donnie said.

We climbed for the trees hand in hand, barefoot and naked, pointers swinging left to right with each step. He led me into a grove of aspens, a circle of white-barked trees with glowing green leaves that fluttered above us in the breeze.

He stopped at a tree. "Gotta take a piss first," he said over his shoulder, hitting the universal pose of a man taking a leak, with his feet slightly apart, one hand on his hip, the other on his dick, looking down at himself.

I hugged him from behind, wrapping my arms around his chest. His skin was still warm from the sun, his butt hot against my bare dick. "Let me hold it for you," I said, reaching down his belly.

"Yeah, whatever turns you on," he said, moving his hand so I could hold his dick. It was warm like the rest of him, curving out, long and firm between my fingers.

"You don't have to ask, you know," he said, taking my other hand and moving it up and down his hairy chest. "I'm all yours. Any time you want to play with my body, just do it. I like it."

My dick twitched up against his butt when he said that. "Your body's all mine?" I repeated.

"Uh-huh. See, it gets me hot to fuck when I feel like I'm turning you on. Know what I mean? Play with me, Billy. Tell me what turns you on."

"Even if it's dirty?"

"'Specially if it's dirty. You ought to know that by now."

"Okay then, I want to watch you take a leak. Up close. That's what would turn me on."

"Go for it," he said, hitting the pissing pose again. "Get your nose right up to it."

I dropped to my knees beside him. "I don't want to drink it," I said. "I don't want to pull a Stanley. I just want to watch you do it and jack off."

I put one hand on the inside of his thigh and rested my cheek against his leg. Inches from my eyes, Donnie tugged at his dick, slowly, waiting for the first squirt.

I stroked Donnie's hairy, muscular leg and toyed with my own cock as I watched. I ran my fingers up between his legs and cupped his big balls in my palm. The shaggy pouch lifted and dropped with each tug on his dick.

"Wup," he said. "Can't make it work till my hard-on goes down. Don't tickle, okay?"

My cock reared up between my legs.

"Come on, piss, dammit," he muttered to himself, frowning. "I wanna put on a good show for you."

The thick tube drooped slightly.

"Aw, yeah," he said. "Here it comes." I watched the little slit open into an oval hole and emit a short stream of clear water. When the slit closed, a drop hung from the tip. I touched my finger to it. The slit opened again, and a strong burst of piss splashed though my fingers.

"Ah-h-h," Donnie sighed, aiming a steady stream of his hot piss into my hand. It spurted from inside his belly in an unbroken line for the first six or eight inches, then separated into beads that sparkled in the sunlight before they sputtered into my open palm. I hugged his leg and held my hand out under his waterfall, fascinated, turning my hand slowly to feel his piss splatter against my wrist, against the back of my hand. He threw his head back and shuddered. The stream slowed to a trickle. His dick lifted twice as he hit my palm with two more bursts, and my hard-on tensed with each spurt.

He shook off the last drops. "Now kiss it," he whispered. "Kiss it hard again."

I leaned closer. He held his dick up for me, milking out one more drop that hung from the tip of it. I kissed the back of Donnie's hand. I kissed his fingers. I kissed the head of his cock, wetting my lips.

"Lick it," he urged me. "Come on. Show me how much you love my dick."

I licked his cockhead. He pushed it between my lips. I opened my mouth and let him into me.

"Here you go, buddy. I saved the last of it for you. Any man who's never tasted a little piss hasn't got any balls."

I felt his squirt jet against my tongue. It was warm, almost tasteless, slightly salty.

"Welcome to the club, big fella," he chuckled.

I swallowed Donnie's piss, shuddering deliciously.

Donnie pulled back and rubbed his dick over my teeth. "I wanna know you love my dick," he growled. He tugged the side of my mouth open with one finger and pushed his cockhead into the pouch of my cheek. "Show me how much you love sucking that cock."

He put his hand on my head and bunched my hair up in his

fist. "Tilt your head back," he ordered. "All the way." He tugged at my hair, forcing my face straight up.

I grabbed his legs and held on, down on my knees between his feet, as Donnie rubbed his hard-on in circles inside my mouth. His dick got rigid. He pointed it straight down, and then bent his knees slightly. With my head back and my jaws wide open, I felt Donnie's dick press against the back of my throat.

"Swallow it," he ordered. "Eat me, buddy. Eat me whole." I opened up around it, somehow, and felt his cockhead go past the point of swallowing. "Oh, yeah," he whispered gruffly. "Show me you love it." My throat tightened around his shaft. Like a sword swallower in a circus, I closed my eyes and let Donnie feed his hard dick straight down my gullet, all the way to the hilt. I hugged his butt with both arms and held my mouth tight against his crotch, surrounding his hard meat with my throat, pressing my lips against his bushy pubic hairs. Saliva dribbled down my chin. I couldn't breathe, but I was going to stay that way until he told me to stop, even if I had to pass out first.

He released my hair and drew the long tube of his sex back out of me slowly, stopping when the end was just between my lips. He looked down his chest at me and smiled. Locking my eyes on his, I touched my tongue to the slit of his cockhead. He put his fingers around the shaft and squeezed out my reward, the sweet taste of his pre-cum oozing out onto my tongue. I knew he understood. I didn't just love his dick. I worshipped it, worshipped every hard inch of his big cowboy cock.

Donnie knelt in front of me. He pulled my face to his and looked into my eyes. "That's what I want to know, Billy. I want to know you're as queer for me as I am for you." He kissed me, slowly working his tongue into my mouth. He put his hand on my dick. Holding it gently, he kissed his way down my neck and across my chest, pausing to suck at each nipple, then planted a row of soft kisses all the way down my belly.

My skin tingled with each touch of his lips. I threw my head back and saw aspen leaves fluttering green and silver above us, supported by a ring of slender white tree trunks that formed a protective cage around us. The leaves overhead hissed in the river breeze as I toppled slowly onto the grass, feeling secure and cozy as his lips nudged at the base of my dick and his tongue darted through my pubic hair. We dropped to our sides in an easy, natural 69 position. I hugged his butt and nuzzled up into his crotch until his balls draped over my nose. Only the damp hair on his belly separated us.

Donnie opened his jaws wide and sank his mouth down over my dick without touching it with his lips. The head of my dick hit the back of his throat and plugged into the tight hole there. He closed his lips around the shaft of my hard cock, swirling his tongue around it, sucking at it softly, then increasing the suction as he pulled his head back. The pulsing, warm, liquid movements of his lips drew my loose cock skin up, released it, sucked it up again, sending wave after wave of hot sexual pleasure up and down my hard-on.

He locked his muscular arms around my hips and reached between my legs from behind, flicking my nuts with his finger-nails, working his fingertip into my asshole, massaging it gently. His fingers danced up and down my crotch, jiggling my balls around and touching all my most sensitive spots.

Donnie's cock pressed against my cheek, a giant sexual stalk sprouting out from the wiry nest of his pubic hair. I chewed on the long strands at the base of his dick, then leaned forward and ran my tongue into the dark thicket behind his balls, into the crevice between his legs.

All mine, I thought again. All mine.

He lifted his leg for me and exposed his beautiful sexual parts, the secret male parts tucked in the fork of his legs. His butt hairs were still wet with river water, clinging to the sexy curves of his ass.

Spreading his cheeks open wide with my thumbs, I found the pink little hole of his ass, hiding inside a tangle of coarse, curly hairs. I parted the hairs and touched him there with my fingertip. He went "MMMH!" through his nose as I stroked the soft ridges and folds of skin. The hole knotted up. I felt Donnie's big log stiffen against my chest, pressing between my nipples.

My heart pounded. I pulled him closer. The cheeks of his butt touched the cheeks of my face. I closed my eyes and smothered my face in the slot between his hairy buttocks.

He pulled away from my dick to gasp "Oh!" He lifted his leg higher, opening up for me. "Yeah!" he whispered hoarsely. "Go for it, buddy. Lick my asshole."

I explored with my tongue, probing through the tangles until

I reached the smooth, hairless ring of skin at the center of his butt. The bare spot twitched at my touch. I pressed into it. His butthole tightened around the tip of my tongue.

Donnie reached for me and got his hand around behind my neck. "Eat my ass, buddy," he whispered urgently, pushing my face into his butt. "Yeah, get up in there good. Get your tongue up inside me. Fuck me with your tongue."

I buried my face in the slot of his butt. He pursed his asshole against my lips, kissing my mouth with his rear end, and then he opened himself for me, relaxed that ring back there inside his butthole, and let me drive my tongue deep into the funnel of his ass.

He groaned, "Uh-huh, buddy. Oh, fuck, that's good. Yeah, eat me out." There was a slightly sour, acrid taste in there, but I didn't mind, I couldn't stop. If that was the taste of shit, well, it was my Donnie's shit, and it turned me on, drove me wild, more than any silly perfume ever could.

I hardened my tongue and ran it all the way up inside the forbidden tunnel of Donnie's asshole, reaching so far inside him I could wiggle the tip of my tongue around inside his guts.

Yes, I thought, yes yes yes, this is what I want. I want to go all the way fucking with a man, and I want him to be a real man. I want a hairy, smelly guy who burps out loud and farts at the wrong time, a man who lets his beard look like hell if he doesn't feel like shaving, a man who gets drunk and falls down and acts stupid and stands up on a rock and beats his chest and hollers at the sky, and then laughs and jumps into the river naked.

I want a man, and I want it to be Donnie, and I want to have all of him, from his sexy brown eyes all the way down to his hard, dripping dick and even into the smelly hole in his ass. I want to lick his sweat and taste his piss and swallow his cum. I want my fuck-buddy, my cocksucker buddy, my butthole buddy. I want my Donnie, rolling naked with me in the bushes, just like this.

"Oh-h-h, Billy, kiss my ass," he moaned, and I did, I did. I licked out the inside of his butthole, and it got me so turned on that my cock strained to explode.

CRACK! A branch snapped behind me. Donnie and I froze. I heard the crunch of dead leaves. Someone was walking by us on the trail just outside the aspen grove.

21

Donnie and I pulled our noses from each other's crotches and sat up slowly. The row of white tree trunks formed a cage around us. A young guy's bare shoulder showed between the trees for a second as he passed, and then we glimpsed the seat of his blue jeans as he walked on toward the river.

"Guess he didn't see us," Donnie whispered. Brushing off the leaves and sand that stuck to our elbows and legs, we got to our feet and peered between the trees at our uninvited company.

It was Preston. He had stopped behind a tree right beside the river and was peeking around the trunk. Donnie and I followed his gaze to the riverbank.

Steve was sitting on a sandbar in the sun, leaning back against a boulder with his arms stretched out, grinning down at his crotch. Deena sat on one side of him, playing with the naked guy's cock. Stanley was kneeling on the other side, jacking off slowly. Stanley said something that made Steve laugh, and then Deena pointed the blond dick up and leaned forward to grasp Stanley's monster with her other hand. She looked at Stanley and said something we couldn't hear, and then bent forward to put her mouth on Steve's hard-on. Stanley bent closer, still talking, as Deena sucked Steve and stroked Stanley at the same time.

"Blowjob lessons," I said. Donnie nodded. We looked around the other side of the tree.

Preston was watching them with his mouth hanging open. I'd always admired his muscular body and the size of the bulge in his jeans, and now that bulge was more admirable than ever. He rubbed his belly and slid his hand down to his crotch. He gave his dick a few squeezes. I felt Donnie's hand on my dick, and I reached for his as we watched Preston massage himself. When he moved his hand we could see the outline of his cock under his jeans pocket. Donnie's dick stiffened between my fingers. My erection had wilted for a while after Preston showed up, but Donnie's hand job was bringing it back to life.

Then Preston's eyebrows shot up and he leaned forward,

looking surprised. Deena was still blowing Steve, but Stanley had raised up on his knees and stuck his dick into Steve's face. Muscles had one hand on Deena's head and his other hand on the donkey dick, slowly tugging the loose skin up and down, staring at it in fascination as Deena's head bobbed in his lap.

We looked back at Preston. He was unbuttoning his Levis. He had to bend over and do a little wiggle of his butt to work his cock loose. When it popped out through his fly we could see why.

"Whoa," Donnie whispered. "That's a two-fister if I ever saw one." His dick throbbed in my hand. We exchanged a glance. My dick was sticking straight out, twitching in his palm. His was standing up rigidly, curving toward his belly button between my fingers.

"Come on," Donnie urged. "Let's go and get him."

I shook my head. "I don't want him. He's an asshole. I don't want anything to do with him."

"Oh, come on. We got him outnumbered. I wanna check out that hunk of meat he's waving around. I'll sneak up on his left and you circle around behind him."

"Then what?"

"Then fake it. Don't you watch TV?"

Preston's hand was bouncing on his cock as he stared intently at the three-way on the beach. I slipped through the bushes behind him, bare-ass naked with my hard-on swinging heavily. I tiptoed carefully through the scratchy brush until I was close enough behind him to hear his hand slapping on his cock. He shifted his weight and leaned forward, absorbed in the action below. Donnie was able to steal up beside him without being seen.

Preston started breathing harder. His hand blurred on his dick as Donnie reached out to grip his elbow. "Hello, Preston," he said pleasantly. "What's up?"

"YAH!" Preston yelled, startled. He dropped his cock and whirled to face Donnie, backing up and moving right toward me. I grabbed both his arms from the rear and pressed his elbows together behind his back.

"YAH!" he yelled again, struggling to pull loose. I squeezed his arms together until his hands met over the seat of his pants. "Wow!" he gasped, since this brought his hands into line to brush my hard dick close behind him.

"Aw, guys, don't," he wailed, trying to avoid touching my cock. Every twist he gave only made his hands move over my hard-on. He stopped struggling and stood stiffly, panting and glaring at Donnie.

"Now, isn't this interesting," Donnie said mildly. "And here I thought you didn't like jacking off with the boys."

"I—was just watching," Preston said flushing. "If you guys are gonna run around naked and fuck in the woods, you can't blame me for looking. . ." His arm muscles tensed in my grip as Donnie reached for his dick; he jerked back against my boner.

"Oh, I don't blame you for looking," Donnie smiled. "Looking is fun. We were just looking at this big dick you got on you." He hefted it a few times, his eyes twinkling. "Shouldn't keep a prize-winner like that all to yourself, y' know."

Although solidly built and muscular, Preston was shorter than me but heavier and stronger, and I knew he could have thrown me if he had tried. But he didn't even struggle as Donnie played with his manhood. He stood rigidly at attention in my grip, staring down at Donnie's hand. I could see sweat droplets forming at the base of his thick neck, just under the close-cropped black hair.

"Yeah," Donnie murmured. "Real nice piece of meat you got on you, big fella." I leaned forward and peered down Preston's front. He was circumcised but there was enough loose skin to bunch up over his cockhead as Donnie tugged on it. "Bigger than mine, I think." Donnie let go and patted the big thing, making it bounce around stiffly. He pinched his own erection between his fingers and stepped close enough to tap his cockhead against Preston's.

Holding the guy and watching the sweat trickle down his bare back was turning me on so much that my cock lifted and pressed against the seat of Preston's jeans. Preston pushed it to the side but this time he didn't let go. With one hand on my hard cock and with Donnie standing right in his face, batting their dicks together, Preston groaned and trembled slightly in my hands. His dick bulged and pointed higher than ever, rock hard.

"Look at that, Billy," Donnie grinned at me over Preston's shoulder. "Our buddy here likes cock-fights."

Donnie put his hand around Preston's boner again and said softly, "Time for you to join the party, big fella. I wanna show this to a friend of mine." Towing Preston by his stiff handle, Donnie turned and led him toward the river. I marched in back, holding his arms, although he wasn't really resisting any longer.

"You remember Stanley," Donnie said to him as we broke into the sunlight on the river bank. "Little guy in our cabin? The one you guys were picking on the other night? I want you two to get to know each other better." He led Preston onto the sandbar.

Steve was still propped against his rock. Deena and Stanley were taking turns sucking his cock. He was stroking both their backs as they leaned over him. He looked up dazedly and frowned when he first saw Preston, but when he saw that Donnie was in full control of the guy's dick his face lit up in a grin. Deena looked up and Stanley looked around.

"Look who we bumped into in the woods," Donnie said with a chuckle. "Our friend here is a wildlife lover, too. We found him doing a little nature study behind a tree."

"Preston, pal," Steve grinned. "Glad you could make it, man. You could have gotten here a lot faster if you'd ridden in with me, you know."

"Get me out of this, Steve," Preston pleaded. "I was just watching you guys. I'm not holding anything against you any more."

"You wanna watch something?" Steve grinned up at us. "Watch this." He aimed his hard-on straight up and motioned for Deena to go back to business on it. Once she was gobbling his dick, he pulled Stanley's big dick toward his face and tried to get his mouth around it, without much success.

Preston shook his head. "Oh, man," he muttered. "Steve, man, how can you do that?"

"I can't really, yet," Steve said, licking his lips. "But I'm working on it. Loosen up, pal. We're all just having fun."

"Almost forgot," Donnie said. "We have a rule around here. No clothes. Hey, Stan, we need some help getting Preston's pants off. Think you could give us a hand?"

"Glad to," Stanley smiled wickedly.

Preston tensed, ready to bolt, so Donnie and I held his arms. Stanley knelt in front of him as Donnie unbuttoned Preston's Levis and let them drop to his knees. His cock still jutted up from over the waistband of his briefs. Stanley slid the underwear down and murmured, "Amazing." Preston's dick was rigid as ever, pointing high even without the waistband support.

Stanley tapped it with a fingertip and watched it bounce. "You know, considering the circumstances, that's an awfully stiff dick for a straight guy," he observed, looking up at Preston and raising his eyebrows.

Stanley untied Preston's sneakers and pulled them off, his eyes focussed on the hunk of masculinity standing up so proudly in front of his nose. Preston obediently lifted each foot for Stanley to remove his socks and pants and underwear. He tossed everything aside, leaving Preston standing completely naked like the rest of us.

Stanley edged closer and trailed his fingers up Preston's bare, hairy legs. "Ooh, nice balls, too," he cooed, tickling them with his fingertips. Preston groaned. Stanley licked his lips, inches from the guy's cockhead. Preston glanced nervously at Deena and Steve. They both smiled back, unconcerned.

"Now's your chance, Preston," Donnie said. "Tell him what you want." He let go of Preston's arm and shifted to his chest, tweaking his nipple. "Tell him what to do."

Preston flushed and muttered under his breath, "Not in front of her. . ."

Steve grinned wider. "Come on, Preston, go for it, man!" Deena nodded.

Preston stuttered a little but finally he got it out. "Suck it," he said weakly.

"Suck what?" Donnie asked quietly, still toying with Preston's nipple. I reached for the other one and gave it a tweak. Preston tensed, making his chest muscles stand up.

"Suck my cock," he said louder but still reluctantly. He had thick lips that usually formed a sneer, but that sneer was turning into a slight smile.

"Say it louder, big guy, like you mean it." Donnie plucked harder at his nipple.

Preston spread his feet further apart. We had both released his arms, and now he placed his hands on his hips, his elbows out slightly, and stared down at his own bulging dick. "Suck my cock," he commanded firmly.

Stanley smacked his lips but didn't move closer. He looked up and blinked innocently. "Who are you talking to, Preston?"

Preston almost whimpered in frustration. "To you, dammit."

"What's my name," Stanley asked levelly.

"Stanley."

"No. What do all the guys call me when they're horny?"

"Di—"

"Say it, Preston." Stanley grabbed the big guy's balls.

"'Dick-face', dammit!" he growled. "They call you 'dick-face'!" He had begun to sweat again.

"Yeah," Stanley smiled in triumph. He twisted Preston's nuts a little. "Now say it to my face, asshole, and say it right."

"Suck my cock, *dick-face*," Preston said, squirming a little and looking confused.

"Uh HUH!" Stanley said, wrapping his fingers around Preston's hard-on. "Now call me 'pussy-mouth,'" he said, smiling up, close to victory. "That's my all-time favorite."

Preston grinned down at him, beginning to catch on. "Eat it, *pussy-mouth*," he ordered gruffly. "Eat every fucking inch of my dick!"

"M-M-M-M HMM!" Stanley moaned through his nose, aiming Preston's cock into his mouth. "See what you get when you're nice to a faggot?" He closed his eyes and slowly engulfed his reward.

As his cock disappeared into the little guy's mouth, Preston put his hands on Stanley's shoulders and threw his head back. "Oh-h-h, fuck, yeah," he groaned. "Eat it, baby, eat it!"

Stanley pulled back long enough to gasp out, "I'm not your baby, Preston. Save that for your girlfriend. It's 'dick-face', dammit. Or 'pussy-mouth'. You only have two lines. Try to get them right."

Donnie and I sprawled on the sandbar next to Steve as Stanley and Preston got into high gear. Deena was sitting between Steve's legs, leaning back against his chest. Steve kissed the back of her neck. He reached around and cupped her breasts as she stared at Stanley sucking Preston's dick.

"I still can't believe you guys all give each other head," she shook her head.

"Giving head is no big deal," Steve answered. "It's getting fucked I can't believe. I mean, I'm still working on taking a finger."

Donnie put his hand on my chest and guided me down onto my back with that firmly gentle touch I love so much. "Okay, folks," he said scooting between my legs. "Let me give you a few pointers about the fine art of fucking butt." He patted my dick and lifted my knees. "Up ya go, Billy," he said, raising my legs into the air.

"First you gotta get it wet. And a little smooching lets your buddy know you got friendly intentions." He bent over and kissed my ass, slurping from my butthole up to my balls and back again.

"Aw, gross," Steve said uncertainly.

"Pay attention," Deena said, watching closely.

Maybe I should have been embarrassed doing it in front of all of them, but I wasn't. What had happened to all the shame I used to feel about sex? Where had all the guilt gone, the feelings of obscenity and dirtiness? I guess Donnie had kissed all that away for me.

"Take a good look, everybody," I called, raising my feet to the sky. "This is how two men fuck!"

Donnie sat back, grinning and pulling on his cock. "Normally at this point the next thing you need is a little grease, but mine's back at the car. It ain't totally necessary, anyway. Just have to remember to spit a few hockies on your main bearing if it starts to heat up too much. In an emergency situation like this, you just skip to step three."

He raised up on his knees and squeezed his dick until a blob of pre-cum formed at the tip. "That's nut juice, boys and girls, slipperiest stuff known to man." He touched a fingertip to it and drew a silvery thread up in front of his nose, smiling proudly. "I'm kinda fortunate in that particular area, 'cause my nuts seem to work overtime, 'specially when I'm fooling with my man Billy here. If you guys run out, just let me know. I got plenty to go around."

Donnie hunched over me, on his knees, running the head of his cock up and down the slot between my cheeks and his eyes holding mine. "I'm so full of cum it's leaking out all over your ass, man. Feel it? That's my buddy-fucking juice. That's what you do to me, man. You make my nuts pump. You make my dick drool. Gonna grease up your ass with my own juice and fuck you. Yeah, buddy, tell me you want it."

I felt Donnie's slippery finger circle my asshole. Once, twice, three times. Each circle made me squirm, and then his fingertip stopped at the center of my hole. He inserted his finger and twisted it around until I shut my eyes tight and begged him, "Fuck me, Donnie, fuck me."

He leaned forward and held his cockhead right at the lips of my asshole. "Talk to me, man," he growled. "Tell me what you want."

"I want your dick, Donnie," I groaned. I opened my eyes and saw his beautiful brown eyes locked on mine. "I want your dick inside me."

Deena leaned over for a closer look. Steve reached for his jutting cock as he watched.

Preston was still staring in amazement, but everyone else was grinning down at me. I didn't care. All I could think about was wanting Donnie to fuck me. "Stick it in me, Donnie," I whispered urgently. "Shove your dick up my ass." I put my legs around his hips and pulled him on top of me, crossing my ankles behind his back, lifting myself up so he could aim it into me.

I watched him point it with his hand and then I closed my eyes again. Every time it's a surprise, how big it is, how much I have to open myself up for it. "Oh, Donnie," I whimpered as I felt that wonderful spreading sensation down there. "Oh-h-h, yes," I whispered as my butthole stretched around the invasion of his big, solid dick. "Uh!" Donnie grunted when his cockhead passed my entrance with a soft pop. Then we both groaned together, "R-R-RUH!," shuddering at the exquisite thrill of that long, luscious slippage as he sank the entire length of it into me.

He wrapped his arms around me and I wrapped mine around him. I had him in me at last. I forgot all about the spectators. Everything was Donnie, Donnie, Donnie, his sweaty smell, his hard muscles, his hairy chest, his stiff cock, inside me, outside me, on top of me, crawling all over me, right where he belonged.

He had me from both ends at once, kissing deep into my mouth, fucking even deeper into my butt. His shoulders pushed my knees up to my ears as he pinned me down, thrusting up into me, straightening out my insides.

I realized that I had never held Donnie face to face while we fucked before. On my back I could kiss him and trace the hard muscles of his arms, grip his shoulders, and follow the flat length of his back down to his moving butt. I grabbed the hairy cheeks and pulled him tighter to me. His buttocks quivered as he pumped his hips at me in that slow, sensual, hypnotic rhythm of fucking me, fucking me, fucking my ass.

I reached down under my butt and up between his legs, fondling Donnie's big nuts. I felt up higher and touched his hard cock, circled my fingers around it, held the thick tube as it slid in and out of my butt. Every push sent his big, heavy balls swinging against the back of my hand, flop, flop, flop.

Somebody's elbow bumped mine. I opened my eyes and looked over. Deena was settling onto her back beside me. Steve was on his knees between her legs, diving for her bush with his tongue out. Donnie sat back and held me by my hips, fucking me slowly.

"Aw right, Steve," Preston called out. "Lick some pussy!" He moved around behind Steve to watch over his shoulder as Steve lapped Deena's cunt.

I looked between my legs and watched Donnie's big dick plunge into my crotch and disappear under my balls. With the bush of his cockhairs pressed against my nuts and my own cock hanging toward my face, I could visualize our hard-ons lined up side by side. I ran my fingers through my own pubic hair and imagined his stiff dick inside my guts, just inches underneath my skin. I touched the tip of my dick. It reached almost to my navel. I knew that was how far Donnie's dick was reaching inside me.

Steve rocked back, ready for the next stage. Deena locked her knees around Steve's hips the way I had mine around Donnie's. Steve moved forward and I could see his cock sliding into her cunt. The ring of a rubber showed for a moment, then that disappeared, too. His blond dick hair met the blonde bush above her pussy. He threw his head back and groaned, "Yeah!"

"God, that must feel good," Stanley said in awe, moving beside Preston to watch.

"It does!" Preston said immediately.

"No, I meant for Deena," Stanley said.

Donnie matched his fucking to Steve's. The four of us gasped and grunted in time with each other. Deena and I locked eyes.

Stanley knelt between Deena and me and put his fingers around Donnie's dick, then reached for Steve's dick with his other hand. He grinned at me, holding both thrusting cocks at once, with his own big hard-on swinging in the air.

Preston laughed, watching us and pulling on his cock. "Double feature, huh?"

But Donnie wasn't watching them. He was looking down at his own dick.

"Feels so good inside you, man," he said, shaking his head at me slowly. He leaned forward again, settling into me, rubbing his hairy chest against mine.

He wrapped his arms around my shoulders and whispered into my ear. "So fucking warm inside your butthole. So good sticking my dick up your fuckhole. Fucking inside you, buddy. Yeah, fucking up my buddy's ass. I just love being up inside there with my dick. Feel it, Billy. Feel my hard dick."

I wrapped my arms around him and kissed his whiskery cheek. "I love your dick, man," I whispered back. "I love taking it up my ass. Get it all the way in me. Give me your dick. Give it to me hard."

He pushed all the way into me and held it there. "Squeeze on it, Billy. Squeeze my cock with your butthole." He was rock hard inside me. I clamped my butt muscles around him. "Yeah, he breathed. "Tighten up on it. Oh, yeah, hold me with your ass. Hold onto me with that hot fuckhole you got down there." I made the lips of my asshole squeeze around it and let go, squeeze and let go, and each time he trembled and whispered, "Yeah, buddy. I feel it. Oh, yeah, buddy. Feels so good when you do that."

He pulled back slowly, then plunged back in, making that huge log of a dick travel all the way in, then letting me feel the whole length of it slide out. It popped loose. When he pushed back it missed and angled off to one side.

Stanley was right there watching. "I'll get that for you guys," he said helpfully. He gripped it and moved it up and down the slot of my ass first, milking out so much pre-cum that my cheeks grew slippery with it. When it was lined up, Donnie entered me again. He started pulling out with each stroke, letting Stanley guide it back in with his fingertips. The ring of my asshole was elastic enough to close each time he pulled out and then open again around his plunging cockhead, opening and closing, taking it all, losing it all, stretching open and releasing.

"Ah-h-h, Billy," my man whispered.

I opened my eyes. Donnie's face was close to mine, his lips parted. Our arms formed a cavity between our chests, a hollow chamber that echoed the intimate little sounds of sex, the tiny squishes of screwing mixed with our gasps of pleasure. Hovering inches from my lips, he stared into my eyes steadily, hugging me and stirring my insides with his dick.

"Yeah," Donnie growled. "Give me your ass, buddy."

"Oh, yeah," I growled back. "Give me your dick, man."

"Oh-h-h, yeah-h-h-h," we sighed together.

His eyes burned into mine. Droplets of his sweat trickled into my face. He smiled at me with a wondrous look of disbelief at how incredibly good our fucking was.

"I love you, Billy," Donnie whispered, at last saying the words I wanted to hear the most. "I love you so much."

"I love you, Donnie," I whispered back.

"Hey, finger-fuck me, Stan," Steve called out beside us. "Finger my ass, man!"

As Donnie kissed my neck I watched Steve squirm over Deena, pumping into her steadily. Each time he pushed at her his buttocks tightened and her red fingernails dug into his back, and each time he pulled back, Stanley caressed the slot of his butt.

Deena murmured something I couldn't make out. Steve hesitated and whispered into her ear. Stanley pointed his index finger into the center of Steve's furry cheeks. He twisted his hand, burrowing into Steve's asshole. Steve lifted his head and whimpered, "Easy, guy, easy. I'm new at this."

"Just relax," Stanley said. "You're an athlete. This is all about muscle control."

Steve briefly looked back over his shoulder. "Well, I never worked on that particular muscle before today."

Stanley spread his ass open and leaned forward to let a drop of spit fall into it. When he entered again, Muscles raised his head higher. "Ah!" he gasped in pleasure.

Stanley twisted his wrist again, working his finger deep inside. Then he added another finger, but Steve just groaned happily, dropping his head down to Deena's cheek. We watched as Stanley fingered more and more vigorously. Muscles raised his head and yelled, "Oh, yeah, man!"

Deena squealed and twisted under the big guy's hips as he kissed her hard and shoved himself into her again and again, with little Stan following every move of his rotating butt.

Preston knelt between Steve's legs, eyeing Steve's ass and playing with himself. Stanley spread Steve's furry butt wide. Preston leaned forward and milked a blob of pre-cum out of his

271

dick, following Donnie's instructions.

"Mmmm, don't stop, Stan," Steve pleaded, his face buried in Deena's neck. "That feels so fucking good — put it back in — I wanna get off with you up my butt—"

Preston braced himself on one arm, the muscles bulging with his weight, and aimed his dick at Steve's butt with the other. His dripping dick started to disappear between Steve's asscheeks. "Yeah," Steve murmured. Preston rocked forward over the fucking couple, grinning as he balanced over them. Another inch sank into Steve's butt, and then another. Steve's head lifted up. "Uh, wait a minute," he started uncertainly. "Stan, that's feels like more than a finger—" He looked back over his shoulder and directly into Preston's beaming eyes.

"It ain't Stan, either," Preston said with a laugh. "Surprise, Steve! You wanted me to join the party, didn't you?"

"Aw, no, man," Steve suddenly panicked. "I'm not ready for that—"

"Loosen up, man," Preston said, his thick cock sinking all the way in. "Like you said, we're all just having fun, right?" He gave another deep thrust. Steve closed his eyes and grunted. "Take it like a man," Preston continued, hunching over his buddy's broad shoulders.

"OK, OK, I'm trying!" Steve gasped. "I'm trying — oh, shit, you don't know how hard I'm trying—" He let out a long groan and his face dropped down next to Deena's.

"Ah-h-h-," Preston sighed happily, lowering his full weight onto Steve's back.

"Yeah, fuck!" Steve gasped, starting to meet Preston's thrusts, squirming between Preston on top and Deena beneath.

"Oh, Steve, it's working!" Deena squealed just as happily.

Stanley clapped his hands. "Look, it's a muscle sandwich." He moved around to their heads and started jerking off in their faces.

"Oh, God, I'm dying," Steve groaned. Deena began gasping uncontrollably, twisting beneath Steve's jerking hips. Preston picked up their rhythm, timing his thrusts so he met Steve's ass on the way up, plunging into him and providing a push as Steve shoved back into Deena. "But I'm going to die a happy man!"

Donnie hunched against me slowly as we watched Deena and Steve kiss Stanley's cock. I looked back at Donnie. His eyes were glazed with pleasure then, narrowed with the look of a man in mid-fuck.

"Ridin' that high trail now, buddy. Up on that rainbow ridge with my fuck-buddy. I just love fucking with you, man. I love feeling your arms around me, feeling your butt holding my dick. I love that look you got on your face. I love reaching down and grabbing your cock and feeling your hard-on in my hand."

"Jack me off, Donnie," I said urgently. "Make me cum. I need that, man. I need my buddy's hand on my dick. I want you to do it for me. Beat my meat while you fuck me. Oh, Donnie, beat me off, fuck-buddy!"

"Yeah, Billy, I wanna feel your dick squirt. I wanna feel you shoot off in my hand. Give me your nut juice, buddy. Blow your load with me, man. Let me feel your hot cum!"

Preston reached over and slapped Donnie's ass. "Go, man! Fuck him, Donnie, fuck him good!"

Donnie's hard body strained against mine. He tightened his arms around my chest, punching into me, ramming his solid male sex hard up between my legs.

I looked into his beautiful brown eyes and surrendered everything, my heart and my soul and my balls and my ass, gave it all up to my buddy, sharing my sex with him until I couldn't tell any more who was fucking and who was getting fucked.

"Now!" he demanded, as he crammed himself into me. "Shoot off with me, Billy!" He stroked my dick faster. "Cum with me!" he groaned with each thrust of his hips.

"I'm cumming," I cried back as my load started to rise through my dick. "I'm cumming!" we chanted to each other, back and forth, louder with each stroke, over and over, until I couldn't form the words any more and had to scream into his mouth. My load spurted up through his fist and sprayed out of my dick onto my belly, and then we were kissing hard and creaming together and all I could feel was his dick and my dick, both of them bulging up huge and spurting out cum. Roaring into my mouth, Donnie rammed his tongue into my throat so deep I thought it would meet the head of his cock coming up through my guts from the other end.

Shuddering and groaning and pumping my ass, Donnie left his mark way up inside me, way up in the vicinity of my heart, I do believe.

"MMMMMH!" Deena squealed beside us.

"GRRRMFFF!" Steve howled with his mouth full.

Steve was getting the best of both worlds, shuddering and twitching and grunting over Deena, firing his load, with Preston's dick jammed full bore up his ass and Stanley's big boner plugged into his mouth. He slumped over her, flushed red all over his sweaty body.

Preston looked up at Stanley and grinned. "Teamwork, huh?"

Stanley pulled his cock away and Steve gasped for air. He groaned when Preston popped his dick out and reared up on his knees facing Stanley. The strange couple leaned back and started beating off over the rest of us. Deena reached up for Stanley's nuts and tickled them as he stiffened and closed his eyes. I wet my finger and reached for Stanley's tiny white butt. "Here you go, little buddy," I offered. "I know just what you need."

Donnie reached for Preston's ass and the big guy's eyes widened with the new sensation.

"Oh, shit!" Stanley gasped. His cum streaked up high, arching into the sunlight and spattering down onto Steve's big biceps muscles.

"Oh, yeah!" It was Preston's turn. His first spurt looped and landed on Deena's arm. He twisted toward us, grinning, and aimed another long white stream at Donnie and me. Another spurt from Stanley landed on Donnie's back as one of Preston's hot blobs splattered onto my arm.

Stanley and Preston twisted back and forth, grinning at each other and hosing us all until they both collapsed between us laughing.

Donnie rolled off me and heaved a deep sigh. "Well, did everyone get what they wanted?" he asked lazily.

"God," Steve groaned, "is there anything left to try?"

"There is for me," Preston said with a smile. He propped up on one elbow and began toying with Stanley's fat, dripping cock. Stanley took a deep breath and stretched, arching his back for Preston to get a better grip on him. "There's some Vaseline up at the car," he said. "We could go get that and I'll show you some tricks."

"Before you go — " Donnie reached into the cool water beside us. He fished out a six-pack and held it in the air. We each picked a can off the cluster.

Donnie raised his can for a toast. "Here's to the two best things in life—hot sex and cold beer."

I lifted my beer. "And buddies to share them both!"

I stretched out beside Donnie and rested my cheek on his chest. "No more Billy Beat-off," I whispered to myself. "No more secrets." I reached down and touched Donnie's soft cock, brushing the delicate skin with my fingertips. "No more hiding what I want."

"What's that?" Donnie asked.

I looked across his furry chest and watched the swirls of the river rush past us. I sighed again. It all seemed so hard to explain. "I said I love you, that's all," I told him, closing my hand gently around his dick.

"Yeah," he said. He burped and patted my back. "Ain't nature grand?"

I closed my eyes and hugged him, feeling myself rise and fall with his breaths, naked and happy with my buddies in the Kingdom of Freelandia.

OTHER TITLES AVAILABLE
DIRECTLY FROM GLB PUBLISHERS

GAY/LESBIAN FICTION/POETRY

The Bunny Book   Novel by
John D'Hondt. The bunny mystique and
AIDS in a feminist setting.
288 pages   Paperback $11.95   _____

A Breviary Of Torment   Poems by
Thomas Cashet. Expressions of our love-
hate relationship with torture.
128 pages   Paperback $13.95
              Clothbound $28.95   _____

The Devil In Men's Dreams   Short
stories by **Tom Scott**.   Gay men's
tales—but the devil made me do it.
246 pages   Paperback $11.95   _____

Good Night, Paul   Poems by
Robert Peters. Poems to a lover—"rapt,
comic, wry, and ebullient" for all lovers.
96 pages   Paperback $ 8.95   _____

***Snapshots For A Serial Killer: A Fiction
and a Play***, by **Robert Peters**. "A startling
and graphic monologue about violence..."
125 pages   Paperback $10.95   _____

                          SUB-TOTAL   _____

Add $2.00 per book for shipping: _____

                      TOTAL THIS PAGE   _____
              (Turn the page for MORE new titles)

Check or money order to:
                          GLB Publishers
PO Box 78212   San Francisco, CA 94107